Love
ON THE
Ninth
Floor
Aries Skye

D1564067

MEDIA

WWW.BLACKODYSSEY.NET

Published by
BLACK ODYSSEY MEDIA

www.blackodyssey.net
Email: info@blackodyssey.net

LOVE ON THE NINTH FLOOR. Copyright © 2023 by Aries Skye

Library of Congress Control Number: 2023900480

First Trade Paperback Printing: November 2023
ISBN: 978-1-957950-03-7
ISBN: 978-1-957950-04-4 (e-book)

10 9 8 7 6 5 4 3 2 1

Manufactured in the United States of America

Distributed by Kensington Publishing Corp.

Dear Reader,

I want to thank you immensely for supporting Black Odyssey Media authors, and our ongoing efforts to spotlight more minority storytellers. The scariest and most challenging task for many writers is getting the story, or characters, out of our heads and onto the page. Having admitted that, with every manuscript that Kreceda and I acquire, we believe that it took talent, discipline, and remarkable courage to construct that story, flesh out those characters, and prepare it for the world. Debut or seasoned, our authors are the real heroes and heroines in *OUR* story. And for them, we are eternally grateful

Whether you are new to Aries Skye or Black Odyssey Media, we hope that you are here to stay. We also welcome your feedback and kindly ask that you leave a review. For upcoming releases, announcements, submission guidelines, etc., please be sure to visit our website at www.blackodyssey.net or scan the QR code below. We can also be found on social media using @iamblackodyssey. Until next time, take care and enjoy the journey!

Joyfully,

Shawanda Williams

Shawanda "N'Tyse" Williams
Founder/Publisher

WARNING

This book is recommended for readers 18 years and older.

The content contains the following: sensitive material, including language and vernacular – cursing, AAVE, and terms that 20-something-year-olds in current times use; unorthodox relationship statuses; intimacy and sex; and mentions of faith-based practices.

While I encourage you to give it a whirl before you pass, please heed the warning so that you can make an informed reader decision. I hope you enjoy the tale of Nissi and Kannon. If you do, please consider leaving a review on Amazon, Goodreads, or your purchasing retailer's website. I'd greatly appreciate it.

NAME GLOSSARY

Because I'm particular about my characters' names, and the readers are too. Here we go:

KANNON: It's KAY-none. (Not can-none or canyon)
BONUS: Nickname: Kann (CANE)

NISSI: KNEE-see (If you mispronounce this, we know who doesn't go to church, lol)

KINSTON: KIN-ston (Not Kingston. The G is not silent. It is non-existent)

AQUILA: It's AH-kee-lah (No, not "quill")

ANGELA: It's Angela. Like Simmons.

CIARA: It's Ciara. Like Russell Wilson's wife and Future's ex.

SHEENA: It's SHEE-nah… (Easy enough, but just in case.)

JOVAN: It's JO-vaughn (Not VAN like a vehicle or the shoes.)

RIVER: Just like Sam Cooke was born down by the river in a little tent.

BENJI: It's BEN-gee. (Nothing new or special, just like it's originally pronounced.)

NISANTE: It's KNEE-sun-TAY (I knew that one was going to trip y'all up.)

ABIGAIL: It's Abigail.

ROXIE: It's ROCKS-see.

KRU: It's CREW.

Chapter One

NISSI

"NOT AGAIN."

Sitting in construction traffic, I peered at my rose gold Talley & Twine watch. It was my fault because I should've left the house on time. Instead of putting my phone in my purse as I intended, I allowed myself to scroll on my new favorite app, TikTok. Of course, one funny video led to another until I found myself deep in an impromptu dance session to a cluster of *"Make it Clap"* and *"Swinging off the Chandelier"* videos. I swear that silly app has been the worst and best thing of my life thus far. It started with my assistant nearly strapping me to my seat during lunch one day to watch a video. Soon, our office became a mini-viral sensation. Every Friday, we posted office day dance challenges, and the TikTok universe ate it up for whatever reason. Hundreds of thousands of people tuned in daily to our office account and even our personal ones to get a glimpse of us dancing or doing some comical, harmless skit. So much so that the other occupants in our building started calling us the Tok-stars, a play on the word *doctors*. Corny, I know, but it was cute. So, we used that as our official hashtag for every video. But now, the app was causing me to run late for work.

I'd managed to limit my morning antics with social media so this wouldn't happen, but now and again, I got snatched into the TikTok realm and was left scrambling in my real life— like today. I wished I could create a TikTok video singing the hook of Ludacris' anthem, *Move, b*tch, get out the way,* to these slow motorists. I could make it on time if they would go just a little faster. Well, as long as I didn't have to wait for that extra slow elevator. We were housed in one of the most top-notch, state-of-the-art buildings and couldn't get a better elevator? It was like they had budgeted for everything else and then got to the elevators and decided that expense would break the bank. I'm sure we could've traded in a few of the no less than fifty Keurigs in the building to do elevator upgrades, especially since we still had the good old-fashioned coffee pots available for those who were Keurig-illiterate. If left to Ms. Dana, the front receptionist, we wouldn't have any upgrades, including a Keurig. I could hear her now in the bathroom: *Who needs lights that automatically illuminate? Just turn them on in the morning and let the suckers run all day. That's how we used to do it.* Energy efficiency and cost savings be damned. At this moment, I couldn't argue with her, though. I would've gladly traded in the illuminating perk for a faster elevator.

A few moments later, traffic started moving, and I knew God had to be looking down on His child. It was just enough movement for me to take the back street and cut through the buildings to get to our building's parking garage. I couldn't scan my parking card fast enough so the gated arm could lift. Semi-flooring my pearl white 2020 Audi RS7 sports car, I whipped into my parking spot and shut off the engine, then quickly pushed my face mask up and grabbed my coat from the passenger's seat along with my messenger bag and crossbody purse. I slung the crossbody over my head, threw my coat across my messenger bag, and slipped it on my shoulder. With a click of my key fob, my car locked as I sprinted to the security booth, which was thankfully free of other employees.

"Running late TikToking, I see," Franklin, the security guard, badgered me jokingly as I flashed my badge.

"Not today, Frank!" I ran through his station with a smile, barely giving him the time to identify me properly.

As I whizzed past him, he darted his head out of the booth and yelled, "She's a runner. She's a track star."

Laughing, I threw my middle finger back at him as I gave truth to the off-key song lyrics while taking flight down the corridor to the elevator. *Sweet Baby Jesus is really on my side today,* I thought when I noticed a few occupants entering one of the lifts.

"Hey!" My hands flailed like a mad woman. "Please hold the doors."

A man sacrificed his hand and foot to keep the doors from closing just as I slid between them, breathing heavily with a light sheen that had developed on my forehead. I'm sure I looked crazed, but I didn't care. Catching this elevator meant I would make it to work on time with five minutes to spare.

The man who held the door huffed. "You're lucky, lady. You must not know how slow these elevators are," he said to the grumbled agreement of the three other occupants.

Slipping my white coat from around my messenger bag, I lightly shook it and turned to address him. "It's Doctor Lady, and yes, I do know. Hence why I was Usain Bolt'ing to catch it."

My statement was met with a few chuckles.

The man put his hand up. "My apologies."

I turned back to look at him. "None needed, but thank you."

"What floor?" he asked, remembering he hadn't pressed the number when I entered.

The building had ten floors, and only numbers 3, 4, and 8 were lit up. The occupant to my left was just about to exit on floor number three.

Staring up at the man, I replied, "Nine, thank you."

He pressed my floor's number along with his and stepped to the side when it lit up.

"Name's Brandon. I work on the sixth floor at Tetro Development."

It took a second for me to realize he was talking to me. When I glanced over at him, I could see him ogling me from head to toe. From what I could tell, he appeared to be a nice-looking, clean-cut, slender, mocha-brown young man behind the mask covering.

Tetro was an app development company, and all the young, freshly graduated techies flocked to their business for a job. From what I'd heard, they had a hell of an intern program, paid new graduates generously, and were big on innovation. A few breakout techies had come from Tetro with cutting-edge technology they'd developed. It was the place to be—*for young folks*. I was young-ish, too. Twenty-six. But I wasn't "twenty-one-fresh-off-my-mama's-breast-milk-and-don't-know-how-to-pay-my-light-bill" young. Those were the crux of Tetro's employees. Graduation on Saturday. Tetro on Monday morning. Therefore, as cute as Brandon may have been, face shield included, he wasn't about to waste my time. However, I would be polite.

"Dr. Nissi Richards, ninth floor with Optimal Dentistry Group. Everyone calls me Dr. Nissi."

His goofy chuckle followed my words, and I could hear the cheesy pickup line before it even graced his lips.

"Can I call you, Dr. Nissi?" he said.

The man who stood slightly behind me boldly laughed as he exited on the fourth floor.

"Good day, everyone," he said, in a bad attempt to mask that he had clowned Brandon No Last Name.

"Well, Mr….uhh…Brandon, I presume you can since everyone else does."

Glancing over at him, I knew that was the wrong thing to say. *He's comfortable now.* Proving my inner thoughts to be true, he leaned back onto the elevator wall and entered "mack" mode. *Bless his young heart.*

"Or maybe I can call you Nissi without the Doctor."

The man upstairs must've heard my silent cries because He answered by way of the elevator, which had come to a halt on the young man's floor. As the door opened, he stood in front of me, awaiting my response. His courage was commendable, but he wasn't going to make any headway with me. Commence the letdown.

"I'm sorry, Mr. Brandon. I'm afraid that won't be possible. Dr. Nissi works just fine for me."

"Come on. Give a young brother a chance to change your mind."

Score. That simplistic pickup line was pretty good. Old school. Respectable. Chance-worthy. Still, it was a no-go for me.

"Sorry, you're fresh out of college, and I am much older than I appear. I appreciate the offer, but I have to decline. Focus that energy on your budding career, and best wishes to you."

He stepped from the elevator just before the doors began to close.

"Again, the name's Brandon, if you change your mind," he shouted as the doors shut, ceasing further come-on attempts.

The doors hadn't been closed five seconds before the woman beside me burst into laughter.

"Shut up, Ciara," I said, turning to her.

"Girl, these young boys never cease to amaze me. You get a new one once a month now. Hey, at least this one had a decent pickup line and wasn't disrespectful when you turned him down. Progress."

Pointing my finger at her, I shook my head while giggling. "Not funny, but you're right."

Ciara Brown worked on the eighth floor. She was a twenty-nine-year-old entrepreneur who owned a life, home, and auto insurance company, CB Insurance. We met when I began working for Optimal Dentistry Group two years ago. She was one of the first faces I met on my first day as a dentist, and she helped quell my nerves. We'd made quick acquaintances and then became fast friends. Since we had to be at work at the same time, we often wound up on the same elevator ride and made it a sport to see how many of the Tetro Boys, as we called them, hit on us with their lame lines.

"And you're talking about you're much older. Girl, you just graduated from the bottle to the sippy cup yourself, calling that man young."

"Hmm, if I'm on the sippy cup, then he's still getting weaned from the boob. We both know he probably just had his first legal sip of alcohol a day ago. Decent pickup line or not, who introduces themselves without a last name? If I *were* to change my mind, who was I supposed to ask for?"

"Brandon, if you change your mind!" we said simultaneously as a barrage of laughter bellowed between us just as the elevator reached her floor.

"Girl, you're a whole mess," she quipped, stepping off the elevator. "I do wish you'd consider dating, in any case. You're going to turn into the old maid." She patted my hand, and her gleaming wedding band almost blinded me.

"Once I find my Zachariah, I'm sure I'll be all in love."

My reference was to her husband, Zachariah Tremble. She held her married name but had founded CB Insurance before they met. So, at work—and she was very clear it was solely at work—she went by her maiden name of Brown.

"There's always—"

"Girl, stop."

My cutoff game was strong because I knew where her next statement was headed—in the wrong direction. She and her husband were forever trying to set me up with his cousin, Iman. Sweet, he was. Fine, he was definitely. Stable and secure, he was not. The man stayed "between jobs" more than he held one, and when he wasn't working, he always claimed to be working on some business venture that never made it past the idea. Zachariah swore Iman needed someone to settle him. He did. Jesus, not me. If Iman couldn't get his own life together, what was he going to add to mine? Surely not value.

After hearing about his lackluster work ethic, I wondered why he always seemed to have a woman by his side. That answer came with a bit of prying from Ciara. From what she'd explained to me, his former girlfriends fawned over him for his bedroom antics, and from having met him twice, I could personally attest that he was a respectful, kind man—a rarity for our millennial roots. Good peen and sweet sentiments were only good for a good time, though. I needed someone I knew could stand in the gap with me, and for me, when the rubber met the road, not someone still examining the road to determine if they should begin construction. Zachariah and Ciara loved their cousin, and they meant well, but Iman wasn't it. Not for me. Hell, not for anyone until he got his life together.

"Lunch?" Ciara called out as the doors began to close.

"Now you know I'm going to always have just enough to eat."

As I walked into my office and slid into my chair, my favorite dental assistant, Sheena, came through the door.

"Look who made it with two minutes to spare!"

I pointed at the door. "No, ma'am. Not before my first cup of coffee, you will not," I joked with her.

"Good thing I got you." She produced a paper cup with a lid and handed it to me. "Just the way you like it."

Taking the cup, I peeled back the plastic cover to the opening, inhaled the fresh aroma of the hot liquid energizer, and took a sip, humming to the feel of it flowing down my throat.

"Orgasmic, isn't it?"

Damn near choking at her comment, I laughed and pointed again. "The door!"

She fanned me off as she walked away and shouted, "Patient at ten."

After my door was closed, I eased back into my leather chair. I loved my life. I really did, but I had to admit, Ciara was right about one thing—I wanted someone to share this life I loved with. I'd never admit that to her or my pesky sisters, Angela and Aquila, though. Truthfully, not to anyone.

Chapter Two

NISSI

My DAY ZOOMED by rather quickly between charting and consultations. It was already five minutes past lunchtime, and my stomach was telling the story. If "hangry" was a person, it would've been me. In my haste to get to work, I left my morning smoothie on the kitchen counter. Served my TikTok-self right. I was only functioning on this morning's cup of Joe and a pack of peanut butter crackers from my now-depleted snack stash in my office drawer. Not to mention, I'd only eaten a grilled chicken Caesar salad the night before. I flaked on my sister Aquila for dinner last night, so I guess that served me right, too.

Forgive me, Lord, but I did not want to hear any more gripes about her husband—my so-called brother-in-law, Joel. It was the same two complaints: he never had time for her or the boys, and their sex life wasn't the same after my one-year-old nephew, Nisante, was born. She acted as if she'd never heard of marriage counseling before. I didn't go to college for that, but I felt like charging a fee every time I had to endure her endless vents, especially those that lacked action.

Oh, and back to the Nisante thing. No, my nephew wasn't named after me. He was named after our father, Nisante Richards, and I have been a little salty toward her since that spiteful move. My parents had thought I was going to be a boy.

17

They were so sure, in fact, that the only name they had come up with was Nisante, Jr. So, my dad changed Nisante to Nissi when I was born, and my mother went along with it. Otherwise, I'm sure I would have some A-name variant like my sisters, Angela and Aquila, derived from our mother's name, Abigail. I'd always told my family, Aquila's thieving ass included, that I would name my first son Nisante. Rather than respect that, she pulled an *Aquila* and named her second-born son Nisante. But let her tell it, she claims she forgot I said that and that it had nothing to do with me but rather to honor our father. Her best excuse was I shouldn't be pressed about it because I had no children—the audacity of a thousand audacities. Since then, I've dealt with her on an as-needed basis, and dinner at her house, while her husband was away on business, was not needed.

Now I regretted not taking Aquila up on the offer. If nothing else, my health-nut sister could cook and was the queen of leftovers. Therefore, I would have had a guaranteed good meal and leftovers today if I hadn't bailed on her. It was a given that I'd hear her disappointment later regarding it. In hindsight, with an impending tongue-lashing and an empty stomach, I should've just gone.

"So, are you coming to lunch today or next week?" Ciara's voice bellowed through my cell phone with an air of cynicism.

"Keep your stilettos on. I'm coming." I stood from my chair and removed my white coat.

"Let me switch my coat and shoes. I'll meet you in the lobby in five minutes."

"Five minutes, or you'll be forced to eat the stomach virus atrocities of 'ewww, egg salad' or 'bubble-gut burritos' from the vending machine," she joked.

"Nasty! Hell naw. I'd waste money on Uber Eats before I ever played Russian Roulette with my digestive system like that."

She hurled in laughter.

"I'll see you in a bit. Let me hop to it."

Draping my white coat on the back of my leather chair, I walked to my door and lifted my cropped jean jacket from the hook, sliding it on my arms over my yellow cap-sleeved petticoat flare dress with a giant sunflower near the hem. It was moving closer to fall, but I carried the summertime mood in my attire with the warm weather still in play. Sitting down, I changed out of my Nike Air Max to my Stella Hues stilettos. Then I stood, grabbed my Kintu New York crossbody, pulled my Optimal Dentistry mask over my face, and headed out of the office.

"Headed to lunch," I called out to Sheena.

"Bring something back for me," she shouted from the computer where she was stationed.

Jokingly, I tossed back, "Ha! You got bring-back money?"

"Nope, but you do," she countered.

Opening the door leading to the main lobby, I snorted through giggles without responding. She knew I would bring her back something anyway. I always took care of my people. Sheena got special treatment, and the others knew it. That's because Sheena and I had a bond like no other. You would think we were sisters. It'd been like that since the moment I hired her during my first week at the company.

Optimal Dentistry Group housed four dentists, including me, and we each carried our own clients and staff under one group name. It also helped keep our clients loyal because if one of us was out or on vacation, the client was routed to another one of us for care instead of being referred out. I loved my career, group, employees, and clients. This slow elevator was another subject, though.

As the doors slowly opened, I shook my head at the wait time while stepping on. Once secured inside, I pulled out my phone to text Ciara.

Me: On my way down. On the slow boat to China now.

Ciara B: Okay, girl. In the lobby waiting on you.

Right after I pressed L for the lobby, the elevator jerked roughly, causing me to stumble and almost lose my footing. I gripped the rail to keep from falling, but not before I rolled my ankle in my stilettos.

"Damn it!" I shouted, kicking the shoe off and grabbing my ankle. *Leave it to me to sprain my ankle trying to be cute for lunch.*

To be on the safe side, I kicked the other heel off. I didn't need to have two sprained ankles. *Welp, there goes my lunch.* As soon as I got to the lobby, I would have to give Ciara money for my food and head back up so one of the assistants could wrap my paining ankle. *Just what I needed.* That's when I realized the elevator wasn't moving, and the buttons weren't illuminated.

Hobbling to the panel, I pressed the button, but nothing happened. I pushed it again, this time in rapid succession. Still no lights and no movement. Keeping my cool, I tried the button to open the elevator doors. Still nothing. Suddenly, it struck me that I was stuck in this decrepit contraption.

"Great!" I threw my hands up. "Just great."

I pulled the emergency phone out and pressed the number. That's how old these jalopies were. It didn't even have the new and improved call button. Who in the hell certified these elevators to pass an inspection? Whoever it was, was either lazy or a complete imbecile.

"Yes, can we help you?"

I breathed a sigh of relief that it actually worked when the security guard answered.

"I am stuck on the main floor elevator."

"Oh no. Okay, which carriage?"

Putting the phone down, I looked up and over at the letter branded on the side of the elevator and then returned to the call. "Carriage B like Boy."

"Okay. Which floor do you think you're stuck on?"

"It never moved from floor nine. It just shifted roughly and stopped."

"All right. What's your name, and are you okay? How many other passengers are on the elevator?"

"I am Dr. Nissi Richards from Optimal Dentistry Group. For the most part, I'm good. I twisted my left ankle when it shifted, though, and I am the only lucky one stuck on the Pony Express."

The security guard chuckled. "At least you're in good spirits."

"Tell that to my throbbing ankle and growling stomach."

He laughed, and even though I was being silly, I was far from joking. My stomach was ready to fight me. Once he was over his fit of laughter, he placed me on a brief hold while he assessed the situation and called for assistance.

"Maintenance has been dispatched, and they are on their way up, Dr. Richards. I am Tim. I'll be monitoring this line for you. Is there anything you need me to do?"

"Can you tell Ciara Brown in the lobby that I am stuck in the elevator? I was going to try to call her, but in case my call doesn't connect, I need to inform her because she's waiting on me."

"Will do. I've also dispatched medical assistance about your ankle. I know you're a doctor, so before you argue, it's protocol."

Scoffing, I asked, "What do you know about doctors and their attitudes about medical assistance?"

"My mama is a nurse, and y'all are the worst patients."

"I resent that, Tim." Stifling back a grin, I added, "Even if it is true."

His deep, baritone voice rattled through the phone as he chuckled.

"You're a mess, but I am glad you're upbeat. It'll make this situation a little better. Hold tight, and I will inform your friend, Mrs. Brown."

"Sure. If you need me, you know where to find me."

Again, he burst out laughing as he hung up the phone. I did the same. By now, my ankle was outweighing my empty stomach, and I knew I had to get off it. All I had was my crossbody and my denim jacket. I was not about to put my pretty yellow dress on the grimy floor. It was bad enough my feet were forced to touch it. *Lawd! And in the middle of a panoramic, my playful term for pandemic. Ugh!* At least we were coming out of this lockdown, and the city was opening back up. Still, as soon as I was out of there, I was going to spray myself with Lysol, leave work early, and head to my bathtub to scrub-a-dub-dub. Easing off my denim jacket, I folded it neatly and copped a squat on the elevator floor while I waited for maintenance.

My cell phone ringing was a welcomed sound until I saw who it was on the other end. Ciara. I knew this chick was about to clown me.

"Don't even start!"

My threat was met with a barrage of sniggles.

"Oh, God! It's true. You *would* be the one to get trapped in the elevator."

"You know what, and I say this with all the disrespect, go to hell." My little snippy, harmless tirade only made her laugh harder. "I'm about to cancel our friendship contract. Keep clowning me."

"I'm sorry, girl." She calmed down. "Seriously, though, are you hurt?"

"I twisted my ankle. I tried to be cute and traded my Air Max for my Stella Hues, only to be barefoot on this dusty elevator."

I could tell she was trying not to give into hysterics again.

"Girl, you gotta stop! I'm trying not to laugh. My stomach and cheeks are already hurting."

I shook my head while grinning myself and asked, "What are they doing?"

"Everyone is gathering around because the entire elevator system is shut down. Maintenance is using the stairs to come and get you now. Listen, I know you're going to be hella hungry, so I'm going to go and grab us lunch. By the time they get you out of there, I'll have some food for you."

"Girl, by the time I get out, I'm going to the house to bathe. My skin is starting to itch as we speak. I swear I see little coronavirus molecules floating around this elevator."

"It could be worse. You could be stuck on there with somebody, breathing in their germs and God knows what else."

"Ewww!"

"Well, let me get out of here. It's getting crowded, and I need to grab this food. But I will check on you. Hopefully, by the time I'm back, your little adventure will be over."

We said our goodbyes, and as I waited for maintenance, I scrolled on TikTok. At least the Wi-Fi was still working. After a few minutes of watching the latest dance craves and comedy skits, I heard a bang on the door.

"Dr. Richards?" a man's voice reverberated through the steel.

"Yes! It's me. Can you hear me?"

"Yes, ma'am. My name is George, and I'm here with my co-worker Ralph. We are going to get you out of there. Just do me a favor and stand away from the doors."

"You got it. Thank you so much."

George and Ralph beat and banged on the doors to no avail. By now, my stomach had tag-teamed with my ankle, and they were hitting me with the one-two combination. My manner was quickly turning from David Banner to the Hulk.

"Do you think you should call somebody else?" My voice came out a little rough with desperation.

"Dr. Richards, this is George. At this point, we're going to have to call Fire and Rescue. We're not able to get the doors open with our tools."

No shit, Sherlock. "Gee, thanks! How long before they get here?"

"Medical is already here waiting for us to get the door open so they can attend to your ankle. Ralph is on the phone with the emergency operator now. It shouldn't be too much longer."

Did he say they are just now calling emergency? Oh, Father in Heaven.

It'd been an hour. I wasn't claustrophobic, thank goodness, but it was warm in the elevator. I was also tired of sitting on the nasty floor, along with the fact that I was battling hunger and pain.

"I'd love for them to hurry."

"I understand, Dr. Richards. I apologize it's taking so long. We'll have you out of there in a jiffy. I promise."

That's what you said an hour ago, George. Thankfully, I had enough couth to say that in my mind instead of aloud the way I wanted. Thank goodness I didn't have to use the restroom. Otherwise, it would have been a real situation in this contraption.

By that point, my mind had begun playing tricks on me. All I could think about was every movie with a faulty elevator or a terroristic threat where they blew up the elevator systems. Hell, I'd even drifted to the Hollywood Tower of Terror. What would happen if I free-fell from the ninth floor? What if when they opened it, I stepped out into another dimension and vanished, never to be seen again? Yeah, they needed to hurry up because I was losing my ever-loving mind. The property management would indeed receive a phone call from my attorney to repair or replace these carriages along with my medical and mental distress claims.

Closing my eyes, I leaned my head into the corner of the elevator, hoping to drift off. Perhaps when they finally rescued me from this hellhole, I'd at least be well rested and none the wiser of how long it took to retrieve me.

After a few minutes, I heard a light rap on the steel doors.

"Dr. Richards?" a man's voice called out.

"Yes, I am here with nowhere else to go."

A deep rumble reverberated from him. *Glad he thinks I'm being comical,* I surmised as I waited for him to speak again. I was well past theatrics.

"I'm Kannon with Fire and Rescue. We're going to get you out of there, okay?"

"Okay." My reply was feeble, a direct result of my exhaustion.

"All right. Just hang tight and sit as far away from the doors as possible."

"Done and done."

As they beat and banged for what seemed like forever, I pulled out my Kleenex pouch and wiped the sweat beads that had developed a sheen on my forehead and neck.

Oh yeah, this day is most definitely a wrap. The way I feel, tomorrow might be, as well.

I could tell a few people had gathered on the ninth floor from all the yells of encouragement to hang in there and questions about my well-being. Suddenly, I heard a loud clank, and the doors slid open to the jeers and cheers of everyone. I even yelled in exuberance for a moment until I laid eyes on the most gorgeous creation on God's green Earth. The firefighter who pried the doors open stood smiling at me, and I swore I'd been transported into paradise. That man was glorious. His fire suit hung off his waist, revealing a plain navy-blue t-shirt, and a fire helmet adorned his head. Underneath the t-shirt were ripped muscles wrapped in honey-brown skin outlined by a tattoo sleeve on his left arm. His perfectly aligned and gleaming white teeth were my next turn-on. What can I say? I'm a dentist, after all. Light brown eyes beamed into me and made the heat index in the elevator elevate another hundred degrees. As my eyes traveled the length of his six-foot and more frame, I didn't even realize the paramedics were attempting to help me out of the elevator. Food and foot be damned. My mind was centered on Fine. Fine-ass Fireman.

"Ouch!"

The paramedic snapped me out of my lustful thoughts when she touched my ankle.

"I'm sorry. I was asking if that hurt," the EMT said.

"I didn't hear you, but I certainly felt you." I shook my head as she apologized.

Her partner lifted me out of the elevator and carried me over to a makeshift triage section they had created. I explained what happened with my ankle, and they wrapped it, assessing it was a sprain. They wanted to take me to the hospital, but I refused. I didn't need an ambulance ride for a sprained ankle. What I needed was food, a bath, and my attorney.

"Girl, it's been an hour and a half. Are you okay?" Ciara asked once the paramedics wrapped everything up with me.

"Other than this…," I pointed at my bandaged ankle, "I'm fine. It felt like I was stuck in there all day."

"I couldn't do anything about that, but I can help with the other problem. Hunger." She held up a bag so I could see it. "I grabbed a Cobb salad for you."

"Girl, I'll have to eat that at home. I'm drained."

Just then, the office manager from my dentistry group walked over with a representative from property management to check on me. I knew the rep was only there to gauge whether I planned to sue and to offer me some crappy settlement to keep my mouth shut. The only thing they received out of me was confirmation that I had hurt my ankle on the elevator and my notice to be off the rest of that day and the next. I would deal with worker's compensation and anything else once home and rested.

Ciara volunteered to drop me off at home, and I agreed because I knew I would need help getting into my house with my belongings. During the ride there, she ragged on me about my ordeal, and I discussed Mister Fine. I could've kicked myself because I couldn't remember his name. It was Keith…or Kevin. Or was it Kenneth? I should've never forgotten that name. It didn't matter anyway because he was probably full of himself, and I did not have time for a man who thought he was God's gift to me.

"I still think you should've gone to the hospital," Ciara fussed as I sat with my leg propped on the sofa and the salad bowl in my hand.

"For what? I have prescription pain meds right here, and you already know they're going to send me to some quack workers' comp doctor."

With her hands on her hips, she gave me an agreed look. "True. So how are you going to get your car back to your house?"

A groan escaped, and it had nothing to do with my current state. "How else? My sisters."

"I can't wait to hear Aquila's response to this one," she said with a finger point as she picked up her purse to leave. "Do you need anything else from me besides the name of that fine-ass fireman?"

I nearly choked on the kale in my salad as I hit my chest. "Ass! But if you could do that, it'd make this entire debacle worthwhile."

She slapped fives with me. "I bet it would." She stood up to go. "Call me if you need me. You know I got you."

After she left, I finished my salad and lemonade, took my pain meds, and made the phone calls that I dreaded making. It's not that I didn't like talking to my sisters—well, especially not Angela, but I didn't want to get the third degree. They tended to baby me even as a full-grown adult, and I wasn't in the mood for their antics today.

"Baby sis! What's good? It's only five o'clock. Aren't you still at the office?" Angela asked in one breath.

"No, I'm at home—"

"Why? What happened? No patients? What's going on?"

Lord, have mercy. I placed my fingertips on my forehead. Angela was anal. She could go off the deep end when she thought something was wrong. I had to figure out how to reel her back so I could add Aquila to the call and tell both of those worrywarts together. 'Cause whew, chyle! They could be trying—loving but trying.

"Calm down, Ang. There's no five-alarm fire. Good grief, sis."

"Forgive me for caring," she said with a scoff. "Next time, I won't worry."

"You lie like a rug!"

We both broke out into a fit of giggles.

"True, but you could act like you appreciate all this love I have to give," Angela spouted.

"And I do. If you didn't, then I'd be concerned."

"Mmmhmm. Seriously though, what's up? Because say what you will about my lovable intuition, but it ain't never wrong."

"So that's what we're calling it these days?"

"Nissi!" she huffed. "Unlike you, some of us are still at work. I'm about two seconds from hanging up on your feisty little ass."

"Fine. Let me call your sister so I can get this over with at the same time."

"Oh, boy, let me sit all the way down," she said, over-exaggeration in her tone. "If you're bringing her in on this, I know it's something serious."

"Don't do that. I speak to both of you equally."

"Girl, neither of us speaks to her equally, so tell that lie to someone who doesn't know you or her for that fact."

Facepalming, I didn't bother to reply to Angela because we both knew she was telling the whole truth and nothing but. With a deep breath, I clicked to add a call and dialed Aquila's number. As soon as she answered, I merged the calls.

"So, the missing-in-action sister finally extends common courtesy and human decency by offering a 'day late and a dollar short' phone call."

That was Aquila. She couldn't even wait to see if there was a valid reason for my standing her up before she plowed into me. I hadn't even had the opportunity to get in a hello. No one could have a change of heart, make a mistake, or do anything that didn't meet her expectations.

"Umm, hello to you, too, and Angela is also on the line."

"Oh, so I have the pleasure of speaking to both the MIA sister and the nonexistent one. What in the Lost and Found is going on here today?" Aquila quipped as snootily as she possibly could. No lie. It *was* funny, though.

An elongated and annoyed sigh came from Angela.

"Hi, Aquila. I'm doing well, and you? Since Nissi called us, maybe we could shift the focus off us to her first," Angela said in one breath. "That's called courtesy and typically how phone calls work, Aquila."

"I shifted the so-called focus to Nissi when I extended a dinner invitation to her, and she failed to show or call. So, tell me again how it works."

"And you have no clue why she bailed, which is why you could try listening for once." Angela paused and huffed. "You know what, never mind. There is no changing you."

"Angela, you are so—"

"Yo! Oil and water, can I please get a word in? Y'all can do this tit-for-tat on your own time. You're both right. Geez. Let's move on."

It was like fight night at the Bellagio with those two every time, and I was the referee. Tonight, I had no interest in playing the role. My ankle was already hurting; I didn't need my head to follow suit.

"Fine." The stubborn agreement came from both of my spitfire sisters.

"So, are you ready to tell us what happened? I really must get back to work before my boss comes back into the office," Angela pressed.

"If you would take your talents elsewhere instead of settling—" Aquila started.

"Like you're settling with Joel," Angela intercepted with a gut punch of a comeback.

I felt that, and it wasn't even intended for me.

"I was trapped in the elevator at work today for like two hours," I blurted out so fast that I shocked myself. I had to. If not, Aquila might have dived through the phone and slapped the fire out of Angela.

"What?!?" they both shrieked.

"That's why I'm at home early. That rickety elevator I usually complain about finally went caput while I was inside. I was the only one, but when it lurched forward, I twisted my ankle. Ciara made sure I got home."

"Why wouldn't you call us immediately?" Aquila shrieked.

"I called you as soon as I could."

"Are you okay, though? Is it just your ankle that's hurt? Nothing else, right?" Angela asked.

"Yes, I'm fine. Other than my ankle, I'm doing well. Just a bit agitated from the day, but I'm good."

"Well, you need to sue the property management—"

"Seriously, Aquila. Can your concern for our sister overshadow your dramatics for once?" Angela snarled.

I just knew Aquila would snap back, but for once, she did not.

"Nissi, we'll discuss that part later…when we're alone. Anyway, how are you holding up? And how did you get out?"

Nestling against my sofa, I took a sip from the Fiji bottled water I'd left on the coffee table last night and adjusted my ankle. "I'm okay, like I said. I probably will be taking the stairs for a while, but besides that, it was nothing more than a blimp in my day. They had to call Fire and Rescue to come and pry that contraption open."

"Now that's a doggone shame," Angela seethed.

"One word: lawsuit," Aquila chimed in.

"*Anyway*, I need one of you to help me get my car back to my house."

"Don't worry about your car, sis. Aquila and I will get together tonight to pick it up. That is if she's available."

"I'm always available for my sisters. Just let me know the time, Ang," Aquila answered, although I didn't miss her slight dig. I'm sure Angela didn't either.

"We'll even stop by your favorite spot and bring you some dinner," Angela added.

"I'll do her one better and bring her some of the food I cooked that she missed out on because she didn't show up as promised. No dig intended."

My head fell back against the sofa cushion, a deep groan emanating from me.

"I'm sorry I missed dinner, Aquila. I should've called. That was rude, and I apologize."

"Apology accepted," Aquila said, sounding like she'd just won a prize at the carnival.

"Well, listen, I hate to run because all I want to do is love on you, but I better go. I need to finish up so I can get out of here," Angela said sadly. "I'll call you when I get off, Aquila."

"Hey! Before you go, don't tell our parents. You know Mama and Daddy will use this as an excuse to try to move me back into the house."

"They only do that because you don't have a man or any prospects," Aquila scoffed. "It's like you're allergic to men."

"I sure as hell wasn't allergic to that fine-ass fireman today," I mumbled, my mind floating back to that mountain of sexiness.

"Oop oop! Wait a minute. Fireman? What fireman? The one who rescued you?" Angela asked.

I rolled my eyes. "I thought you had to go?"

"That was pre-fireman. Spill it! Telling us about an ankle and leaving out the good stuff," Angela fussed.

"I know that's right!" Aquila dittoed her sentiments.

Look at the impromptu "Amen" choir. They could argue about everything under the sun, moon, and stars, but when it came to my love life, they were suddenly bosom buddies.

"There's not much to tell. Before prying the doors open, he identified himself by name, but I can't remember what it was. All I know is that he was six foot and more of caramel and fineness."

"Oh no! We have to find this man. I've never heard you speak about anyone like that. He must have been fine, fine," Angela said.

"He was, and how am I going to do that? Call every fire station in the city?"

I heard Aquila snap her fingers before she said, "Use that TokTik thingy you and your office are so famous for?"

Slapping my hand against my forehead, I laughed. "It's *TikTok*, and how is that supposed to work?"

"Wait, Nissi. Aquila may be on to something. Your office is a viral sensation. If you put out a TikTok explaining what happened and asking everyone to tag the Fire and Rescue to locate him in our area, it just might work. I mean, how many firemen were out today rescuing dentists from an elevator?" v

"See, even Angela agrees with me," Aquila said. "Try it."

"What if he never hears about it or responds? Isn't this a bit desperate?"

"If he doesn't, you tried, and someone asking to meet the person who saved their life is not uncommon," Angela said.

Aquila agreed. "Besides, what do you have to lose?"

Chapter Three

NISSI

TWO DAYS LATER, my ankle felt much better, but I was still taking appointments virtually from my home office. The workers' comp doctor had not yet released me to return to the office, so I did what I could from home. Low key, I enjoyed the break. It allowed me to make my own schedule and partake in some much-needed rest and relaxation. It dawned on me that I hadn't had a vacation since I graduated from dental school. My days had been consumed with gaining the remaining knowledge I needed through my hands-on interactions with patients, studying what I had learned in school, and preparing myself to one day go into practice for myself. A vacation seemed like something of the past and only attainable when I reached my next set of goals. How wrong I was. I didn't understand the importance or benefits of this level of rejuvenation. If I could figure out a way to perform oral surgery from the house, I'd never return to the office.

"Dr. Richards' office," I said, answering my cell phone playfully.

"Ha. Ha. Play it up. Some of us have real work to do," Ciara chuckled.

"You just miss me."

"I do," she whined with the cadence of a three-year-old. "When are they releasing you? These days are long and boring. Besides, it's your turn to get hit on by the tech guys."

My belly rumbled with laughter. "I haven't a clue yet. Don't worry. It won't be much longer. I'm sure they are giving me space and time to reconsider slapping the property owners with a lawsuit. Besides, when I come back, you'll still be getting hit on by the tech guys. *'Cause, baby, it's the stairs for me. It's the stairs for me. Climbing up the one, the two, and up the three. Stuck where? Ha ha! Not there.*"

The crooning sound of the revamped TikTok song serenaded her ears.

Ciara wailed out so loud that she snorted. "On Gawd! That right there is why your office is TikTok famous. I swear you don't have the good sense God gave you."

"On the contrary, I do, which is why it's the stairs for me!"

"Shut up! Just stop it right now, I say!"

After a few moments, Ciara and I calmed down, and she got down to the real reason for her call.

"Since I see you are doing just lovely—which was the reason for my call, by the way… umm, when are you going to do that TikTok asking about Mr. Fine-Ass Fireman? And don't blame it on the injury. Clearly, your hands, mouth, and phone work, as evidenced by your being on the phone with me and blessing my bored soul with that beautiful TikTok P. Diddy remix."

If she could see my eyes, she'd probably say they were going to get stuck in my head from the deep rolls I had going on.

"Last time I ever do something to help the bored and lonely. Just unappreciative."

"You can try to divert this little conversation all you want, but I know you are interested in at least finding this man."

"Can I get healed first? Geesh!"

"Pray tell. What does your ankle have to do v   ~ur mouth?"

Grrr. I hated when she had a comeback that I couldn't come back from. It was a rarity, but it did happen every once in a while.

"Y'all just want to see me thirst-trapping over that man."

It was the only card I had left to play.

I could hear her chair slide back as she let out an "oooh," which usually meant she had an *Aha!* moment.

"Lord, have mercy." I sighed dramatically. "What is it, Ciara?"

"I never thought I'd see the day that Nissi Richards was scared." She clapped her hands together. "You are scared to make that video because you're afraid he might ding your bell. Then you'd have to provide the real reason you reached out, which is you're attracted to him. You're running scared."

She had found my hidden card, but I wasn't going to cop to it.

"Nissi Richards isn't scared of anything."

"Except Mr. Fine-Ass Fireman, you little chicken shit."

"Girl, fuck you."

"No, that's what you want Mr. Fine-Ass Fireman to do to you."

It was my turn to cackle. She was right about that. I didn't even know the man, but if my memory served me correctly, one glance at him and I could've slid out of the elevator myself from the pool of wetness that gathered at the apex of my thighs. What kind of wizardry was that? Scratch that. He was a straight-up sorcerer. Never in my life had I wanted to be spread eagle for a man I didn't even know except for Mr. Fine-Ass Fireman.

"Look at the time. I have a patient call in five minutes."

"Run all you want from me but stop running from the fireman."

"If you're going to address him, say it right. Mr. *Fine-Ass* Fireman."

"My bad. I stand corrected."

"And I STAN for Mr. Fine-Ass Fireman. Bye!"

I hung up before she had a chance to retort. I knew she wouldn't call back only because she didn't know if I honestly had a patient or not. Even though she didn't have a chance to respond, her words lingered like garlic after a meal. They beat loudly in my head and were relentless in plaguing me.

After my last patient, I made a quick sandwich and took a bath. Sitting in my short shorts and School of Dentistry t-shirt, my view of the television was random and aimless. Perhaps the real reason I couldn't settle my spirit—no matter what I'd done—was because the urge to do that stupid TikTok had me on edge. After a few more minutes of struggling to kill the thought in my deepest memories, I finally gave in.

"Forget this." I lifted the remote and zapped off the TV.

Easing from the sofa, I grabbed my cell phone and headed to my desk. There, I hooked up my phone to my tabletop tripod, adjusted the lighting, and clicked the red button to record on TikTok.

"Hey, TikTok fam. It's your girl, Dr. Nissi Richards. Right quick, I need your help. As many of you know, I am your favorite dancing dentist. Two days ago, I was trapped in the elevator at work and had to be rescued by Fire and Rescue. No lie. True story." I waved my hands, signaling I was cool. "It's okay. I'm fine. Just healing and resting up from that incident. But that is not the purpose of this video. You see, there was a fireman who broke open those doors and saved me, but I don't remember his name. Ugh! So, I need you all to help me find him. Please tag every fire station in Miami and help me find my rescuer. If you are out there, I'd love to treat you to dinner as a thank you. So, please, you guys, tag and reshare. Together, I know we can locate Mr. Fire and Rescue. Much love, and I'll be back jiggin' real soon!"

After one review, I posted the video and decided to let it work its magic. I didn't want to dress up or do too many takes. That would let the public know I was looking for this man for more than a thank you. Knowing the TikTok bullies, they'd draw that assumption anyway. With a little over twenty-four thousand followers, I hoped it was enough to make my video go viral. Or viral enough for Mr. Fine-Ass Fireman to notice.

Putting my phone on silent, I sat on the sofa under my blanket and snuggled up to catch up on all the drama Netflix could provide.

I woke to the sound of hard pounding on my front door. Sitting up, I stretched and realized I had dozed off. The incessant knocking at the front door brought me fully out of my sleep-induced fog. *Who the hell is this?* My thoughts went rampant, flipping from irritated to curious. Curiosity won the battle as I flung my feet off the side of the sofa and hobbled toward my front door. Glancing at the clock on the wall, I noticed the time—9:00 p.m.

Whoever this is better have an excellent reason for popping up at my house unannounced and at such an ungodly hour, I thought, then with irritation in my voice resounding loudly, I asked, "Who is it?"

"Your sister!" Angela barked. "Open this damn door."

Quickly, I unbolted the door and flung it open. "Angela? Somebody better be dead, desperate, or destitute, or I'm gonna fight you about this foolery."

My words sliced through her as she pushed past me into my home. Closing the door, I turned to face her.

"Where is the freakin' fire?"

"On your phone!"

"Huh?" *I know this chick didn't pop up at my house because I didn't answer the phone.*

I'd never hit either of my sisters, but she was asking for a swift left hook if that was the case.

She searched around frantically until she saw my phone on the coffee table. Then she stalked over to it and picked it up.

"Look at your phone! Me, Aquila, Ciara—hell, even your assistant—have been trying to reach you." She shoved the phone into my hands. "Look!"

Grasping my phone, I slid my finger so the screen would wake up, and the first thing I saw was the numerous TikTok notifications, all 100-plus of them. My eyes ballooned, and my hands trembled as I opened the app. I shared my "Mr. Fire and Rescue" video only three hours ago, and it already had over fifty thousand likes, two thousand comments, and three hundred shares.

"Holy shit!" My hand flew to my open mouth. "What the hell?"

"Girl, not only did your dental office share it, but so did the property management, a few Miami-based celebrities, and several TikTok influencers! You've gone viral for your man!"

Going viral on TikTok was nothing new to me, but I'd never gone this viral this fast. Moreover, why did my mouth feel as if it was full of cotton, and where did these flutters in the lining of my belly come from? There's no way I could be this excited. I didn't even know if any of these replies were from the fireman. I needed to take a deep breath and calm down. There was no need to lose my mind over nothing.

Calmly, I asked, "Has anyone located him?"

"That's what we were trying to reach out to you to ask!" Angela walked around and plopped down on my loveseat. "People have tagged so many stations, and firemen from all over have been trying to locate the guy. Girl, people are all in the comments asking have you found him and everything."

"My DMs are blowing up right now. This can't be real." I walked over to the loveseat and showed my sister. "This is crazy."

"Honey, people are a sucker for this type of story." She pointed at a comment. "And apparently thirsty, too. Look at these men in your comments. @Bigelow1963 says: *If you can't find him, I'm available, baby.* And @DeuceL2 says: *I'ono dude, but he's a lucky MF'er if he can bag your fine ass."*

I pointed to another. "And @lucyburgirl says: *Damn, sis! Thirsty much?"* I rolled my eyes. "Which is exactly why I didn't want to do this."

Instead of responding to me, Angela pulled out her cell phone and started clicking away. When my phone dinged, I knew it was her. *@AngSoRich replies to @lucyburgirl: 1st it's the audacity with a name like Lucy B Ur Girl & 2nd of all, she got a mad army behind her & soon a whole fire department, so tread lightly!* Her comment caused me to sling my phone on the sofa with a gasp. Normally, I would've been upset about her retaliatory remark because we're both professionals and clapping back to trolls ain't my style. But this is one time I was glad my big sister stepped through.

With a huff, Angela folded her arms and fell back against the loveseat. "Sorry, sis. I know you ain't about entertaining the trolls on that app, but I ain't made it that far in my petty journey. When they go low, I'm dragging their bitter asses to hell, especially when it comes to my baby sister. Hell, even Aquila. Only *we* can give her hell."

She was right. My sisters and I could be oil and water, but that blood stuck together when it came to outsiders. Professional or not, I'd snatch a lace front with a quickness over my sisters, and the same went for them. Believe that.

Reaching over, I hugged her tightly and kissed her cheek. "I swear I love you."

That made her smile, and she kissed me back on my cheek.

"I love you, too. Now, scroll through those DMs and see if he responded."

When I picked up my phone, I hollered and showed her the comment under hers. *@TheAquilaOliver replies to @lucyburgirl:*

And 3rd of all, poof, be gone! Your comment too strong!" Angela and I both barreled over. Aquila was never on social media, but leave it to her to make a grand entrance. Before I could call her, she called me.

"Girl, I hope you find this man soon before I end up in jail behind one of these little thots on this TokTik app."

"It's *TikTok*," I screamed, rattled with amusement.

"What the hell ever!" she spewed. "Did you find him?"

"No. I was asleep before Angela pounded on my door and woke me up. I have to scroll through a ton of DMs."

"You would fall asleep while we're all engrossed in your TokTik-TikTok-on-and-on-and- it-won't-stop drama."

Pointing to my phone, I looked at Angela. "Get your sister."

"No, ma'am. That's your sister!" She shook her head and fanned her hands with the "no" motion.

"That's all right. I'll bet you claim me when you find him."

"And you won't let me live it down, either."

"Damn sure won't. Listen, I have to go check on the kids. Call me when you know something."

"I will. Love you, Aquila."

"Love you more."

After hanging up, I slid back against the arm of my sofa, bringing my feet underneath me.

"And when did Aquila get on TikTok? She doesn't do social media."

"The night we got your car," Angela replied. "She asked me to download the app on her phone. So, I did. She said she wanted to make sure she could follow the drama that unfolded behind you and the fireman. She only follows me and you and, of course, hasn't posted any videos—not that she ever would—but it's apparent by her comment that she's been sucked into the videos."

"I know, right? Talkin' about some '*poof, be gone!*' Girl, I don't know why she acts like she doesn't like to let loose and be ratchet sometimes. That comment was classic."

Angela shrugged. "My guess is because she's married to Chef Joel Oliver, master chef and restauranteur to the stars!" she quipped with an air of arrogance.

"If anything, she should be on there more than us. Social media is a restaurant's marketing bread and butter."

Angela sucked her teeth and fanned me off. "Yeah, if she was a part of the business. You know good and well Joel keeps his business separate from her. She knows as much about the Oliver brand as we know about the Oliver brand."

Then looking at each other, we simultaneously said, "Not a damn thing!" and slapped a high-five at our jinx comment.

"Anywho! Forget about Aquila's marriage and try to get into one of your own. I ain't over here at this hour to talk all night. I want to know if that man has responded."

Rolling my eyes, I slid my phone into my hands and opened the TikTok app. I'd probably been scrolling for about fifteen minutes when I saw Angela's head lolling to the side. Instead of going back to her condo, she was fighting a good night's sleep just to be nosy. Now that was dedication. She knew she had to be to work in the morning yet was worried about some off chance in hell I'd…

"Holy shit!"

Angela jumped up, hitting her knee on the coffee table. She grabbed her knee and hopped up, bouncing around and hobbling to try to subside the pain I knew she felt.

"Damnit! What?"

"Are you all right, sis?"

"Girl, I know you better have some news while I'm here getting injured."

"That's because you should be home in bed instead of being in my business."

"Go to—"

Before she could finish her tirade, I bounced up and down. "I got a message!"

"From him?" Her eyes lit up like Christmas at Rockefeller Center. She wasn't in pain anymore suddenly. "Let me see!"

Snatching my phone back, I wagged my finger at her. "It's not from him, per se—"

"I swear I'ma knock you out if you don't cut the shenanigans. Who is it from?"

"Okay, feisty! It's from another fireman who works with him. He said he responded to the call with him. His name is Jovan, but according to Jovan, my knight-in-fireman's armor name is Kannon. Kannon Jordan."

Without any further questions, Angela ripped the phone from my hands and hurriedly scanned the message I had been referring to.

"It says here he was off today but that he DM'ed him the video and texted him about it."

"Yeah, exactly what I was going to tell you before you rudely snatched my phone."

It was her turn to hit me with the eye roll. "You were taking too long. Anywho...OMG, sis! What if he messages you? Then what?"

"I'm going to thank him and invite him out for drinks."

Angela's facial expression turned to one of shock. "*You* are going to step outside your box and invite that man out?"

"Don't act like I'm a prude. I would totally ask a man out. It just has to be the *right* man."

"I know you would, but typically, you're on the shy side when it comes to approaching first, especially when eyeballs are on you. In this case, almost all of Florida knows about this."

I wasn't necessarily shy about taking the initiative but more old school. I liked to be approached and pursued. With men these days, you had to know they were genuinely interested in you because using women was more common than not. However, this was a one-off situation and wouldn't be a date. It would be a casual meet and greet.

Shrugging, I took my phone back from my sister. "I admit I'm nervous, but shoot, I've come this far. Might as well ride the wave."

"If he is as fine as you portrayed him, you better ride more than a wave," she said while sexily slow-rolling her body. "Eowwwww."

"You know what. It's time for you to go home. Nasty. I'ma tell ya daddy."

"He'd be proud. How you think we got here? He and Mama were riding that same wave."

Ha! This chick is crazy.

"The door!"

"Fine." She grabbed her keys and clutch and headed to the front door while I followed her. Once she reached the door, she turned around and hugged me. "Seriously though, sis. Don't let this opportunity slip away. I want to see you with a man who makes you happy."

Not my sister putting ten thousand on one situation. My head fell back, exhausted from her futile matchmaking attempts. It was too much.

"It'll just be a thank-you outing...if he responds."

"That could lead to an opportunity." She threw me a mean side-eye that almost made me recoil.

Not one to be defeated, I clapped back, "I could say the same for you, ya know?"

"We," she fanned her finger between us, "are not the same, and you know that. And before you get started, goodnight."

Before I could give a rebuttal, she spun on her heels and walked away.

"Text me when you make it home," I yelled to her backside.

With a bob of her head to acknowledge my request, she threw up the deuces before getting in her car and driving off.

Pressing my back against my closed door, I considered what Angela said. My career had been my focus for so long, and Kannon was the only man who had caught my eye. Perhaps it was some celestial sign that I was supposed to connect with him. Either that or Angela and all of TikTok land had my head gassed. Either way, I decided if Kannon reached out, I'd take a chance and give him a fair shake. If he didn't, it would be his loss, and I'd move on with my life. No harm. No foul.

Chapter Four

KANNON

"DUDE, WHAT ARE you talking about?"

The words came out of my mouth as soon as Jovan answered his cell phone.

"Yo, I'm talking about lil' mama—the dentist chick you rescued from the elevator on that professional office building call a couple of days ago."

Scratching my head, I looked at my phone with confusion. I knew what call he was referring to, but I was lost as to why he texted me about it. Our days were long, and I rarely touched my phone when I was off. It was my way of decompressing both from the job and the world's depressing news of the day. We received enough of that from our emergency calls. So this left me a bit curious.

"Yeah, I remember. What about her?"

Jovan sucked his teeth. "Dawg, do you not check your phone at all?"

"As a matter of fact, I don't. Not much anyway when I'm off."

"Well, you might want to check it. Specifically, your TikTok DM. The one from me."

"What's up with the games, dawg?" I shook my head as I plopped down on my sofa and flipped to TNT to catch my Heat battle it out with the Lakers. "Just tell me."

"Nah, chief. This is one DM you need to see for yourself. Listen, my girl just pulled up. I promise you'll thank me later. I'm up."

"A'ight. Later."

When I hung up, I turned my attention to the game rather than TikTok. Jovan was always on some dumb stuff. He stayed on these apps more than his kid. I got it. Living at the station most days was boring, so social media and television were life. At home was an escape from all that for me.

Besides, knowing Jovan, it was probably some TikTok after-dark video. While I appreciated a nice female body just as much as the next man, it didn't thrill me like it thrilled him. I preferred to have a real woman in my arms, not one I could only lust over on some social media app. That was worse than the strip clubs, where most strippers were personally off-limits. Sure, there were certain situations where you could bed a stripper, but it wasn't like how it's portrayed. Many of those women were about their bread and their bread only. I couldn't blame them. Who wanted to be touched and sexed up by every horny man vying for their attention? I know I didn't want every woman who wanted me. It was called standards or, as my mom used to say, *being grown*.

At some point, a grown man understood that tits, ass, and box were the same. Not equal. But the same. There had to be more. I was the "more" guy. Jovan was the…let's just say, *non-standards* guy. If his girl really knew everything that was up with him, he'd be the *murder victim* guy because that Jasmine was a real one. I'd never tell her about his window-shopping ways and aisle nine stays because, I mean, there was the bro code, but I did at least try to steer him in the right direction.

All that aside, after watching my Heat get assassinated by the Lakers in the first half, I was sick of the game, and curiosity had taken over about this whole DM. It had to be more than just some fine chick, and as I processed it, it dawned on me that somehow the lady I rescued and the video had to be related. Why else would he mention her?

I was just about to check out the situation when my cell phone rang. Seeing that it was my brother, I slid the bar to answer and walked to the kitchen to grab a beer.

"Sup, bro?"

"Bro, nothing much. I was calling to ask have you seen that TikTok video?"

Now I knew something major was going on. Kinston was only ever on social media to post his workouts, exercise classes, and fitness tips. He was not a scroller. He was about his business. So, if he was calling me about this video, it was definitely news.

"Nah, man. Jovan texted me about it about an hour ago, and I called him. He told me that he sent it to my DM, but I haven't seen it yet. How do you know about it?"

I took a swig from the beer bottle.

"Man, one of the other trainers tagged me in the video and asked if Mr. Fire and Rescue was you. The only reason I entertained the comment was because of when we talked the other day. Remember you told me you had your first elevator rescue? I didn't think it was you, but then I got to thinking, how often do people get stuck on elevators that require Fire and Rescue?"

Realization struck me at my brother's point. *It had to be her. Nah, it couldn't be. Could it? Had to be.*

"Man, this is wild. Now I know it's the dentist. Jovan mentioned the same thing. I'ma go check it out. At first, I thought Jovan was just sending me some foolishness about a TikTok model."

Kinston's deep baritone voice rumbled at my assessment. "I can see that, but nah, man. This is legit. You need to check it out. That's all I'm gonna say."

Curiosity held my attention for real this time. Jovan might have been on some BS, but never Kinston.

"A'ight. Let me go check this video out, and I'll holla at you later."

"A'ight, baby boy. Love."

"Love."

Strolling back to my living room, I hiked my grey sweatpants up on my waist, kicked off my Adidas slides, and stretched out across my sofa with one arm behind my head. With my phone in my other hand, I scrolled to the app and checked my DM, which had blown all the way up. When I found Jovan's DM, I clicked on it and clicked on the video, which took me to the profile of @ThatDentistChick.

A smile a hundred miles wide spread across my face as I watched the video. The sentiment was hella sweet. Not to mention Dr. Nissi Richards was gorgeous. All I could see was her upper body in a dental school tank, her beautiful milk chocolate face, and her curly hair pulled high into a ponytail on top of her head, but she was divine. She was the type of woman a grown man drooled over. Not those ass-shot vixens. She was royalty personified.

When I went to respond, that's when I noticed the video had amassed over two hundred thousand likes, and the comments and shares were in the thousands. Talk about viral.

Who is she?

A quick peek at her profile showed me that she had over fifty thousand followers compared to my five thousand, and she mentioned her dentistry group's page. When I went there, it showed they had an account that amassed six hundred thousand followers.

Yeah, she's TikTok famous.

That's when I knew a comment or DM wouldn't get her attention. I decided my response would have to come via Stitch. Since she'd seen me in uniform, I'd stitch it the next day when I was all suited up at the fire station.

After deciding how I would respond, I got consumed with reading the comments. There were plenty of encouraging and funny comments and a ton of thirsty men and hating females, too. It's amazing how people projected their own misgivings on someone and spewed them as facts. Some of the females talked about how she was thirsty and how I wouldn't appreciate it. As if they even knew me or what I would or wouldn't appreciate. *People*, I tell you.

When I looked up, I'd been going through comments and her videos for two hours. Shaking my head at myself, I stood up, stretched, and then headed to my bedroom to jump in the shower. But first, I texted my brother.

Me: Yo, bro, I saw the video.

Kinston: She cute. You gonna reply?

Me: Yeah, I'ma stitch it tomorrow. Just thanking her, ya know.

Kinston: Just to thank her?

Me: Man, FOH. She just wanted to thank me.

Kinston: That's what she said in the video. Let me know what her mouth say.

Me: LOL! You wild, boi.

Kinston: And you famous. Your pussy points going up from this one, my boi.

Me: You know pussy ain't never been a problem. It gets old.

Kinston: Yeah, I know, bro. You gotta admit that video is kinda sexy.

Me: It was sweet. I appreciated it.

Kinston: Downplay it all you want. I know it has you tender.

Me: LOL! Bruh, I'm going to bed. Love.

Kinston: A'ight, Mr. Fire and Rescue. Love.

Chuckles erupted from me as I plugged in my cell to charge and headed to the shower. While washing, I couldn't help but meditate over Dr. Richards' video. Her words replayed in my mind like a broken record. Before I knew it, I was smiling like a Cheshire cat. Man, this was the craziest turn of events. No cap, though. As much as I wanted to play it off, the gesture did make me tender in the chest.

Chapter Five

KANNON

$\mathcal{J}$UMPING OUT OF my Ford F-150 truck, I re-tucked my blue fire engine company t-shirt in the back of my turnout pants and made my way into the firehouse. As soon as I entered, everyone in the kitchen area turned and screamed, "Mr. Fire and Rescue!"

I couldn't help the eruption of laughter from me if I tried. The whole situation was wild. This boisterous greeting had to be fueled by my good buddy, Jovan, because I knew at least half of my crew didn't have a clue what went down on social media, let alone with that video. I had no doubt it had been shared around the station multiple times with the anticipation of my arrival.

"I just have one question," Captain Morris said, slapping me on the shoulder. "What did you do to that beautiful young woman to make her put out a viral APB on you, Jordan?"

Jovan jumped into a chair and started moving his pelvis like a snake. "He was putting the fire in the rescue!"

The entire crew bellowed at his foolery.

"I just did my job. That's it!" I replied while fanning my hands to dispel Jovan's antics before they became rumors.

"Sounds like she's looking to reward you for it, too," one of the older men said, much to everyone else's agreement.

"See, there y'all go putting a million on one dollar." I wagged my finger at him. "That woman clearly said she wanted to thank me."

They all took a page out of Jovan's book and started gyrating in their seats or where they stood.

"Then let her thank you!"

These men were out of control. No cap. It was hilarious, and I couldn't do anything but enjoy their playful banter. No matter how much I tried to downplay it, I was flattered by such a grand gesture. This job was life-threatening and, for the most part, thankless. I didn't mind putting my life on the line regardless, but it felt good when someone took the time to acknowledge us. Dr. Richards' gesture was extra special. Cards or a pop-up visit were the norms when we did get recognized, but a viral video? That was one-of-a-kind.

"So, did you respond?" Jovan asked as I put my items in my locker.

When I turned to answer, all eyes were on me. Everyone was invested in this. My brother even called me this morning asking about it. They weren't the only ones. I watched the video again, and by now, the video had over five hundred thousand views. Who knew a quest to say thank you would garner so much attention? I knew what they wanted to see—a sappy damsel-in-distress/heroine love story. It was cute in theory, but it wasn't reality. Still, I was lowkey amused by the attention, so I was going to do my part to feed the people what they wanted—a response.

"No, I didn't. I'm gonna respond in a bit."

They all jumped up. "Can we be in the video?"

Look at these grown men on some big feminine energy vibes. Ridiculous.

"No," I scoffed. "I'm not trying to make this lady think we're over here discussing her. I'm not trying to make her uncomfortable."

"Man, you ain't no fun!" Jovan scowled, sucking his teeth.

Glancing around, they all looked like sick puppy dogs, so I had a change of heart. I would add to the moment's entertainment in the spirit of the energy on TikTok and, apparently, my fire station.

"Okay, if y'all act like gentlemen in the video, then yes. She's a dentist, so let's keep it professional. And by *us*, I mean all of *you*."

Captain Morris thought of a great idea, which was to have all the men line up outside of the fire station with our arms folded across our chests and serious expressions on our faces. He'd announce that we are the firefighters of Engine Company 79, and then I would step out into the camera. Of course, Jovan had his tripod ready in anticipation to be a part of the video, which he probably purchased for his own extracurricular activities. That wasn't my business, though. At any rate, we set it up.

Using my cell phone, I stitched the part of her video asking people to help find me, and then we rolled the camera. *Action!*

"Hi, we're the firefighters of Engine Company 79, and it's a pleasure to serve our community."

I stepped out and put on my best smile.

"What's up, Dr. Nissi Richards? I heard you were looking for me, though." I fanned my arms outward. "Here I am, Kannon Jordan, your rescuer. Although I was only doing my job, I appreciate the heartfelt search. It was my pleasure, and here is my thanks to you. Salute."

I ended the video with a two-finger hand salute and a bright smile.

We all reviewed it and were amazed that we captured it perfectly on the first shot. I created the caption: *@ThatDentistChick*

Heard you were looking for me. Welp, here I go @KingKannon94. I'd never tell my brothers-in-arms, but I was nervous as hell when I posted that video. For good measure, I followed her and sent it to her DM. After that, I texted my brother to have him look on my page for the video. I figured I'd give her the rest of the day to see it and respond because now, I was hyped up about it. To stay true to my word and not come off stalkerish, I turned my phone on silent and went about my day.

Chapter Six

NISSI

IT WAS FRIDAY night, and I was giddy as hell. Mr. Fine-Ass Fireman, aka Mr. Fire and Rescue, had responded that morning. I hadn't watched the video, though. By my sisters' order, we would watch it together that night, so I decided to make it a girls' night. I also invited Ciara and my assistant, Sheena, who shared the video on our dental group page. I ordered finger foods from my favorite delicatessen, so we had a mixture of chicken wings, rice, meatballs, cold cuts and cheese trays, finger sandwiches, and bottles of white wine.

By eight p.m., I was opening my door for the always fashionably late Aquila. Everyone else was there, and we'd been snacking on the good food and great wine.

"Sorry I'm late. I had to wait until Joel got there to get the kids," Aquila said, exasperated as she floated past me. "You know you could've asked me to cook."

"We wanted to eat tonight," Angela said as we made our way into the living room. "Not next week. Nobody had time to be waiting on you, especially seeing you're an hour late."

Aquila hugged Angela. "It's good to see you, too."

"Ooh, I love the way you say 'screw me' so sophisticatedly," Angela quipped as they sat down.

"Y'all are a mess. I'm not fooling with you two tonight." I shook my head at them.

Aquila swatted at me before turning her attention to Ciara and Sheena. "I promise I am not this rude, but my sisters love to aggravate me. Hey, Ciara and Sheena. It's good to see you again." They both spoke to her before she got back up to make her a plate of food. When she returned, I was sitting with my phone in my hand and more nervous than a kid about to get their teeth cleaned for the first time. Earlier, when I had taken a break at work, I opened TikTok and saw the mention. Before I could go to his page, Angela and Ciara called almost at the same time. It was as if we had been on the same wavelength. None of them had seen the video, opting to watch it together so they could see my reaction. Truth be told, I wanted to see theirs, too, and I needed the support. If he were a grade-A asshole, I would need moral support.

"Don't let me stop you. Go ahead and check the video," Aquila said, munching on a sandwich. "And don't say nothing about my tardiness," she added, pointing her finger at Angela just as her lips parted.

"For once, I agree. This is already nerve-wracking enough," I commented, then got up and sat on the sofa between my sisters as Ciara and Sheena squeezed in.

"I can't believe you finally admitted you're scared about this," Ciara threw out as they all looked at me in surprise.

"I didn't think it would spread like wildfire, and now, I guess I'm kinda feeling the pressure. People have come up with their own narratives about what will happen, and I'm just hoping this man doesn't think I'm short some screws and marbles."

Sheena threw her hands up. "Girl, I swear you are putting too much into this. He's probably not as fine as you imagined anyway. You were tired, hot, and hungry. You probably daydreamed him."

There was a pause before we fell into a deep guffaw. I swatted Sheena's leg as I came down from my giddiness.

"I swear I can't stand you!"

Swiping tears from her eyes from the hilarity, Angela shrugged. "Well, only one thing can solve all this. Watch the video."

My eyes fell across the room, and my girls bobbed their heads in unified agreement.

They were right. Why was I so nervous? It wasn't like we knew each other personally or had anything further than this moment of TikTok fame. I would watch the video and be done. We'd have drinks if he wanted. Life would return to normal. We'd be nothing more than an old fad in a few good days.

I unlocked my cell phone and pulled up the app. Immediately, I felt the heat from all around me as the ladies leaned in to get a good view. I noticed he had followed me, so I took the liberty to follow him back. When I clicked on the video in my DM, the stitch appeared first, and then we saw a line of men. After they introduced their engine company, the most gorgeous man I'd ever seen stepped forward and began to speak. His deep light brown eyes surrounded by full lashes were encased around beautiful sun-kissed amber-hued skin with a short bed of wavy hair, muscles for days, a tattoo on his arm, and teeth so bright, white, and perfectly aligned it made my dentist's heart soar. That's when I realized it was him—my rescuer.

When the stitch ended, a collective sigh flowed through all of us.

"Forget what I said, girl. You ain't made a damn thing up! He is *fine, fine*," Sheena hollered as the ladies went wild.

"Play it again!"

"Let me grab my phone!"

"That is one fine-ass man!"

"Lawd Ham Mercy! Who made him? Who?"

My sisters and friends scrambled around for their phones so they could go to his page and watch the video, which now had a little over five hundred thousand views. I sat there paralyzed and mesmerized. Kannon Jordan was perfection. The way my name rolled off his tongue dampened my panties the moment I heard the smooth tenor in his voice. Then he ruined them again with that smile. Standing there with the sun glistening off him in his turnout pants and fitted t-shirt didn't help the cause. Whomever his mama and daddy were needed to be slapped or crowned because the DNA they poured into making that scrumptious bucket of creamy caramel was either sinfully sweet or heavenly crafted. From the gentle way he addressed my video, he seemed heaven-sent.

My eyelids fluttered as I was brought back to attention by a set of fingers snapping in my face.

"Earth to Nissi," Angela summoned. "Girl, that man got you gone!"

"Not just her. He has *all* of us gone," Ciara purred as if she didn't have a whole husband.

"This is probably the best idea I ever gave you because Ciara is right," Aquila mused, biting her lip while watching the video again on her phone.

My eyes bugged out, and I wasn't alone in the shock. Aquila had never been so forward. Not Mrs. Prim and Proper.

"And what would Joel say?"

Aquila's eyes bounced up to me. "Joel wouldn't say a thing because I won't be watching this around Joel, which is why I'm here. I have to thirst trap in peace."

The neighbors probably thought a bomb had detonated from the thunderous hoots and hollers as we all jumped up and down in excited unison. Yep, Kannon had to be heaven-sent because he'd turned into a miracle worker. Anybody who could get my strait-laced sister to loosen up was a godsend.

Once we finally settled down, Angela picked up her glass of wine and broached the most anticipated subject of the evening.

"My question is are you going to respond?"

Boldly, I stood up. "So, who's going to record?"

These girls fell over themselves as they clamored to get the tripod and my phone. I guess it would be safe to assume that's what they hoped I would do.

While they set up, I checked my appearance. My fitted distressed jeans and "Black Women Dentists" tank top served just the right amount of cuteness—nothing over the top. My kinky coils fell loosely around my face, and my glammed-up make-up was still fresh. I slipped on my Stella Hue stiletto pumps and walked back into my living room. Once Angela let me know the setup was ready, I stitched the last part of his video and spoke while looking into the camera, standing as cute as my size ten body allowed.

"Hi, Kannon! Thank you so much for responding and for saving me that day. I know it's all in a day's work, but a little appreciation goes a long way. Shout out to Engine Company 79. You men rock—especially you, Jovan, for linking me to Kannon. So, Kannon, drinks on me as an official thank you?" I said, then hunched my shoulders as if to say the ball was in his court—well, because it was.

I reviewed the stitch, admiring my hella simple yet sexy vibes in the video.

Am I shooting my shot? Hell yeah.

Kannon Jordan had me smitten, and I knew this man and I had to meet up. We just had to.

Chapter Seven

KANNON

WHEN IT CAME to women, I'd had my fair share. That's why I'd been chill the past three years. My brother and dad called it the settle-down syndrome. All the things that used to excite me just didn't anymore. I didn't care for the random DMs, fake IG models, or ease of sex through sites like Pornhub or Twitter After Dark. It didn't impress me. Sure, I appreciated a nice body like the next man. No cap. But I wasn't out here scrounging around for it like some sex-deprived teenager after his first piece of the box.

That's why I wasn't ecstatic when I received Dr. Richards' reply to my video. Jovan, all the men at the fire station, and even my brother were overhyped about her and trying to coax my mind into ulterior thoughts. Now was she cute? Nope. She was *beyond* cute. Honestly, she was one of the most beautiful women I'd ever seen. A *certified* baddie. But that didn't mean I needed or even wanted to get in her pants. More importantly, it didn't mean she wanted to get into mine. What it meant was that a very grateful and *beautiful* young woman wanted to thank me for my service. No more. No less.

"Where are you meeting up again?" Kinston asked as he spotted me during my last set of reps on the bench press.

"Three, two, and one," I said, then pushed up the bar holding two hundred and fifty pounds of weights while Kinston guided it to the holder. "Brick."

"Nice." He snapped his fingers as another question came to his mind. "Is it cool for y'all to meet—you know, with COVID and all?"

"I'm sure she's good with it since she invited me. Like me, she probably tests frequently because of her profession. Besides, the city restrictions have been lifted, as you know, and the bar is still practicing social distancing."

"A'ight. Just looking out. That's good the bar does that. Hell, we still sanitize around here. Lysol and Microban COVID right up outta here," he joked though he was serious. "So, are you meeting her today?"

"Yeah." I wiped my sweat with the towel and threw it down beside me. "At five p.m. We're just meeting up for drinks and appetizers."

Kinston sat on the bench across from me, picking up a dumbbell. "And it's *cool*?"

Snickering, I couldn't help but shake my head. My brother always had my back.

"Man, it's cool. It's a *friendly* visit. She wants to thank me with a couple of drinks and some snacks. I respect it."

"Snacks, you say?" Kinston laughed. "What kind of snacks, bro?"

"You nasty as hell, bro. I swear," I said behind a chuckle, but he shrugged off my comment.

"Are y'all gonna have cameras there? I mean, since you are both TikTok famous now."

He wasn't lying. The original video had now amassed over two million views, and our response videos were in the high hundreds of thousands of views. Even our followership had grown. Dr. Richards was now sitting at about three hundred thousand followers, and my list had grown to a little over one hundred thousand followers. While I enjoyed the initial banter over the videos, I wasn't into being in the limelight. I enjoyed the interaction with people...well, the sane ones...especially while working at the station because it passed the time away. Some major companies had even contacted me to be a brand ambassador with paid partnerships. That part definitely wasn't bad. In fact, I'd secured a deal with a protein powder company and an underwear line. I received my items free, a forty-percent commission off the products, *and* a sign-on bonus. So far, I'd made a nice little grip.

All the attention wasn't bad attention. I just preferred my private life to be private. It's a rare phenomenon these days, especially with my generation, but I didn't believe everything called for a social media announcement. However, I was cognizant that the entire reason I had this newfound TikTok fame was precisely because of that. Still, no cameras would be rolling on me and the good doctor. We would probably give each other a shoutout, and that would be that.

"Boi, get the hell outta here." I pushed him on the knee. "You know I'm not about that life. I don't mind the bonuses that have come from this whole situation, but I'll be glad when my privacy can be restored."

"I'm just clowning you, bro. I know you're not about that life in real life."

I stood and stretched. "It's all good, bro. You ain't the first person to clown me over this whole thing, and you won't be the last. I'm getting used to it now."

Staring at myself in the mirror, I felt an emotion I hadn't ever felt with a woman—nervousness. My outfit was on point with my black fitted slacks, gray polo shirt, and black Marc Nolan sneaker loafers. My cropped wavy hair was glistening, my five o'clock shadow beard was nicely trimmed, and my Versace Eros cologne added the lingering hint of freshness I loved. With the addition of my Talley & Twine watch, I knew I was dressed to impress. Still, I felt unnerved, and I had no clue why.

My phone buzzed in my pocket. I pushed ignore and then activated my Do Not Disturb feature. I didn't have time to entertain anyone's foolery. Grabbing my wallet and my Heat facemask, I headed out of the door on my way to Brick to meet my TikTok partner-in-crime.

When I arrived, I asked the host if she had arrived, and she said no. It was nice and breezy out, so I opted to sit outside with the live band. Since Dr. Richards and I had exchanged numbers, I texted her to let her know I was there and where I was seated. She texted back that she was on her way. Of course, she was fashionably late. I had ordered my first drink and was vibing to the live music while sipping on my Henny when I realized ten minutes had passed. After checking my phone again and seeing a text from her stating she was there, I relaxed.

I had just taken another sip of my Henny and placed the glass down when I turned around to see a vision of perfection saunter through the doors. She stood there for a moment, scanning the bar until she landed on me. It was as if our eyes were magnetically pulled to each other. Even though she wore a clear face shield, I knew her TikToks did her absolutely no justice. Her coiled hair framed her face perfectly, and the strapless, form-fitting, Mediterranean-colored dress hugged every curve of her body. The strappy stilettos on her feet showcased her sexy, toned legs and cute pedicured toes. When she smiled at me and waved, my heart damn near exploded. Like seriously, what the hell was going on with me? When she got near, she removed her shield and placed it by my Miami Heat facemask. Then I stood, and all six-foot-two-inches of me hovered over her tiny frame.

"Dr. Richards?"

"Mr. Jordan?"

We both cracked flirty smiles and then hugged. She felt so soft against me, as if I were cuddling clouds. Her sexy fragrance tickled my nose. My God. She smelled divine. As soon as we disconnected, I felt as if I'd unplugged from my life source. Yeah, I was going crazy because that made no sense. I didn't know this woman, but her essence felt familiar. Pulling myself out of my thoughts, I remembered my gentlemanly manners and pulled out the chair for her, then scooted it up before reclaiming my seat across from her.

"Wow. It is so good to finally meet you," she said with a hint of a blush.

"You, as well. I appreciate this kind gesture, but it really wasn't necessary. It was part of my job, and I love what I do."

"I know, but I just felt the need to thank you anyway."

"Welp, who am I to turn down free drinks and food?"

We shared a laugh, and it felt like we even laughed in sync. This was by far the most comfortable yet awkward moment of my life.

"You look gorgeous, by the way."

This time she did blush, and I swore something rumbled in my gut.

"Thank you, and you look very debonair yourself."

Just then, the waitress came over and took her drink order and my new one. We also decided to order some food to soak up the alcohol we were consuming. I knew Dr. Richards had every intention of paying, but there was no way I would allow her to foot the bill, even if it were my thank-you gift. We'd been enjoying the view and the music when the waitress returned with our drinks.

"Shall we make a toast?" I asked, holding up my glass.

She lifted hers. "What should we toast to?"

"Rescues, good times, and new friends."

Her smile lit up as she clinked glasses with me.

"To rescues, good times, and new friends," she repeated, then took a sip before setting her glass down. "So, Mr. Jordan, tell me more about yourself and the life of a fireman."

"Well, Dr. Richards, what would you like to know?"

"Call me Nissi, please. And whatever you feel comfortable enough to reveal."

"As long as you call me Kannon."

She giggled. "Fair enough, Kannon."

My name oozed off her lips like butter, and I almost rescinded my offer for her to call me by my first name just to make sure my man down below didn't overreact if she spoke it again.

"There's not much tell, I guess. I'm twenty-seven years old, and I've always wanted to be a fireman ever since I saw one save my friend from a burning building in elementary school."

"Wow. Talk about scary and interesting at the same time."

"I know. My father always said it was strange that I'd gotten encouraged to become a fireman from that incident. He thought it would have the opposite effect on me—that I'd run scared."

"You don't strike me as someone who runs from scary situations."

"That and my daddy didn't raise no punk."

That caused her to burst into a fit of giggles. At the same time, my heart erupted with something unknown.

"That he did not." Raising her hand, she quipped, "I'm a witness."

Concern taking the forefront of my thoughts, I gently clasped her hand into mine without thinking. I paused before speaking, surprised at my impromptu level of intimacy and waiting for her to smack me for such a bold action. Instead, her hand relaxed in mine as if this was our natural interaction.

I softly caressed it and continued, "Speaking of, how are you feeling? How's the ankle?"

Eyeing her ankle, she twirled it around in a circle so I could see it for myself.

"It's fine now. I doctored it very well. Thank you for asking."

"That's good to hear. Although, I figured you were better from the video you took in those stilettos. Ain't no weak ankles modeling those shoes."

"All facts." She paused for a beat and cleared her throat. "So, you liked that video, huh?"

Finally releasing her hand, I sipped from my drink and bobbed. "Very much so. I loved them both. At this point, I think I'm a bit of a fanboy of all your TikToks."

Her face lit up before she laid her hand on my arm. "And I, you. I see you and those sponsorships. You betta! Congratulations!"

Her giddiness was infectious. I swear.

"You bouta make me blush, woman. Thank you. So, why don't you do any sponsorships? I know you've had to be approached."

Before she could answer, our waitress brought our food. Both of us said grace before we began devouring the crispy chicken nachos. *She also believes in God. Noted. But why, though? Why did I make a mental note of her beliefs? Surely, I won't need to know that information.*

Wiping a dab of sauce from her luscious lips, she answered, "I'm leery about it because I don't want to be in breach of contract with my job. As a dentist, I receive many sponsors wanting me to showcase dental hygiene products, but some of that stuff isn't FDA-approved, and I can't risk my job or my license. Now, I have been approached by some hair care companies as of late, so who knows? I may. My second reason is that I'm very particular about what I use on my skin and hair, so I have to vet it first."

She didn't have to tell me. Her skin sparkled like diamonds, and her hair glistened. The fruity scent of her shampoo kept wafting in the breeze along with her perfume, sending my senses into overdrive. A lesser man would've tried to get between her legs by now. 'Cause, no cap, baby girl exuded a sensuality that made you want to explore more than just her conversation.

Leaning in, I whispered, "I can tell you take care of yourself. Very well, baby girl."

She blushed again. Even that was otherworldly. I wondered if she knew just how desirable she was without even trying.

"Tell me about becoming a dentist. You seem rather young to be so accomplished."

She lifted her glass and tilted it to me before taking another sip of her Pink Lady. "And I am. I'm twenty-six, and I busted my tail to accelerate through college and dental school. I earned my degrees and title with grace, so I wear that doctor badge with pride."

"*Twenty-six?*"

I was floored. I just knew she was older than me. Not that she looked older, but because she was a dentist. I would've pegged her to be around twenty-eight or twenty-nine because of that accomplishment alone but not younger than me. *Wow!* She was beauty *and* brains, and that made her desirability shoot up two hundred percent.

"I'm impressed." I nodded with appreciation and a bit of shock. "Truly, that's outstanding. I know your family is proud."

"Yes, they are. I'm the baby of the group, so they are proud, nosy, overbearing…alladat!" she joked. "My sisters might be at a table stalking us right now." She looked around as if scanning for them, which amused me because I understood.

"Shoot, my brother and best friend would probably be with them."

Her brows lifted in curiosity. "Mmm, best friend? That would be Jovan, right?"

"How'd you guess?" I joked, knowing Jovan was the reason we were able to reconnect.

Her expression turned serious, and the way she smiled demurely made my heart gallop, feeling as though a stable of Clydesdales were beating on my chest. *What in the world is happening to me?*

She followed that with the most thoughtful sentiment. "Well, I couldn't argue with him if he was. I mean, we might not have this opportunity without him."

The way she expressed that made me bite my lip to keep them off her lips. Momentarily, she seemed caught up in the same trance. We couldn't tear our eyes off each other. The synergy was intense, and I was two seconds away from pulling this woman into my arms. But then, she cleared her throat and glanced away. It was the correct move. Not the one I wanted, but it was for the best.

Pulling out her cell phone, she waved it in front of me. "I guess we should make them and the rest of the TikTok universe happy and record a video. That's if you don't mind."

"Mind? I'm all for it. At least it will halt all the questions if they see the video. As much as I appreciate your gesture and some of the opportunities that came along, people have been on my nerves about my private life."

"Same!" she nearly shouted. Her hand landed on top of mine and lingered. "Let me apologize. I don't do personal on any app like that, but my sister said it was the best way to try to locate you. I even debated it for a couple of days. I didn't realize when I posted it that it would snowball into the *Nissi and Kannon Show.*"

Motioning my hands in refusal, I clarified, "No, please don't think I'm upset about it. I think what you did was extremely thoughtful and nice. It's just—"

"You appreciate your privacy. I get it. I swear I do."

I was relieved she felt the same. Being a good sport, I pulled out my phone.

"Let's make two videos—one for your page and one for mine. That way, we have everyone covered. Same caption and all."

Giddily, she replied, "Let's do it."

I scooted my chair beside her, and since I was taller, I took the phone from her hand and held it out once she had the app ready.

"So, are we freeballing it?" she asked.

"That's the only way to go. If we practice, it'll seem scripted. I say go with the flow."

She nodded, and after ensuring we were both in the frame, I pressed the timer. Once it counted down, she waved with the brightest smile.

"It's your girl, Dr. Nissi, That Dentist Chick, and look who I linked up with, you guys—Mr. Fire and Rescue." She pointed at me, and I beamed brightly.

"What up, TikTok land? It's your boi, King Kannon, aka Mr. Fire and Rescue," I stressed for silly effect. "And yep, I'm out on the town with the beautiful and sweet damsel in elevator distress. Thank you all so much for helping her locate me. My thank-you dinner and drinks are amazing." I faced her and smiled. "Thank you, Dr. Nissi."

She leaned in, embracing me giddily, and I had to ensure I kept my life together.

"Aww, you're welcome," she said before looking back at the camera. "Just wanted to update you all and say thanks again to everyone who tagged and shared."

"We up," we said together.

It shocked us both that we ended the video that way because it wasn't rehearsed. After reviewing the footage, we decided to reshoot the same message on my phone. Once we finished our impromptu videos, we posted them simultaneously.

Both of our captions read *Miami Nights*. *#MrFireAndRescue meets #ThatDentistChick*. We then put our phones on silent and returned to our evening out, enjoying each other.

After the video, we finished our food while talking about anything we could think of—our careers, hobbies, aspirations, siblings, disdains, and likes of different music, food, and essential topics. We even discussed the weather. Before we knew it, we'd been sitting there for three hours. I only took notice because I saw her shiver from the night winds that had begun to stir as the sun set on the horizon.

"I didn't mean to have you out this long. You're cold."

"No," she said, shaking her head. "I was enjoying myself. Don't feel bad. But I am getting a little chilly out here."

"I have a jacket in my truck. What do you say we get out of here and walk along the beach?"

"You're not sick of me yet?" she giggled.

"Your allegiance to the Dolphins almost ran me away, but I'll give you that because of Dan Marino."

She rolled her eyes and lightly swatted me. "How can you call yourself a Miamian and not root for the Dolphins?"

"The same way my brother roots for the Lakers."

She cringed at the thought.

"It could be worse. I could be a Jaguars fan," I added.

She nearly choked on the last of her drink. She wiped her mouth with the napkin as I patted her back during her coughing spell.

"You almost killed me with that notion! Got me out here sounding like a case of coronavirus." She laughed heartily. "Now, you being a Jag fan would be a tragedy. That option is one step worse than the Buccaneers."

"Tom Brady is the goat. Fuck outta here."

"The goat of cheating and controversy," she quipped. "I mean, I give the man his props. He's exceptional, but don't act like people didn't cater to him and for him. Mr. Fourth Down, but the game was over."

Howling, I choked out, "The man made a mistake!"

"The man had a concussion from getting planted on his butt. Getting hit is his kryptonite," she challenged me. "That and inflated footballs."

I threw my napkin over the empty plates. "You know what, I think I'm sicka you." It was my only comeback after that Deflategate jab. "And I was gonna let you wrap in my jacket as we strolled along the beach and everything," I teased as if rescinding my offer.

"Aww, I'm sorry, not sorry, but I'm sorry," she cackled, amusing herself.

Her little feisty banter amused me, too, but I pretended it didn't. Despite putting up a valiant effort, I failed miserably. This woman was hilarious, witty, charming, laid back, and super intelligent—all wrapped in one fine-ass bow.

Spotting the waitress, I raised my hand, and she came over. "Check, please."

The waitress smiled at us and nodded before walking away.

"Oh, so you're really ready to get rid of me now?" She reached into her purse to pull out her wallet. "I see how it is."

Wagging my finger at her, I quipped, "You're a mess, Nissi. I'm just trying to give these people back their restaurant and finish this conversation privately."

"Oh, he still wants to spend time with me." Her eyes gleamed with excitement.

I caught the glint in her eyes, and I wasn't going to fumble it either. Leaning forward, I licked my lips, turning serious. "If that's what you'd like. No pressure, but I'm enjoying myself. So, if you'd like to continue without freezing…" I rubbed my hand on her shoulder. "I'm down."

My newfound emotion from earlier emerged for the first time since I'd met Nissi. Nervousness. She swallowed hard and diverted her eyes from mine as she attempted to create warmth by rubbing her arms. She was nervous, too. Recognizing the emotion, I lifted my index finger to her chin and gently turned her face back to mine. I wanted to assure her there was no need to feel anxious around me. When our eyes connected this time, there was that magnetic energy again that we seemed lost within. I couldn't pull away from her on my own recognizance if I tried or wanted to. The "wanting to" was the portion I was struggling with. Nothing and no one else mattered in the space and time I was trapped inside with Nissi. Our heads moved closer to each other, but before our lips could touch, the waitress returned with the tab.

Nissi jerked back and cleared her throat. "I have that right here."

She fished for her card in her wallet, but I had already slipped the waitress my credit card before she could dig hers out.

"No worries. I got this."

As the waitress went to walk away, Nissi stopped her.

"No, wait. This was my treat, and I insist."

The waitress stalled to see what she should do, and I put my hand up.

"It's fine. You can use my card," I offered to the waitress, who still stood there, unsure of whose instructions to follow. Then I turned to Nissi. "I appreciate the offer, but the invite was thanks enough. Besides, I wouldn't dare allow you to foot a bill for me."

Her head tilted to the side. "But I wanted to thank you."

"And you have." Capturing her hand into mine, I added, "I was raised old school. I wouldn't feel comfortable, and my father would kick my ass—grown man or not."

She recoiled with a girlish smile that was soft and adorable. Finally, she nodded to the waitress that it was all right.

"At least allow me to leave the tip."

With a deep sigh, I relented. "If you must do something, I guess the tip is a decent compromise."

Before I changed my mind, she fished out forty dollars and placed it on the table.

"Thank you for allowing me to pay. I know you wanted to treat me, but your presence and time have been the biggest treat."

Her eyes danced, and I knew I'd left an impression on her.

"Now *that...*" She slid her finger across my hand. "That earned you more of my time."

And my brawny six-foot-two self blushed full-on. "So, a beach walk it is?"

"It is."

The waitress brought my card back, and while I was signing, Nissi gave the lady her tip, which she almost fell out over. It's a shame that paying something as simple as the gratuity made a waitress's day. It was awful that people paid below the bare minimum or nothing at all.

"Thank you both so much," the waitress said. "I don't mean to interrupt or be offensive, but are you two, Mr. Fire and Rescue and That Dentist Chick?"

We looked at each other, sharing knowing glances. Finally, I nodded.

"Yes, that's us."

"OMG! I thought so, but I didn't want to intrude. Do you mind if I take a picture with the two of you to post on my TikTok and IG?"

Nissi and I agreed, and the waitress slipped her phone from out of her back pocket. She snapped a few photos and was kind enough to allow Nissi and me to pick the best one. While still standing in front of us, she posted the picture with the caption:

Look who I served at my restaurant! Yep, it's @kingkannon94, aka Mr. Fire and Rescue, and @ThatDentistChick! They are so dope!

After that, she thanked us again before walking off.

"Are you thinking what I'm thinking?" Nissi asked.

I hit her with a head nod. "Yep, let's go before someone else recognizes us."

With that, we both stood to leave.

Chapter Eight

NISSI

I NEVER UNDERSTOOD THE phrase "having an out-of-body experience" when meeting someone. I didn't believe in instant attraction or love at first sight until Kannon. He made me a believer. Lawd, that man was everything. When I first spotted him in the restaurant, I nearly buckled. If I thought he was fine in his videos and even in my frazzled state when he rescued me, it was nothing compared to the man I walked in on at Brick. He was fresh dressed, and his woodsy cedarwood scent made my juices brew. When he stood to embrace me, I nearly passed out. All six feet and more of him embodied with muscles, a charming smile, and gorgeous hair had me and all my highly educatedness stuck on stupid. His *everything* was just sexy as hell.

To get over my astonishment at his outer sexiness, I surmised he was all brawn and no brain, but I was wrong—not just wrong, but dead wrong. He was intelligent and could converse about something more than himself and his muscles. He wasn't arrogant as most guys would be, and he respected my space and how he spoke to me. He was a gentleman through and through, and I knew then that his parents raised him right. He further reassured me when he insisted on paying for the meal. Obviously, I was prepared and more than willing to pay for it. That, of course, was my reason for inviting him out. However, the fact that he took such great pride in taking care of the check meant he wanted to be the man and provider in the relationship, not a boy posing as a man. The kind of poser who looks for a woman to take care of him. No, Mr. Kannon Jordan was all man, a thoroughbred.

When I followed him to the beach, I was grateful I had my Chanel slides in the back of my car. He allowed me to change out of my heels, and keeping his word, he draped his jacket over my shoulders before we began walking. He was the consummate gentleman. We walked and talked for several minutes before deciding to rent a privacy-covered cabana to lay inside and look out at the ocean and night sky. Once we settled inside, he ensured that I was taken care of.

"Are you good? Comfortable?" he asked, his face full of concern.

Nodding, I pulled his jacket tighter around me. "I'm good."

"Good." He lay back with his arm behind his head and the other draped around my shoulder. "Man, I can't remember the last time I've had so much fun, relaxing and enjoying myself. Thank you for this."

"Shoot, I should be thanking you at this point," I said, and I was serious.

He glimpsed down at me, inquisitiveness furrowing his brow. "Why do you say that?"

I motioned around me. "This. The whole idea of it. You know, for as long as I've lived in Miami, I've never done this—rented a cabana on the beach."

"I'm not shocked at that." He shrugged. "Most people travel the world looking for wonders that can be found in their backyard. I've learned to appreciate the moments surrounding me," Kannon said as I snuggled against him, enjoying the warmth of his body.

Christ. This man has a way with words.

"It's when you say things like that, that I wonder where you came from."

"I'm a rare breed, but so are you."

Intrigued, I glanced up at him and asked, "How so?"

He paused for a moment as if contemplating, then answered, "Your vibe. You have every right to act like a high-sidity woman with her ass on her shoulders because of your accomplishments, but you don't. You're chill and down-to-earth. Then, you're not a typical Miami chick. You enjoy things like social media, but for the reason it was intended—to connect and have fun. Not to flash your body for likes and sell your soul for attention. It shows me that you're rooted in the same kind of stable foundation I am. Even the fact that you almost boxed me to pay the bill. A lot of these women not only expect a man to pay the bill but take issue with *how* they pay it. If you've got cash, then your credit must be bad. If you pay by credit card, you're irresponsible and have no money in the bank, and if you pay by debit card, you have no credit or bad credit. It's a never-ending cycle of what she can get from him instead of what value she can add to him. Likewise, men are just as bad. I'm not ashamed to tell the truth about that. Many of them run after those types of women and then complain about them but will bypass a woman like you and say she's too independent or headstrong. Our generation got the game all wrong, and most don't even know themselves, let alone what they want from another person. You and I…*we* are rare, but rare is gold, in my opinion."

Just like that, my lace thongs were drenched. My heart skipped ten beats, trying to find the one that could calm me down. I had no idea I'd been staring at him until he flashed a half-smile as his forehead creased.

"What? Did I say something wrong?" he asked.

Contrary, he'd said everything right. Done everything right. Showed me everything right about him. I saw value in the pursuit and wanted to be sought after, but how rare was it that a person didn't have to pursue what they hoped one day to find? Fate decided to hand deliver us to each other, no pursuit needed. My sisters and friends' words replayed in my mind. No idling in wait. I'd take the plunge. I'd take it…for Kannon.

I didn't answer his question but instead brought my mouth to his and gently kissed him. He pecked mine back, being careful not to force more, but I longed for more. So, I deepened the kiss, and I felt his resistance.

"Nissi," he breathed out.

I brought my finger to his lips. "Tonight, you've taught me about living in the moment. Live in it with me."

This time when our lips collided, it felt like mini explosions erupted in the pit of my stomach. I could feel his excitement, too, as our tongues danced methodically, savoring each other. By the time we finished the kiss, our breathing was erratic, and I was on fire. I had never been adventurous, but for Kannon Jordan, I learned quickly to seize the opportunity. I climbed on top of him, peeling out of his jacket and wrapping it around my waist. He was hard as steel, and the feel of his imprint told me that he equally anticipated our connection. That, and I'd be enormously pleased when he released it. His wallet lay above his head, and I lifted it.

"Condom in here?"

"What are you—"

"*Condom.* Is there one in here?" I repeated, letting him know my urgency.

He swallowed and nodded, then opened it and lifted the gold packet. While he fumbled with taking the condom out of the wrapper, I made it my business to undo his belt, unbutton his pants, and slip that luscious thickness out of its boxer briefs confinement.

Once the condom was out, I took it from his hands, much to his surprise. His eyes lifted, but when he realized what I was doing, he folded both hands behind his head, giving me access to take the wheel. Masterfully, I rolled down the covering over his shaft, gently stroking him along the way.

"Shit, Nissi," he said breathily.

Once our safety net was secured, I felt his hands caressing my voluptuous hips as he rolled my dress upward to my waist. He touched my thong and ripped the thin fabric, discarding it in a heap beside us. Apparently, he loved how my rotundness felt as he palmed it and tapped it several times. My moans were low and sensual. I loved the feel of his hands on my body. They felt as if they belonged there.

I'd be lying if I said I wasn't nervous. I was apprehensive because I was super tight yet wetter than I'd ever experienced. It'd been nearly a year since I had been penetrated with something that wasn't battery-operated. Of the two sex partners I'd had, neither made me feel how Kannon was making me feel. I'd known Joshua throughout my childhood. He had been my longest relationship from senior year in high school to our sophomore year in college. We'd had sex when we were freshmen in college. Those feelings and experiences were new; we were young, so it felt good. But compared to what? Benji, I'd met in dental college. He wasn't my boyfriend, but rather a great friend and study partner turned beneficiary. We'd been what each other needed. Sure, he wanted more, but I wasn't into him for anything more than study and sex. He had been a good guy, intelligent, funny, and attractive, but at the time, my goal wasn't to get serious with anyone. We carried off and on throughout dental school, and just as we entered our professional careers, he decided if I weren't going to give him more, he'd rather find someone who would. Even my times with him were of no comparison. Kannon felt and made me feel as he declared…rare.

Kannon's sensuous teasing as we continued to kiss drove me insane.

"Ooh, Kannon," I said, moaning his name.

It was as if his name on my lips flipped a switch in him. When he stared at me this time, his eyes revealed a lustful animalistic need for me. He pulled his bottom lip between his teeth and bit down on it before lifting me so I was positioned just right to slide down his length.

"Ride me, baby."

His command came out in the deepest tenor, and I sprang into action—gliding down on him inch by glorious… painstakingly glorious…inch. The moment we were completely connected, we groaned. *Damn.* It felt…*like*…like *home.* The pain felt so good as I felt my walls expanding, making room for him inside my oasis. Slowly, I rode him until we found our rhythm, and our moans filled the space with our wanton needs. And I was so wet, so gotdamn wet.

"Ooh, you're so tight but wet for me, baby. It feels so good," he said, confirming what I already knew.

He took control of my body by gripping my hips and rolling forward and backward, making me take all of him. He filled me to the hilt. It pained so deliciously good. It didn't take long for my depths to open completely to him, and that's when I put my back into it and rode him like a stallion, losing my mind in the process. My juices rained down, and delirium took over. Kannon could've asked me anything at that moment, and I would've agreed.

"Oh, Kannon! Oh, *gawddd.*" My moans rippled out. "Take it," I panted softly.

Kannon's face tightened, and he bit out, "*Fuck!*"

Those obvious days of training in the gym paid off because he held me in place and lifted me so his back was against the back of the cabana rather than lying down completely to give him better leverage. He flipped down the front of my strapless dress and bra with one hand. My breasts plopped out, and he helped himself to a mouthful, gliding his thick tongue over my nipples and encasing them in his full mouth. He sucked and licked with fervor yet tenderly while continuing to roll my hips back and forth on his girth. It felt so good that I held both my breasts in my hands and fed them to him as if he was gaining nourishment from them. He was milking me dry, and I loved every second of it.

My moans became ragged as he pleasured me within the confines of the cabana. He felt the shift in my body and knew I was almost there. Lifting his face, he gripped me with both hands and pulled me down harder on his shaft, exploring and stretching my depths with skilled perfection. It felt so good that my head dropped to focus on my impending orgasm. I was going to explode harder than I ever had in life. I knew it. I *felt* it.

"Nah, look at me. I want to see your face when you cum for me," Kannon ordered.

As if I belonged to him, I obeyed his command. The moment I gazed into his lustful, determined, and confident eyes, I came undone. My love faces caused him to smile sinisterly.

"I'm cumming!" The roar came from a voice I didn't recognize—even though it was my own.

"Oooh, that's it, baby. Cum for me."

His tone was pleased, obviously happy to be the one to unearth me. And cum, I did.

"It's so good. Mmm, Kannon. *Oooh, Kann…Nonnnn!*"

I exploded and collapsed on top of his chest. So much pleasure had been released that, for a minute, I lost consciousness. *What has this man been blessed with?* His sex baptized me and almost eulogized me. While I was certain I was lying near death's door, he wasn't finished. He held me tightly, flipped us over without losing the connection, and thrust upward with measured and snake-like movements.

"Yes, baby. Let me please you," Kannon whispered.

Spent and in a pleasure overload, I could do nothing more than hold on for the ride. I managed to cuff my hands around his chin and plant a deep kiss on his lips, moaning out the sounds I could no longer formulate into words. I was gone. Our orbs honed and peered into each other, even amid the still darkness of the night. Our gazes were transfixed as if we were imprinted on each other's souls, feverishly lip-locking and entangled in a moment that was so much more than our carnal lust. The gaze, the kiss, and our lustful moans must've done it for Kannon because I felt his body tense as he worked as if he were unearthing lost treasure.

"Shit," he whimpered as his head fell back. "Ahh!"

The growl that emanated from him made my love button twitch. I couldn't believe it, but as he came, I came again.

"Nissi, *gotdamn!*"

"*Kannonnnn!*"

Chapter Nine

KANNON

WHAT IN THE *entire hell have I just done?* I had the most amazing sex of my life with one of the most beautiful and sexy women I didn't even know. How could that be? How could she turn me on beyond a level that women I knew...women I had dated... hadn't done? When she sank on me, it felt like I'd found a missing piece of me that I had unknowingly lost. She was new to me but felt familiar. *What in the ancestral plane is going on here?*

All I could do was hold her when she collapsed against my chest after we both came. I had to make sure she was real. What we'd done together had to be an illusion. Not because I didn't believe it happened but rather because we sexed each other in a way that could only be matched by lovers who knew each other...*loved* each other. I had met Nissi only hours ago, less than twenty-four of them. I wouldn't have believed it if I hadn't experienced it myself. These feelings had me both excited and confused. No cap. I had to will myself from whisking this woman away to my house and never allowing her to leave. It wasn't even about the sex. Okay, that's total cap. It *was* about the sex but more about the feelings I'd been trying hard not to experience since she walked her sexy self through those doors at Brick. Nissi had me questioning everything about myself, my beliefs—hell, about life.

When she snuggled up to me and gazed up into my face with hazy, dream-filled eyes, it was at that precise moment I realized I had messed up in more ways than one. I refused to be *that* dude while being guilty of being *that* dude.

Weakly, she sat up, flipped her bra and dress over her breasts, and gave me a smile that broke my heart into a thousand pieces.

"I'm normally not this forward. I've only had two sexual partners before tonight. I was caught up and feeling so much about you and—"

I brought my finger to her lips to calm her. I knew from the tightness that baby girl wasn't getting any on the regular. Her oasis felt virginal. Besides that, she didn't have to explain what was understood. We were grownups who were feeling each other and had a grownup moment. Plain and simple. At least, for her, it was that plain and that simple.

"You don't need to explain your decisions, least of all, to me. I enjoyed it, baby girl. Believe that."

Vulnerability crossed her face as her shoulders hunched up, and I knew she was about to hit me with the question I dreaded.

"*So*, where do we go from here?"

I drew in a deep breath, but before I could speak, nervous Nissi intervened.

"I mean, there's no pressure. If it was a one-time deal, I can accept that. I don't want you to feel like I'm stalkerish or clingy. I just…it felt like so much more there to be explored to me, and I was wondering if it felt like that for you because—"

"I have a girlfriend." I ripped the Band-Aid off.

She swallowed and fell back against the cabana. "What? A what?"

The disappointment in her voice was what I would have paid to avoid. Yep, I felt every bit like the crap she probably perceived me to be. Regret filled me. Not because of what we did but because of what I had revealed and how I knew it hurt her to hear it.

Peeling off the loaded condom, I straightened my man below back into my pants before attempting to explain myself. "Listen, Nissi. I have a girlfriend, but it's not what—"

The slap knocked the words clean down my throat. She may have been about five-foot-three and only around one-hundred-and-thirty pounds, but that slap felt like a knock from a defensive tackle. She leaped from the cabana with the agility of a panther, straightening her dress and scouring for her Chanel slides.

Throwing the condom in the receptacle, I straightened my clothes while begging her to hear me out. "Nissi, please listen to me. I'm sorry."

"Sorry?" She stared up at me, pushing her hair behind her ears. "You just went into an entire soliloquy about bum dudes our age, and then you sit there and admit to me after five hours together, flirting and..." She stepped closer and lowered her voice to a whisper. "...*fucking*, that you have a girlfriend. You're trash, bro!" She located her other slide. "Where's my purse?" she bellowed, looking about frantically.

As bad as it hurt to hear her call me trash, I deserved that. She wasn't lying. I was every name in the book for sexing her without telling her. In my defense, I only planned to have a thank-you dinner with a woman I rescued—not enjoy her, feel anything for her, or fuck her. But here we were.

"I tried to tell you. I wanted to tell you."

My words came out scrambled as she leaped into the cabana to retrieve her purse. She spun around so fast that her butt plopped down on the cabana bed, and I seized the opportunity to block her there so she could hear my side of the story.

"*Tried to tell me?* You couldn't tell me within five hours?" She shook her head in disbelief. "Move."

"No, not until you let me explain."

"I'll scream. I swear to God."

"Go ahead, Nissi. There's nobody out here. So, scream. Go ahead."

"Are you threatening me?"

"What? No. Come on." I hurriedly took it back because I didn't want her to believe I was a psycho. "I would like to apologize and explain my poor actions. Everything you've said, I deserve. I own that. Just let me explain, please."

She sat there for a little while contemplating my words. Finally, she said, "Fine. Explain yourself so I can go home, and move so that I can stand up. I need to breathe."

I stood back and attempted to help her out of the cabana, but she swatted my hand away. So, I stepped back out of her space. She stood stoic before me with her arms folded across her chest. Yep, with that admission, she had already shut me out.

"Talk," she demanded with such authority I thought my mama had appeared from the grave and issued the command.

I didn't even waste any time, either. "My girlfriend—"

"A damn girlfriend," she spat, her nose flaring and head shaking. "Unbelievable."

"Nissi, *please*."

She threw her hands up. "I'm quiet. You've got one minute or less."

Running my hand over my face, I wondered why I was trying to explain the situation to her. Easy answer. Even though I was wrong, I was selfish, too. I wanted her to enjoy this beautiful moment we had shared without dwelling on the fact it never should've happened. The exact fuckboy persona I'd just denounced.

"River and I have an open relationship. You see, she's a painter, an artist. She travels a lot with spoken word artists and musicians, performing live paintings. She's always been upfront that she doesn't want to put restrictions on our relationship because things happen. With her being gone for weeks, she may have the urge to satisfy a need just like I may have one. So, we agreed to have an open relationship."

"Wait. So I'm just some notch on your open relationship belt? Wow."

"No, you're not." I released a deep sigh. "See, we agreed to tell the person we want to have a sexual encounter with about our significant other. If that person is cool with the situation, River and I discuss it. If we approve, we're free and clear to be with that person. It keeps River and me on the up and up with each other while being straight up with our temporary sexual partner. With you, I hadn't planned any of this. It was only supposed to be drinks and appetizers. River even thought the idea was cute. I didn't expect to meet you and feel things or have sex with you. When you first kissed me in the cabana, I tried to say something, but the way you had me feeling in there—hell, this entire night, I didn't want you to stop. *I* didn't want to stop. It was selfish, and it was wrong. I feel terrible, and I'm sorry. Still, I'm not sorry about what happened between us. I'm only sorry I didn't handle it properly."

"So what am I supposed to do with this information now? The deed is done."

My worried eyes met her gaze. "I'm not sure," I lied.

I wanted her to tell me that she would agree to be with me as my girl even though I had a girlfriend because I wanted every ounce of Nissi Richards. This one-and-done situation was not something I was feeling. What I *was* feeling was her—so much so that I considered picking up my cell right then and admitting my transgressions to River. I would beg her for her forgiveness while being upfront that Nissi wasn't some random I wanted to let go of. I wanted a chance to explore whatever was happening with Nissi, even knowing how wrong I was for wanting it.

She shoved me. "You're such a liar. I can see it in your face. Now that you've had a taste, you want me to agree to this cockamamie ideology of two girlfriends and an open relationship. Say I'm lying."

The fact that she read right through my bullshit blew me. How was it even real for her to know me as if we'd been dating for years? Sheer insanity. I had already not been as forthcoming as I should've been initially, and she had me pegged. I wouldn't lessen my image by throwing out a blatant lie. One that, apparently, she'd see right through anyway.

"I can't say that, Nissi."

She turned to walk away, and I gently grasped her arm. She snatched it away but stood there.

"It's weird. It's wrong. It's downright messed up, but I know I won't be able to shake you. Regardless of how upset you are right now, you felt something festering between us, and I'm not just talking about sex. You felt it, and I felt it, too. And I would love to explore that."

She turned completely to face me with the most incredulous look and her hands on her hips. "You have bigger balls than Goliath. I can't believe you had the audacity to gas me this entire night, screw me, then admit you have a girlfriend, and *then* try to bate me into being a part of your collection of concubines."

"I don't have any concubines. I've never even done this before."

"So you've never cheated on your girlfriend until tonight?"

"Cheated" felt like a slight, but I realized she was right. I had cheated. And with her. My odds kept sinking, and so did my outlook.

"Technically, you're right. River and I have been together for two years. I've slept with River and two other women in that timespan. Both were only a couple of times, only about sex, and River knew about them ahead of time. So, it wasn't cheating." Sadly, I admitted the cold truth. "And yes, tonight, I cheated."

Sheer disgust spread across her face, and I would've taken it all back to redo it just from that look alone. It gutted me.

"I'm not even going to entertain this." She raked her hand through her hair and then slapped her thigh. "But you know what? It's my fault. I should've asked before I went there because I know I can't trust a man to be upfront. I should've known better. But now I do. I don't care how *open* your relationship is. You have a girlfriend, period. And that is a no-go for me." She took a deep breath and softly said, "Thank you for rescuing me. Thank you for dinner and drinks. Now lose my number, and don't worry, I won't ever contact you again."

She stomped off, and I grabbed my wallet and ran after her.

"Nissi, wait. Please. Come on," I pleaded with her as we reached our cars. "I'm sorry. I understand if you want to walk away from this. I don't blame you. Can we at least be friends?"

Friends? I'd entered fuckboy mode behind this woman. We both knew the friend's plea was so I could keep tabs on her and hopefully convince her to be mine. No one had made me feel the way Nissi made me feel, not even River. But I wasn't ready to drop everything for Nissi. That would be a lie. I loved River. We'd been together for two years, but the things I had experienced with Nissi in one night were unmatched. True, I didn't know her, but I knew in my core that I needed her.

"*Friends?*" she scoffed. "Look, Kannon, and I say this with all the disrespect… Fuck you!"

When she reached for her door handle, I didn't stop her. She had made her position plain. I had to respect it, even if I hated to do it.

Once she was nestled in her car, I leaned over, placing my hands on my knees, and peered into her driver's side window.

"I'm sorry," I shouted through the closed window.

My apology was met with her middle finger as she drove away.

"Damnit!"

I punched the air before pulling my keys out of my pocket, entering my truck, and heading back to my apartment.

Chapter Ten

NISSI

UNCONTROLLABLE TEARS POURED down my face as I drove home. Why was I even this upset over what could be dubbed a one-night stand? Even as I questioned myself, I knew why—because I liked his lying, cheating ass. I more than liked him. I was connected to him in some intergalactic way. How else could I explain that I'd had the best and worst night of my dating life on the same night? Something told me only Kannon Jordan could do that, making me hate him as fiercely as I probably could've loved him. *Loved? Did that thought honestly cross my mind? Oh yeah. He sexed me senseless.* Whether love or lust, it would take me a good minute to get over Kannon because of the caliber of man I believed him to be. That thought upset me that much more because I didn't even know him to be this gone over him. *Did he put spices and herbs from love potion number nine in my liquor?*

When I made it to my condo, my tears had subsided, but my heart was aching. *How could I be so stupid and sleep with that man on the first and now, the only date?* I picked up my phone only to find my TikTok notifications had gone crazy again. I opened the app and saw nearly fifty thousand people had already viewed our date night post. Not to mention, the waitress had tagged me on her IG page, and even she had about two thousand likes from the photo. Going back to TikTok, I decided I would unfollow him there first and then on all the apps. That's when I noticed his comment underneath our video on my page. *@kingkannon94 good times with you, Dr. Nissi. You're rare. Thank you.*

Slick bastard. He knew if we commented on each other's posts, people would assume we were dating or friends. If I unfollowed him at this point, people would dig deeper as to why. Trolls. I hated them about as much as I hated Kannon. It'd be messed up if I commented back for him to tell River I said hello. Instead, I liked the comment and replied: *@ThatDentistChick replies to @kingkannon94 you're welcome, Mr. Jordan.* Short and direct to the point. I hoped he could feel the coolness in my written tone. Since social media was hot, I blocked his number instead. If he did try to reach out to me, he would have to do it in a public forum. I prayed he didn't because I didn't know if I could resist airing him out if he did.

Easing out of my car, I sauntered inside my condo. As I closed the door, the feel of something around my waist caught my attention—his jacket. I still had a piece of Kannon with me. Unraveling the jacket from around my waist, I lifted it to my nose as my back collided with my closed front door. The smell was a mixture of his scent and mine—a tale of our night of passion. My eyes leaked again as thoughts of the throes of passion pinged around in my head. As angry as I was, I wanted that man so badly. If he had no one, I had no doubt I would be in his bed or him in mine right now, sexing each other until exhaustion forced us to stop. Then that thought angered me because he was a liar and a cheat, and I was ashamed to have been with him and even more ashamed to want him still.

Wiping my eyes, I tossed his jacket on the nearby barstool and went to the master bathroom. By the time I finished showering Kannon's smell off my body and getting in bed, it was a little after midnight. All I wanted to do was sleep the night and the next day away.

As soon as I closed my eyes, my phone dinged. Without paying attention, I opened the notification, which went straight to my TikTok DM.

> **kingkannon94:** Tried to call and text, but I see you got the trigger finger with the block. Nissi, I am sorry. For real. I know it's too late, but I mean that.

I didn't even have the energy to discuss it. I was just done.

> **ThatDentistChick:** There's literally nothing for you to feel sorry about to me. Save that for River. I won't block you on social media because of nosy followers. But understand, we have nothing more to say to one another. Goodbye, Kannon.

I closed the app and placed my phone on the nightstand. Tears trickled down my face as my heavy-lidded eyes closed.

I jumped for my life when I heard my phone clatter to the floor. The light filtering through the blinds told me it was morning and early. Glancing at my clock on the nightstand, it read 8:05 a.m. *Who would have the nerve to call me this early on a Saturday?* I knew that answer even as I thought of the question. Angela. She was an early bird. Then I remembered I promised to call her when I arrived home from my dinner with Kannon, and I hadn't. Turning my body to the floor, I lifted my cell phone, and sure enough, I had about six missed calls from her. Falling back in bed with my phone on speaker, I dialed her number.

"Just answer me this. Are you over at his house, or is he over at yours?"

Groaning, I swallowed back the tears that seemed like they didn't know how to quit.

"Neither, Angela."

"So y'all just parted ways or something?" she asked confusingly.

"I got home around eleven-fifteen last night."

"So why didn't you call me then? I was up at least until about twelve or twelve-thirty."

"No reason. Just went to bed."

By now, I was fighting hard to keep my breath steady.

"Oh, hell no. What happened? Whenever you give short answers, some foolishness went down. Who do I need to fight?"

"No one, Angela. It's just..." I paused, and a few sniffles escaped.

"Oh, I'm on my way. Right now!" She hung up before I could protest.

Knowing Angela would break every traffic law to get to my place, I got out of bed, slid on my slippers, washed my face, brushed my teeth, and then headed to the kitchen to put on some cups of coffee—French vanilla for me and regular with half-and-half for her. By the time our cups were ready, my doorbell rang. Going to the door with my cup in hand, I opened it. As soon as she saw my puffy face, she embraced me.

"Oh, Nissi."

Usually, I'd be full of playful banter, swatting away her affection. Today, I needed that... like, really *needed* it. So, I allowed her to coddle me as silent tears raced down my cheeks. These waterworks had a broken faucet. It was as irritating as it was releasing.

She stepped into my apartment and followed me to my living room. While she made herself comfortable on the sofa, I went to the kitchen to grab her coffee.

"There you go." I handed her the cup and sat beside her.

She took a sip before placing the mug down on the coaster. "Honey, what happened?"

"Honestly, it was the best five hours of my life. The only thing that compares was graduating dental school and pledging Alpha Khi Alpha."

Confused, Angela flailed her hand. "Wait. Hold up. Five hours? Then why are you upset and in tears this morning? What's going on? 'Cause this ain't adding up."

I took a huge gulp of coffee before I replayed the best-worst night of my life for her. From when I saw him at the restaurant up to his last TikTok DM, I told her everything.

"That *mother*—" Angela paused and rubbed my knee. "How do you have a whole girlfriend and wait until after you get the box to say that? I swear men ain't shit."

"Same thing I said."

"And I'm upset because he seemed so promising."

I let out a sigh as my eyes watered again.

"Yeah, he did." I wiped my lids before the droplets could fall.

Angela sat there looking at me strangely. "Sis, I don't want to add fuel to the fire, and even though you have a right to be upset, it seems deeper."

How could I tell my sister that it was? The whole experience made no sense to me. There's no way I could convince anyone that this man left an imprint on me as if I'd known him all my life. How could I explain I caught feelings in five hours? Was it even feelings, or was it lust? Nah, I wasn't crazy. Sex did many things to me, but it didn't have me crying my heart out the next day.

Angela's eyes grew with realization. "Sis, did you catch feelings for this man?"

It made no sense to lie, so I didn't.

"I think I did. I really did." I blew out a weighted breath. "I know it sounds crazy."

With an empathic smile, Angela rubbed my back, soothing my tired soul.

"No, it's not. It's called love at first sight. You fell for him on sight. Something within y'all souls connected, and that's why he's all bent up about what he did, and you're so hurt by it. I'll bet he's just as hurt and confused as you are. If you fell, then he did, too."

"Yeah, he fell alright. He fell into my loose legs and got what he wanted at the time while waiting on his girlfriend to come home."

"That may be true on some level, but he felt something."

"How do you know?"

Angela pulled out her phone. "Well, this was posted early this morning on his TikTok page. He's got it bad."

She showed me her phone, and it was a video of him in different positions on his sofa, shirtless and wearing grey sweatpants with the snippet of the remixed Whitney Houston song, "I Have Nothing." His video caption read: *When You Can't Sleep Because She's on Your Mind.* The comment caption read: But who gonna save me? #woesofmrfireandrescue

"It makes sense now. I thought he was teasing the people because they knew y'all went out for the first time, but the man was serious," Angela admitted.

I handed her the phone with an eye roll. "Girl, that was probably for River."

"You know that ain't for no River. Besides, he wasn't thinking about no rivers, streams, or waterfalls except the wetness at your apex when he was asking you to cum for him."

Only she could make me laugh in my heartbroken condition.

"I swear I hate you."

"You love me." She snuggled up against me on the sofa.

"Why are you so soft on him? He hurt my feelings."

"Oh, I still plan to kick his behind, even if I have to go to Engine Company 79 to do it, but I guess because listening to you describe your night and how you guys looked in those videos you posted, you could see it in both of your eyes. There was magic between you. Magic doesn't happen with everyone, even if they do have a girlfriend."

Making light of her words, I declared, "It was probably gas. We had nachos."

Angela burst out and threw a throw pillow at my head. "And you talk about me!"

"I get it from you. You're older."

Angela hugged me close. "I love you. You must do what you must do to protect your heart. I feel that. I also feel your heart may be with Kannon no matter how you fight. Gas or magic, there was a deeper connection, and we both know that."

I lay up under my sister, considering her words. It couldn't be possible that I had fallen for that man in one night. I refused to believe that. However, as I sat there, considering that last night was all we would ever have, my heart ached with a hurt I'd never felt before. Not with Joshua. Not with Benji. No one. And that made me question everything I thought I knew about love and relationships.

Chapter Eleven

KANNON

FOR TWO WEEKS, I'd been miserable. I'd had one night with Nissi, and that woman consumed my dreams, thoughts, and masturbation. River was due home this week, but instead of being excited about her return, I was moping around about my lack of contact with Nissi. *It was one night.* That's what I kept telling myself, but she consumed my every thought every time I turned around.

Even being a brand ambassador was troublesome because once I posted those sponsored ad videos, I went from Nissi's personal account to her work account, looking at TikToks. I had even graduated to stalking her Instagram and Facebook pages. The place she posted regularly was the work TikTok account. The only video posted on her personal account was of herself on the beach, which showed the crashing waves and her pretty toes. The caption on the video and in the comments simply said: *Serenity.* Instagram only had one photo of her back in the office with the caption: *Back in the Saddle.* Nothing on Facebook had been updated. It drove me wild. I needed to see her happy and doing her thing, not just with her dentistry group.

I felt responsible, like I broke her, and I needed to know she was repaired. Although I felt the only person who could repair the damage was me, it bothered me because I didn't know how to do that. She wouldn't talk to me or interact with me, and her seeing me again was out of the question. More than anything, I missed her energy, her conversation, and her time. Yes, I missed her after one five-hour night.

"If you didn't plan on helping Kin and me, you could've stayed home, son. You were already late," Kain, my father, said as he threw another piece of rotted wood in a heaping pile.

Kinston looked at me with a smirk and shook his head before discarding the pieces he had been removing. Our father had called us to his house to help replace the steps on the front porch. I didn't mind at all. I loved my father and would do anything he asked of me. My mind was, unfortunately, otherwise occupied.

"Now, Pops, you know I was at the dentist earlier."

"Well, you must still be there 'cause you sure ain't here," he countered.

Grinning, I shook my head. "Sorry, Pops. A lot is going on."

My father stood straight, removed his gloves, and wiped the sweat from his brow. "Uh oh. I know that look. Spill it. What's that artsy girl got your britches in a bunch about?"

Eyeing my father strangely, I replied, "She doesn't have me upset about anything. She's on the road." I picked up some wood and discarded it.

When I turned around, my dad had a grin on his face.

"Ahh, shucks now. It's another woman."

"Pops, what are you talking about?"

"Don't BS me, boy. I'm a country negro from the backwoods of Georgia. We don't grow, but our asses ain't slow. I've seen that look before. Had it a time or two when Marie was living. That look has a woman written all over it. So, what girl—who ain't your girlfriend—got you all twisted up?"

Kinston stood up. "You may as well tell him, bro. You can't fool, Pops."

Kain pointed at him. "Not on your best day!" he cackled.

The last thing I wanted to do was talk about Nissi. She consumed enough of my time. Since my brother confirmed what my father speculated, I had no choice. Then, I considered the positive possibilities of this conversation. Perhaps he could offer some insight that would be helpful. Right now, I could use all the help I could get.

"Can we sit?" I asked my father.

My request caught him off guard. After straightening to his full height again, his gaze fell on me as he briefly assessed me. Then, he began walking toward the house.

"Aw, hell. It's deep and serious. Kin, stop chucking that wood and come sit down. We gotta help your brother get out of the mess he's done got himself into."

I wanted to protest that it wasn't that serious, but how could I? It felt *that* serious to me, so I know that's how they received it. Following my father, we all sat on the porch and drank cool water from his water cooler.

After a few sips, my father looked over at me. "Speak your piece."

"Remember the lady I told you I rescued in the elevator a few weeks back?"

My father snapped his fingers. "The one who caused all that ruckus on that app thing over you. That lady?"

Kinston and I laughed. Pops was old school for his age. He didn't give two damns about technology. He said all he needed a phone for was to talk and send those messages when he couldn't get us knuckleheaded boys on the line. "Those messages" meant texts.

"Yeah, that one. We met up at a restaurant as her *thank you* and had dinner, drinks, and great conversation."

"Mmmhmm." My father rubbed his chin. "So, if that's it, why is she still on your mind?'

I shrugged and put my head down. "It's a little more complicated than that."

"Aw, hell. You gave her the Peter, and she gave you back Sunshine. Now you're over there like the white boy—*you ain't never going home again*," Kain joked, referencing the movie *Harlem Nights*.

The fact that his off-collar comparison was accurate was mindboggling.

Kinston wagged his finger at our father, cackling. "Pops, you wrong for that one."

"Just as wrong as I am right. Ain't I, Kann?" He swatted my arm to get me to admit it.

Running my hand through my curly waves, I responded, "You're right, Pops."

"I knew I was right!"

"But, Pops, it ain't just about the sex. I can get sex anywhere. It's—"

"The connection," he finished. "Sex with a woman is just a means to an end—an urge fulfilled. Sex with the *right* woman is lovemaking. Lovemaking can only happen when you in love. That sunshine was more than sunshine, son. You done messed around and found your heart."

"What do you mean, Pops? I just met that woman. I've been with River for years. I love River. The issue is that Nissi got mad with me because I told her about River after we had sex. It left me looking like a fool. I apologized, but I felt bad. Horrible. But it was just one time. I need to find a way to shake Nissi out of my mind."

My father took a swig from his water cup and directed Kinston to sit next to me. Once he was finished with his water, he glanced at us and leaned back in his chair.

"Let me tell both of you boys something. Yo' problem is you think she's on yo' mind when she's in yo' heart. Hell, truth be told, it ain't even 'bout the woman. It's 'bout love. Love don't give a damn if you been with a woman for a minute or a decade. When the right one comes along, it just happens. Like y'all youngsters say, it is what it is. You have love for River. She a good girl. Sweet. Travel too much for my liking, but hey, that's yo' thing." He threw his hands up. "But I always knew she wasn't the one. Yo' eyes don't beam when you with her. She don't make yo' chest puff out or yo' shoulders square up. What I'm saying, son, is you care for her, but not the way a husband loves a wife. She ain't the one." He poured more water and drank a little before pointing it at me. "Now, this woman— Nissi—she the one."

"How do you know that, Pops? You've never even met her."

"Don't need to. I see how you respond just talking 'bout her. You ain't never did none of this over that River girl. She can book up tomorrow and be gone months, and you move like you don't have a care in the world. You can't be with that Nissi girl 'cause she mad at you, and you moping around here like you lost yo' cat and yo' dog died. I'd say that's a whole lot of emotions for a one-time deal. You ever get this sick over River when she leaves?"

"No, but the situation is different."

"The only thing different is that you fell in love at first sight with Nissi, and River is just the lady you loving on…whenever she's in town."

I didn't protest because my pop had said what he said. Trying to rid my thoughts of the possibility of my dad's words, I sat back and stared up into the sky. *Lord, if she's the one, I need a sign.*

My father stood and patted my knee, then tossed his empty cup in the trash and pulled up his trousers over his semi-protruding belly. "You ain't got to believe me. God got a way of showing us better than He can tell us. Y'all ain't ready for each other right now. But when you are, there won't be anything River or any man can do to stop what's taking root in yo' heart and hers. And don't ask me how I know she's feeling the same. I know because you are. Feelings like that ain't lopsided. They're shared."

He began to walk off the porch. "Kin, help get yo' brother's mind off it for now. When you boys are ready, come help me finish up these steps."

Kinston leaned forward with his hands on his knees, bringing steepled hands to his lips.

"So, how about the Heat?"

"Let it go, bro." I laughed at my brother's attempt to steer me off the conversation.

He shrugged. "Hell, I tried."

"And failed miserably."

"Shut up, bruh." He playfully punched me.

I jumped to my feet, and he followed suit. We play boxed with each other like we used to do when we were children. Those were the days. Pops would be in the yard doing something because he was always in the yard. Mom would make a batch of ice-cold sweet lemonade, and Kinston and I would play on the porch. Back when times were slow and simple.

After a few minutes, Pop cleared his throat. His quiet way of telling us that was enough and to get back to work. We'd known that signal since we were scrappy little boys. I got in one last lick before we made our way to our father.

Kinston looked back at me and whispered, "I'on know if I believe everything Pops said, but I know one thing he said was on point."

"What was that?" I listened attentively.

"River ain't it." He looked me square in the eyes. "She's a good girl, and whatever that thing y'all had set up may have worked in the past, but it and *she* ain't what you want. Maybe it was at one time, but you've outgrown her. Everyone around you realizes that. It's about time you do, too."

With that, he patted my shoulder and sauntered over to the piles he'd been working on.

After listening to my pops and Kinston, I wondered if there was any truth to what they had said. There was a reason I had cheated on River after all this time. Was it because my heart and soul knew what my mind couldn't accept—that I was ready to move on with my life? Or was it the old me resurfacing because Nissi was just that irresistible? Something about her had spoken to a part of me that hadn't felt alive in years, if ever. However, I couldn't help but wonder if it was because Nissi was the one or because River wasn't.

Chapter Twelve

KANNON

After a long day of working on the steps and the yard with my pops, I was finally home and about to shower and rest. I decided that I would hang out with my brother and Jovan tonight. The mask mandate had been lifted, and we all needed a break from COVID and life. I especially needed to rid my system of Nissi. All I had done besides work was sit in my apartment and eat, sleep, and think all things Nissi Richards. I had run out of TikTok and Instagram videos to watch and pictures to ogle over. Tonight, I planned on having at least one Nissi-free night of enjoyment and relaxation to clear my mind. I had to. River was due back any day, and I could not, under any circumstances, be stuck on this woman with whom I'd had one encounter while my girlfriend of two years was in my presence. Not only would it be inappropriate, but it would also be mad disrespectful. If she screwed a man behind my back and came back with him on the brain, I would send her packing right back to him. Therefore, I owed her the same respect.

As soon as I stepped into my bedroom, my cell phone dinged. I retrieved it from my back pocket and saw a text from Jovan. When I opened it, I noticed a video was included with his text.

Jovan: Not sure if you saw this, but I thought you could use a pick-me-up. LOL!

Everything in my spirit told me not to click on the video. I think my mama's spirit whispered to me not to open it. I was stubborn and hard-headed, though. So, I opened it. As soon as I did, I knew when I saw Jovan later, I would murder him. On the spot. DOA.

Nissi's sorority had done the "Don't Rush" challenge on TikTok. However, she had posted the twenty seconds of her portion of the challenge on her personal page. The theme was professional to personal. She started off modeling herself wearing medical scrubs, a white coat adorned with an AKA pendant, an AKA mask pulled under her chin, and her medical bouffant cap. Then at the song's drop, she showed herself in professional attire: green pants, a black and white polka dot blouse, and black Louboutin shoes, with her hair framing her face and her AKA jacket dangling from her finger. The kicker was the personal look. She did the AKA stance in front of the camera. When she pulled back, her curly hair was in a bun high atop her head with one loose curl dangling in front, her make-up was on-point with lip gloss that had her lips popping, and she wore a tight pink dress that accentuated her breasts and barely covered her backside, with cut-outs on the sides. The dress was so fitted and hitting in all the right places that it looked painted on. That voluptuous ass sitting on that Coke bottle figure took my mind back to the cabana in a heartbeat.

Kannon: What you doing even looking at her page? Don't you have a girl?

Yeah, I was heated because he sent it, but also, I was blown because he was looking. Jovan was my boy, but I knew how he was. Since Nissi was never really mine, he was grimy enough to shoot his shot. To him, it wasn't breaking bro code unless she was your woman. Nissi may not have been mine, but to hell with all that. He could find anybody else. He wasn't going to mess with Nissi. That I meant.

> **Jovan:** Bro, I was just looking. Ain't no harm in that, I thought. But I mean, as far as the girl comment, yeah, I do. Just like you got one. Ain't stop you, though.

Did he just try me up? Oh, he wanted it for real. Yeah, he was itching to catch a fade tonight, and I was going to scratch that motherfucker, too.

> **Kannon:** What's that supposed to mean, bro? Real talk. Stop stalking her page, and don't even think about stepping to her. I swear that's on God, bro. I'ma see you tonight.

> **Jovan:** My boi, are you BIG mad, frfr? I was clowning with you, but I see where you at wit' it. FOH. See me tonight then.

I threw my phone down on my dresser. I had planned to chill, but apparently, Jovan had plans to reemerge old Kannon. That Kannon addressed disrespect straight up with no talk, all action. Best friend or not, I was about that action tonight. He was out of control, and if his woman couldn't reel him in, I damn sure would.

I jumped in the shower, praying it would calm me down enough to take a nap, but I was so amped that all I wanted to do was fuck or fight. Hell, both. Nissi had me on brick, and Jovan had me ready to throw hands.

As I showered, everything Nissi and I had done flooded my brain. Then I was consumed with everything I wanted to do to her. Throw her legs up over my shoulders and pound inside that tightness. Dive my face into that sweet pussy and swoosh around all up in it. I wanted those juices all over my face like a milk bath. Drill her from the back and listen to the sound of my nuts and her sweetness make music. Fuck the "act right" right into her.

I hadn't realized my eyes were closed thinking about it until I felt pressure on my man below. As I stood there with water and suds cascading down me into the drain, I held my hardened thickness, squeezing and pulling on it. I had to get this nut off. I was too wound up. I jumped out of the shower and dried myself off. Pulling on some athletic shorts, I grabbed my cell phone and went to Nissi's TikTok DM.

@kingkannon94 to **@ThatDentistChick** hit me back now.

I put my phone down and plopped on my bed. My legs danced as I awaited her reply. After five minutes, I checked my phone and saw she had seen the message but didn't reply. Maybe she was busy. It was Saturday. She wasn't busy. But perhaps she was. I decided to give her five more minutes. By then, I was pacing a hole in the floor, frustrated to the hilt. I checked again and even refreshed the feed. She still hadn't responded. That's when I knew she had no intention of doing so. She was lucky I didn't know where her hard-headed ass lived. I'd pull up. Pull up and sex her senseless in the doorway of her place because my urge couldn't make it further than that. I wanted her so damn bad.

Lying across my bed, I settled for my backup plan. I opened my nightstand's bottom drawer and retrieved my washcloth and lotion. Pulling my shorts down, I lay back, pulled up the video Jovan had sent me, and went to work. I had never beat my meat so ferociously in my life. I paused the video at an angle where her booty was tooted and started thinking about that night we had. I clutched my chest because the way I was about to bust made me feel like my heart was about to explode.

"Oh, Gawd!" I beat until my legs and back were lifted off the bed.

Just as I was climaxing and about to growl her name to the top of my lungs, River walked into my bedroom with a smile on her face. But I couldn't stop the release. However, I managed to bite my lip until I drew blood to keep Nissi's name from spilling from my mouth.

"Ugh," I garbled as I skeeted, my seed shooting out like a volcanic eruption. "Arghhhh!" I gasped to pull breath into my lungs.

"Wow," River said, folding her arms across her chest. "I've missed you, too, bae."

Believe it or not, that release, which was the best masturbation I'd ever experienced, wasn't enough. It took off the pressure but didn't kill the urge. As soon as my eyes zoned in on River, my primal instincts took over, and I scurried off the bed toward her.

As soon as I pulled her into my arms, I kissed her so passionately that her knees buckled. I didn't even give her a chance to respond. I picked her up over my shoulder and tossed her on the bed caveman style. My phone bounced off the bed from the toss, and I caught it. Luckily, my screen had darkened, so I cut the phone off and tossed it on the dresser. Before it could land, I had pounced on the bed atop River.

"Bae, what's gotten into—"

My mouth was on hers to quell her words. She swooned from the amount of passion behind it. I didn't need to talk and didn't want to. Jerking her tie-dye dress over her head, I grabbed her petite cream-colored breasts and gobbled them. Her brown curly locks were in a wild ponytail, and I pulled it, forcing her lust-filled hazel eyes to roll backward. Kissing my way down her body, I ripped her thong apart, too hungry to pull them off her. Although my mouth watered to taste her, I changed my mind. My erection needed attention the most, so I decided to handle that urge.

I was about to slide into her moistness when River sat up on her elbows. "Condom."

I wanted to protest but thought better of it. Neither of us wanted kids right now, and truth be told, I considered that she might've cheated on me. Why? Because I'd done it to her. If I couldn't trust myself, how could I trust her? We *were* in an open relationship, right?

I slid the top drawer of my nightstand open and retrieved a condom. Once the covering was in place, I lifted her petite bottom and slid inside. Every nasty thought about Nissi came to mind as I went to work on River. As I searched for my satisfaction, I didn't even care if she was a willing participant. I drilled her slim body mercilessly. Then I flipped her over to her knees and dug trenches as I gripped her little cheeks tightly and pounded inside. None of it helped. She didn't feel like—her. I was chasing something that couldn't be found in River. Not anymore.

"Yes, daddy, just like that!" she wailed.

Hearing her voice almost deflated me. Five hours. Five hours with Nissi erased two years with River. Just. Like. That. So, I had to test the theory. I prayed for forgiveness, but to stay hard, I imagined it was Nissi underneath me. As soon as I did, my girth hardened and thickened so much that it had River running from it. She'd had this prize for two years; this was the first time she'd run. It was also the first time I remember being this aroused, though. Only it wasn't thoughts of River that aroused me. It was all Nissi. Sweet, tight, sunshine Nissi. That damn dentist chick…*Nissi*.

"Nah, don't run." I gripped her hair from behind and pulled her ponytail backward. Leaning over, I growled into her ear, "*Take. It.*"

My command wasn't because I wanted River. I wanted to finish the illusion of wild sexing on Nissi. And wild sex her, I did. River screamed all kinds of obscenities. At one point, I thought she would summon Jesus to beg for a release from my primal punishing. When my seed began to pump out, I was damn near standing up inside her. With one foot planted on the bed, my hands gripped her waist while I slammed her butt back into me, meeting it with deep, determined thrusts. I howled to the moon like the sneaky wolf I was and filled that condom up— all the while trying my best not to call Nissi's name.

When I released her, she collapsed onto the bed. I didn't even know if she had cum. That's how I knew this thing between us had run its course. I was never *that* dude. Even with the women I had no feelings for, I would at least ensure they were satisfied before I got mine. I'd been so consumed with wishing River was Nissi that I didn't care what she experienced, be it pain or pleasure. I didn't like that. I was converting into a man I didn't know, and this version was even worse than the man I used to be. Truth was, I had outgrown the current space I was in. I knew it. But how could I let go of River when she'd done nothing but love me the way we agreed to be loved? That seemed like a crap deal. I had crapped on River enough lately. I couldn't be a complete asshole.

I collapsed on the bed beside her. My eyes were closed to conceal my thoughts when I felt River ease over and snuggle against me. I could feel her staring at me, so I took a moment before I opened my eyes. She knew me. She knew I wasn't asleep.

"So, Tiger, what was that all about?"

"You're not tired?" It was my way of diverting the question.

Falling onto her back, she lifted her hands above her head in a deep stretch.

"Yes, I'm exhausted, of course. It just seemed like you were pumping some aggression away or pent-up sex. I don't know. You were just different. Excellent. But different."

"It was pent-up sex. I've missed you. I haven't spoken with you in two days. It's just hard when you're not around."

The lies poured out. And with a straight face. This was so wrong.

She turned on her side to face me. "Aww, bae. I love that. I've missed you, too. No worries. You get a full month of me. I'm a little tired from the back-to-back trips, so I'm not taking anything else on for a month to rest, relax, and *ride*." She kissed me on the cheek and turned to her side. "I need more of that when I wake up. Or you could just wake me up with it. Your choice."

Before I could respond, she was out like a light. Great. She wanted more of something that wasn't even inspired by her or desired from her. How much further in this sinking sand could I drown?

By the time River woke up, I was getting dressed. I'd slept lightly on the sofa for a couple of hours, then got up and re-showered to go out. Kinston and I were meeting Jovan and another guy he knew at Jovan's house, and then we were headed to the club. Yep, I was still going out. I had a couple of points to prove. One, to confront Jovan about those text messages, and the next, to prove that Nissi was not embedded in my system. Not after only five hours.

"Where are you heading?" River asked as she stretched and yawned.

I gave myself the once-over, taking in my light tan short-sleeved Polo shirt, dark denim jeans, and tan Cole Haan leather sneakers.

"Jovan, Kinston, and I were gonna hit up a spot tonight. It's been a minute since I hung out, and I just need to unwind. Ya know?"

She stood up in all her naked glory with her arms folded.

"Kannon, I just got back in town today. You screwed me to exhaustion, told me you missed me, then I said I wanted that treatment again when I woke up. But now, you're heading out with your boys? Make it make sense."

Turning to face her, I shrugged. "River, this night was already planned. I didn't expect you until two days from now. I did miss you, and earlier *was* bangin', but I want to hang for a little bit and destress from my week." Unfolding her arms, I held her hand. "We can always do what we did earlier. I got a month of you, right?"

Rolling her eyes, she shook her head and walked toward the bathroom. As she walked, she muttered, "Weird."

I didn't have time to entertain her attitude. I needed to head out so I wouldn't be late. As I picked up my keys, River emerged from the bathroom with a towel wrapped around her body.

"Are you going to be here when I return?" I asked.

"Maybe. I might be at my place."

Yep, her attitude was in full effect.

"River, don't be like that."

She closed her carry-all bag and spun on me. "*We* haven't had time. You could go out with your boys any time. You see Jovan at work. I know I got home early, but any other time, you complain because I'm not back fast enough. Now I'm here, and you're out. I don't know what is going on, Kannon, but your vibe is off, and I don't like it."

Her words were the truth, but they still irritated me.

"Well, let me see if I can pass the vibe check elsewhere. I'll see you later…or not."

Behind my back, I heard her audibly gasp at my comeback as I walked out of the apartment. I wiped my hands down my face when I got into my truck. Inside, I slowly felt like I was losing the battle to keep my life in order. I was out of sorts and out of character. River didn't understand. I needed the time away from her to reel myself in and be better *for* her. She wouldn't understand that because she didn't even know why it was necessary. Tonight, I was determined to begin my attempt to repair what I had broken with River and within myself.

Chapter Thirteen

KANNON

AFTER I SCOOPED my brother, we headed to Jovan's, and I filled him in on the text messages between him and me. Conveniently, I left out my wild afternoon of sex with River, although I told him she returned early. Kinston sat and listened attentively the entire time. He was like that. A good listener. I appreciated it because he let me get everything off my chest before he spoke.

"First things first. Are you sure you wanna hang with Jovan tonight? I think y'all need some space, especially until you can get your head right."

"I was on one earlier, but I'm calm now. We can hash it out like gentlemen. He's my boi at the end of the day."

Kinston gave me a weary look, but I ignored it. Jovan said what he said. I said what I said. It was done. Besides, I couldn't be around here being a warrior for a woman who didn't want me. It kept my mentality in upheaval, and I was tired of running off unstable emotions. My remedy? A little music, a few drinks, and a good turn-up, and then I'd be back on my regular schmuglar with River.

When I pulled up to Jovan's place, Kinston hopped out with me.

"You can wait in the truck, bro. It won't be too long."

Kinston eyed me seriously. "Nah, I don't let my brother walk into any situation where he's had beef with another man, foe or friend."

One thing I could always count on was my brother having my back. A smirk crept across my face, and I tapped him on the chest with the back of my hand. "Love."

He gripped my shoulder. "Love."

As soon as I rang the doorbell, Jovan met me with one other guy in the background.

"You still seeing me?" he asked with a slight attitude.

"Man, come on, and let's head to this club."

Jovan stood there for a second to gauge my temperature before holding out his hand. We slapped hands together and pulled each other into a one-armed embrace.

"My boi!" he bellowed spiritedly. "I thought you had lost your mind, but you back." He turned around and waved the other man over. "This is my boi, Shawn, that lives a few doors down."

We all gave introductions and started heading to our vehicles to follow each other to the club. Since Jovan knew where the new spot was and I wasn't familiar, Kinston and I would trail Shawn and him.

"Aye yo, Kinston, did you see Kann's lil' baddie in that Don't Rush challenge video?" Jovan said, addressing Kinston before directing his gaze back over at me. "I gotta admit, Kannon, I wish I had gone up for that elevator call instead. That Dr. Richards is one bad broad. The way she had you gone, I'd be rid of Jasmine in a heartbeat for that."

Rage swelled inside of me before I had an opportunity to calm down. The next thing I knew, I stoled on him, and Kinston and Shawn were left trying their best to break us apart. My brother—being the most muscular of us—was able to maneuver himself between Jovan and me and pull me off of Jovan. If he had been anybody else, I would've swung on him for interfering.

I pointed at Jovan, still attempting to break free from Kinston's death grip.

"I told you. I *warned* you. Leave Nissi's name outta your mouth. You better not even think about stepping to her, or I'll break your jaw!"

"You didn't break it this time. Do it!" He spat out a glob of blood as Shawn held him back. "We supposed to be best friends, and you wildin' out on me over some chick? For real, Kann?"

"You need to respect her." I shrugged out of Kinston's clutches. "I'm good," I hollered so he could give me some space.

"Respect her? I'on even know her." He shook his head. "I'm good," he shouted at Shawn, who stood back with his hands raised. "You don't either, for that fact. Defending her like she's your wife. Fuck you talm'bout."

Quickly, I closed the space between us, pointing my finger in his face.

"That's your problem. You have no respect. You don't have to know her. I'm putting the play down. As my boi, respect me enough to pick it up."

"Oh, so you putting the play down, huh?"

"Yeah, I put the play down!"

He clapped and nodded his head. Then put a hand on his waist. "How you putting a play down on a chick that ain't yours, my boi?" He turned to look at Shawn with a backward finger pointing at me. "This boi screwed this chick *once* that he only knew for *five* hours, and his chest is tight. Can you believe that?" His native New York accent shone through heavily.

Shawn looked back and forth between us. "I ain't in it, bro. I just wanna go to the club and have a good time, man."

"That's what we were supposed to do until this ma'fucka got his boxers in a bunch." Jovan sneered, turning his focus back on me.

"A'ight now. Let's just cool down, Jovan," Kinston intervened.

"Cool down? Kin! It's your brother who needs to cool down. Up here acting like a bitch—"

"Whoa! Whoa!" Kinston stepped between me and Jovan, placing his hands on Jovan's chest. "You not about to come at my brother like that, man."

"Nah, he ain't, Kin. But let him say what he gotta say," I intervened. "Go on. Speak your mind since apparently there's a lot on it."

Jovan shook his hand. "Man, I'm out. Let's go, Shawn."

Fanning my hands, I spat, "Nah, don't bitch up now. Say it, bruh."

Jovan stepped back with his face frowned up. "*Bitch?* Nah, I bang *bitches*. It ain't in me." He paced and then stopped. "A'ight, you want some truth?"

"Yeah, go on and give me some truth," I clapped back.

"Here are facts. You confronting me over *Nissi*? She ain't River, my boi." He pointed at me. "*That's* who you need to be worried about. How 'bout keep that same energy for *that* broad? River is the one in the streets banging other men with your permission, and you worried about a female you knew for one night? *Bruh.* You sound mad dumb right now!"

"Now you got an issue with my relationship with my girl? *Wow.* You sound mad jealous right now."

"Nah, fam. I have no issue with you or River, and damn sure not y'all's relationship. *But you do.*" He wagged his finger. "You know what the whole truth is, Kannon?"

Tilting my chin up, I asked, "What's that?"

"You mad because you're just like me, and Nissi brought that up outta you. Exposed you. Now you tight 'cause you don't know how to put that jack back in the box."

"What you mean?" I asked, brushing him off. "I ain't nothing like you. You don't do nothing but play your girl out. Cheating on her and stringing her along."

"Yeah, I do, but I know who I am, famo." He pointed to himself. "I never denied I'ma nasty ma'fucka. I own that shit. I ain't shit, and I know I ain't shit, nor am I trying to be shit. Jasmine stays 'cause she wants to. I ain't begged her to stay a day 'cause I know what I do is all the way foul. I know I'm wrong, but I accept that because that's me. It's where I'm comfortable. But when I'm ready to settle down, whether with Jasmine or whoever, I'ma know that, too. And I'ma handle mine properly.

"That's your problem, Kann. You out here with River in this *open relationship*, and all it's doing is allowing you to pretend to have a real relationship while you're still doing what you wanna do—still being an *ain't shit* ma'fucka. True fuckboy status. 'Cause if you really wanted to be with that girl, ain't no woman could take you from her. I don't give a damn if she was gone all three-hundred-and-sixty-five days of the year. You'd just make Jergens the number-one brand in lotion!"

He stepped right up into my face with his hands on my chest.

"And *big* facts, Kannon, you were so busy pretending you had changed that when you ran up on a woman like Nissi, you didn't know how to be who you claimed you were. That's why you are moping and upset. You're pissed off with yourself because the *you*—that you wanna be—wants a woman like Nissi, but the *you*—that you are—knows you ain't built for nobody but a woman like River. Nissi rang your bell, and you can't answer the call because you know deep down that she ain't about to play River's games with you. With Nissi, you gotta step up or step out.

But you ain't gotta worry about that 'cause Nissi stepped yo' ass out for you. So, don't be mad with me because you worried about the next man being with Nissi just because you ain't ready to step into who you know she'll require you to be." He stepped back and waved for Shawn. "Let's go to the club, Shawn."

As they walked toward his car, he turned around. "Jovan still got love for you, my boi. Nissi will never be on the table for discussion with me again. But your problem ain't with me, Kann. It's with yourself. When you ready to talk for real, I'm here."

Jovan and Shawn kept walking, and I stood there frozen about the reality check I'd received, unable to process it fully. On several levels, what he said was factual. I had some hard truths to discover about who I was and what I wanted out of life. Whether that was with River, Nissi, or the next woman, I had to discover who Kannon was—for me.

"Bro, you can take me back to the house. I don't even feel like hanging tonight," Kinston said, snapping me out of my trance.

Slowly, I turned to him. "What do you think about what Jovan said?"

He patted my shoulders. "It doesn't matter what I think. It matters what you know." He cuffed his beard and shook his head. "Bro, that's person number three who told you River ain't it. As messed up as some of the things he said were, he ain't lying." He took a deep breath. "Look, you're my brother, and I'ma always stand beside you ten toes down from the earth to the dirt. But you gotta get a handle on yourself, and you and I both know that starts with dealing with what you ain't willing to face. You gotta deal with it, bro. So, deal with it."

While driving Kinston home, I contemplated my actions and what everybody said. I knew what I had to do. It involved prayer and a special visit. This was something I had to do for myself. Not River. Not Nissi. Me.

Chapter Fourteen

NISSI

AFTER A MONTH of pining away over my botched connection with Kannon, I finally felt better. He had occupied many of my day and night dreams. It was one of the reasons why I'd been scarce on social media. Every time I went on TikTok, someone asked about us. If it wasn't a commenter, it was the turmoil of seeing his sponsorship videos scroll by on my following or "For You" page. Not to mention, his "Who Gone Save Me" video went ultra-viral. That sent people on a tailspin, wondering if he was joking or if there had been an issue with us. All kinds of stupid theories started flying. So, two days later, I decided to comment, "Superheroes don't need saving," with a winking eye emoji. He liked the comment and pinned it to the top. That calmed the fodder and gave the impression that he'd been joking and simply missing me. Thank goodness he never responded.

In fact, I hadn't heard any more until two weeks later when he messaged me on TikTok, demanding I respond to him. Like that was going to happen. First of all, I didn't appreciate the tone of that message, and secondly, what did I owe him to give him a response, especially to a demand? So, I left him on read like I should have done before he got my goodies. But you live, and you learn. I learned that Kannon Jordan was a no-go for me.

Since there hadn't been any further communication, I was getting back to myself pre-elevator catastrophe. Even social media had calmed down and gone back to the followers loving my silly skits and dance videos with the dental office instead of being all up in my personal business. The unexpected hole punched into my heart by Kannon had finally closed, and I was healing. For that, I felt like rewarding myself because it had been a crazy emotional road back to me, but I was back. A lot more guarded, but back!

It was time to unwind after being back at work, settling my claim with the property owners, and finally putting Kannon behind me. Ciara, Angela, and I decided to have a girls' dinner that Saturday night. I tried to get Aquila to come, but the wife of Joel Oliver had a mandatory family night. So, I would have to catch up with her another time.

Giving myself the once-over in the mirror, I looked like new money. My fitted, ripped knee-length jean shorts popped in all the right places, the white bustier gave my breasts the lift and fullness I wanted, and the white three-quarter-sleeved blazer was the perfect addition. It added a splash of sophistication to my bad-girl ratchet style. I wore my cream-colored wide-brim fedora by Wear Brims and silver angel wing stilettos to complete the look. I'd even straightened my kinky coils. For added flair, I sprung for some custom press-on nails by Butterfly Spirit Nails. I couldn't wear acrylic nails with my profession, so I had a stash of press-on nails for special occasions, and tonight was considered special to me.

Once I headed out the door, I scooped up my big sister, Angela, and we made our way to the restaurant to meet Ciara.

"Girl, I'm so happy we are hanging out. I needed this—like *needed* this," Angela said right before we entered the restaurant.

"Not a lie was told in that statement, sis. I know I need this."

"I know you do, too. That man—whose name shall not grace our lips—had you wound up tighter than a virgin's coochie."

As I staggered into the restaurant, my head dropped from the ripples of laughter that rushed through me.

"Shut the hell up!" I hollered. "I promise I can't stand you. This is the last time I will take you anywhere. The last."

Pursing her lips, she quipped, "Then you'd never have a good time."

Ugh. She was right about that. I could've knocked her batting lashes off, though, for speaking the gospel truth.

"This is why Aquila loves me more," I said, spitting my favorite comeback.

"Aquila needs to love Aquila more."

And I oop. She had a point there.

Our eyes met in solemn agreement as I wagged my finger at her. "True that."

Once the hostess showed us to our reserved seats, we found Ciara waiting for us. We hugged each other, took our seats, and removed our face shields. The first thing we did was order a round of drinks. Of course, Angela dived right in and gave us more than the tea on everyone she could think of. It was so much information that it was more like spilling hot coffee! Noticeably, she was sure to withhold her own coffee, tea, or water. That was Angela. Ready to be about somebody else's business, but she'd never reveal her own. No lie, Ciara and I enjoyed it, though. Who doesn't like a good piping hot cup of Joe?

In between her spillage, we ordered more drinks and food to soak up that premium liquor. Once Angela had spilled all she could think of, Ciara went in, too. Much to Angela's pleasure, we exchanged water cooler gossip. The never-ending tales of undercover lovers, freaks, and crazies were continuous in a place with multiple companies in a ten-story building. I was glad not to be on the receiving end of it now that the whole Mr. Fire and Rescue fiasco was over.

"Speaking of breakups to makeups, I guess your boy worked everything out," Ciara said before taking a bite of her bread and crab dip.

My brows furrowed as I sat my margarita down.

"What boy?" From my peripheral, I could see Angela trying to shake her head discreetly, so I turned to her. "And what are you trying to signal to hide?"

I pursed my lips and narrowed my eyes at her.

Releasing a deep sigh, she tossed an annoyed glare at Ciara. "See, no more liquor. Just team too much." She flailed her hands.

Ciara shrugged apologetically. "My bad. We're still not mentioning him?"

Angela slapped the table lightly. "What drink did you have? Don't get anymore, please," she scoffed. "Good Gawd Almighty."

With my arms crossed, I stared back and forth between my sister and my friend, growing aggravated. "So, are one of you two heifers gonna clue me in on the big secret?"

Ciara mouthed another apology to Angela before downing the remainder of her drink.

Angela turned to me and swallowed. "Well, we know you had been trying to deal with your emotions behind the man whose name shall not grace our lips, so when you didn't say anything, we didn't mention it. Ciara, Aquila, Sheena, and I made a pact that we wouldn't bring him up to you—or anything about him— unless you did. Now Ciara is over here flapping her drunk lips."

I didn't want to say her lips must stay drunk twenty-four hours a day, so I sat there on mute, waiting for her to finish.

"What are you talking about?" I asked after she didn't volunteer any further information.

"You aren't going to let this go, are you?" Angela asked.

"Not a chance in hell."

Huffing, she pulled out her cell phone from her purse and unlocked it. She scrolled, typed something, and then handed me her phone. "Here."

I wiped my hands with the cloth napkin before taking the phone. It was Kannon's Instagram page. The third photo I saw was of him with a biracial woman with curly hair. They were sitting side-by-side with their heads tilted together, making silly faces. The caption read: *Our silly selves #TheKannonRiver*. Another picture had to be taken by someone or a tripod. They were sitting in a gazebo swing, and Kannon had his arm draped around her as he planted a kiss on her temple, and she beamed brightly. The caption read: *Her. #TheKannonRiver*. Another picture was with River holding the phone as if she was taking a selfie, but you could see Kannon in the background in the bed underneath the sheets with his bare chest visible. He was on his phone, not paying attention as River smiled for the photo. The caption stated: *@ riversmeadow thinks she is slick. Late Nights. #TheKannonRiver*. When I clicked on River's handle, it didn't take me long to see the same photo on her page. Her caption read: *My nightly view. Blessed. #RiversKannon #TheKannonRiver*. I clicked back to his page. All the photos were posted within the last couple of weeks.

Looking up, I saw Ciara and Angela's eyes beaming back at me in anticipation of my reaction. I handed Angela her phone and shrugged.

"Good for them. Looks like they worked it out. I'm glad."

With that, I picked up my margarita and took a sip.

Ciara reached out and touched my arm. Her face wore a concerned expression. I guess waiting for my reaction caused her to sober up a bit.

"Honey, are you sure? It seems so fast."

"Girl, we only met each other once. He's been with her for two years. I'ma need y'all to relax."

Angela grabbed my hands. "Turn around and look at me."

"What?" I asked with a scoff.

"You heard me."

Groaning, I turned so that we were face-to-face. She eyed me closely, paying close attention to my eyes and facial expressions. After a couple of minutes, she exhaled and rubbed my hands.

"Okay, you seem like you're handling it well. Seriously, we wanted to ensure you were over him and everything that transpired. We didn't want to pour salt in a healing wound."

I reached over and hugged her closely. "Thank you, sis." I then turned and faced Ciara. "I love you, guys, and I appreciate your concern for me. I promise I am perfectly fine and happy he could move forward with his girl. I am good."

They both smiled brightly, and Angela picked up her glass. "Well, all right now. Let's get this party started."

We all cheered and clinked glasses.

Angela could always see through me. That's why I had perfected the "Angela Avoidance" stare. It was an expression I'd practiced over the years to keep her from determining my innermost feelings, therefore putting one thousand over something that was only a ten. I knew she only wanted what was best for me and would always be overly protective of her baby sister, but some things weren't worth the time or energy. Because when it came to me—and even Aquila—she made time and had all the energy. Situations like this one were why I was glad to have perfected the Angela Avoidance stare.

As we continued drinking, eating, talking, and joking, my mind kept reverting to Kannon and River. I won't lie. A part of me—a micro, morsel part—felt a pang of hurt. Perhaps even a tinge of jealousy toward River. True, Kannon and I had never been together as a couple, but all those feelings of wanting to pursue that with Kannon rushed back to me. It was like a needle prick to my heart.

What pained me the most was his caption: *Her.* That one word. *Her.* It held so much weight and reeked of unspoken volumes. To me, it meant everything he desired, needed, and had was in…*her.* River. *Her.* Not Nissi, but River. To me, that sentiment deduced that his attempt to keep me around was solely to have me as a sidepiece. *Wow.* I liked it better when I thought he held some budding feelings for me. It felt forgivable—like even if he had made an emotional and horny mistake, it was due to a reason. Now, I felt like a notch on his belt. A time passer until the woman of the honor returned…*Her.* With that one-word comment, I felt cheapened. My mind began to spiral about how he or any other man saw me.

No, don't take yourself down that rabbit hole. He's a horrible individual.

Mentally, I coached myself between superficial giggles and irrelevant conversation.

I am unique and worthy and—forget Kannon and all the rivers, streams, ponds, lakes, waterfalls, bayous, seas, oceans, and fucking water puddles in the world. They could load up on a *riverboat* and sail off into the sunset. *Kannon Jordan. Asshole.*

"Sis, you good?" Angela tossed concerned eyes at me, bringing me out of my Kannon and River mental bashing session.

"Huh? Yeah, I'm good. Why?" Confusion etched my face.

"I asked did you want another margarita twice, and you were zoned out," Angela said, eyeing me suspiciously. "I know you're not over there thinking about—"

"Girl, no. I think I've had one too many margaritas." *Lies. Lies. Lies.*

Narrowing her eyes, she spat, "Sis, please! You've only had two. You can usually drink four before you get buzzed." She smacked her lips. A clear indication that she doubted me.

"I had a couple of wine coolers at the house before I picked you up." *More lies.*

Angela sat there for a few eyeing me unbelievably, but I'd perfected the Angela Avoidance face so well that she dropped her suspicions. Releasing a sigh, she tilted her head.

"All right. But no more drinks for you. You drove me. You can't be DUI."

"Exactly why I am not drinking anymore," Ciara added.

"Girl, I'm surprised at you. You usually hold liquor better than me," I said, turning my attention to Ciara to get the focus off me.

She slapped the table and bucked her eyes. "I know, right? I don't know what's going on with me. Zach would have a fit if I drove home drunk. Let me order some water."

"Yeah, you do that." I pointed at her. "And you know I would not let that happen. He'd ban our friendship over his wife. I would call him and let him be pissed while picking you up than for you to pop up at home like that, and God forbid you get in an accident."

The waiter brought over two waters and another margarita for Angela. I secretly wanted another one, but I had to pretend I was good. Thankfully, the bar and grill decided to crank the music a bit, and "Popstar" by DJ Khaled and Drake flooded the speakers. Everyone started bopping to the music as soon as it ripped, turning it into a mini-club atmosphere. I got so lost in dancing with my girls and having fun that I had completely forgotten the brief sour mood that man—whose name shall not grace my lips—had put me in. I was so turned up that Angela gave me a sip of her margarita. I needed it. To let go and let loose.

Put aside the stress of my personal and professional life and be on my Nissi shit.

"Look at you acting up."

I turned to the familiar voice and gasped, covering my mouth with my hands. His smile radiated back at me as excitement filled me to the core.

"Benji!"

Before I knew it, I was in his arms, squeezing him tightly. He held me back just as tightly while I held him. With a deep breath, I stepped back out of his embrace. It had been over a year since I'd seen him, and his presence elated me. We stood there entranced and smiling like two goofy teenagers until I heard a voice from behind him.

"Oh, my bad," Benji said. "Nissi Richards, these are my boys, Adrian and Pete. Y'all, this is Dr. Nissi Richards."

"*The* Nissi, huh?" the one identified as Pete said before shaking my hand, and Adrian followed suit.

Batting my eyes at Benji, I said, "I see my reputation precedes me."

Nervously, Benji chuckled, and Pete waved his hands.

"All good things, I promise," Pete intercepted.

"Good to know." I smiled at them. "Forgive my rudeness. Benji, you remember my sister, Angela. And, Angela, meet Adrian and Pete."

Angela hugged Benji, then shook the other two men's hands. I also introduced Ciara. Pete quickly tried to hit on her until Ciara clarified that her name was *Mrs.* Ciara Tremble. Pete apologized, and he and Adrian headed to the bar while Ciara and Angela continued dancing.

Benji and I stood there in awkward silence. I didn't know what to say to him as I'm sure he didn't to me. We had known each other now for the better part of six years. We'd been classmates, study partners, friends, and friends with benefits, and of all that shared experience, it felt like we were two familiar strangers. Truth be told, I missed his friendship more than anything. I wasn't sure of that until that moment. If we had been nothing else, we'd been great confidants.

"My apologies. I just can't stop staring at you." He shook his head. "I didn't think you could get any more gorgeous, but look at you. You're stunning, Nissi. Absolutely."

"Thank you," I cooed, blushes reddening my face. "No disrespect to your lady if she's here, but you look as handsome as ever."

And he did. Benji stood at five feet ten inches with gray eyes, a tapered haircut, and a thin chin beard. He'd never been overly muscular but rather gave off sexy dad-bod vibes. I always joked that he resembled the actor Jesse Williams. Everyone did. He often joked that resembling him meant nothing if he couldn't pull the ladies. Liar. Many women had wanted Benji Eloi, but he couldn't see that because his sights had been set on one person—me.

"No worries. No girl."

"Oh, she's at home?" I inquired slickly.

"She doesn't exist. I'm single," Benji said, staring at me with intent.

Just then, Adrian returned and handed him a beer. He drank a swig, then looked back at me.

"What about you? Are you taken?"

For some reason, his question unearthed me. I recoiled timidly, pushing my hair behind my ear. "No, I'm not. I'm still single."

A waitress came dashing by, trying to squeeze past him with a tray high above her head, forcing him to scoot into my space. He placed his hand on me to brace himself and shield me if the waitress tipped her tray. She shouted a quick sorry in our direction while continuing along her path. He remained standing in my space, grinning down at me.

"I guess I better get out of the way." He glanced up to see everyone partying. "Wanna dance with me?"

"Sure." I shrugged as he took my hand, and we found a nice spot.

Our conversation ceased as the deejay flipped from rap to dancehall to Miami bass music. We danced and slow-grinded on each other, and I twerked with my girls for what seemed like forever. No lie, it was a good time. Excellent, in fact. By the time we grew tired, we had been at the restaurant for three hours. Ciara broke the trance by calling it a night, which led to Angela throwing in the towel, too.

"Well, I'm the driver, so I guess I better go." I faced Benji. "It was so good seeing you again."

His eyes danced as he asked, "Nissi, do you mind if I walk you to your car?"

When I told him I didn't, he let his boys know what he was doing and headed out of the building, walking beside me while Angela and Ciara walked ahead.

"So, tonight was fun," he said casually.

"It sure was. I haven't let loose like that in a long time."

Agreeing, he added, "Me either. I almost reneged, but I'm glad I came."

Pushing up against his shoulder, I grinned. "You are?"

A throaty chuckle escaped from him. "Get outta here, Nissi. Don't play. You know I am. Any time with you is a good time." He stopped me, turning me to face him. "Real talk. I miss you."

"Aww, I miss you, too—"

"Not on any buddy friendship." He shook his head. "I miss *you. Us.* I know it was never official between us, but a brother is always gonna be soft on you. You're the one who got away for me."

"Benji—"

He put his hand up. "You don't have to explain. You owe me no explanation. It was your choice. I just…I wanted you to know how I felt. How I *still* feel."

"So how come you never contacted me to tell me?"

His eyes widened, and he scoffed. "Nissi, I gave you an ultimatum, and you told me not to let the door hit me where the good Lord split me. I couldn't come back from that. So, I let it be. I've dated a few times, but seriously, no one does it for me like you."

"So what are you saying, Benji?" I sighed.

"We're both grown. We're dentists. We're single. I hope you believe, like I believe, that tonight isn't a coincidence. Maybe college wasn't the right time."

He eased closer to me, taking my hand into his. The alcohol mixed with his Armani cologne wafted in the air, tickling my senses and threatening to engulf me in all things Benji.

"But I'm hoping now may be the right time."

"Benji, I don't know. I just—"

My sentence was cut off when he brought his hands to my face and his lips to mine. His familiar kisses ignited in me, and we kissed each other slowly and deeply for a few minutes. Ending it with a few pecks, he pulled back, crushing my soul with those deep gray eyes.

"A chance. One chance. That's all I ask." His solo finger was held up as he glanced at me with pleading eyes. "We already know each other, so it wouldn't be like starting over. It'd be like starting again. Please, bél mwen," he said, calling me beautiful in Creole.

His gaze pulled me in, and I could see he had always wanted me. Nothing about that had changed except time and distance. Perhaps I'd been wrong about Benji. Maybe he was supposed to be the one for me. He had one thing right. After all this time, we were both single and available. Perhaps Kannon was meant to be with River, and I was meant to be with Benji. Benji had put in the time and effort and had proven to be the man I needed. He deserved this chance, and honestly, so did I.

Nodding, I smiled, biting my lip. "Okay."

Excitement danced in his eyes. "For real? Okay?"

I laughed and softly swatted at him. "Yes, nut. For real."

He embraced me warmly, and it felt good. When he pulled back, we exchanged cell phone numbers and made plans to meet up the next day. With one more kiss, he saw me in my car and said goodnight to Angela and me.

"Okay, Benji," Angela teased as I pulled out of the restaurant's parking lot. "So that means Kannon really is yesterday's news."

"Kannon who?" I joked as she hollered and slapped hands with me.

Chapter Fifteen

KANNON

$\mathcal{S}$ITTING IN THE breakroom at work, I ate a bowl of cereal and read a magazine. It was lowkey this morning, and I was bored as hell. But this morning, I was particularly happy about the lowkey boredom. I was also at peace for the first time in a long time.

My life had been in an upheaval since Nissi, but especially after my blow-up with Jovan. We still weren't communicating. Luckily, we ended up on differing shifts the past couple of months. He hadn't reached out, and neither had I. Honestly, my failure to communicate was more about me dealing with my crap than being upset with him. Despite how disrespected I felt, I couldn't deny his words held truth. When I reflected on it, he had called my girl River a whole broad, and that didn't even make me flinch. But the mention of Nissi's name on his lips almost caused me to lose my friendship with him—or *had* caused it.

At any rate, I thought I was on my way to getting my life back on track because that next day, after the fight with Jovan, I visited my mother's gravesite. Even though she was no longer with me in the physical form, being near her spirit always seemed to give me clarity. Speaking with her seemed like the only time I could genuinely express myself. As I sat, my mind wandered back to that moment two months ago.

Walking to her final resting place always felt like I was walking the green mile. No matter how many years passed, this was the worst part of visiting the gravesite. The walk. It was something about passing by so many lost loved ones that was as saddening as it was humbling. When I reached the grave of Marie Georgette Jordan, I did as I always did—touched the top of her headstone with my fingertips, bowed my head, and prayed the prayer I always prayed, which was unique and special between my mom and me.

"Heavenly Father, thank you for the time we had. Heal me of the hurt from the time we lost. Give me hope for the time when we will reunite. Clarity, peace, and love abound. Amen." I kissed my fingertips, placed them on her marker, and then set the fresh flowers in her vase. "I love you, Mama."

Tears fell from my eyes as I stood there staring up at Heaven. Damn, I missed that lady so much that it was unreal. Whenever I wanted to be angry about the weddings she'd never attend, the grandkids she'd never get to hold or mold, and the accomplishments she'd never see, I could hear her voice telling me that everything was in God's time, even death. Then I'd suck it up and appreciate the time He blessed us with her physical presence.

"Mama, I messed up," I admitted. "You know me and River have been kicking it for a minute. I love that girl; I do. She's good people. She's been good to me. But I met a woman named Nissi. I'm sure you were laughing in Heaven at the story."

I paused, breaking into laughter about how Nissi and I had crossed paths.

"Anyway, we went out for dinner and drinks so she could thank me, and I slept with her. I know. I know. You always told me that taking my Peter out of my pants too soon would soon land me in trouble. And it did. I swear I was not trying to dip and ditch her, but everything felt so right in that moment. It was like the moon, the stars, and the planets permitted us to explore each other. When it was over,

and reality struck, I thought I was doing the noble thing by telling her about River. I know that conversation was a day late and a dollar short, but I wanted her to understand that I told her because I wanted to be honest and correct the error of my ways. I also told her because I was hoping she'd want to continue...I don't know...something... with me. Boy, was I wrong. She was livid, and I knew she had every right to be, Mama. I just hoped she could forgive and forget. Well, she damn sure forgot. I haven't heard from her since I reached out to apologize again. Thing is, she has been on my mind heavy ever since. Like, real talk, Mama, I can't shake this woman. It was one time after five hours. Why is she still living rent-free in my head like this? I just need clarity. I want to do right by River—be the man I know I can be for her, but I can't get Nissi out of my system."

I stood there for a few moments letting the breeze blow. I felt her spirit all around me. I felt peace, comfort, and love. I knew she was there because my spirit began to feel better. I dropped my head at the realization. The only way to move forward would be to confess to River and see where our chips landed. Then we could decide if we wanted to repair ourselves or walk away. While this had nothing to do with Nissi, it could lead me to understand why I felt those feelings.

Lifting my head, I smiled and touched her headstone. "Thank you, Mama. Even in Heaven, you're parenting. Continue your rest, and sorry to disturb you. I love you."

With that, I left with a plan to discuss everything with River. I had it all mapped out on how it would go down. By the time I got back to my apartment, River was sitting in the living room in complete silence. Her legs and arms were crossed.

"Hey, babe. I wasn't expecting you."

I walked into the living room to notice her demeanor. Confused, I glanced around, trying to figure out why it looked like I had walked into the middle of a shakedown.

"Ugh, babe. What's going on? Why are you just sitting here?"

River's eyes flashed up to me, and anger reflected in them. "You slept with her, didn't you?"

Taken aback, I stepped back, scratching my beard with a perplexed stare.

"Huh? What? Who? What are you talking about?" She had seriously caught me off guard.

She jumped up and threw her phone at me. "Her! The chick you rescued." She made a silly mocking gesture. "That dentist chick! You fucked her, didn't you?"

It was true, but hell, how did she know? My mind immediately went to Jovan, and I swore I would kill him if he snitched. For real, this time.

"Umm, babe. Where's this coming from?" I attempted to buy time.

She pointed at the phone I had caught. I flipped it over, and the video of Nissi and me at the restaurant was playing repeatedly. It touched me tenderly, so I hurriedly put my poker face on. I didn't want my mind to ramble over that night because that would've been a dead giveaway.

"River." I gazed up at her with sympathetic eyes.

Her hand flew up, her chest heaving.

"Don't." She paced with her hands on her hips, a habit of hers whenever she was upset. "I know you, Kannon. And I know that look on her face. She was feeling you for sure. And the way you showed all thirty-two teeth, she wasn't alone in her feelings. Admit it. This is why you've been acting brand new. You've been sleeping with this woman behind my back. Haven't you?"

"No, I haven't been sleeping with her, River."

That was the truth. Her statement implied an ongoing scenario that was not happening. Once. Yeah. But I needed time for that reveal.

"Kannon!" she whined. "It was a cute little deal. You were supposed to go out for dinner and drinks. That's it! Even if you wanted to screw the broad, you could've asked me. We have an agreement!"

My temper flared, and I tried to quell it. Instead of speaking, I bit my lip and turned away from her for a second.

River's eyes flashed. "You're pissed. Why are you pissed, Kannon? Because it's true? You and your little dentist broad have been putting on for TikTok, and you got a whole woman!"

"First of all, she ain't no damn broad!"

It ripped from me before I could resist. Hearing River disrespect Nissi ignited a fire in my soul. I had let the first insult go, but time number two was on me.

Her mouth snapped shut, and the shock knocked her back a few steps as if I had physically pushed her.

"Wow. So she really got in your head? You're under fire with your girlfriend about cheating, and you just defended her. I can't with you."

River stormed into my bedroom, and I was fast on her heels.

"Babe, wait." I placed my hand on her arm as she reached for her overnight bag. "I'm sorry. Can you listen to me and hear me out? Please. If you want to leave afterward, I won't stop you. Let's talk about this. That's all I ask."

She swiped a lone tear from her eye as she turned to me. Crossing her arms, she nodded as she stood there, shaking her leg to calm down. "Fine. Explain yourself."

It was my day of reckoning. I refused to be anything but a man, so releasing a deep breath, I confessed.

"The truth is I have not been sleeping with Nissi. However, I did sleep with her that night."

River gasped, and her eyes ballooned with rage as tears swelled in her eyes. With it being the closest thing within her reach, she threw the shirt off the bed, hitting me in the face.

"I knew it!"

The tears poured down her face with the outspoken truth of my deceit. As badly as I wanted to console her, I stood back because I knew *she didn't want me near her. Instead, I continued giving her space and made my plea from a distance.*

"River, it was one time. I swear." I held my hands up to my lips in the steepled pose. "I'm not saying that to force anything on you. I'm telling you because I should've already told you. I should've told you the moment it happened. I messed up, and I'm wrong. I want to do whatever you feel you want to do about it. Your answer doesn't even have to come today."

"Kannon, how could you?" she asked through trembling lips. "We have an open relationship, so you didn't even have to cheat on me. We did that so this…" She fanned between us. "…wouldn't happen."

"I know. You're right. No argument here. To be honest, we were in a moment, and it just…"

My unspoken words lingered and fizzled into the atmosphere. Clearing my throat, I skipped to the less hurtful facts.

"Immediately afterward, I told her about you. I know I should've told her before, but right after we… I didn't waste any time telling her."

"So that's why you were defending her?" she snapped.

Leaning my head back, I inhaled before explaining.

"I'm not trying to make you feel a way about that. I defended her because all of this was on me. I'm not trying to hype her, but she was sweet and seemed like a good person. I believe she would've walked away if she had known. I don't think it's fair to blame or judge her for something that is a thousand percent on me," I ended and patted my chest with an open palm to emphasize my fault.

Shrugging, River asked, "Okay, so she's innocent or whatever. What am I supposed to do with this information? You still slept with her behind my back."

"I did, and I accept whatever consequence you want to delve out. I'm not going to fight you on whatever you want to do. I want you to do only what you want, and I will follow your lead."

She paused, considering what I had said. That was all I could offer. River deserved peace of mind and happiness with or without me. I was man enough to accept if she was no longer willing to keep me as part of that equation. We'd had a great relationship, no matter what her decision. However, I chose to give her my hundred percent if she kept me.

"How do I know I can even trust you?"

The question floored me. It wasn't because it wasn't valid, but because it made me realize my deception had brought a factor into our relationship that had never been an issue. Distrust. I loathed that. I'd always considered myself a straight-up man. To hear that question fall from her lips shredded the very fabric of my being.

Easing up on her, I clasped her hand and gently brought her to me. It pained me that she couldn't bear to look me in the eyes.

"The whole truth is that before I came in this door, I was going to confess to you anyway."

She scoffed, disbelief shrouding her face. Gripping her chin in the crook of my index finger, I turned her face, forcing her attention back to me.

"I'm serious. I went to the gravesite for solace and guidance. I wanted to make this right with you even if I can't make it whole. I put that on my mother."

She blinked back tears, and her face softened. "I know how you feel about your mother. You put nothing but truth on her."

I raised my hand. "So help me, God."

Releasing a deep sigh, she eyed me and said, "I mean, we have an open relationship, so I'm a bit conflicted. Technically, I would've permitted you to do what you did anyway."

"But it's the trust and honesty that's the issue, not the permission." I nodded my head toward her. "I get it."

She put her hands into mine after an extremely drawn-out and awkward moment.

Aries Skye

"*Before I make this decision, I have to know. That's it with her, right? Nothing else. No more times. You took your free pass, so don't even think about asking me for one with her ever again.*"

"*That was it.*"

It was the truth. Nissi wanted nothing to do with me, so I accepted that. River deserved my best, so I accepted that, too.

Closing her eyes, she nodded. "We can work through this, but I'ma be honest. I don't want the open relationship on the table anymore. I can't deal with that after this."

"*Done and done. I told you. It's whatever you want.*"

"*And any other TikTok you make better be with and about me—Instagram, Facebook, and whatever else.*"

"*You got it.*"

Her hardened expression eased at my agreeance to all her terms and conditions. Neither of us knew what to make of our new dynamic, but if we wanted it to work, we would have to give it a committed effort. River may not have been who everyone thought was for me, but she'd held me down, even now, after committing the ultimate offense. For that, I owed her all my energy and heart. Maybe that is what love was. Perhaps it wasn't some glorified whimsical tale but commitment and sacrifice.

Her hands captured my face. "I'm trusting you."

And that's how it had been for the past couple of months. She trusted me to get it right, in a sense. The new River was a bit more insecure. She'd been about proving her status in my life and driving me insane with it in the process. I tried my damndest to prove my loyalty and dedication to this relationship, but the extraness was bothersome. That was not who we were. It wasn't who we had ever been. However, I understood I forced that dynamic to change, so I rolled with the punches. But damn, if the punches weren't rolling over me. That was why I was happy to be bored sitting in the station house—because my personal life was miserable. I'd take boredom over misery every day of the week.

I noticed a presence sitting at the table with me, bringing my attention back to the present. When I looked up, it was Jovan. He was eating a breakfast sandwich with an energy drink. He gazed at me, smirked, and then picked up his sandwich. It was a shame our brotherhood had come to this. I missed his wild behavior and rudeness. Above all else, he was my boi.

I put down the spoon and magazine and looked up at him, forcing him to look up at me. The scowl on his face was etched so tight I thought I would have to tackle his giant muscular ass to the floor if he popped off.

"What?" he asked, still with a mean mug on his face.

A few seconds passed before I burst into laughter, and he belted the same.

"Bruh, quit flexin'," I howled as we stood and reached across the table, slapping fives. "I'm sorry, bro," I said, offering my apology.

He nodded. "It's all good. My bad, bro."

We sat back down, knowing that all had been forgiven and everything was right between us. Still, I felt I owed him more than a one-line apology.

"No matter what, we're bros." I sat back and ran my hand over my head. "I was caught up in my feelings."

Jovan shrugged. "I get it." He sat back and folded his arms. "To be honest, I was out of line, and I shouldn't have said that about Nissi or you, bro."

"I appreciate that for Nissi, but as for me, although it may have been out of line to say, it wasn't necessarily a lie." I hunched my shoulders in agreement. "But I'm working on that."

Jovan smirked. "So you told River, huh?"

I nodded with a sigh. "Had to. I've got my faults, but I couldn't be that dude to her."

"She got your ass doing cartwheels, I see. I took one look at your TikTok and was like, yep, my boi in the doghouse on that #coupletiktok bs," he joked.

I couldn't help the roar of laughter that belted from the pit of my stomach. That was the Jovan I was used to. Again, he was right. No offense to the couples who enjoyed it, but it had never been our thing. However, actions had consequences. Consequently, I had to make her feel comfortable in our relationship. If that meant putting on for the 'for you', Gram, and the city then I had to put on.

"Yeah, man. She got me on those sucker vibes," I said sheepishly among our shared laughs.

"Real talk, bro. Do what you gotta do," Jovan said, and we touched knuckles in respect. "I do have one question, though, my boi."

"What's that?" My eyes furrowed inquisitively.

He leaned over close to me. "The dentist chick. Was the pussy *that* bomb?"

I reared back as we both chuckled, giving him the "you already know" look.

"*Bruhhh.*"

Grinning, he threw his hands up. "Say less, my boi! Say less."

Chapter Sixteen

NISSI

FRESH OUT OF the shower, I oiled myself down, then eased into my fitted leggings and tank top. I twisted my curly locks into a bun atop my head and headed to the kitchen to pop the popcorn and make drinks. Margaritas for me and Amaretto Sour for Benji.

A smile crept on my face thinking about him. We'd been dating for two months, and I enjoyed our relationship. Though we had known each other intimately already, we started slowly. I allowed him to court me instead of resuming where we had left off. He appreciated it. He said it allowed us to get to know each other more deeply. He was correct. Benji and I learned some things about each other in the past, but we didn't honestly know and understand each other. Having dated these past couple of months allowed us to explore and learn. That was a good thing. Sex had not been a factor in our relationship, but I can't lie—I was beginning to feel an urge that needed urgent attention. Benji turned out to be a far better catch than I expected, and I had to admit he had me smitten with him. So, if sex came up, I was ready…ready for Benji.

Once I set everything up in the living room for our movie night, I heard a knock on my door. I jogged to the front door and opened it to find him soaked.

"What in the world?" I asked as he rushed inside.

He brushed a quick peck on my lips as I stood back.

"Hey, baby. It started raining on my way here, and I left my umbrella at home. All I had was this jacket in the backseat."

"It's cool. Hang your jacket in the coat closet to dry, and hand me your tennis shoes, socks, and clothing. I can throw them in the dryer. I have a robe you can wear. Sorry, it's girlie, but I won't snitch if you don't." I giggled as I ran back into my bedroom to grab it.

When I returned, I handed him the robe and quickly gathered his belongings to rush them to my dryer. I started with the clothing and put the shoes in a net bag to toss them in when the clothes were done. When I returned to the living room, Benji was sitting on the sofa with my silk robe wrapped around his body and holding up a jacket.

"Whose jacket is this?"

Instantly, the color drained from my face. *Kannon.* I wanted to lie because how could I explain a jacket twice my size hanging in my closet? For a split second, I considered saying it was my father's, but the design was too youthful. Benji may have been many things, but stupid he was not nor would ever be.

My palms sweated as I rubbed my hands together, knowing only the truth would suffice. I mean, Kannon and I weren't ever a couple. We didn't even talk anymore. What happened was well before Benji and I made our relationship official. So, what did I have to worry about? Nothing. Exactly.

Slowly walking to the sofa, I sat beside Benji.

"Uhh, it belongs to a guy I saw once."

There I said it. I picked up the remote and turned on the television to detour this conversation.

Benji eyed the jacket in his hands, furrowed his brow, and then laid it on the ottoman.

"A guy you saw once?" He repeated my answer as if trying to make sense of what I had said. "Once, as in, you dated, or it was literally once? And when did this 'once' happen?"

Here we go. This was the part I wanted to avoid because he would want total answers not half-truths. I would, too, if I had seen another female's clothing in his house. Just like I would feel entitled to an answer, so was he. I didn't want to bring it up because it was Kannon. I didn't want to recall him or anything about him.

"Well, it was before we reconnected. I want to make that very clear." Turning to face him, I propped my elbow on the sofa and leaned my head onto my open palm. "Remember when you asked me about the viral TikTok when I was trapped in the elevator?"

Slowly, he nodded his head. "Yeah. You told me you and the fireman met for drinks and dinner."

Casting my eyes downward, I felt ashamed. I didn't tell him the entire truth about that night. I didn't feel it was necessary to rehash it, especially since Kannon and I hadn't been a couple. Still, that five-hour date was returning to bite me in my rear end again.

"I didn't tell you everything." My eyes flickered upward. "We…uhh…after dinner, we walked on the beach. He'd given me his jacket to cover over because it was cool from the ocean breeze. We rented one of those private cabanas, and we…kinda sorta…umm, slept together on the beach."

His eyes flickered with confusion and then ballooned. "You slept with him?"

His response came out as both a statement and a question of shock. Swallowing the invisible lump in my throat, I nodded.

"Yes, if you must put it that way. We had sex."

He sat up, leaning forward with his hands clasped together. "So, are you still seeing each other? What's the deal? Because that, as surprising as it is, doesn't explain why his clothing is in your house." He turned his face to mine. "Should I be concerned?"

"No." I sat up and pulled his hand into mine. "We're good. It was a one-time deal. Afterward, he confessed to having a girlfriend, and I blew up. He apologized, but it was too little too late for me. As for the jacket, I still had it wrapped around my waist when I left him, and that's the only reason it's still in my house. I don't think he remembers I have it, and I haven't contacted him to tell him that I do."

Benji was quiet for a while. I was sure he was contemplating whether to believe me. His mind was probably scanning all the times we'd been together or not together to determine if what I had said was the truth.

"Why would you hold on to his property?"

Shrugging, I said, "I don't know, Benji. I didn't want to see him again, so I hung it up and forgot about it. Why is it such a huge deal to you?"

"Probably because I don't want another man's clothes in the house where my woman lives," he responded sarcastically with a scowl. "Come on, Nissi. Even if you didn't want to see him again, which I agree with because that was a punk move, you could've donated it to charity or something. It doesn't have to sit in your coat closet like a shrine to a man with whom you had one 'hit it and quit it' date."

"I mean, I wasn't even thinking about it, and it happened well before we reconnected. It's not like I was your woman then. I don't want to toss his belongings like that. It isn't right."

The look of bewilderment on Benji's face was damning. He pulled his hand from me and stood.

"So you're seriously going to hold on to this man's stuff? What is the end game? 'Cause either give it back to him or donate it."

Now I was in my feelings and matched his vibrato. "Are you making demands of me over some man's jacket with whom I have zero contact? Seriously?"

"Are you saying you wouldn't make the same demands if it were some female's clothing in my house? Seriously?"

I hated to admit he had a point. It was valid, and I knew it. My feelings were neutral with the entire situation. A part of me wanted to reach out to Kannon for the return, but the part that knew how hard I had battled to rid myself of the infatuation with Kannon did not want to meet up with him.

Tossing my head back, I offered a solution. "I'll figure out a way to get it back to him. Does that make you happy?"

Benji stared at me blankly and then scoffed, shaking his head. He snatched his keys off the coffee table and headed toward the laundry room. I jumped up, stalking behind him.

"Benji!" I boomed, gripping his arm. "What are you doing?"

"Leaving," he said through gritted teeth as he took off the robe, snatched his clothing out of my dryer, and slipped on his basketball shorts.

I threw my hands in the air in frustration. "Over a freaking jacket?"

"Over what you're not telling me!" he boomed, his voice elevated. He stepped into my space. "Nissi, it's a jacket. You act as if I'm asking you to make a life-altering decision. The fact that you are this worked up over simply giving this man back his property or chucking it means there's a lot more you aren't telling me. How serious did you and this guy get?"

"We didn't get serious," I belted, inhaling sharply. "It's not even something I can explain, okay? All I can offer you is that nothing between Kannon and I materialized past that day."

He stood back as realization crossed his face.

"But you wanted it to. That's why you're so hung up about this jacket."

Rather than answer, I swallowed and lowered my gaze.

"Jesus Christ," Benji said, folding his hands atop his head in disbelief. "Are you still hung up on this man? What about us?"

"We're good, Benji!" The panicked words bellowed out of me in a plea. "Did I want something to materialize between Kannon and me? Yes, I did. However, it didn't. I'm with you, and I'm good. *We're good.*" Tears found their way into my eyes, and I sniffed them away.

One glance into my saddened face softened Benji. He exhaled and moved into my space. His intense gaze nearly burned a hole through me, and I looked away from him to survive. Caressing my face in the palms of his hands, he forced my attention to meet his. His words were so solemn and sincere.

"Do you know how much I love you?"

Love? Did he just say he loved me?

The word came out of my mouth as both a call to repeat and a question. "Love?"

Boring a hole through my soul with his intense gray orbs, he bit his bottom lip and repeated with luster what he had already declared.

"Yes, *love*, bél mwen. I'm so all in with you that it scares me. These past two months have breathed new life into me, Nissi. I didn't even know I was drowning until you gave us a chance again. I think I've always loved you. Since the first day of class in dental school."

We shared a knowing chuckle, and then he licked his lips.

"But these past two months have been nothing short of amazing. I don't just love you; I'm *in love* with you, Nissi."

My eyes ballooned, and he smiled.

"You don't have to feel obligated to those feelings, but I want you to understand how deeply I feel for you and how serious I am. So, no, I don't want another man's clothing in your house unless it's your father's."

We cracked a giggle at that as I continued to process his words. I couldn't believe his confession. Actually, I could. Benji had always given all of himself to me. Now, with the admission of his true feelings, I had to do the same for him. I wasn't at the "in love" level yet, but I cared deeply for him and wanted to put him at ease. My loyalty lay with him, not some fly-by-night one-night stand. So, I fully committed to nourishing our budding relationship because Benji was my present and possibly my future.

"Baby, I'm sorry, and you're right. I don't want you to have any doubts. I'm in this with you. Therefore, I am going to give it back to him."

We stood there while he continued to drink in my facial features as if committing them to memory.

"I asked before but must ask again to be sure." His gray eyes found mine, and I could see the fear reflecting in them. "Should I be worried?"

No details were needed because I fully understood the scope of his question. Although Kannon had infiltrated my heart, Benji had no reason to be concerned about him or any other man. Benji had been all man for me since day one—before I even appreciated the man he was to me. There was no way I would ever betray that, and he deserved to know it. So, I gave him the peace his heart needed.

My hands cradled his face as I said, "Benji, you have nothing to worry about. I am all yours." I stepped back out of his embrace and lifted my tank top over my head. "In fact, I want to show you how much I'm committed to our relationship."

The expression of love turned into lust at the sight of my bare breasts. We stood there suspended in times of yesteryear as the reality of my intentions took root. As if a switch clicked in his mind, Benji didn't waste a moment as he moved swiftly toward me and swooped in on my exposed breasts. His taut hands cupped them sensually before he tilted his head, gently suckling on my left nipple. His hand glided over my right breast and flickered his thumb and forefinger over my nipple. Moans escaped my lips as I eased my hand behind him, softly cupping his head to my chest. Relinquishing my breast from his lips, he lifted me into his arms, and I wrapped my legs around his waist. Our lips met as we kissed with wild passion, and he carried me into my bedroom, laying me gently on my bed.

He followed suit, easing on top of me and gripping the hem of my leggings and panties. His seductive gaze momentarily caught my eyes as he slid them down my legs and yanked them off at the toe before standing back up at the foot of the bed.

Is this happening? Oh yeah, this is happening.

Even though we were not new to each other, I felt excited energy coursing through my veins—a renewing. His familiarity called out to me, and I was ready. More than ready. Lying on the bed, fully exposed to him, I bit my lip as I gazed at him sexily and spread my legs so he could see my glistening lower lips.

"Ooh," he whimpered, pulling his bottom lip between his teeth. "Bél mwen."

His determination was evident in the swiftness of the removal of his basketball shorts. What sprang forth was an old friend I hadn't realized I had missed until I saw him come alive. My yoni twitched with a familiar excitement as he climbed on the bed to rejoin me. Before we got carried away, I pointed at the nightstand. He nodded his head with acknowledgment, reached over, and slid the top drawer open. Reaching inside, he removed a gold foil packet. As he worked to shield himself, I took my two fingers and played with my sweetness, making sloshing noises with my wetness.

I moaned as my head lolled backward. "I'm so wet."

Benji's eyes were transfixed on the sight of me pleasuring myself, and that turned me on even more. Watching his facial expression turn from wonder to wonder-lust was enough to take me over the edge. Before I could, Benji removed my fingers and placed them in his mouth. Slowly, he suckled my juices off them one by one. He took his time licking all around and between my fingers, slurping up all my sweetness. My skin felt ablaze, causing my treasure to burst into a raging inferno. Benji was proving his grown-man status in his sexual endeavors, exploring far more than he did when we were in college, and I loved it.

He moaned after removing my fingers from his mouth. "The sweetest juices in the world, I swear."

Wrapping my arms around his neck, he leaned on top of me as we kissed again. The taste of myself on his tongue heightened my arousal, and I wrapped my legs around his waist as our tongues tasted each other. Benji circled his tongue around my lips as he positioned himself at my opening. My body tingled when he pushed inside me, and he grunted, pausing for a nanosecond to savor the reconnection. This was not the same Benji I used to sneak quickies with back in dental college. He pressed himself deep inside my walls and began to work my body over. His slow, sensual thrusts were painstakingly delicious.

"Mmm, Benji." My moans spilled out as I gripped his back, taking in his deep strokes.

"Hmm, Nissi. You feel so good."

I wanted to roll over and ride, but he pushed my arms back against the bed as he stared into my eyes.

"No, baby. Just like this. Let me have you *just…like…this.*"

I wanted to protest, but with each syllable, he dove deeper and deeper into my core. And damn if it didn't feel so good. My eyes rolled back as he slowly stroked me out of my mind. It was like he was on a mission to make me forget Kannon and any other man who might've held my attention or heart. He was doing an excellent job at his attempt to eliminate the memories, too. As my moans increased, so did his speed. My erotic confirmations of pleasure were turning him on. When he sped up, the suction sounds of my yoni and his balls clapping together had my head spinning.

"Hmm, shhh!" I yelped. "Bennnjiiii!"

His name on my lips must've done it for him because he pounded my pretty yoni like he was digging for lost treasure.

"Ooh cum with me, baby!" he wailed out. "I can't hold it much longer. This pussy is so incredible."

I wasn't ready for it to end. He felt so good—better than I ever remembered. I wanted to will him to continue, but I knew it was a losing battle. His body tensed, and his face scrunched up, indicating his impending climax. Lifting my legs higher on his waist, he sank deeper, tapping the center of my core. My juices started pouring out when I did that, and Benji yelped in delight.

"I'm 'bout to explode," Benji panted.

I chased my climax as he pounded my yoni into submission. When he screamed out, I burst, which made him scream again.

"Nisssssiii!"

After the waves of passion subsided, he rolled onto his back and pulled me against him to snuggle. Easing into the crook of his arm, I nestled my head against his chest, fulfilled and content. My mind was clear, and I was grateful we were back on track. I was just about to float into a dream state when he spoke.

"I love you so much, Nissi." He kissed the top of my head. "Hands down, the best lover I've ever had."

"Aww, baby." I cooed.

His sentiments made me happy, but it was all I could offer. Despite the beauty we had just shared, I wasn't in love with him… yet. *Ugh.* I hated to admit that. Tucking those thoughts away, I continued to bask in our time.

"Thank you, baby. We needed this. *I* needed it. And thank you for understanding about the whole jacket situation. I trust you to handle it, and I figured out how you can do it. Just message him and ask for his address. Ship it to him."

"Yeah, baby, that's what I'll do." I leaned up and kissed him, then climbed on top of him. "But I don't want to talk about that or anything right now. I'd much rather enjoy us."

Licking his lips, a grin graced his face. "That's my girl. I swear I'll do anything to please you. You've got me wrapped. You know that?"

I nodded and leaned in as we kissed again. We kept going until we both were aroused and ready to go another round. Thank goodness I was able to stop his rant about Kannon. For one, thoughts of him were not good for me sexually, especially during sex with my boyfriend. For two, he had no clue that I was delivering the jacket in person. It was a decision I made when he brought up the entire thing.

My dental group was paired with a healthy kids' initiative with the city to speak to children about dental health. The issue was that these health fairs were being held at different fire stations around the city as the base. Of course, due to our TikTok fame, my group got scheduled with elementary age groups set to be at Engine Company #79. Yes, Kannon's station. I had to speak to a group of first graders that would be there. I figured it would be the perfect opportunity to return his jacket. I would know he received it, and I'd be too occupied to have a personal and private conversation with him. It was a win-win. Besides, it wasn't like I was making a special trip. I was already going to be there for the kids.

Chapter Seventeen

NISSI

ONE WEEK LATER, I was preparing to head to Station 79 to discuss dental health with the kids, and I was excited to meet the children. Youth inspired me more than anything. The admiration in their eyes seeing a young black female doctor made all those grueling nights of study and sacrifice worthwhile. Who I was not excited to see was Kannon. I guess *uncertainty* was more the feeling. I hadn't seen or spoken to him since that night, and I was anxious about our reactions to each other. At the end of the day, we were in relationships, so any interaction we had would be a non-factor.

As I prepared to leave my house, I stood in front of the mirror, eyeing myself. My curls hung loosely around my face with barely-there makeup. My fitted yellow capris accentuated my bottom in all the right places, and my nude camisole tucked into my capris was sheer at the top and silk-blend at the bottom. My beige three-inch block-heeled shoes were the perfect addition—cute and sophisticated wrapped in one five-foot three-inch bubble. Slipping on my white coat, I made my way out the door with my purse and Kannon's jacket, jumped into my car, and headed to the station. My assistants, Sheena and Roxie, were set to meet me there with the goodie bags for the kids and the supplies for the class.

Thankfully, Sheena and Roxie arrived right when I did, so I exited the car and greeted them. After the greetings, I helped them unload and proceeded to the fire station.

As we walked, Sheena pulled me back out of earshot of Roxie. "Are you gonna be cool?"

I nodded. "Girl, yes. I've moved on with Benji. Kannon was a one-time non-factor."

Sheena gave me the side-eye. "Yeah, Benji is nice or whatever, but he ain't no Kannon Jordan. Just saying."

Shrugging, I frowned. "Who cares if Kannon is well-built? He still screwed me over, and Benji hasn't. He's been there for me like a real man should. He's mine and—"

"You gone stick beside him?" she joked.

Her quick-wittedness brought me to howling laughter. "Shut up, nut. But yeah, I guess so. I'm gone stick beside him."

Sheena smiled. "All right. Whatever you say."

We caught up with Roxie just as she rang the bell at the fire station door. That's when I realized I had left Kannon's jacket in my car. However, I decided to let it be. I would give it to him on my way out. That way, there was no extensive conversation due to time constraints.

As soon as the door opened, an older man stepped out.

"Hi, I'm Captain Morris. Please allow me to help with those boxes. Taylor, Mason, come and help these ladies."

Soon, two more firemen appeared and grabbed the boxes from us. Then they all led the way to an open area where we would present to the first graders. As soon as they sat the belongings down, I turned to the captain with my hand outstretched.

"Hi, I apologize for our rudeness. I am Dr. Nissi Richards from Optimal Dentistry, and these are my assistants, Sheena and Roxie."

He shook each of their hands.

"No worries. It's a pleasure to meet your acquaintances, ladies. Let me introduce you all to the crew."

With that, he called all the men into the room, and when they filtered in, I kept my head down to avoid awkward contact. He introduced everyone, with all of us waving hello. When he got to Jovan and Kannon, I could've passed out. *Jesus.* Both men were fine as hell, but Kannon was extra scrumptious. My gaze was brief because I wasn't about to get sucked into the #KannonRiver show.

"And I believe you know Kannon Jordan," he said with a smirk that I didn't find slick or amusing.

The fakest smile I could plaster adorned my face as I glanced in Kannon's direction. He held a somber expression on his, and I retrained my attention back on the captain.

"Yes, we've met. Thank you."

My words were so cool that I'm sure they sent a chill down everyone's spine.

"Well, alrighty then," Captain Morris said with a bit of awkwardness.

To break the stiff air, I followed through with, "Thank you for that introduction, Captain Morris." I nodded my appreciation to him and addressed the firefighters as a unit. "I am Dr. Nissi Richards, and these two young ladies are my wonderful assistants, Sheena and Roxie. We want to thank you all for graciously allowing us to enter your space for the greater good of our community."

My words were met with handclaps before Captain Morris spoke.

"Don't sweat it. We enjoy the kids and are happy to partner with you and your practice."

After that, we excused ourselves to help prepare for the little ones. Goody bags were prepared in one box, and then we set up the demonstration table with the fake teeth, toothbrush, mouthwash, and dental floss. As soon as we finished, Sheena pulled me to the side.

"Girl, what's up with that awkward exchange between you two?"

I rolled my eyes. "We haven't seen or talked to each other since that night, so I knew things wouldn't be all gumdrops and rainbows."

"He seems like he wants to talk to you, and you were giving major ice queen vibes."

"I was giving major 'I'm here for a job' vibes." My tone was stern. "Listen, I don't want to spend all morning dwelling on my past, especially a past that was only one day and not even a full one."

Sheena held up her hands. "I feel you. I wanted to make sure you would be okay being around him."

Her words touched me, and I realized I was being harsh. I had to release that energy because the kids would pick up on it, and it wasn't anyone's fault that Kannon played me for a fool except for us. Besides, why was I upset? I'd been strong with Benji for three months, and he was the most amazing guy ever. I had a beautiful career, a great family, and supportive friends. I could not get sucked into one night from hell and let that change who I was. So, I took a deep breath and let go of my reservations, putting Kannon and all that drama behind me. It was above me now.

"I'm good, sis. I promise." I offered a genuine smile. "Thank you."

Bumping my shoulder, she giggled. "It's his loss anyway."

I pointed at her and tossed a serious glance in her direction. "That part!"

While in our private talk session, Captain Morris came over to announce the first graders were there. We walked out to the main area to greet them with the firefighters, and soon, three classes comprised of sixty first graders came barreling into the fire station with their three teachers and a few parental chaperones. After Captain Morris and I introduced ourselves to the teachers and parents, he informed the teachers that my presentation would be first and then the fire truck tour. That worked for me. It would serve as my get-out-of-jail-free card to slip away from the fire station and avoid Kannon Jordan altogether.

"You're the TikTok dentist, right?" one of the teachers asked.

With a slight chuckle, I answered, "Yes, that's me—That Dentist Chick."

"Yes, I'm so glad it's you. We sent waivers to the parents of the kids, just in case you wanted to do a TikTok with them. That way, you have permission."

Kids? These teachers wanted to be in a TikTok. They weren't slick.

"You didn't have to do that. We weren't going to do a TikTok because of the legal constraints with the children."

The other teacher turned from Captain Morris. "Please don't say that. These kids have looked forward to meeting That Dentist Chick from TikTok."

"Really?" I was surprised.

"Yes, your dances are viral, and a few parents followed the whole Fire and Rescue saga. I don't know if you've heard, but you're very famous in Miami," the first teacher confirmed.

"So, please don't tell these kids they won't get to do a TikTok with you. They will probably lose it and start crying."

My hands flew over my heart. "Aww, well, I can't disappoint the babies."

With that, the teachers and parents gathered the kids to sit on the huge carpet on the floor while Sheena, Roxie, and I took center stage. The firefighters sat at the table behind the action so they could watch the entire presentation, Kannon included. Then, one of the teachers introduced my assistants and me.

"Hello, everyone! As your teacher said, I am Dr. Nissi Richards, and I am so happy to be here with you all today."

One by one, their hands flew in the air.

I pointed at the first little girl. "You, my little lady in the hot pink shirt."

"Are you the dancing dentist from TikTok?"

Nodding, I offered her a bright smile. "Yes, I am!"

Once again, hands were raised, but even more this time.

I pointed at another little girl. "Yes, sweetie?"

"Can you do a TikTok with us, please?" she asked, and they all kicked in with the pleases like a harmonized chorus.

I motioned with my hands for them to calm down, and they did instantly. It had to be the "celebrity" status because their teachers were shocked and appalled at the immediate obedience.

"I'll tell you what. I'll do a TikTok with some of you if you all allow me to finish my demonstration."

They went berserk at that news.

"I have time for one more question before I have to get started."

One little boy raised his hand, so I acknowledged him. "Yes, sir?"

"Hi!" He waved sheepishly, and I waved back. "You're really pretty," he said behind his hands, blushing much to the other youngsters' snickers and oohs.

A blush crossed my face, as well. "Aww, thank you, sweetheart. What's your name?"

"Drew," he said boldly.

"Well, thank you, Drew."

"Can I be your boyfriend?" he blurted, causing everyone to burst into hysterics, including himself.

"Well, Drew, that is awfully sweet of you, but I promise you will not be checking for me when you get my age." All the adults snickered at my answer. "But I tell you what." I wagged my finger with a wink. "If it's okay with the teachers and parents, I can call you my little boyfriend for today."

His starry eyes flew to his teacher, and she nodded a playful yes. He then jumped up and down while pointing at his other male friends.

"I told you she was gonna be my girlfriend."

Barrels of laughter erupted between the teachers, parents, firefighters, my assistants, and me.

"Okay, boyfriend!" I egged him on.

He strutted his stuff with his little chest puffed out for a second before I quieted the room full of excited first graders back down. Then, I went into my spiel about the importance of proper dental hygiene and showed them how to floss, brush their teeth properly, and rinse with mouthwash. Afterward, I answered their questions about my job and dental care. It ranged anywhere from why dental floss was so thin to why didn't I wear fake nails. These kids were so smart and intuitive, far more than I was at their age. I loved every bit of my time with them.

"Dr. Nissi," one of the students called out, "aren't you in one of those turntees?"

We all looked around, unsure of what she meant until she further explained.

"You know when you all do this." She stood up and started "pretend" stepping, which was hilarious.

"Why yes, I am. I'm in a *sorority*. The Alpha Khi Alphas."

"Can you step?" she asked eagerly.

"Yes, I can."

Why did I say that? I was met with little pleas to show them how to step. Even the firemen and teachers asked. And yes, Kannon was just as boisterous about it as his counterparts. So, I asked my assistant to play the instrumental version of "Everybody Mad" by O.T. Genasis. I stood with my head leaned back with my palms faced down and fanned out on either side of me as the music came on. When the beat dropped, I did a quick two-step combo with the sorority pretty-girl hand gestures and ended with the official hand sign and my ankle crossed at the knee. Those kids went wild with excitement, and I received a standing ovation from everyone in the room.

My boyfriend, Drew, jumped up and hugged me, and I embraced him.

"Can we do the TikTok now?" he asked.

"Sure can. I'll let you choose, boyfriend. Which song should we do?"

He put his finger up, thinking, and another little girl ran over to him and whispered in his ear. His face lit up as he turned to me and said, "Poof, Be Gone!"

I hollered. "You kids are trying to make me go to physical therapy, I see."

Sheena waved it off. "Don't believe that. She's got knees like Megan."

Her statement amused everyone as we guffawed.

"See, what we're not gonna do is encourage that today!" I pointed playfully at her.

Kannon cleared his throat with a cough and straightened himself in the chair. All eyes were on him.

"Excuse me. My apologies." His eyes bore into me.

Quickly, I darted my eyes away from him because even that innocent encounter sent an uneasy shiver down my spine.

"Okay, we can do Poof, Be Gone. I choose my boyfriend, of course, and the young lady who helped him decide."

"Marisa!" she shouted and came forward.

"I need one more and a volunteer to record."

The main teacher in charge chose a student named Nina, who had been selected as student of the week, and she came forward. The volunteer to record came from the back. When I looked up, it was Kannon. Of course, it was Kannon because who else out of the no less than fifteen adults in the building would record? I'm pretty sure it was a conspiracy on the firefighters' end because as soon as one of the parents was about to volunteer, she was politely asked to put her hand down by the only male parent, who gave Jovan a nod. Like, I didn't see that.

"I got you, doc," Kannon said as he stood towering in front of me with a flirtatious smirk.

Resisting the urge to roll my eyes, I pursed my lips and replied, "Thank you."

My assistant brought my cell phone to me, and I set it on TikTok with the song before handing it to him. "Here. It's set already."

He smoothly caressed my hand as he slid the phone from my grasp. Licking his lips, he stared at me. "Like I said, I got you, doc. Have fun."

He winked at me, and those deep-set light brown orbs were like a tide waiting to snatch my soul into their murky waters.

Nope. Not today, Satan. I didn't waste a second moving away from him. He was attempting to suck me into his aura, and I wasn't having it. He was certifiable—fresh off couples TikTok and flirting with me. *The whole ass nerve of this man.*

I lined up my assistants with the three children, and we did a practice run first. Each adult was paired with each child, my boyfriend and I being first as everyone else fell into succession with the dance. When we got ready to record, I slipped off my white coat and sat it on a nearby table. Once I did that, I looked over at Kannon to give him the green light to start the countdown, and I could have sworn I saw that man bite his lip while looking down the length of my body. I shook it off, and he began the recording. My boyfriend and I took off with the dance, followed by Marisa and Sheena and then Nina and Roxie. We all hit our poses and snapped at the end. We ate that dance up! The adults and kids roared after we finished—even Kannon, who was fist-pumping in the air.

"Thank you, guys. I will do one more TikTok so we are all included. Volunteer, you still good?"

"I got you, doc." He winked at me again.

I was so engrossed in the moment that his sexy wink produced a slight blush that I quickly cleared, refusing to be undone.

"Okay, choose the song 'Can't Stop Jiggin'," I directed.

After that, I told the teachers and my assistants my idea was to put the caption: *When they say you're only a dentist, but you're influencing the future.* I would start walking away from the camera to the beat, followed by my assistants and then the students, and I would double back around to ensure the camera caught the teachers and parents. Then I explained to Kannon to continue letting the beat ride so we could catch them all. He gave me the thumbs-up and hit record. Looking into the camera with a scowl, I started bop walking to the beat, followed by my assistants, the kids, teachers, and parents. I walked backward so Kannon could catch everyone while I beefed up all the kids as they walked by and then the teachers and parents. By the time we finished, everyone was in high spirits and jumping up and down. When I retrieved my phone from Kannon, he returned it without any inappropriate actions. Thank goodness.

The main teacher and Captain Morris thanked me for my time and then corralled the first graders to go outside to see the fire trucks. Before they left, we handed each child a goody bag filled with a toothbrush, toothpaste, dental floss, and a cup of Play-Doh. My boyfriend gave me another hug before joining his team, and I told him to stay good and do well in school. He promised he would, and I believed him. I loved the light in his little eyes. As stoked as I was to be around those first graders, I was happy they were moving on to the fire trucks because a sister was tired, tired. I rushed over to help Roxie and Sheena finish packing up our things.

"Whew, chile, I'm exhausted." I fanned my face a bit as I packed the last box.

"You should be…entertaining two boyfriends up in here today," Sheena joked as Roxie hooted and hollered, then I lightly pushed her.

I knew she couldn't wait to rag on me. "Shut your mouth, and let's get out of here before he finds a way to come running to talk to me."

We rushed outside to their vehicles while all the firefighters were preoccupied. I placed the items in Sheena's car, hugged them each, thanked them for their help, and advised them that I would see them in the office. I'd gotten in my car to leave when I remembered Kannon's jacket was in my backseat.

"Shit." I hit the steering wheel.

Just give the man his jacket and stop being dramatic, I chastised myself as I eased out of my car and grabbed the jacket. An idea hit me. I would give the jacket to the captain and avoid having to see Kannon again. As I approached the captain, he smiled brightly.

"You did a great job with those kids today, Dr. Richards. You should go into pediatrics. You'd earn a killing."

"Aww, thank you so much." I gestured my gratitude for the compliment. "I wanted to thank you for your hospitality and ask if you'd give this to Kannon."

"Oh, nonsense. You can give it to him."

Before I could protest, he whistled, causing all the men to look up.

"Jordan, come over here, please."

Kannon jogged over quickly, and the captain looked at me. "It was a pleasure, Dr. Richards. Have a wonderful day."

He walked off, patting Kannon on the shoulder as he approached me.

Exactly what I didn't want to happen. Holding his jacket in front of me, I said, "Here you go. This belongs to you."

He took the jacket and tossed it over his shoulder. "Appreciate it. You could've kept it, though."

I shook my head. "No reason to do that."

He laughed, stroking his hand down the front of his wavy hair. "I mean, it has your scent in it."

"I don't make it a habit of taking things that don't belong to me."

His facial expression dropped, and I knew that stung. He walked right into that one. What else was I supposed to say? He was trying to be slick, and I was keeping it real—something he should've done with me regarding his relationship with River.

"I know you don't believe me or accept it, but I am very sorry, Nissi. I handled you wrong, and I'll regret that for life."

Something about how he said that felt so sincere that I felt emotions creeping through my system. *Nope.* I didn't care if he meant it; I couldn't allow his apology to take root, even if it were sincere.

Shrugging, I attempted to make light of the situation. "It's in the past now."

His expression turned solemn as he slid his fingers over his beard. "Nissi—"

Just then, my phone chimed. Thank God for small favors. It was my actual boyfriend. Kannon looked down at my phone as the words MY BAE-BENJI scrolled across my screen and then looked back up at me with shock.

"Bae, as in boyfriend?" he asked with knitted brows and his lip curled upward.

I nodded. "Yes, my boyfriend. Almost three months," I responded as the phone call went to voicemail.

He rubbed the back of his neck. A mixture of emotions flooded his face. Shock, angst, and disbelief were some of the ones I caught.

"Oh," was his simple reply.

"Well, I really need to go. I must get to the office, and I need to call my man back. You understand, right?"

His lips tightened, and he sniffed, flicking the tip of his nose. "Yeah, I got you, ma."

This time those words came out peppered with irritation and anger. I knew good and well that he wasn't upset or jealous even. He had *her*. River. His *RiverKannon, KannonRiver*. He didn't need or want me. Since the next man had me, he couldn't tolerate it. Petty ass. That was why I was glad I had left him and his antics behind on the beach that night.

"Well, have a nice life, and I wish you and River the best."

With that, I turned and trucked to my car, leaving him standing there and staring after me, but I refused to turn around. I marched until I reached my car, got inside, and drove away without a backward glance at Kannon Jordan. Connecting my phone to my car's Bluetooth, I pressed redial.

"Bél mwen," Benji's sultry voice floated through my speakers.

"Hey, baby," I cooed with a blush.

Chapter Eighteen

KANNON

I STOOD THERE FOR what had to be a while, staring after Nissi long after she left the fire station. My mind was reeling at the fact that she had a boyfriend. Apparently, she had gotten one merely a month after our encounter. Like, for real? She could tuck what we had shared away that fast, huh? But what right did I have to be upset about it? None. Our encounter happened when I had a whole girlfriend. Still, that didn't stop me from being pissed about her having a man. I knew it was possible because a woman of her caliber should get snatched up quickly. But to a man named *Ben*? He sounded lame as hell—ole cornball.

"I take it you didn't tell her you were single and free to mingle?" Jovan's voice infiltrated my thoughts.

My head dropped, and I rubbed the nape of my neck. "Nah, man."

"Why not?" he quizzed. "You've been waiting on this day."

Looking over my shoulder at him, I admitted the truth. "She got a man."

With that, I walked back into the station house and found a nice comfortable spot to lay my head back and try to sleep off this continuous nightmare, forgetting all about the youth outside.

It was true. River and I had been broken up for a month now. We gave it our best, but it wasn't enough to mend our fences. Honestly, we could've mended our fences, but one person was preventing that—Nissi. I don't say that in the figurative sense, either.

River had been gone out of town for two weeks on business. During her absence, I talked to her daily, and we even had phone sex a couple of times. However, my thoughts drifted back to Nissi whenever I was alone in my apartment. Every. Single. Time. I couldn't turn it off. Trust, I tried. I even avoided social media, thinking that seeing her pop up on my "For You" and "Explore" pages was what kept driving thoughts of her in my mind. None of it helped. At all. My dreams were laden with more nights on the beach with Nissi. I even dreamed she was walking down the aisle to give me her hand in marriage. In fact, that was the dream that did it. I had asked God and my mama for a sign, and they'd given me one. One hell of one, too.

River had been home a couple of days, and we'd made love fiercely that night. Like, I seriously thought I was over this whole Nissi situation. Our lovemaking was that beautiful. When we drifted off to sleep, I began having a glorious dream of my wedding day. The beauty of the memory could only be about dreaming of going to Heaven or marrying the woman who felt like Heaven on Earth. It was like that. I remember feeling such a sense of calm and peace during that dream. It was as if my soul was satisfied. It felt so miraculous that I never wanted to let go of that feeling. My mama was sitting in the front row, smiling at me and blessing my day. When the bride walked down the aisle, I knew God sent her just for me. I was so in love, so proud, and so happy. When the veil was lifted, I stared into the eyes of Nissi. I remember calling her name and planting a kiss of thankfulness on her before the ceremony even began.

When my eyes popped open, I gasped, and when I turned, I saw River had her back to me. I knew then I had to let her go. Even if I never had Nissi again, there was no way I could continue that relationship knowing she would never be enough for me.

I dragged my hand down my face in angst. It would undoubtedly be the worst thing I had to do in my life, second to burying my mother. River was a great woman. A great woman who loved me despite my flaws and faults. A woman who had put her own feelings aside to allow me to have extra women on the side and dealt with the fact that I'd still ultimately cheated. She didn't deserve any of this, and it pained my heart that I was about to break hers. However, I'd rather let her go than waste any more of her time or life. She had already wasted two-plus years for no reward or gain.

When I reached out my hand to touch her, she recoiled. It shocked me because I could've sworn she was asleep. I didn't understand why she would pull away from me, so I called out to her.

"River," I whispered into the night.

"Don't." Her words came out pained behind sniffles. That's when I realized she was crying. "Just go ahead and say it, Kannon."

Confusion was etched on my face. "What?"

The question eased out because I was honestly unsure where she was going with this conversation.

She turned over, and her face was drenched with tears. Her lip trembled, and her nose was red as droplets of tears continued to roll down the tip of her nose. She swiped at them and thwarted my attempt to reach out to her.

"We both know what you were about to say to me. Just say it. Rip the Band-Aid off."

Her words brought me back to when I confessed to Nissi that I had a girlfriend. I had thought those same exact words. Words I'd gotten from River. That was her favorite saying. Rip the Band-Aid off. The realization that she knew I was about to leave struck me, and my eyes ballooned in wonderment. Before I could even formulate the question, she explained.

"*You said her name in your sleep.*" *She looked up at me with hurt in her eyes.* "*Nissi. You said her name with so much passion, so much confidence, and so much…love.*"

I attempted to grab her hand, but she pulled away.

"*No. Don't patronize me. It's her. You love her. Don't you?*"

With my eyes closed, I softly shook my head. I couldn't believe I had said Nissi's name aloud, or that River had heard it, or that this was even happening. I loved River. I just wasn't in love with her.

"*I…don't…I don't know. I…just.*" *I looked over at her awaiting face and sighed.* "*This is so hard. I don't know what it is. It's just something. I love you, River. I do.*"

She reached out and caressed my hand. "*That something is love.*"

"*It was one time and one night!*" *My frustrations poured out of me at my heart's unwillingness to let Nissi go.* "*I love you.*"

"*But you need her.*"

Those words broke me. Tears poured out of my eyes because that was exactly it. I needed Nissi Richards in my life. Surprisingly, she eased over to me and held my head in her hands while she wiped my tears away.

After several minutes, River's voice broke our silence. "*I understand now, Kannon. Even if you don't.*" *Lifting my face, she stared directly into my eyes.* "*You're in love with her, and that is what love at first sight is. You fell in love with her the moment you saw her. She's who you were meant to be with. She's your soul tie. And neither I nor any other woman could compete with that.*"

"*I'm so sorry, River. I really am. I'm so sorry.*" *I pelted out through sobs.*

Blinking back tears, she shook her head from side to side. "*Don't be. That is not on you. That is ordained, Kannon. Sent from Heaven. I only hope that one day, I can find my forever like you have.*" *She took a beat before she declared,* "*I should go.*"

She moved to get up out of the bed, but I gripped her arm gently.

"It's three o'clock in the morning. Please stay. Let's have these last few moments together. Then..."

She placed her finger on my lips and eased back into the bed. We snuggled against each other, and I held her tightly for as long as I could until sleep won the battle. When I finally cracked my tired eyes open the next day around nine in the morning, River was gone. All the stuff she usually kept at my place was gone, too. On my nightstand, there was a note:

Kannon,

Thank you for showing me that love at first sight exists. Just promise me that our breakup will not be in vain. Accept your feelings for Nissi and go to her. I love you...always.

Next Lifetime,

River

Lifting the paper to my lips, I kissed it and then tucked it away in my nightstand drawer. Reaching for my cell phone, I pulled up the Instagram app and went to Nissi's page. The moment I saw her face, I knew everything River had said was true. I wanted that woman. I needed her. I loved her. I had to have her. I just had to figure out a way to do that.

I thought that opportunity had fallen into my lap when I learned she would be at the station today. I planned to tell her that I was single and plead for us to start over. She had almost slipped away from me if it hadn't been for my jacket. I was so excited when Captain called me over that I nearly floated. Only to find out she had a man. *Ben. Cornball.* I'd wasted too much time. She slipped away from me. The only thing was, if I still felt like we were meant to be, she had to feel the same way, right? Perhaps she needed a minute to come to her senses. Whatever it was, I knew I couldn't move on, and I prayed like hell she hadn't either. I was living proof that you could be with someone and not truly be with them. And I hoped that was the case with her and Ben because what else was I going to do?

Chapter Nineteen

NISSI

IT'D BEEN A long day in the office with a day packed full of clients, two of whom wanted alternative treatment options because they felt our costs were too high for their out-of-pocket expense, and they had no qualms about letting it rip about how unfair that was. I understood. Dental expenses could be a beast, so I empathized with them. All I could do was assure them that their issues would be resolved once the procedure was done, unlike some other healthcare procedures. That, of course, didn't matter as much as how much it would cost them to get said procedure completed.

After feeling like I had gone through several heavyweight boxing rounds, I was relieved when it was time to meet Ciara for lunch. We opted to eat in her office, which was a welcomed break for me. Not only did she have the perfect window view, but it also gave me the escape from my office and the peace to spend my entire one-hour lunch break eating and chillin' with my girl instead of fighting traffic for most of the time.

Even though the elevators had been upgraded, I still took the stairs to her office. Shoot, my body had gotten a bit toned from using the stairs the entire time the elevators were under repair and beyond. Not bothering to change any of my attire, I eased down the flight of stairs to the eighth floor, wearing my medical scrubs, white coat, and Air Max for comfort. As soon as I pulled the glass door open to CB Insurance, I was greeted by her lovely receptionist, Ms. Linda, whom everyone adored. After a few pleasantries between us, she allowed me back to Ciara's office.

Thankfully, her door was already open in welcoming anticipation of my arrival. When I walked inside, I took a second to inhale and release. Her space was absolute Zen. From the window view to the aromatherapy candles to the colors and placement of her plants creating a feng shui, I felt an instant settling in my spirit. The calming effect, Ciara called it. She said she liked to make sure her clients were comfortable, which, more often than not, assured securing insurance premiums with them. She was thriving, so I guess all that feng shui-Zen stuff worked. It did for me, anyway. So who was I to argue?

When I plopped into the chair in front of her desk, she pulled out two plates from our favorite Jamaican food truck and sweet teas, and my senses went into overload. One whiff of the plate had my stomach clawing for a taste.

"Let me hurry up and feed you, bringing that musty energy into my establishment." Ciara slid the white Styrofoam tray in front of me and a large white Styrofoam cup filled with tea and a straw.

I opened the plate and thought I'd been transported to Heaven. The restaurant's ackee and saltfish and beef patties were my favorites. When I opened it up and saw both dishes inside, I knew there was a God who sat up high and looked down low and that He sent my friend Ciara just for me. Praise Him!

After unraveling my plastic fork out of the rolled-up napkin, I lifted my hands in the air.

"My God. This is grace, and I thank you."

Ciara's eyes shot up at me, and her hand flew to her mouth, trying to hold in the contents from laughing at me. "Girl, that prayer went straight to God's doorstep!"

Biting into my ackee and saltfish, I hummed my enjoyment and bopped in my seat joyfully. No lie. This meal was making love to me. Great taste, fulfilling, and oh so satisfying. I might've even moaned a couple of times. Yes, it was that good.

"I know you're enjoying your little meal and all, but you're not about to sit up in my office grunting and groaning. You know why you're here. Speak on it," Ciara said, then took a swallow of her tea.

"You know, for a person who wants me to get over Kannon, you sure want me to keep dwelling on him." It was my shotty attempt to get her to drop the subject.

Glaring at me, she slid her food into her mouth and slowly dragged the fork out, then twirled it around to point toward me. "That must be why you have that stank energy, but oh no you don't. If you're having an issue getting over Kannon after all these months, that's on you, sis. Don't try to flip it on me because you still can't mention the man's name without your heart and coochie rates increasing."

I nearly choked at that. Coughing and beating my chest, I took a moment to gather myself. "You almost killed me!"

"Nah, sis. You were simply choking on the truth." She rolled her eyes at me. "All I asked was for a recount of events, not about your feelings for the man."

I needed friends who liked to sugarcoat shit. The ones I had—including my sisters—were too much to handle at times, especially when I was in the hot seat.

"Fine." I pouted and went into detail with my friend, telling everything from when I arrived at the fire station until I drove off.

She placed a hand up. "Wait. How did he seem when you received the call from Benji?"

"Pressed as hell." I giggled. "He even verified it. Talking about '*Bae, as in boyfriend?*' The expression on his face when I told him that Benji was, in fact, my boyfriend and had been going on for three months was priceless. He looked highly perturbed and borderline ill."

"Not fresh off of couples TikTok," Ciara chimed in.

I threw my hands in the air. "That's the same thing I thought, girl! Like dude has a whole girlfriend in these relationship streets. In fact, he had her when we had our one-time fling. So, why is he so pressed about what I got going on?"

"To me, it sounds like he's pressed because he's still impressed," Ciara said while cocking her head to the side and sliding her last morsel into her mouth.

I tossed a skeptical glance in her direction.

"What? Don't give me that eye. Obviously, having a woman didn't deter him from wanting you before, so why should it now? Based on what you're saying, he still wishes he had a little Nissi action in his life."

Whipping out my cell phone, I glared at the time. I had ten minutes, but I wasn't going to spend it drudging up the past. "I need to run, girlie."

"I bet you do," she teased.

"Anyway." I stood. "I'll holler at you later."

I strolled out of her office, thinking about what she had stated. I couldn't help but wonder what was Kannon's motive. Just as my thoughts began to swirl, I stopped myself. *Nope, not my issue. Benji is my present, not Kannon.* With that renewed thought, I decided to go about my workday.

My personal cell phone vibrated in my jacket pocket as I reached the office, and I lifted it to view the message that had come through. It was from Benji.

Dinner at my place tonight?

Smiling, I texted back: *Sure, what time?*

See you at 7 pm. I love you.

See you then, bae.

And just like that, my focus was right back where it was supposed to be—on Benji. No, I couldn't tell him that I loved him yet, but we were in an honest relationship. That's what mattered most to me—well, that and the fact Benji could cook his ass off. So, hell yeah, I was ready for dinner anytime this man asked. In fact, I was ready for dinner *and* dessert. And I ain't talking Betty Crocker!

Chapter Twenty

NISSI

'THE LOVE OF my life," Benji said low and sultry, swooping me into his arms and holding me there as he inhaled my scent.

I swear he made it easy for me to fall in love with him. I couldn't wait for the day I could reciprocate those feelings wholeheartedly.

"Aww, bae." I pulled back, caressing his face in my hands.

When I dropped my hands, he leaned his forehead against mine, and we stood there for a while, basking in the energy of each other. When the intimate connection became too much for Benji, he sucked my bottom lip between his lips and drew me into a deep, passionate kiss. Our tongues swirled around, tasting and exploring each other. Pulling my arms tighter around his waist, I deepened the kiss, and Benji devoured my mouth as we stood in his open doorway. A guttural groan escaped my lips, and Benji pulled me inside, closing the door with one hand and then gently pushing my back against the now-closed door without ever breaking the kiss. With one hand around my waist and the other placed flatly on the door, he hovered over me and moved his kisses from my lips to my neck, and I was about ready to come undone.

"Hmm, bae," I moaned as he trailed kisses from the middle of my neck to the collarbone as his left hand slipped under my blouse and caressed my breast.

"I've missed you, baby," Benji said huskily before attacking the other side of my neck.

I was about to unzip my jeans when a beeping sound went off.

"Shoot!" Benji pulled back abruptly. "Let me grab this food. I almost forgot."

Giggling, I pecked him on the lips once more. "Yes. I don't like anything extra crispy but my chicken."

Benji's Adam's apple bobbed as he guffawed while running into the kitchen. I walked into the living room and made myself comfortable on the sofa. That's when the savory smell wafting from the kitchen penetrated my nose.

"Something smells good in there."

Benji emerged with a smile, tossing the oven mitt on the countertop beside him before leaning on the doorframe, his long legs crossed at the ankles.

"You smell better." He licked his lips, and I felt a blush surface on my face.

My eyebrows hiked as I brushed my tongue across my lips. "Your kitty points went up for that one."

A sexy glint showed in his eyes at my remark. He rubbed his chin, and I saw his long legs start to make quick strides. His manhood flopped in those black sweatpants as he padded across the floor to me. Towering over me, he used his knee to push my legs apart, and I leaned back on the reclining sofa as he lowered himself onto me.

"Can I cash in my points tonight?" His voice was thick with emotion.

"Yes," I whimpered as he leaned in, kissing my neck again. "But you gotta feed me first."

His head fell forward in a snicker.

"I guess my points are on hold right now," he said, staring lovingly into my face.

Sliding a lone finger down the side of his face, I nodded. "I need sustenance."

He licked his lips. "So do I."

Bursting into laughter, I swatted his shoulder. "Nasty."

"You like it," he teased, returning to a standing position.

"I do."

He took my hands into his, helped me to a standing position, and held me in his arms.

"Mmmhmm," he said, kissing my lips and lifting me.

As I wrapped my legs around his waist, we never broke our kiss. He walked us into his dining room and sat in a chair where I straddled his lap and continued with our kiss. The feel of his manhood beneath felt as though he could have chopped logs. My eyes rolled back as Benji ground his hips, causing his manhood to glide across the apex of my thighs.

"Bae," I moaned as we continued to kiss.

"Yes," he whispered into my mouth.

"I want this, but the smell of that food is making me hangry."

Benji chuckled in my mouth, stopping the kiss. We broke away, leaning forehead to forehead as we continued to bask in each other.

Benji lifted his head. His grey eyes penetrated mine with a mixture of lust and love swirling in his reflection. "Let me feed you so you can stop interfering with my wet dream."

With that, he patted my butt for me to lift, and I obliged.

"I told you I needed sustenance, and nobody told you to be able to cook that well," I said while following him into the kitchen.

"One of us has to."

Feigning offense, I gasped, my hand pressed to my chest in disbelief.

"Benji Eloi, are you claiming that I cannot cook?"

Benji placed the lid down on the countertop and turned to me.

"There are two things I won't ever do." When I looked at him with my arms folded, he continued, "Question a woman's age nor question her cooking skills. So, I'm not claiming anything, but I will say I'm grateful my grandmother's knack for culinary skills passed through my gene pool."

I threw the dishtowel at him. He laughed and pulled it from his face. Pursing my lips, I smirked.

"Asshole. For the record, I *can* cook. Just not as well as you, Mr. Eloi."

Wrapping his arm around my shoulders, he pulled me into a sideways hug and kissed my forehead.

"Aww, thank you, baby. You know I'm always open to showing you anything. Any time you want to burn in the kitchen, I got you."

"Uh. Hold on there, Reading Rainbow. I never said I wanted to go that far on the culinary journey," I joked. "I like having a man who can cook better than me. I feel liberated."

Spooning some of the roasted potatoes, he lifted it to my mouth. "Well, bring those liberated lips here and try this."

He blew on it and slid the spoon into my mouth, and I swore I was in foody heaven. The olive oil drizzled off the potatoes, and the garlic flavor melted on my palate. A moan escaped as I feasted on the perfect bite. I may have been joking, but the man really could cook.

"Good, isn't it?" he asked, nodding in approval of my reaction.

"Bae, it really is. What else are we eating?" I asked, watching him make my plate.

"Bacon-wrapped asparagus, spring mix salad, and honey garlic salmon." He passed me the plate. "That is until I can get to you."

I grinned playfully, taping him before I turned and nearly ran to the dining room to sit down and eat. After Benji made his plate, he brought us some white wine and water. Then we said a prayer and dove in. Dinner was filled with us discussing advancements and medical theories in dentistry and catching up on our families and happenings. He had attended a conference the past weekend, so we hadn't seen each other since last Wednesday. It was why we were all over each other.

Benji grabbed the linen napkin and wiped his mouth. "I meant to ask you how it went when you gave the guy his jacket back?"

The question stunned me, and I picked up my glass of water to take a sip. "What?"

Benji's eyebrows hiked in wonderment. "You went to the fire station and returned the guy's jacket, right?"

Feigning remembrance, I tapped my forehead with the palm of my hand. "Oh, oh. The jacket. No, nothing happened because I mailed it to him instead."

The lie flowed out so easily, and I didn't know why. It wasn't necessary, but I didn't want him to know the truth. Why? I didn't even have that answer for myself.

Leaning back, Benji scoffed, looking even more confused.

"What made you do that instead of giving it to him at the fire station?"

Shrugging, I surmised, "I thought he might not be at work that day. Also, I didn't want to waste time at the fire station. I had a ton of work to do. No big deal." This time, I took a swig of wine. Switching subjects, I asked, "How did your dad make out with the restoration of his old model Chevy?"

"It turned out well. He says he needs one more fresh coat of paint, and it's all done."

Smiling, I said, "Good. Tell him he has to take me for a spin when it's complete. I'd love to see it. Your dad loves that car."

"My mother claims he loves it more than he loves her," he joked. A beat passed before he said, "Speaking of parents, I'd love to meet yours this Sunday when you go over for the famous Richards' Family Sunday dinner."

It was good that I already had my wine glass tilted to my mouth because my throat immediately parched. *Did he just invite himself over to my family's house for dinner?* It wasn't that I had an issue with Benji coming over, but he couldn't wait for me to invite him on my own. Who invites themselves over to someone else's parents' house? Benji apparently. The man declared his love for me and put the gas on all other parameters in our relationship. I didn't want to offend him, but he needed to pump the brakes a little. He didn't even bother to ask how I felt about that.

"Don't you think it may be too soon for something like that?"

Benji ate the last helping of his salad before wiping his mouth and hands with the linen napkin. "Too soon? You've met my parents before."

Now he had my attention. Surely he was not trying to compare what he was asking to how I met his parents.

"Umm, bae, I met your parents because your dad needed someone to pick him up from the auto shop when he dropped your mom's car off. We were out, and it was closer to pick him up than to take me home. So, I met your parents by happenstance."

"Still, you've met them. They love you, and so do I. Don't you think it's about time I met your parents?"

"Benji—"

"Now it's Benji." Exasperated, he sat back and smoothed his hands down his sweats.

"That is your name. Isn't it?"

"And you only call me by it when you're upset. What is there to be upset about with me wanting to meet your parents?"

"I'm not. You're trying to compare a planned dinner with a chance meeting."

"Does it matter, though?" Benji asserted. "We're a couple. Going to dinner on Sunday with your parents. It's not that difficult."

"Yet, you've never invited me to Sunday dinners with your family," I mumbled, irritated with the entire conversation.

He picked up his cell phone from the table. "Do you want me to call them now? I can arrange that."

I dropped the fork and glared at him as it clattered onto the plate. "Why are you making such a big deal out of this?"

He stood.

"And why aren't you?" He wagged his finger before gathering his plates. "Now that's the true discussion that needs to be had because, in all honesty, you and I both know what I proposed is reasonable for two people in a committed relationship."

He stormed out of the room with his plates and headed to the kitchen so fast that it seemed he was a blur. Although I was still a bit heated from our back and forth, I had to admit he was right. He wasn't being unreasonable, especially not for two people in a relationship. Why was it so difficult? It's not like I needed to be in love for him to at least meet my parents, so that wasn't the problem. I swallowed at the realization of what the issue was. It was the word he had used before he stormed out of the dining room. *Committed.* Benji and I were on two different levels within our relationship. For him, I knew he saw engagement, marriage, and a family with me. He didn't have to express it because he showed it. He showed it in his actions. He was committed. Me, I was comfortable in our relationship. I was taking my time and going with the flow—no expectations of him or myself. I was monogamous, not committed. And that was the issue. While I didn't have a problem with my parents meeting a man I wasn't in love with, I felt I needed to be committed to the man to allow him into my sacred family space.

Standing, I picked up my plates and strolled into the kitchen. I stood in the doorway, observing Benji as he moved around cleaning up. When I walked to the sink to place my dishes inside, he started scrubbing the countertop with the scouring pad. Turning to him, I was about to explain my position when his words left me stupefied.

"Is there someone else, Nissi?" He paused from cleaning, bracing the palms of his hands against the counter, unable to look at me. "Perhaps the fireman?"

That question knocked the wind out of me, and through a shaky voice, I uttered, "Bae, no."

He swallowed hard and looked over at me. His eyes danced with emotion.

"Then why is it so hard for you to let me in? What more can I do?"

His plea broke me down. I didn't have an answer for that. By any woman's standard, he was doing everything he was supposed to do. Whatever my hang-up was, it was mine, not his. He deserved all of me because I had all of him. The least I could do was try to move toward commitment.

Releasing a sigh, I moved closer and rubbed his back with my hand.

"Look at me, Benji, please."

He faced me again, and I caressed his face.

"You're right. I don't know why I'm hung up here. You're everything I could ever want. Please don't think you're not. And I owe it to us to try. If it makes you happy, then dinner on Sunday at the Richards' house it is."

His face lit up like Christmas. "Are you sure?"

"You really want me to question this decision right now?"

"You're right."

He scooped me into his arms and twirled me around. Placing me back on my feet, he held me close. My eyes fluttered upward to meet his intense gaze. The love radiating from him made my eyes water. This man truly loved me.

"Just meet me halfway. That's all I ask."

Nodding, a single bloated tear streaked down my face, and he wiped it away with his thumb. Grasping his hand, I kissed the inside of his palm. I wasn't ready, but I owed Benji this opportunity to draw as near to him as he was to me. Lifting my chin, he kissed my lips with soft pecks that turned succulent.

Grabbing his hands, I led him to his master bedroom as we continued to kiss and explore the depths of each other's mouths. He stumbled a bit, but his focus was on me, not where to plant his feet. When we finally got to the room, he fumbled as he attempted to undo my blouse. I grew a bit frustrated as he wrestled with the buttons.

"Bae, I can do it."

"I got it, baby." He continued struggling until he popped one of my buttons.

"Benji!" I shrieked. *I know this man did not just ruin my blouse.*

"Sorry, baby." He pecked my lips.

I placed my hands on his. "I have the rest."

He stood back as I undressed and struggled to remove his clothing. I couldn't understand why a t-shirt and some sweatpants were such a task until it dawned on me.

"Are you drunk?" I asked after he finally disrobed, which took longer than I did unbuttoning a blouse and jeans.

Benji flopped down on the bed in all his naked glory as I lay across the bed with my bra and panties on. He scooted further on the bed and lay back with his arm sprawled across his forehead.

"Yeah, I think so." He released a huff. "I had about three shots of tequila when you were in the dining room."

And there it was. Wine mixed with tequila shots was not a good combination, especially since he mixed dark and white liquor. I could do nothing but shake my head. It had been over a week since we'd last indulged in each other, and now, I was left to deal with sloppy drunk sex.

"Maybe we should just—"

"No, baby." Benji rolled over, pulling my body close to his and nuzzling his face between my breasts. "I need you tonight. Please."

I placed my hand atop his head and stroked his low-cut faded hair. Soon, I felt sweet kisses on my belly, easing down to the crease of my panties and inner thigh. My head fell back at the feel of his lips on my skin, and once again, I was set ablaze. Benji leaned back on his knees, hooked my panties in the crooks of his fingers, and eased them down my body. Biting his bottom lip, he stared at me with a sexy glint in his eyes that made my folds slick with juices. He leaned forward and eased my arms out of my bra, and I unclasped it, discarding it to the side of the bed.

Not bothering to ease under the sheets, Benji resumed his position, hovering over me and taking my breast into his mouth. I moaned as his tongue flickered back and forth over my nipple; his warm mouth gently clasped around the areola and suckled ever so softly. He continued moving from one breast to the other until I was panting in delight.

Wrapping my legs around his waist, I pulled him closer to me. He trailed his tongue between the peaks of my breasts to the side of my neck, then released a grunt.

"I want you so bad," he whispered, his words ragged.

He wasn't the only one. He captured my lips in a crushing kiss. Extending my arm, I felt around until my hand found the nightstand and slid open the drawer. Reaching inside, I fished out the entire box. Benji broke our frenzied kisses long enough to take the box from my hand. His coordination was so off that he ripped the box, and gold packets flew everywhere. We giggled at his mishap as he picked up one and ripped the gold wrapping open with his teeth. As I lay back against the pillows, I watched him sheath himself with excited anticipation.

Once protected, he eyed me like a lion with his eyes on its prey and crashed his lips back into mine. I moaned under the heated kisses as our tongues mingled wildly.

"Oh, bae." I stretched out when he nibbled on my earlobe.

Pressing against me, he entered me roughly. I welcomed the feeling because he had never been so aggressive, and I loved it. He had always been so gentle and smooth. It felt good to feel him give it to me, rough and rugged.

"You're *so* tight. Damn it, Nissi."

His declaration caused my sweet spot to soak. All I wanted him to do was talk dirty and pound into me with fierceness.

"Oh, Benji. Just like that, bae," I hissed out.

Benji leaned all the way forward, pumping wildly.

"Yes, baby. Yes. I can't hold it. I'm cumming."

"Wait, bae—"

Before I could say or do anything to stop the sensational ride we were on, it ended just as quickly as it began—just like the attractions at a fair. It gave you a fast and hard rush, and just when you started to enjoy it, your two minutes were over. Thrilled but not satisfied. Yeah, it was like that.

Benji fell over to my side, huffing and puffing like he would blow his house down.

I know damn well that's not the end. Couldn't be. Perhaps this is an intermission to get the first nut off, not the complete show. I rolled to my side to face him. "Come on, bae. Let's go another round."

Benji lifted his arm off his head and peered over at me. "Are you serious? I'm done for the night. I can barely move, baby." His head fell back on the pillows. "And my freaking head is spinning. I need a nap."

You've got to be kidding me right now. I just knew he was not going to leave me hanging like that. Before I could protest, I heard a soft snore and looked down to find him asleep. *This mutha is like dead-ass eyes closed, arm sprawled, mouth slightly ajar sleep.* I knew drunk Benji wasn't going to fulfill me. Here he was, out like a light with the condom still matted on his seeping shaft while my kitty was ready to karate chop me for lack of completion. I shook my head at our precarious situation. That was my cue.

Easing off the bed, I went to his master bathroom's linen closet, grabbed a washcloth, lathered it, and washed at the sink, or as my mother would say, I took a prostitute bath. Afterward, I dressed quietly and texted Benji's phone, letting him know I left and locked up, then headed to my house to partake in a night of candles, cocktails, and cumming on my own with my new rose vibrator.

When I got home, I wasted no time setting up my nightcap scene. I peeled out my clothes and tossed them into the laundry room. Walking into my kitchen, I slid my hand along the cool marble island countertop and drummed my fingers as I mulled over my wine selection. Deciding to go light with Moscato, I opened the drawer on the island and fished out my wine opener. Then I turned around, pulled the bottle from the wine rack, opened my stained-glass cabinet door, and took down a champagne flute. Using the wine opener, I popped the cork of the Moscato and poured the glass about midway. Taking my glass and the bottle to my bedroom, I took a long swallow of wine before placing them both on my nightstand. Then I lit my champagne-scented candle and slipped my robe on that lay sprawled across the foot of my bed. However, I left it open since I was ready to get started with my "me" time.

Opening my bottom nightstand drawer, I pulled out my purple velvet bag, untied it, and reached inside to retrieve the box that housed my rose toy. *Please be charged.* I opened the box and pressed the button on the side to feel it vibrating in my hand, all ten speeds ready to go for my evening pleasure. Although I had tried all ten, I favored speed three, the constant high-powered one. It took me there fast and furiously as many times as I could stand. The one ride that ended when *I* wanted it to and not when it was ready.

Thinking of Benji, I picked up my cell phone and texted to let him know I had made it home safely. When I placed my phone back on the nightstand to get my night started, it vibrated, and I picked it up, pressing the accept button.

"Nissi?" said a voice I didn't recognize.

I stared at my phone and staring back at me was the shocked face of Kannon Jordan. Quickly assessing myself, I realized he could see me and half of all my naked glory. I jumped, dropping my phone on the carpeted floor, which was no better because he could now see what he had missed in full glory. I quickly stood up and tied my robe before picking the phone up off the floor. Gathering my bearings, I looked back at the phone to see him grinning like a hyena with an overwhelming look of approval on his face. That's when I realized he had called me from the Instagram app, which made sense because I'd blocked his number.

"What are you doing calling me?"

I was two shades red from embarrassment, which was a feat considering my milk chocolate skin tone.

"I meant to send you a voice message and hit the video-call button instead," he explained in a much calmer tone than I could muster. "The question should be, why would you answer for me if you were otherwise preoccupied."

"I didn't answer for you." I shook my head. "I thought you were—" My voice trailed off.

His face contorted in realization. He snapped his fingers. "Ahh, your *man*," he said, stressing the word man in a way that made my eyebrows hike in surprise.

"Yes, my *man*. Who else would I answer the phone for knowing I wasn't fully clothed?"

His face fell like the saddest puppy, and he shrugged his shoulders. "I guess no one. You're right. I'm sorry to have bothered you."

Seeing his hurt expression, I felt like crap. I didn't have to be such a butthole just because I had pent-up frustration. I stared at him as he sat lying back on his sofa. His light brown eyes hung low in a sleepy haze, and his wavy black hair had grown out a bit, making him appear a little disheveled. He'd grown his beard, adding to his sultry bad boy appearance. His fitted white t-shirt caressed his muscular build, and his tattoo sleeve seemed sun-kissed against his rich caramel tone. I couldn't see past his waistline, which appeared adorned by a pair of grey sweatpants. My throat went arid at the thought, and I coughed and rubbed my hand along my neck, hoping moisture would seep back into it.

Lifting my flute, I took a sip to quench my thirst before asking, "Umm, well, what was the reason for your call or intended voice message?"

Taking a deep breath, he went to speak, but then his mouth snapped shut as he shook his head. "It's not important. I'm sorry to have bothered you. Have a good night with your man. I apologize for interrupting."

The somberness in his voice chipped away at the iciness around my heart. Sure, I had Benji, and he had River. But what happened between us was now water under the bridge. If I wanted to believe I had honestly moved forward, I needed to be able to know I had released my past. Being evil toward Kannon only seemed to show I hadn't recovered from our encounter. And I had. Or I believed I had. So why continue to be surly?

"Listen, Kannon. You weren't interrupting me." Rubbing my temple, I emanated a tired exhalation. "I'm adult enough to move forward from what happened. What is it that you called me about? I'd like to know."

His eyebrows furrowed as he gawked at me. Disbelief lined his face as he sat up, adjusting himself. "Wow. That's great. That's...I'm...," he stammered. "Forgive me. I wasn't expecting this. It has me a little bit flustered. Bear with me, please."

I tilted my head, allowing him grace. "Take your time."

After a few instants, he cleared his throat. "I know you have someone, and I don't want to interfere with that. So, if I'm out of line, please tell me." He paused, but when no objections came, he continued. "Nissi, I don't want you to think you were a notch on my belt that day or that I intended to deceive you. I only intended to have dinner and drinks with a woman who wanted to thank me. Hand to God." He raised one of his large hands for emphasis. "But the connection—both emotionally and physically—was there. I hate how everything went down, but no cap, I do not regret our time. I would like to meet with you to offer my formal apology. This time, instead of it being on you, it's on me. Friendly, I promise," he guffawed lightly, his light brown orbs casting an unintentional spellbinding and sensuous glare. "I think we ended on a horrible note, and I can't live with myself knowing how I left things with you. In fact, I haven't been living too well with it in my heart. Please don't say no. Please."

An array of feelings coursed through my body, from nervousness to giddiness. Meet with Kannon? Could I subject myself to another face-to-face interaction with him? No. That would be wrong. Benji would hate me. But it was only an apology. I was a grown woman who had moved on. I could keep my faculties under control around a man with whom I'd only had one night. Benji and I had a history. He was my present. Kannon was a moment in time. I could do this.

My silence must've alarmed him because he quickly intervened with, "I didn't mean to make you uncomfortable, but—"

"No, you didn't." I snapped out of my contemplative thoughts. "I can do that. I can meet you."

His eyes widened. "Wow. Can you? You will?"

A grin crossed my face. "Yes, Kannon. I'm going to need you to stop weirding out on me, though."

"My bad. I'm sorry. It's just that it's been so much animosity and awkwardness between us since then. It's hard to digest this new space you're in right now."

I nodded in understanding before he continued.

"Can I cook for you?"

"Cook for me?" It was my turn to be surprised.

"Yes, I would take you out, but you have a man. I don't want to risk Mr. Fire and Rescue and That Dentist Chick being spotted and becoming a TikTok sensation again."

"Good point," I agreed.

He was absolutely right about that. I, for sure, couldn't afford for Benji to find out about this impromptu rendezvous.

"As long as you don't poison me. I'm good with that."

"I can burn. Don't doubt my skills."

"Mmmhmm. We'll see," I teased as I eased back on my bed.

For the next few minutes, Kannon and I went back and forth with each other about our culinary skills. The jokes were a welcome distraction, and it felt good to chill like this over the phone with him. It felt easy. Before long, we found ourselves in a barrage of mirth around useless but feel-good conversation. I hadn't laughed this much or this hard in a long time. When he stood to walk to his kitchen, I caught a glimpse of those grey sweatpants. The way my yoni reacted was a betrayal of epic proportions. Her disloyal behavior had me internally ashamed.

"Kannon, I need to go," I said abruptly. "I…uhh…I have your address, so I'll see you for that apology dinner."

Kannon looked confused but quickly seemed to rid his facial countenance of the wonderment. "Okay. I understand. I didn't mean to hold you this long. I'll let you get back to whatever you were about to get into…with your man. Goodnight, Nissi."

"Kannon—"

Before I could say another word, he ended the call. In haste, I jumped up, sat on the side of my bed, and video-called him back, but he didn't answer. He did the right thing by not responding. I clutched my phone to my chest as I lay back horizontally across the bed, thinking of Kannon. He was the last person my mind needed to be on, but seeing him on the phone reminded me that my body was on fire. Rather than having Benji on my mind as I should have, it filled with all the things I wished I could've explored with Kannon. I was wrong, but it was a simple fantasy sparked by that fine specimen that called me. *A girl can fantasize, right?* I was, and I didn't have a choice because that image of Kannon lying on his sofa was not going away.

Undoing the belt of my silk robe, I let it fall open, then felt for my rose toy and pressed the button. Still lying horizontally, I placed the rose at the apex, and the sensation began to heighten me. My moans grew as the feel of the rose awakened my insides. However, I couldn't get the angle I needed, so I sat on the side of the bed with my rear end on the edge and moved the rose to a better position. My phone slipped off the bed onto the floor with my movement, but now, the rose was right where I needed it to be. So, I continued allowing it to massage my clit instead of worrying about my fallen device. With the rose taking me to a place of bliss, I moaned in pleasure with thoughts of Kannon consuming every crevice of my mind.

"Ahh, right there!" I belted out.

With my legs spread as I clung to the edge of the bed, my head tossed back, and sweat beads formulating on my forehead, I used my left hand to spread my lower lips wide and my other to place the suction of the rose right on top of my love button. My toes curled into a ballerina's point as I wailed in ecstasy.

"Ooh, Kannon! Yes, Kannon! Ooh shhh. Right fucking there!"

I released with a hard jolt and thrashed back and forth on my bed. My juices splashed all over my rose and fingers. My body twitched as my thighs clutched together, squeezing the toy as the last remnants of my orgasm spilled out. Dropping the rose on the floor, I lifted my fingers and sucked my juices off each one, humming to the taste of my nectar.

When I bent down to retrieve my rose and my phone, I saw it was still on the Instagram DM with Kannon, but I noticed a second outgoing call and a hang-up. The time on my cell read 12:54 a.m. The call I had mistakenly made went out at 12:45 a.m. The display showed the call ended at 12:52 a.m. Hoping the timestamps were from our first call connection, I reviewed when Kannon had last called me, which was at 12:15 a.m., and that call ended at 12:40 a.m.

Did he see and hear me?

I slapped my hand on my forehead. One thing was for sure; I wasn't about to call him back to find out. Mostly, I didn't call out of embarrassment because I knew he had. Instead, I plugged in my cell phone, cleaned my rose with my toy cleaner, jumped in the shower, and went to bed. When I closed my eyes, a smile creased my face, imagining Kannon's expression of watching me pleasure myself—something he could no longer have. Then a vision of Benji flashed in my mind, and I felt horrible. Absolutely horrible. Horrible…yet satisfied.

Chapter Twenty-One

NISSI

SUNDAY, THE DAY I dreaded. Not that I dreaded every Sunday, just this one. It was the day Benji was set to meet my parents. Besides the fact that I wasn't comfortable with this forced introduction, I was also dealing with the guilt of pleasuring myself to Kannon a mere two days ago, especially since I was 99.999 percent positive he saw and heard me doing so. I had recently promised to give my relationship my all and flat-out declared that Kannon wasn't a factor, when now I'd proven myself wrong. One sneak peek at Kannon's profile had me losing my ever-loving mind. At the time, I had been truthful, but that truth didn't even last twenty-four hours before it became an outright lie. Therefore, even though I dreaded this Sunday, I willed myself to endure because I owed Benji this, especially since I had no plans to tell him about what went down in my bedroom the other night or my upcoming apology dinner.

To ensure I didn't flake out, I asked Benji to pick me up and drive us to my parents' house. This way, it guaranteed I would show up because I'd be left with no choice. I also figured if he drove, it would raise his comfort level that I was keeping my promise to him. Only I knew that both were a cop-out. My mind swirled with the most recent events in my life, and all I could focus on was how to keep my mind off Kannon and focus on Benji.

The feel of Benji's warm hand caressing mine and interlocking my fingers brought me back to the present. We were headed to my parents' house as I rode shotgun beside him. I took my right hand and patted the top of our intertwined hands.

"You all right over there?" he asked, glancing at me.

Heaving a breath, I nodded, then leaned on the open palm of my hand as I rested my elbow on the door's armrest. "I'm good. Just a little tired, I guess."

"My bad. I didn't mean to keep you up all night," Benji said with a grin, and I couldn't help the smirk that graced my face.

It was true. Benji had made an impromptu visit at about nine o'clock last night. We'd spent the night cuddling in each other's arms, watching movies on my sofa, and by midnight, the movies were watching our show on my sofa. I must admit Mr. Eloi rectified his drunken episode from Friday night and had me spread out in a game of sexual twister. I had not known how versatile we could get until Saturday night. Our tryst lasted until we both were spent at about three in the morning. He left at about nine this morning to get himself together for today and his work week. I hated that he had gotten up so early because I had a bad habit of not being able to go back to sleep once I was fully awakened, which is precisely what happened. It was four in the afternoon, and I was paying for my lack of rest.

Offering him a lazy smile, I grinned at his devilish expression. "You lie like a rug. You meant that with every fiber of your soul."

He laughed as he turned down the street to my parents' house. "Get all your little jokes out now. We can't talk about this when we pull up to your parents'. I must make a good impression, not let your dad know I was beatin' down his daughter last night."

His words struck me. Not even the words that should've struck me about beatin' me down. It was one singular word in particular...*impression*. Of course, he wanted to make an excellent first impression. It wasn't that, so much as it was the *reason* he wanted to. It would be different if it were solely to have my parents' approval, but I had the sneaking suspicion it was because he wanted my parents to see a future that included him as my husband.

Nisante Richards was an easygoing man. As long as a person was respectful and courteous, he got along with them. Judging a man to see if he was fit for his baby daughter was a whole different level. Benji would need more than one Sunday dinner to gain that type of approval. Even then, he would probably only get as far as a ninety-five percent approval rating. Nisante would always reserve five percent in case he had to remind a man that his daughters had a father who gave all the damns about them, even if they didn't.

As we pulled into the driveway of my parents' home, Benji placed the gearshift in park and then turned his attention toward me. Nervously, I cast my eyes in his direction, and he slipped his hand into mine.

"Typically, I am the one who should be nervous." He took in my expression before searching my eyes. "Should I be worried?"

I released a nervous grin. "No, no," I reassured, clasping my other hand atop our already connected ones. "My parents are chill people. They'll love you." I hunched my shoulders. "It's just the first time I'm bringing a guy over to meet my parents since senior prom."

A smirk crossed Benji's face, and he rubbed his thumb across my chin. "That doesn't necessarily make me feel better. Special, yes, but less nervous, no."

Leaning over, I planted a quick peck on his cheek.

"You should be a little nervous. Next time, be careful what you wish for." I grinned at him and wiped the lipstick off the side of his face. "Let's go."

Filled with nervous excitement, Benji hopped out, but I took my time. While looking up at my parents' Mediterranean-styled home, all the feels came back to me. Growing up here was filled with love and laughter. By the time we approached the three half-circle, multi-color stone steps, my father had already stepped outside.

"My Nissi Pooh," he cooed, giving me a big bear hug.

I wrapped my arms around him and squeezed him just as tightly.

"Hey, Daddy. I swear you act as if you don't see me at least once a week."

Pulling out of our embrace, he lifted my chin and smiled at me. "And every day I don't see you is too long." Looking past me, he eyed Benji. "This must be your special guest."

Stepping back, I reached my hand out to Benji, and he took it. Then I pulled him forward to stand beside me.

"Daddy, this is Benji Eloi. Benji, this is my dad, Nisante Richards."

"And I am her mom, Abigail," my mother said, racing out the door, hugging me first and then shaking Benji's hand. "You went to dental school with Nissi, right?"

"Yes, ma'am." Benji wrapped an arm around my shoulder. "She was more focused on her studies back then, but the universe has granted us a second chance."

My mother pointed her finger at him. "I like that. Smooth. Very smooth."

My dad eyed my mother. "But not too smooth."

My dad's words made Benji jump back, flailing his arms. "Never too smooth, sir."

Giggling, I agreed. "Yeah, Daddy, Benji is a straightforward man."

My father stepped down and wrapped his arm around Benji's shoulder as my dad's slightly taller frame towered over him. "I'll be the judge of that. For now, welcome to our home, Benji."

He led him into the house as my mother and I followed behind. As soon as I stepped inside, the smell of my mother's famous peach cobbler invaded my nostrils, and I was immediately transported back to when I was ten. Aquila and I would fuss over who would get the first corner piece. I don't care what anybody says; the crust of the peach cobbler is more important than the peaches in the cobbler. Period.

As we traversed through the foyer to the family room, I swear nothing had changed. The foyer was still lined with pictures of us girls, with the addition of our latest family portrait taken two years ago, a family photo of Aquila, Joel, and the boys, and countless photos of the boys themselves. The fireplace was ablaze in lieu of turning on the heat, which Daddy hated. The warm earth tones of the combined space between the family room and the kitchen gave the house a homey feel. My parents may have lived in Miami all of their adult lives, but they were rooted in their North Carolinian upbringing traditions—all of which were instilled in us girls.

In the family room, my dad hiked his khaki pants up at the thigh and sat down in his La-Z-Boy, interlocking his fingers as Benji and I took a seat on the sofa. My mother ran off to be sure dinner was well prepared.

"Nissi Pooh?" Benji whispered in my ear.

"Call me that again, and it will be the last thing you ever utter," I whispered back with a tight grin.

"So, Benji, how'd you link back up with my daughter?"

I slapped my thigh. "Dad!"

He shrugged. "I'm just trying to get to know the man."

"But can you warm up to it? Geesh."

I was irritated. My dad used to be the beat-around-the-bush type of man. Nowadays, he was going in straight raw dog.

Benji patted my hand. "It's okay, baby. I don't mind answering your father's questions. I like that he gets straight to the point."

My dad gestured his hand toward Benji. "See, he doesn't mind."

Thankfully, my mother floated into the family room to save the day.

"Why don't you take Benji to show him your new and improved man cave while Nissi helps me in the kitchen, hmm?" She patted my dad's shoulder.

We both knew it wasn't a question, though. It was an order, and my dad didn't skip a beat in obeying her unspoken command. Hell, neither would I.

He stood. "Come with me, Benji. We can chop it up as men in my new man cave."

Benji stood and bent to kiss me, but I turned my face, offering him my cheek only. He kissed my cheek and then waltzed off into the back of the house with my dad. After they disappeared down the hall, I joined my mother in the kitchen.

"Good save, but I know you just wanted me out of the way so Daddy could drill him."

I picked up one of the apples from the fruit bowl, washed it at the sink, and bit into it as I leaned on the kitchen island.

My mother slapped my hand. "First of all, he'll be fine, and second of all, we have every right to drill any man you girls bring home. Lastly, why would you eat that apple knowing dinner is almost ready?"

She tied her apron and leaned on the island with her elbows, shaking her head at me.

"Well, first of all, I'm hungry, and second of all, I wish you all would've drilled Joel 'cause he ain't it."

My mother cackled at the unsuspected comeback. "Crazy girl. But why do you think your dad is doing that now? One Joel

is enough for this family, and he is one too much if you ask me."
She threw her hands up.

I threw my hand in the air as if I were sending up praise.
"Ooh, preach, preacher!"

My mother turned back toward the gas range to ensure all
eyes were turned off.

"Speaking of, does she still call you to complain about him?"
I shot her a knowing glare. "Are you still claiming to be
forty-five instead of—"

Turning with the swiftness of a ballerina, she pointed at me.
"Say my real age, and I will swat you with this spoon and send
you home hungry. And you know you can't cook."

I scoffed, slapping my hand on the countertop. "I can razzle!"
"But you sure can't dazzle."

Apple chunks flew everywhere, and my mother rushed to
pat my back.

"See! You almost killed your favorite child," I jokingly said as
I drank the water she hurriedly poured me.

"Shouldn't have been eating before dinner anyway."
"Ooh, burn. You're so cold-hearted."

She turned me to face her to be sure I was all right. "Good.
Then you girls know exactly where you get it from."

We hugged each other, giggling at our antics. She was spot-
on about that one. Our smart-aleck remarks and quirky comebacks
were all courtesy of Abigail Richards, the clapback queen.

"Well, keep on being there for your sister. I know it's hard to
keep listening sometimes, but rather a shoulder to lean on rather
than a pill to depend on."

Point taken. "I got you, Mama. Speaking of, will she and
Oliver The Great grace our presence for dinner?"

My mother fanned her hands in irritation. "No. She said something or other about clients of Joel's and having to schmooze with somebody or other."

"I'm surprised he included her."

"Chile, she probably invited herself. That man only wanted a wife for babies. I'm convinced."

I lifted my hands as if I wasn't in it. "You said it. I didn't."

"And I'll say it again and again if I want to—to your face and hers," she snapped back with her hand on her hip. "And speaking of not saying things, you made sure you didn't tell your father and me about this TipTop hook-up."

I had to stifle my giggle. My mother was such a Boomer. She was Aquila's mother, that's for sure. *TipTop? Fix it, Jesus.* Then it dawned on me. How the hell did my mother know about my *TipTop* hook-up?

"Hold up. Wait a minute. How do you know about that?"

"Didn't I tell you when you were growing up that I had eyes in the back of my head?"

"And how did this conversation revert to me? We were talking about Aquila."

"And now we're talking about you."

"Well, I just want to talk about the fact that I get the corner piece of cobbler and that Aquila left me alone with Angela all by myself," I fake whined, clearly trying to deter my mother from all things Kannon Jordan.

"I heard that, you little bi…snot!" Angela walked into the kitchen and hugged our mother, rolling her eyes at me and shooting me the middle finger.

"Nah, say what you were going to say, sister." I had to bust her out because we both knew the B-word was hanging on the edge of her tongue.

"She better not either in or outside of this house." My mother pointed at her and then at me. "That goes for the both of you."

When she turned around, we mouthed *bitch* to each other.

"I saw that!" Mama fussed with her back still to us.

"We didn't do nothing!" Angela and I sang in unison.

Our mother turned to face us. "At least I know you'll still ride and lie for each other."

"It's ride or die, Mama," Angela giggled.

"Nah, it's ride and lie. 'Cause that's all your bad tails used to do growing up." My mother shot a glance at Angela. "And before you argue, when I asked about your sister's TipTop romance, you acted like you didn't know what I meant."

Angela and I looked at each other and groaned. "Aquila."

"Yes, Aquila. She may have her issues, but I wouldn't know anything if it weren't for her." She pulled the ham out of the oven and turned back to us. "So why didn't you tell me about the TipTop?"

"Mama! Please, for the love of modern technology. It is Tik. Tok. TikTok," Angela said as I leaned over into her in a fit of delighted tears.

"Oh, TipTop, TikTok, Bullet Shot. Who cares? That's not the important thing. That hook-up is what's important."

Ugh! I could've smacked Aquila. I swore her name should've been Agua because her mouth flowed like a river. Ugh! *River.* Ugh! Stream. Flowed like a stream.

I didn't want my parents to know because my mother would have a million and one questions. The questions would've been warranted if it had worked out between Kannon and me, but it hadn't. Now, months later, I had to explain to my meddling mother about my TipTop hook-up, all while Benji was in the house.

"First of all, there's nothing to explain. We went out for dinner as a thank-you, and that's it. Besides, can we not talk about this while my man is in the man cave with Daddy?" I finished the apple and tossed it into the receptacle.

It was my mother's turn to scoff. "Who? That wonderful young man in there that you are trying to pull from the frozen tundra of the friend zone?"

My eyes widened as I turned frantically, searching for Benji. "Mama!" I shrieked when I didn't see him.

Angela just covered her mouth in astonishment.

"He is my boyfriend."

She eyed me. "I birthed you just like your sisters. I know you. If you want to keep pretending, that's on you. I hope you fake it until you make it, baby. I can tell he's a good man with a big heart, but as you told me about Joel, he ain't it."

Just then, Daddy and Benji could be heard coming down the hallway, and I couldn't have been more grateful for that reprieve.

"Oop, here come Daddy and Benji," I happily announced.

"Let the church say amen to that," Angela whispered as she turned her eyes to Daddy and Benji.

"Amen," I concurred.

Daddy gave Angela the same bear hug, and Angela greeted Benji. The men headed to the dining room while Angela and I helped Mama bring the food out and set it on the table. Our dining room had been the staple of many family dinners. Something about the gold and burgundy trimming, the china hutch, and the cherrywood table and chairs breathed tradition, family, and love.

As we joked and talked around massive helpings of ham, macaroni and cheese, butter beans, squash casserole, candied yams, rolls, and peach cobbler, I noticed that Benji fell right in with my dad. Those two hadn't stopped conversing since we'd arrived. It felt pleasant and awkward at the same time. Once we were finished, Benji joined my dad in the living room to watch football while my mom, Angela, and I cleared the table, put up leftovers, and cleaned up.

"Honey, leave the trash there. I'll take it out when everyone leaves," Dad called out.

"Oh, now you want to contribute," Mom joked to everyone's amusement. "The trash."

"Oh, shut up, woman, and come sit over here with me by this fire."

My mother blushed. Angela and I were amused at their antics. After thirty-two years of marriage, they still loved and adored each other. Forget those celebrity couples who stunted for the Gram. My parents were real couple goals—hell, black love goals, too. The way my father looked at my mother and she melted under his gaze—if I had a man to look at me like that for years to come, I'd never leave either.

Once we finished cleaning the kitchen, we gathered in the family room and watched television. We all sat there giving sideline analytics about the game until it went off. The Dolphins had beaten the Patriots. It seemed it was the only team they could ever beat, but we loved them all the same. The thought brought me back to my conversation with Kannon, and I laughed out loud.

"What's so funny, baby?" Benji asked, patting my knee.

His voice jarred me, and I jumped. "Oh, nothing. Umm, it's nothing." I cleared my throat with guilt consuming me. "Are you ready to go?"

"Whenever you're ready," he answered, and I was glad.

Every black person knew that meant they were ready to go, too.

When I stood up, Benji stood with me, and Angela used our exit as her black card cue to head out with us. We grabbed our to-go trays and all headed toward the front door. Angela said her goodnights first, making sure to leave Benji and me behind. Duly noted.

"Well, Benji, it was a pleasure to meet you. You are a breath of fresh air," Mama coaxed as she hugged him. "You're welcome back anytime." With that, she hugged and kissed my cheek. "You still must tell me about that TipTop," she whispered for my ears only.

All I could do was shake my head as she went back inside the house. When I turned around, my dad and Benji were saying their goodbyes. They both turned toward me, focusing their attention on me. I walked down the steps and onto the driveway where they were. My dad beamed at me the entire time.

"My Nissi Pooh," he cooed with pride.

My cheeks had to be rosy red from the blush that crossed my face. I so loved my dad.

"Aww, Daddy."

Benji smiled at our exchange, then leaned over, placed one hand about my waist, and kissed me on the cheek. "I'll be in the car."

I nodded, and he threw up his hand at my father as he backed away.

"It was a pleasure, Mr. Richards. Thank you again for having me."

"My pleasure, Benji," my dad said, waving at him.

Once in the car, I turned to my father. "So what's your verdict?"

A hearty laugh escaped him. "He's a nice young man. I can tell he comes from good stock. You landed some cream of the crop."

My head fell forward, and I nodded. "Yeah, I did."

My father crossed his arms about his chest, making his broad shoulders and muscular physique stand out more in his soft blue cotton sweater. "Too bad he's not the man you want."

Surprise filled my face as I lifted my eyes back to him.

"No, I'm just moving slowly. I like Benji. We're good."

"You know I was born at night but not last night, right?"

"You and Mom act like I'm the Ice Queen around Benji."

"I mean, you do have some Elsa vibes going with the man."

My father cackled as I pouted. Realizing I was slightly offended, he held me by my arms.

"Aww, Nissi, I'm not saying that to be mean, but your mother and I know our girls." He lifted his hand to his lips and then snapped his fingers. "Remember when I asked your mother to sit with me earlier tonight? I saw the expression in your eyes and the smile on your face. That's what you should look like when your man looks at you or kisses you. I didn't see you smile once around Benji, outside of jokes, not on your face or in your eyes. I know he's a good catch, but if you don't want him, let him go."

Leave it to my father to offer nuggets of wisdom that I didn't ask for but didn't know how much I needed to hear. *Am I really stringing Benji along?*

My dad pulled me into a tight embrace, and I hugged him back just as deeply.

"He asked me for my blessing to marry you, Nissi," he whispered into my ear and held me tighter so I wouldn't react.

A shiver rippled through my spine. *He asked my father for permission to marry me?* I couldn't believe it. He and I were nowhere near marriage. At least I wasn't. What was I missing? What I thought was just a tiny blimp about the status of our relationship was more like a boulder of differences. I wasn't upset that Benji asked my father. It actually flattered me. My issue was why I couldn't see in us what he saw.

When my body relaxed, my dad pulled back, still holding my arms. "If he's not the one, don't drag him along. Just think about it. I love you no matter what you decide."

Hugging him again, I said softly, "I love you, too, Daddy."

Chapter Twenty-Two

KANNON

O NE GLANCE AT the clock let me know I was behind schedule. My goal was to be done with cooking before Nissi arrived at my house. A deep rumble flooded my stomach at the thought.

I'm about to see Nissi at my house.

I don't know what kind of favor my mother asked God to grant me, but I was grateful for the saving grace. The opportunity of a lifetime was within reach, and I would not allow it to slip through my fingertips this time. I promised a friendly dinner, and I didn't lie about that. It would be. The last thing I wanted to do was pressure Nissi and make her feel duped. I would use this chance to show her the man I am and allow natural progression to do its thing.

After my breakup with River, I did some deep soul-searching. I realized my relationship with River would never work because we were pinning a relationship tag on our situationship while it was shrouded by singleness. Some may not see it as that, but it's my truth. I agreed readily to the terms because it alleviated the pressure to conquer my libido and avoided the responsibility of faithfulness. Essentially, we toed the line between the two, and that was all fine and dandy until I met someone I couldn't shake. Nissi hooked me in her clutches and brought up the harsh reality that what I had with River was temporary. What I felt with Nissi was what I desired on a permanent basis. And on God, I wanted it with her. There was no rhyme or reason to it other than to say: *when you know, you know.* And I knew.

The sound of the doorbell caused me to toss the dishtowel over my shoulder and jog to the front door in anticipation of my welcomed guest. I was stunned by a vision of beauty when I opened the door. Nissi stood before me in a fitted sweater dress and knee-high boots made for the runway. Her loose curls framed her gorgeous cinnamon-toasted face. Her doe eyes batted at me as her plump lips parted into a gleaming smile. Whatever Nissi Richards was selling, I was sold—a satisfied customer who was willing to be a repeat shopper.

"Hey," I greeted her.

"Hey," she returned breathily.

Opening the door fully and stepping back to allow her inside, I moved so she could ease past and caught a glimpse of her sexy frame as she glided by in her stiletto boots. I couldn't stop the lip bite that happened if I wanted to.

Joining her in my living room, I spread my arms out. "Welcome to my humble abode. Thank you for agreeing to talk to me."

Placing her purse on my sofa, she nodded. "It's no problem. You have a lovely apartment. Quite clean for a bachelor pad."

Somehow, I knew the "bachelor pad" jab was her way of assessing that a woman...River...was responsible for my impeccable upkeep. I took that stab and curbed it with my truth.

"Most times, I'm at the fire station, so I don't have an opportunity to dirty it up. I'm so used to cleaning the station that I naturally do the same here."

She bobbed her head as she quickly glanced around.

"I'm impressed," she regarded me with dreamy-eyed surprise. Then she tilted her head upward and sniffed. "Smells delicious. What are you making again?"

Flashing all my teeth in a wide grin, I motioned with my head. "Come with me and find out."

She trotted into the kitchen behind me as I lifted the lid on the pot I'd had on simmer.

"Come close," I instructed as she leaned over. I waved my hand, wafting the aroma over to her. "My famous one-pot crispy chicken with rice."

Gasping, she stood back with astonishment splayed over her face. "Are you kidding me right now?"

"I kid you not."

Her hand flew over her heart. "It's just that when my sisters and I were younger, my mother said she didn't have time to cook full-course meals because she had to tend to us girls. So, she made all these one-pot meals. It used to drive my daddy crazy, but she was the queen of the castle. So, he had to accept it or trade places. He loves us with all his heart, but being the sole caretaker for three little girls while his wife worked was not in his game plan. When we got older and more independent, she began to graduate to bigger meals, but those one-pots were some of my favorites. God, you brought back such a nostalgic memory."

Seeing her fawn over the memory made my heart swell. My mother was genuinely working her angel magic for me today.

"Well, I'm glad it does. I learned to make these quick meals to feed a large group at the station house. My mother was a grade-A cook and taught her boys to work around the oven. She always said we needed to be prepared—"

"In case your wife doesn't cook, right?" She playfully giggled, leaning on the countertop.

Turning the oven off, I wiped my hands with the towel and turned to her.

"Actually, she said every grown man should know how to defend himself. When it came to the household duties, my mama was an equal opportunity employer."

Amazed, she smirked. "Smart woman. I wish I could meet her."

Her words stung me, and my eyes watered. Blinking, I cleared my throat.

"Indeed. I wish so, too," I agreed as I glanced at her. "She passed away a few years back—lupus." I paused for a moment, then said, "Why don't you have a seat at the table? It's been set. I'll bring over the one-pot."

Her hand covered mine, and when I lifted my eyes, hers were pooled with sadness.

"I'm sorry, Kannon."

Lifting my hand, I brushed the side of her cheek. "It's all good. She would've loved you."

We took a beat, simply staring into each other's eyes before I spoke again.

"Please take a seat."

As she sashayed to the table, I prayed my man down below could contain himself. I was already struggling with my heart and couldn't fight the battle for the both of us. Grabbing the simmering pot with potholders, I placed it in the center of the table on top of a placemat, then trekked back to grab the chilled bottle of Pinot Grigio. When I returned, I popped the cork and poured wine into both flutes on the table. Then I grabbed the serving utensil and spooned two crispy chicken thighs and rice onto her plate and mine.

Taking my seat, I extended my hand, and on cue, she placed one of her hands into mine, and I led us in grace. Once we finished blessing the food, I raised my glass, and she followed suit.

"To new beginnings," I toasted.

She echoed my sentiments, and we touched glasses before taking a sip.

"This is good." Nissi hummed at the taste of the wine.

"I'm glad it's to your liking," I said after taking a bite of the crispy chicken.

It was perfection if I had to say so myself. The best version of this one-pot I'd ever made. Before I could ask how she liked it, her eyes closed, her shoulders relaxed, and she moaned to the savory flavor on her palate after having forked a spoonful into her mouth.

"Oh, my goodness, Kannon. This is fantastic. I can't believe I'm admitting this, but it's better than my mother's." She dabbed her mouth with the napkin beside her plate. "A chef's kiss!"

With that, she brought her fingertips to her lips and blew the kiss into the air.

"Thank you. Thank you. And I promise I won't tell your mother that my one-pot is better than hers," I said with a hearty chuckle. "I'm so glad you're pleasantly pleased."

Nissi took a sip of her wine, placed the glass down, and tapped it, eyeing me curiously.

I took notice, and when she didn't say anything, I queried, "What's on your mind?"

"These pleasantries are nice, and dinner is phenomenal, but I'm interested to know why you called me over. For all intents and purposes, we'd gone our separate ways merrily."

Merrily. The term she used struck a chord with me. It wasn't so much the word as the intent. Was she trying to insinuate that she and her boyfriend were content, or was she throwing a sneer my way? I couldn't readily decipher it, but it held a certain undertone that didn't quite sit well with me. I would address that in a second. First, I had to handle the business at hand.

Recapturing her hand into mine, I took in her beautiful brown doe eyes.

"Well, as I stated over the phone, the ending of our encounter hasn't sat well on my spirit. I've wanted to apologize to you during a time when you could fully embrace it." Lost in her eyes, I leaned forward so we were inches apart and continued my plea. "Now that time has passed, and we've had time to recoup from the events, I need to unequivocally say I am sorry for not being honest with you upfront. I am sorry if you feel I took advantage of you in any way. I am sorry I had someone at the time and couldn't fully embrace what we were feeling and what we could've been. Can you find it in your heart to forgive me, please?"

I held her gaze for seconds long before I slowly leaned back against my seat and began eating again.

She sat there dazed before finally clearing her throat and softly whispering, "Yes, Kannon, I do."

She drifted back into her seat and slowly continued eating her meal.

I do. Those words from her lips almost made me lose my mind. This time it was I who sat quietly, allowing the contentedness between us to marinate. Gradually, we picked up our conversation, which was lightened after that. We discussed everything from current events to updates on our personal lives and the outcomes of our TikTok fame. Everything except River and *her man.* Those two were the elephants in our room. However, I wouldn't press. *Friendly.* That's what I was sticking with.

Leaning back, she rubbed her belly. "I am going to pay for this, but it was delicious. This was one hell of an apology tour, Mr. Jordan. My inner fat girl thanks you."

Holding up my finger, I quipped, "I have one more surprise for you."

Her eyes lit up, but then she protested. "Kannon, whatever it is, you do not have to. You have owned up to your apology marvelously. This is all enough. Really."

She could contest if she wanted, but I was already out of my seat and headed toward the oven. Opening the oven door, I pulled out a glass dish and brought it to the table, placing it on another placemat. Then I ran back to the refrigerator, opened the freezer door, pulled out a pint of vanilla ice cream, grabbed two bowls and spoons, and returned to the table. She gave me the eye as if I was doing too much…that is until I scooped a corner piece of the contents out of the glass dish.

Her hands flew to her heart as if she had just now paid attention to what I had placed on the table.

"Kannon, I know this isn't peach cobbler!"

Placing the bowl in front of her, I nodded. "Yes, it is. The first corner piece of peach cobbler with a scoop of ice cream on the side, just the way you like it."

Her eyes flashed with giddiness this time as I made my bowl and resumed my seat beside her. She slid the first forkful into her mouth, and I had never been so jealous of a utensil. Her head lolled backward as the sweetest groan emanated from her being. *If my food can make you feel like that, imagine what I can do.* That's what I wanted to say, but I quelled the thought.

"This is not only some of the best cobbler I've ever had, but you also added the ice cream." She faced me. "How'd you know, Kannon? This is my favorite."

Shrugging, I admitted the truth. "That night at Brick, you told me that your parents were from North Carolina and that your mom's staple dish from her home state was peach cobbler. You told me that you loved the first corner piece with ice cream on the side but that you all have foregone the ice cream because your mom is now lactose intolerant. Since I was on my *apology tour*, as you've deemed it, I wanted to prepare something special so you would know I listened that night as much as took." Wiping my mouth with a napkin, I squared my shoulders and peered into her luminous eyes. "You weren't a placeholder or a notch for me that night, Nissi. You were…*are*…a jewel. Wonderous…

breathtaking," I said, pushing a curly tendril behind her ear. "I was honored to share time and space with you, even if only for that moment."

Tears pooled in her lids, threatening to spill over, but she turned her face from mine, halting their trek down her beautiful cheeks.

After a few blinks, she stared down at her bowl and said, "You remembered?"

Slowly inching my hand toward her face, I placed the crook of my forefinger under her chin and lifted it so we were eye to eye. "I remember everything about that night. Everything."

The kitchen fell quiet, and I felt the earth tilt on its axis. All that could be heard was my erratic breathing and the soft puffs of air she released as her chest softly heaved up and down. If she made the first move, I would claim her as mine. I had no one to hold me back, and *her man* would be nothing more than a distant memory. On God. But she would have to give me that sign. I had played my hand and laid my cards out there, so there was no doubt in my mind she was picking up what I'd put down. Still, I couldn't rush this with her. It had to be on her terms so I could be certain I was the one she wanted because she for sure was the one I wanted.

Piercing the stillness, she wiped her hands and pushed back from the table.

"Kannon, I need to go." She stood, and I had to follow suit hurriedly. "Everything was lovely, and dinner was amazing," she said, rushing to the living room to retrieve her purse.

"Nissi, wait, please."

She stopped on her way to my front door but didn't turn to face me. Slowly, I chanced it by easing up behind her and gently placing a hand on her shoulder.

"Don't run, please."

"I have a man. You have a girlfriend." She shook her head. "This is messy. I can't do messy with you. You apologized and promised it'd be friendly—"

"I don't have a girlfriend, Nissi," I said.

She swung around and faced me with questions in her eyes.

"River and I broke up," I admitted.

A gamut of emotions flooded her as she shook her head. "Well, I still have a man."

That remark cut me, and the brashness in me rose. "I know... *merrily*."

"What?"

Flicking the tip of my nose, I repeated, "Merrily. Earlier tonight, you said we'd moved on merrily. It wasn't me you were referring to. It was you. So, you're *merrily* with him?"

The words were more brutal than I intended, but the fact that she kept bringing up this cornball when it was visible to a blind man that she didn't want him slightly infuriated me. She would rather hold on to some fake semblance of a relationship than try for something real with me.

"Yes, merrily." She squared up. "And you said friendly."

"Have I been anything less than that?"

Swallowing, she shook her head. "No, it's been very friendly." Turning away from me, she muttered, "Too friendly," then continued her pace to the front door.

She opened it, and I wanted to slam it back shut, but I acquiesced. I was serious about her showing me the sign. And she did. She wasn't ready. No matter how much I was, I could not nor would not force her hand. *Freely.* She had to give into this freely with me, though I held out hope even as her last few steps signaled my opportunity was fleeting.

She turned once she was just outside the threshold, and I thought a change of heart was coming.

"Listen, Kannon. I appreciate this. The apology tour were something I didn't know I needed from you, but I did. And I forgive you. Let's leave it there."

"Nissi—" I went to protest, but she placed a soft finger on my lips.

"Girlfriend or not, I can't. I…I…I have a man."

We sat in her reality for seconds long before her red-rimmed eyes cast the saddest stare at me.

Hunching her shoulders, she surmised, "Maybe one day."

Rather than allow the heartache to break me, I relented. Exhaling, I bobbed my head.

"Maybe."

Tearily, she said, "Thanks for the cobbler and ice cream."

And with that, she turned and walked away, leaving me and my feelings on the front doorstep.

Chapter Twenty-Three

KANNON

THE SOUND OF a finger snap pulled me out of my reverie. I looked up to see Jovan eyeing me strangely.

"Boi, what's got you spaced out?"

I was so far gone that it took a moment for me to remember I was at the station house, sitting at the table. Looking over at Jovan, I shook my head slightly before returning my attention to the bowl of soggy Frosted Flakes in front of me. I dipped my spoon in the milk and cereal and brought a spoonful to my mouth. Swallowing that nasty mixture made me gag before I placed my spoon inside the bowl and shrank back in my seat, smoothing my hands down my uniform pants. A perfectly good bowl of cereal was ruined.

"Nothing. Just my mind wandering."

Jovan picked up the napkin beside his protein shake and wiped his mouth. "My boi. Your mind is on the same thing it's been on for the past few months—Nissi. I thought you said you were going to reach out to her. You need to because all this moping around you've been doing ain't healthy, and it ain't solving nothing."

Shrugging, I lifted my hands. "I did."

It was all I was willing to offer to Jovan. There was no way I could tell him that she threw her man in my face and then mistakenly called me back, only to have me witness and hear her pleasuring herself and calling out my name. And there was definitely no way I could admit I had her in my home, cooked for her, basically bared my feelings on the cross, and nothing materialized. He would've knocked me in the head for not finding out where she lived and doing ninety on the freeway to get to her. It wasn't because I didn't want to; it was my way of sparing myself. She would have pushed me completely away, and I would never have a chance with her again. It wasn't likely now, but I had to hold on to my modicum of hope. Instead, I had to be content with our lovely dinner and the lasting memory of watching that fine, sexy vixen enjoy a beautiful climax with a smile on my face and a stiff erection in my palm, knowing that I had brought her to such amazing ecstasy. I'd hung up before she caught me and my drooling mouth so I could finish my release. I came so hard thinking about Nissi that I almost had to be resuscitated. Masturbating to memories of Nissi was not new and something I had done since she walked out of my house talking about her little boyfriend, and I felt like a simp for even admitting it to myself.

I'd initiated my "apology tour" because I was honestly sorry and sick of playing the back and allowing some chump named Ben to have who I knew belonged to me. Now I was in even more of a funk than before the mistaken video call and "friendly" dinner because I knew all I needed was one shot at making her mine, and it would be bye, Ben. All I needed was time to convince her that what I felt for her…what we felt for each other…was real. Perhaps telling Jovan would help. As wild as he was, at times, his advice was golden.

"I called her over Instagram, and she threw her new man in my face faster than I could say hello. What am I supposed to say to that when she won't even entertain a conversation with me without making it abundantly clear that she's off the market?"

I revealed the only portion I was willing to admit. I could never tell him about the other two significant events.

"Tell her that you still want her to be off the market, just not with a cornball named Ben. Who the hell names their child that? I know he got clowned every day in grade school."

I tried to stifle my laughter with my fist to my mouth, but I couldn't. I wagged my finger in his direction, and my brow arched.

"As valid as that point may be, that cornball pulled my girl."

"Ahhh shit now," Jovan said, leaning to the side. "*Your girl?* You stomping hard in them Nissi streets, I see."

My lips turned up at the realization that I had spoken my true feelings aloud. I swiped my hand over the goofy smirk on my face and interlocked my fingers on my lap.

"Hell yeah, and if she let me, I'd beat the whole damn block in them streets."

Jovan reached across the table, and we gave each three fast hand slaps.

"That's what I'm talking about, my boi! I'ma figure out a way to help you out. In the meantime, I'ma help you relax and get it off your mind."

"Man, I ain't trying to go to no club—"

Jovan pumped his hands at me. "Pipe down. This ain't that. You gonna put some respect on my maturity."

With a hearty chuckle, I tilted my head in agreement.

"You're right. My bad," I said, fanning my hand out. "Please continue."

"Thank you," he said, his voice full of sarcasm. "Anyway, one of my friends at the gym is hitting the stage tonight at this local artists' music showcase, and he invited me. He's nice on the microphone and a true lyricist. Come with me. We can drink, listen to some decent music, and figure out how to boot Ben."

Mulling it over for a bit, I gave in. I had declined Jovan's other attempts at outings, and Kinston was super busy preparing to open a new gym location these days. So, he hadn't had time for much other than a few quick check-in phone calls and text messages. Perhaps clearing my head would clarify what I should do about Nissi or at least clear my head from constantly thinking of her. Either way, a night out away from the job and the confines of my apartment were needed, and I was going to take advantage.

Slapping hands with Jovan, I agreed. "A'ight. I'm in."

I had to admit my fresh was on point tonight. It was evident to me by every woman who took a double take as Jovan and I strolled by. The music showcase was an upscale event, so I went all out with a silk black and white button-down shirt, black slacks, and black and white twill peacoat with my Marc Nolan boots. Everything pulled together for me. The low curls on top of my head were on point, the new cologne had a fiery nighttime fragrance that lingered long after I'd passed, and my only accent was my silver big face watch. If I wasn't so caught up on Nissi, I could've had one hell of an afterparty with any of those women.

"Ole Rico Suave," Jovan joked as we entered the building. "You got me looking like your bodyguard with the way these chicks are checking for you."

"Bruh, cut it out," I joked, playfully tapping him on the chest.

He lifted his hands. "My bad. I thought you were trying to bag Nissi, not all the chicks in Dade County. 'Cause, boi, you clean tonight!"

"Let's just hope we haven't missed your boi do his thing."

Jovan waved me off. "Nah, he just texted me back and said he doesn't go on for another thirty minutes. So, we're good."

The newly renovated building had an entertainer's vibe to it. The low set lights gave off that "smoky, chill, yet romantic vibe if needed" ambiance. Deep burgundy color booths with dark marble tables lined the back walls for the VIP patrons on a raised platform. The middle of the floor was spaced with black round marble tables with four cushioned chairs, and on the sides of the floor were smaller marble tables with two cushioned chairs. The bar was illuminated with a blue neon light around the liquor shelves and the counter's top and bottom. There were cushioned bar stools with backs placed around the bar. The stage, of course, was upfront on a raised platform to give visibility to the artists. The stage was lined with LED lights and an above-head running light track to provide the professional shine needed onstage, doubling for excellent professional photos. There was a microphone and stand front and center with a bar stool on stage, and the band and their equipment were off to the side in the back. The velvet curtains were the perfect backdrop. In the center of it all, there was a dance floor. I was thoroughly impressed.

Our waitress led us to the opposite side of the bar to the marble tables with two seats. It was one of the few unoccupied. Moments after we sat down, Jovan's friend spotted us from near the front and made his way over to where we sat.

"My boi!" Jovan slapped hands with him and brought him into a brotherly hug. "Keith, this is my boi, Kannon Jordan. Kannon, this is my boi, Keith. Tonight, he goes by Kru."

Kru and I dabbed each other up.

"Nice to meet you, bruh. Good luck on that stage tonight."

Kru bowed his head. "I appreciate that, bruh." He patted Jovan on the shoulder. "I'm just humbled that both of you came out to support me tonight. It means a lot."

"You got talent. Besides, when you blow up, I want tickets to those shows. Remember who was there from day one, my boi."

We all shared in that laughter.

Kru elbowed and then side-fist bumped Jovan. "A'ight, I got you. For real. I gotta get back."

"A'ight. Kill it."

He threw up the deuces as he walked back up front. The dim lights lifted as he eased to his table, and the next artist took the stage. Looking up at the stage to the back, I saw River seated on a stool with an easel in front of her. It caught me off guard. I hadn't seen her in her element in over a year. She'd typically be on the road, but I should've figured she would be featured at the new local hotspot. It was a cesspool for untapped and independent talent. Seeing her again warmed me. I was happy to see her living. She looked refreshed and renewed as if she had hit her stride in life. A far cry different from the last time I saw her.

"My bad, man. I didn't know she would be here tonight," Jovan offered sincerely.

Shaking my head, I shrugged. "It's cool."

We watched and listened intently to the smooth sounds as River did her thing. When the music artist finished, she turned the easel right side up to reveal a striking portrait of the musician. The audience erupted in applause and catcalls as the two ladies held hands and took a bow. After their set, the crew began the clean-up as River took her tools and the portrait and headed off stage.

Just as I was about to get up to congratulate her on the successful set, the waitress approached us. She was a tall, lanky chocolate beauty donned in leather pants and a black t-shirt that bore the bar's name.

"Hello, gentlemen. What are you drinking tonight?"

Pointing to the table with River, I said, "Can you take those ladies a refill of whatever they're drinking?"

She turned to follow my gaze and then pointed to be sure. "The two ladies that were just performing on stage?" Verbally, I confirmed, and she said, "Sure. Do you gentlemen want anything?"

"Hennessey and Coke for me," I answered.

"Crown and Coke," Jovan answered, eyeing the waitress with a sly smile.

She caught his glance and licked her lips while jotting our order on her pad. Tapping her pen when she finished, her face shone with seduction as she moistened her lips once more and stared at Jovan.

"I'll make sure that comes right out."

Jovan propped his elbows on the table, fisting his hands together, then sucked his teeth. His gaze traveled her length before he responded.

"You do that, sweetheart. We appreciate it. And don't forget to ask the ladies at the other table." He slapped my shoulder. "It'd mean a lot to my friend."

She stepped into his space. "What about you?"

The words glazed out of her mouth like honey.

"Me? I'm just out here supporting my friends," he responded with a wink.

She looked back toward me for confirmation. When I shrugged, she turned back to Jovan and winked.

"The drinks are coming up, and I'll be sure to ask."

I noticed the extra bounce in her step as she floated off.

Turning my focus to Jovan, I asked, "Don't you have a lady?"

"I have a main, but what's a dish without sides?"

I almost choked, trying to stifle my laughter. Why did I even ask? I should've known Jovan would have a classic and reckless comeback. Though I laughed solely because it was funny, I wished he would get himself together because his girl was a good one. But who was I to judge? River was good, and I did the same. I guess deep down, I always knew River wasn't the one. Maybe that's what Jovan felt. Admittedly, even if she were Jovan's "one," he wouldn't care because he was adamant he wasn't settling until he was ready.

The waitress was back in no time with our drinks, then left us and walked over to hand River and the musician their drinks. When she placed them down, I saw their confused stares, and the waitress pointed back toward Jovan and me. When their eyes landed on us, River's eyes lit up, and the musician mouthed *thank you*. I lifted my glass of Henny and Coke in the air toward them. River nodded, leaned over, and whispered in the young lady's ear. Pushing her seat back, River stood with her drink in hand and waltzed her way to where Jovan and I were seated.

We stood when she reached our table. Jovan spoke first.

"What's up, Miss River?" he asked, giving her a quick hug.

"Nothing much. How have you been, Jovan?"

"You know I'm still being Jovan."

Her lips pursed as she lightly swatted his shoulder. "Mmmhmm. Still a mess."

Our knowing laughter was palpable.

She turned to me, and there was a brief awkwardness between us before she placed her drink on our table and outstretched her arms. I pulled her into a warm embrace, and we lingered there for a moment. I didn't know how I would feel if I ever saw her after our breakup, especially how it went down, but I was grateful to see her, especially in her element. She may not have been the one for me, but she was still someone I cherished in my life, even more so after sacrificing her happiness to ensure I had mine.

We pulled back, and she smiled up at me.

"How have you been?"

Scratching the side of my beard, I huffed and answered, "I've been."

Her mouth formed an "O" expression as she nodded. "Still haven't been able to lock her down, huh?"

A sheepish guise found its way to my face, and I folded my arms across my chest, feeling uneasy about the conversation. "It's been a little complicated."

Sensing my discomfort, she patted my hand. "Don't worry. Things will work themselves out eventually."

"You don't have to say that."

She placed one of her petite hands on my chest. "I mean it. No pity parties, jealousy, or sympathy. I want you to have who and what is best for you. Just as I know you wish the same for me."

This woman was a godsend. I couldn't do anything but pull her into another embrace. There weren't many people in the world who could be as forgiving and carefree as River. Her level of maturity and care were otherworldly. The man who locked her down would indeed be a blessed one.

By the time we pulled back from the embrace, Kru had taken the stage, and rather than River going back to her seat, she nestled back against me as we stood hooting for Kru. His flow was melodic, with marked precision on each rhyme. He had the entire audience swaying and dancing to his smooth lyrics. Most people were feeling him so profoundly that they moved to the dance floor, including River, who took my hand and led me out to the sea of people bopping and swaying to his music. River and I swayed with each other, falling into a familiar two-step as we immersed ourselves in Kru's music. We lived in the moment, enjoying life.

The deejay churned out the latest hip-hop craves when Kru's set was done, and we grinded on the dance floor with everyone else. As the next artist prepared to come on, the deejay slowed down the mood, and the artist took the stage. The woman looked familiar to me, but I didn't have time to process it before River slipped her arms around my neck.

When I looked down at her placing my hands around her waist, she had tears in her eyes. My eyebrows knitted together in confusion. Her sudden emotional shift stung me for a second. Wiping her eye when the one bloated tear flowed down her cheek, I peered into her glossy eyes before my lips parted.

"What's wrong?"

River went to speak, but her lips trembled, and she sucked her bottom lip between her teeth. The ramifications of my one night with Nissi had manifested into the pain that stood before me. River had so gracefully bowed out of our relationship that it never occurred to me that she was hurting. Disappointed, possibly. Upset, definitely. Hurt, I never imagined. I pulled her into my arms, and she shrugged away.

"Please don't, Kannon." The words came out so softly that I had to bend to hear her.

It pained me to see her coming undone. I wanted to do anything I could to help her.

"What can I do?"

She shrugged. "Reverse time. Never meet Nissi. Fall in love with me."

And there it was. The elephant in the room had stampeded through. My heart sank at her admission. I felt horrible, not only for hurting her but for being unable to do the things she had asked. I couldn't reverse time. I didn't regret meeting Nissi. Most of all, I wasn't in love with her. I loved her as a person, as a friend even, but not in the sense she longed for. And I wouldn't pretend because that was worse than the truth. The truth was that a cinnamon-toasted, feisty, intelligent, and oh-so-sexy woman stole something from me one night at dinner and on a beach. While our time had been short-lived, it thwarted two years of my life with River. I owed River more than the lie that I could be what she needed me to be. So, I said nothing. I only hugged her again to quell the pain of her loss, hopefully.

When she pulled back to say something, the woman—who had been singing and was now obviously finished with her set—walked past me with two other women. One of which was...Nissi. My Nissi. My heart pumped voraciously as my eyes drank in her smooth velvety milk chocolate skin, those curls that made me want to entangle my hands in them and pull on them as I sweated them out, and her slender mid-section that shone through her mid-riff cream turtleneck top and brown wide-legged pants. With each stab of her stiletto boots, I wanted to pull her into my arms and show her why she didn't need that rose toy and a memory of me to fulfill her needs. I was ready and willing to make all those fantasies come true. My thickness jumped at the sight of her, and I had to force Jack not to jump out of the box in the middle of the club.

That's when my attention went to the young lady beside her who had been on the stage. I knew I'd seen her before. Sheena. She was one of the dental assistants who had come with Nissi to the fire station. When Nissi and I met glances, her eyes ballooned when she noticed the woman in my arms...River. Her face morphed from surprise to anger, then transformed into disgust. All the while, I stood with my mouth agape as I stared at her.

River's eyes traveled between Nissi and me, and realization struck her as she shook her head and walked away. Simultaneously, Nissi shook her head and headed to the door. Both women took off in opposite directions from me, but my instincts took over, and I ran after the woman whom I wanted in my future, not from my past. Shuffling through the crowd, I pushed the door open as I stopped to scan the area where the women had walked. When I spotted Nissi, I took off in her direction, yelling her name.

"Nissi!" I ran to catch up with them before they reached the parking lot. "Please stop."

She didn't. She and the other two women kept their pace. However, I gained on them quickly.

When I finally got close enough, I yelled, "Please let me explain."

Abruptly, Nissi turned in my direction. Her heated gaze stopped me dead in my tracks.

"You don't have to explain why you are out with your woman. I will spend time with my man, and I'm definitely not explaining that to you. But for someone who just had me up in your home on your *apology tour*, claiming you'd broken up with your girl, you've proven you're exactly what I thought of you the night I met you. Trash. River deserves better. And I surely have better."

Her onslaught shredded me to pieces.

"That isn't fair. You don't know what is going on, and it's wrong of you to make assumptions."

Nissi looked visibly vexed by my words. "Yeah, well, I guess we're just two wrong-ass individuals. And you know what they say about two wrongs." She paused as my eyes silently pleaded with her. "They never make a right."

Dejected, my shoulders dropped at her intended assessment.

"Nissi." Her name came out pained.

Putting her hand up, she stopped any further pleas from me.

"Have a nice life, Kannon." Her words came out with a vibrato that teetered on tears.

With that, she spun on her heels and stormed away. The one woman whom I didn't know rushed off with her, but Sheena paused and shot me a warning glare of daggers.

"Just leave her be," Sheena shot at me before turning to catch up with Nissi.

As much as I wanted to run after her and force her to listen, I knew tonight wasn't the night. Her friends would take me out before they ever let me get near her, and Nissi was far too distraught to listen.

When I turned to go back inside the venue, I saw River exiting. She looked up at me, put her hand up to stop me from approaching her, lowered her head, and took off toward her car. I didn't have the strength to battle River's feelings. Besides, I couldn't provide what she wanted, and I refused to put on to sugarcoat her wounds. As bad as I felt about how we ended, we had, in fact, ended. Following up with her was why I was now in an even worse position with Nissi. In her words, I had to rip off the Band-Aid to move on. And that's what I chose to do, hoping to one day repair Nissi's vision of me. Seeing her emotions, I knew something still lingered in her heart for me. All I had to do now was figure out how to tap in.

Jovan exited the venue just as I was about to enter. He held up his hand.

"Let's go back to my place and have a drink. You need it, bruh."

"That's the best thing you've said all night."

Jovan gripped my shoulder as we headed toward the parking deck for his vehicle.

Chapter Twenty-Four

NISSI

"UGH! AND WHY did we agree to come to the gym with you again?" Angela whined, throwing a hissy fit like a toddler in their terrible twos.

"'Cause y'all two skanks..." Aquila pointed her finger between Angela and me. "...are forever going out without me. So, I have to plan time to spend with both of you since I'm never included in your plans."

My eyes rolled in her direction. "In our defense, you're invited, but you always have responsibilities with the kids and Joel at home."

"Whatever. All you both do is drop over to my house long enough to spoil my kids with crap you buy and raid my refrigerator. Then you're *poof* like a gust of wind."

"But at least we visit. When's the last time you visited us?" Angela sucked her teeth as we opened the door to the gym and walked inside. "Hell, don't you have a home gym? We could've done this at your house."

"First of all, visit y'all for what? To die of malnourishment from the lack of meals you both cook? Second, going to the gym gives me a break from my babies. Third, my trainer is here. And lastly, bring your arses on, and please don't embarrass me."

She marched ahead, and Angela and I looked at each other with annoyance. Still, we trailed behind her just as we had always done since we were little kids—following our eternal big sister leader. Once Aquila got us signed in, we headed to the room where she was to meet her trainer. While we waited on him, Aquila prepared for the exercise session while Angela and I joked around, much to Aquila's dismay. She was on her mat stretching as we stood there cackling.

"You know we could've just talked on the phone," Aquila said, her attitude boiling over. "Instead of standing there laughing, you might want to stretch now because my trainer doesn't play around. I don't have time to be in the ER because one of you shredded a thigh muscle."

Groaning, Angela and I headed over to where Aquila was and put our mats on the floor. I swear she thought she was our mama instead of Nisante and Joel Jr.'s. Then again, she had acted like she was more our parent than our sister since we were kids. I can't even count the times I'd heard our mother say, "Who is the mother, Abigail or Aquila?" To which my father would always jokingly respond, "Sounds like Aquila." She had always taken that oldest role to heart. We knew Aquila was just being...well, Aquila, but it still didn't irritate the hell out of us any less.

"You'd think all this exercise would loosen her tight ass up," Angela said to me as we stretched to ensure our bodies were loose for the workout.

"My ears work just as well as these hands," Aquila said flippantly.

I couldn't help the snicker that came out of me. Aquila's clapbacks were classic. As tough as Angela was, there were times when she was no match for her. This was one. Angela playfully pushed me as we snickered about what Aquila had said.

"Can you two skanks be serious for once? I take this workout seriously, and my trainer does, too. Play with it if you want. You'll be crying later."

"I concur."

We all turned our heads to the male voice emanating those words. A tall, muscular bucket of caramel with golden dreadlocks waltzed inside, and I forgot all about Benji for a minute. That golden-brown archway had us—well, at least Angela and me— feeling like McDonald's. *Ba-da-ba-ba-baaa. I'm loving it!* I saw why Aquila got away from the house. I'd choose that Adonis over Joel's arrogance any and every day of the week. Between him and Kannon, it should've been a sin of God to make men that fine. It just didn't make any sense.

Shaking my head, thoughts of Benji permeated my mind, cutting off my lustful thoughts and reverting me to my present reality. It was then that I realized Aquila had jumped up to speak to who undoubtedly was our trainer. When I glanced over at Angela, her mouth was partially hanging open, and her eyes were fixated. I wasn't sure if my sister was even breathing until I took my hand and lifted her chin to close her mouth.

She swatted my hand away. "Girl, stop."

I leaned over and whispered into her ear, "Well, keep your mouth closed before you catch a fly."

She turned to me with her eyes squinted and then smirked. "Well, you do catch more flies with honey."

With that, she licked her tongue out sexily as if she were slurping on something, and I knew exactly what that something was.

"Eww." I shook at the thought.

Aquila turned around. "Okay, ladies. I've spoken with my trainer, and he's agreed to go easy on you today since you both need to be whipped into shape."

Angela stood with her hand on her hip. "Ahh, chick, speak for yourself. Ain't a damn thing wrong with these curves that Mama blessed me with."

"You ain't lying."

The subtle words pinged in the room, causing us to turn toward the trainer and eye him. Because did he really just say that out loud? Okay, trainer.

His hand flew to his chest. "My bad. My apologies."

Angela tossed her hair. "If you weren't right, I'd probably be upset."

At that, all of us fell into a barrage of cackles.

"Geezuz! I swear I can't take y'all nowhere." Aquila slapped her hand on her forehead, then turned to the man who was still lingering between embarrassment and chuckles. "Allow me to introduce everybody. Ladies, this is my trainer, Kinston."

We waved, and he offered his best smile and a wave back.

"And Kinston, these are my sisters, Angela and Nissi."

Kinston's smile dropped immediately and was replaced by an indiscernible facial expression. He eyed me inquisitively, and my first thoughts were that he had seen me on TikTok. My sisters eyed him suspiciously as they caught how he'd honed in on me. His face contorted, and then he gasped with realization.

Releasing a deep breath, I said, "Yes, I am the TikTok dentist chick from Tokstars."

"No," he said between confusion and a grin. "It's not that. Well, it is that, but it's not that at all."

Aquila turned to him. "Umm, Kinston, I need you to relax a little. This feels a bit cringy." She turned to us. "I'm sorry. He's usually not like this."

That's when he seemed to snap out of whatever transfixion he had on me.

"I'm so sorry. I don't want you ladies to feel like I'm some weird stalker or anything. It's nothing like that. It's just that I know Nissi."

Talk about confused. I had never met that man a day in my life. Hell, I'd remember such a man as him. That's for sure.

"You must have me confused with someone else because—"

"Not personally," he interrupted, putting his hands out. "You went out with my brother, Kannon Jordan. I'm his older brother, Kinston Jordan."

The color drained from my face as Aquila gasped, and Angela smirked slyly. Of all the trainers in Miami Dade County, Florida, my sister had to choose the gym and trainer who was related to the one man in the world whom I did not want any contact with when all I wanted was an activity to decrease my stressors. My mind was transported to the time nearly two weeks ago when I saw him at the Indie Lovers Club. A time I dared not even mention to my sisters out of embarrassment.

Ciara and I had gone out together to support Sheena's debut performance for a single she had just released entitled "Love Rapture". Sheena could blow with a light and airy voice. Her falsetto was easily comparable to *thee* Mariah Carey. I'd been so ecstatic for her that night until seeing him. Kannon. With River. Kannon's River. I was stunned because he was fresh off the heels of our impromptu apology tour and out with his...*Her*. Part of me had contemplated that maybe they had ended things when he messaged me, and I actually believed him when he told me they were over. But that theory was quickly derailed when I saw River's arms wrapped around his neck and his hands about her waist. When he saw me, he looked like a baby caught with their hand in the cookie jar—cheating bastard. I'd never met the likes of a man so utterly conning. And for a minute, he almost had me. Not this time, however. He was not about to convince me of any more of his lies. She could believe the lies, but I wasn't built nor beat for it. So, hell yeah, I was in my "middle fingers up to Kannon Jordan" mood, only now to run into his copy-and-pasted version—better known as his big brother, Kinston.

Kinston must've noticed my flushed and flustered appearance because the next thing I knew, he was in my face with a cup of water.

"Here. Drink this," he said, concern splayed all over his face.

Blinking my eyes, I snapped back from the abyss, grabbed the cup, and guzzled the water down. "Thank you," was all I could manage to spit out.

"Are you all right?" Kinston asked, still unsure of my shocked state.

Just then, Angela walked up beside me, rubbing my back. "Yeah, sis. Are you?"

I could tell by her tone that she had jokes for days. However, I honestly could not engage in her brand of bullshit. I was still reeling off the news that Kinston was Kannon's brother, and I was standing there in his class.

"Yes, I'm…I'm good," I clamored. "We should get started with the class."

His brows crinkled. "Are you sure?"

Nodding, I gave my confirmation. "Yes, of course."

Deciding not to pressure me, he walked back to the front. Before he gave instructions, he glanced at me. "No worries. This is a safe zone. I'll respect your privacy regarding my brother. Consider the conversation off the table."

A breath I didn't know I had been holding escaped me, and I felt my blood pressure drop. I nodded, and it was as if all was understood.

He started the music and showed us how to stretch. Aquila wasn't lying. Kinston was brutal, and we were supposed to be going easy. I couldn't tell. If that was easy, I hated to see hard. While Aquila was zipping through, I was struggling because our trainer was spending a whole lot of time assisting Angela. When he called for a break, I was more than ready and ran to the water cooler.

"I told you to be prepared," Aquila huffed as she approached me by the water cooler while I was downing my cup.

"If you wanted to kill me, just say that," I huffed as she snickered. "I'm glad my slow death amuses you."

Aquila jutted her hip to the side and fanned me off. "You'll survive," she said nonchalantly. "Speaking of survival, I want you to know I had no idea he was related to Kannon. In all sincerity, I apologize for that. Are you okay? Really?"

As shocked as I was, I knew my sisters were even more shocked. Kinston looked just as flabbergasted as us, so I knew speaking on their personal lives had never been a topic of discussion.

"I give you a hard time, but I know you'd never knowingly walk me into an ambush, Aquila. I trust that you both knew nothing about the other." I leaned forward. "Now, if it were Angela…"

We gave each other knowing looks with raised eyebrows and pursed lips.

She turned so that we were facing the other side of the room. "Speaking of which, Kinston seems to have a thing for our sister."

"And our sister doesn't seem to mind."

"At all," Aquila joked as we stood and watched the flirty private conversation that stirred between the two.

Just then, Kinston glanced at his watch. My head fell back in agony because I knew he would call us back to the torture chamber. Just as he was about to speak, a woman came through the doors, granting us a few more minutes of rest. *I knew there was a God.*

"Cami!" Aquila squealed as they ran toward each other.

"Aquila!" Cami shrieked, and the two hugged each other tightly.

"Cami, I told you about trying to steal my clients," Kinston playfully scolded her.

She broke away from Aquila and waved him off. "Next time, don't miss a day, and your clients won't fall in love with me."

Suddenly, Aquila looked over at Angela and me as we drank water and took in the scene. She pointed in our direction and introduced us.

"Cami Nilson, these are my sisters, Angela and Nissi. Sissies, this is my backup trainer who keeps trying to steal me from Kinston, Cami."

She walked over to us and shook each of our hands. "It's nice to meet you. I see Aquila finally wrangled you guys here."

"Bullied us is more like it," Angela joked, eliciting laughter.

"Pay her no mind, Cami. Mama and Daddy were on that ooh wee back then, and it caused permanent damage," Aquila joshed.

Angela clapped her hands together. "Oh, you got comebacks, sis. You know I can do this all day with you, Mama and Daddy's Lil' Miss Mistakenly-hit-the-mark-down-in-the-park."

By now, all of us were in stitches with tears rolling down our faces, even Kinston. The hilarity of growing up in the Richards family never ceased to amaze me, especially not with my two older sisters. Frick and Frack were a whole comedy show by themselves.

"Oh, my goodness," Cami wiped her eyes. "I can't with you two. Let me tell you all my reason for interrupting your class before I pass out from laughter." She took a deep breath. "You know next weekend is my big day. Travis and I are tying the knot, and I wanted to ensure I extended my invitation to you, Aquila. We're having a wedding and reception at the Hilton ballroom. I'd love it if you and your husband could come." She then turned to Angela and me. "You two, as well. I know we don't know each other personally, but I love you ladies' energy."

"What if we have a plus one?"

That came from me. I didn't mind going if I could bring Benji. I was not about to sit with Aquila looking like the lonely and desperate tag-a-long.

Cami shrugged. "The more, the merrier. I'm excited for everyone to see me marry my man!"

"She ain't lying," Aquila said, playfully nudging Cami.

Angela turned to me. "Heifer, how you gonna leave me out there like that? I'm supposed to be your plus one."

Raising my hands, I quipped, "My bad, sis."

By then, Kinston had walked over to the small semi-circle we'd formed. "You could always come with me as my plus one."

The silence that took over the room was deafening. Our eyes landed on him, seemingly at the same time. He stood there like a deer caught in headlights. It was as if he had forgotten how to breathe as he gulped and pulled air into his lungs.

"You are mighty bold to ask her that in front of us. You know that, right?" Aquila quipped with a raised eyebrow as she folded her arms across her chest.

By then, Kinston was sweating bullets, and it didn't have a thing to do with his class. A part of me wanted to scream that she would not be suckered into the likes of a Jordan. I knew siblings were as different as night and day, just as my sisters and I were, but birds of a feather also flocked together. I had already been taken through the wringer with Kannon. I'd be damned if Kinston dragged my big sister through the mud. Being divinely gorgeous wouldn't save him if he toyed with my Angela. On God. However, I had learned long ago that the best way to piss off my sisters was to get into their business prematurely. I had to get Angela alone to gauge her temperature on this little situation with Kinston before I offered my unsolicited opinion.

"Okayyy," Cami said, holding her hands up in surrender. "I'm just gonna head out." She turned to us and hugged Aquila.

"Aquila, it's always a pleasure." She pulled away and waved at us. "Ladies, it's good to meet you finally. My offer stands as a single invite or a plus one." She turned her head and winked at Kinston playfully.

After she left, Angela walked over to Kinston, and Aquila and I pretended to be engrossed in our conversation while eavesdropping on theirs.

"You're tuned in, right?" Aquila questioned with a whisper.

"Girl, ear hustle on a thousand." Looking at Aquila, I leaned in to be sure my following words were indeed private. "He's cool, right? I mean, given his pedigree."

"As far as I know, he's straight up. But I don't know him on an intimate level." Sensing my concern, she touched my arm to calm me. "He's not Kannon, sis. You gotta give him a chance to muck up first."

"He's the closest to a Kannon," I grumbled, then relented. "Fine. I wouldn't want anyone judging me based on you or Angela."

Cocking her head back, she scoffed. "I don't know if I should agree or be offended."

"I don't know, but you should hush so we can hear what the hell they are about to say to each other."

Angela approached Kinston with extra sass.

"Forward much?" Sauciness oozed out as she folded her arms.

A nervous chuckle escaped Kinston. "Bad timing a lot, too. But I meant what I said."

He stared back at her with a confidence that had replaced his previous uneasy demeanor.

"You don't even know me, man, and just what would your lady say?"

Kinston leaned back against the wall with one foot propped against it.

"Let me ask her," he replied while rubbing his chin beard.

Angela frowned. "Wow. So you're really gonna ask me to go out with you—to a wedding, no less—and you have a whole woman at the house?"

"Nah, she ain't at the house."

"Wherever she is," Angela snapped, her neck rolling from side to side.

"Welp, lemme ask her then." Kinston leaned forward closer to Angela's face. "I need to ask you something. Do you mind if I take this beautiful woman named Angela to a wedding next weekend? She seemed a little apprehensive about taking my offer, so I wanted to ask you. Hopefully, she'll be all right with going with me."

I had never seen Angela turn beet red until that very second. The gesture even made Aquila's mouth drop, which was hard to accomplish. I was impressed, but on the other hand, I'd seen that type of impressive gift of gab. It was attached to another man, last name Jordan—birds of a feather or rather *brothers* of a feather.

Clearing her throat, Angela placed a hand on her chest. "I… umm…you think you're slick, don't you?"

Kinston gently shook his head. "Nah, you asked if my woman would mind, so I asked." He shrugged. "She hasn't answered me yet, so I don't know."

Angela's stoned expression turned into a giddy-faced attempt not to burst into laughter.

"Boy, you're a whole mess." She wagged her finger.

"And you still didn't answer my question," Kinston said.

Angela spun on her heels and then peeped back over her shoulder. "You didn't ask me one. You asked your woman. Let's get back to work, trainer."

Kinston beamed and nodded. "Yes, ma'am."

When she walked over to us, I pushed her with my hip. "Okay, Kinston."

Aquila and I slapped high-fives as we teased Angela with googly eyes.

"Whatever. He's about to start up again."

As we sauntered back into our lineup, Aquila stretched and made her position on funding today's session abundantly clear. "I don't think flirting with my sister should be added to my tab, Kinston. We're gonna run over fifteen minutes because of these delays."

Kinston started the music. "Don't worry about it. This session is on the house."

He tapped his chest to let her know he had it.

Aquila slung a glance at Angela. "Aww, okay, I'ma have to bring you more often."

Angela pursed her lips with an eye roll. "Let's just get back to work, please."

And work we did. I don't know if Kinston was trying to work off the fire Angela had stirred inside of him or if he was beating her into submission, but we all paid the price for whatever emotions he was experiencing. Of course, Kinston made sure his favorite girl in the session was handling the exercises perfectly. Not saying he didn't do his job and check in on Aquila and me, but he catered to Angela most assuredly. By the time our session ended, all I wanted to do was fall down and not move for the next year. I knew he had outdone himself when I saw Aquila huffing and puffing.

"Well, Kinston, thank you again for a great workout. Sissies, I have to skedaddle to get home to your nephews." She hugged us, then tossed her gym bag over her shoulder. She turned and pointed to Kinston. "See you at the wedding."

He saluted her. "And hopefully with a plus one."

He shined that dazzling Jordan smile in Angela's direction.

"As long as it gets me a friends and family discount, I'm all for it," Aquila joked.

"I got you for today definitely," Kinston reminded her.

248

"Then I need your potential plus one to start plus one'ing." With that, she bucked her eyes at Angela, who shot her a bird before leaving.

When I looked back, Kinston and Angela were deep into a stare-down of wills, so I decided to mill around the room, pretending to gather my things and check out the equipment while keeping my ear lifelines open.

"You said I didn't ask earlier, so I'm asking now. Would you accompany me to Cami and Travis's wedding next Saturday evening?"

"I don't know—"

"Why wouldn't you? Give me one reason."

"Boy, I don't even know you."

"Simple. My name is Kinston Percy Jordan, named Percy after my grandfather. So, don't laugh. I'm thirty-two years old, and I'm a fitness instructor. Oh, and I'm single unless you want to fulfill that wish for me, too. What else do you want to know?"

Angela held her hand up. "That's enough for now. So how about you don't know me," she said defiantly.

"Simple. Tell me. Tell me now or over a cup of coffee and some breakfast this Sunday. I know this nice little spot that makes the perfect eggs benedict."

Hearty laughter escaped Angela. "I can say one thing; you do not play around. You were a bit nervous before, but once my sisters didn't pounce on you, you pressed that gas full throttle, no brakes, sir."

With a shrug, he replied, "When I see something I want, I go for it...*like a motherfucka.*"

He allowed his words to linger with a stare so intense I could see my sister coming undone.

That's when I knew it was time to go. I was all for eavesdropping, but knowing my sister's panties were marinating in juices from Kinston's enticing words was where I drew my limit. These Jordan men were dangerous. I prayed that if my sister gave Kinston the time of day, he wouldn't waste her time like his brother had done with me. In fact, I hoped Angela hurried up to finish their conversation because being around Kinston had begun to drudge up thoughts that I had worked hard to bury into the deepest crevices of my mind for the umpteenth time. I let off a cough, which brought Angela back from the depths of Kinston's advances and brought them back to the fact that they were not alone.

"I drove my sister, so I really need to go." She began backing away from him. "I appreciate your offer, but I think I will pass."

She hightailed it over to me, and I handed her the bag that was hers. I knew she was ready to go because Angela was the type to hold her own in any situation. Kinston had found a sliver of a tunnel and almost cracked her code. Therefore, she had to abort the mission to keep her heart tucked away.

As we turned to head out, Kinston met us at the door.

"Thank you for all the help in class. I'll take the tips to heart," Angela said.

I held out my hand to shake his, and he gently captured it. "It was a pleasure to meet you. This is a great class you have."

"Thank you, Nissi, and likewise. Thank you, ladies, for attending, and feel free to sign up anytime." Then, he reached inside his bag, pulled out a business card, and handed it to Angela. "Call me if you want a session, that breakfast, or that plus one."

Their grins were infectious, and I had to blush myself. He was relentless. Who could blame him, though? My sister was a catch, and anybody would be blessed to have her grace the presence of their life for even one millisecond.

She slid the card out of his hand and tucked it into her bag. "I'll remember that."

"You do that."

"Goodbye, Kinston Jordan," Angela said, walking backward out of the room.

"See you later, Angela Richards."

The stroll to her car was quiet, but I screamed and started slapping the dashboard as soon as we got inside.

"Say what? Not fine-ass Kinston trying to holler at you!"

"First off, if you tear up my car, you're paying for the damages."

"Quit trying to act like that didn't just happen."

She shook her head and giggled as she backed out of the parking spot.

"No lie. I honestly see why you fell so hard for Kannon. 'Cause, babyyy!"

I pointed at her. "You see my pain!"

"Girl, who raised those pretty ninjas? 'Cause, baby, my coochie was doing somersaults trying to hop out of my yoga pants."

"And that was when I knew it was time to go." I pinched my fingers together for emphasis. "I ain't trying to witness all that."

"Shoot, real talk, you probably saved me."

Taking a page from Aquila's book, I became the voice of reason. "Just because Kinston is related to Kannon doesn't mean they are the same."

"I know, sis. I know."

The fact that she willingly accepted that logic confused me because we both knew by actions—seen and unseen—that she was feeling him as much as he was feeling her. I tossed a confused stare at her.

"So why did you turn down his offers?"

"Girl, that man is only looking for ass to tap. He is not about to screw me into insanity. I like my mind and my peace."

My head fell back against the headrest. "You don't know that, Angela."

"But I do know that even if he doesn't want ass now, he'll want ass later. And again, I'm not about to let him fuck me into insanity. Have me out here in the daytime with a flashlight trying to search for his ding-a-ling like I'm Dora the damn Explorer."

When I finally found my breath, I hollered, "Bishhhh! I hate you."

"Why?" she managed to ask between fits of laughter.

"Because I was Doraaa!"

Thank goodness we were at the red light because she and I started stomping and slapping the car in a barrage of giggles and tears. Those damn Jordan boys.

Chapter Twenty-Five

KANNON

*M*Y HEAD COLLAPSED backward on the headrest once I parked my F-250 truck in the parking spot. Everything inside me wanted to put the gearshift in reverse, head back to my home, and curl up in bed. The past couple of weeks at work had been rough. It seemed like everyone in Miami had an emergency—from car wrecks to medical emergencies and down to house fires. You name it, we were called for it, which is precisely why I didn't want to be at my brother's gym at o-dark-thirty this morning, especially since it was my only day off until Saturday. That unusual fate happened due to a sweet shift trade with one of my co-workers. Ain't no way I would pass up two days off in one week. That thought alone brought me back to the question as to why my brother insisted I come in early this morning to work out. I usually got my workouts late at night or mid-day, but Kinston was determined to have me come before Jesus rose.

A groan escaped my lips as I reached to turn off my ignition. I forced my tired muscles to reach over, grab my gym bag, and exit my truck. *His ass had better have hit the lottery or something for dragging me in here, knowing I've only had about four decent hours of sleep.*

When I entered the weight area of the gym, I saw Kinston in the mirror doing bicep curls. I waved at the few gym heads scattered about, who loved to be there before the roosters woke up. As I continued toward Kinston, his business partner, Roman Patterson, breezed up to me, and we slapped hands together.

"Mr. Fire and Rescue!" Roman belted. "What are you doing here this time of day?"

Pointing in the direction of my brother, I said, "Ask him."

Roman chuckled. "I should've known. The only thing that sees you at five in the morning is sleep and the fire station."

"You got jokes, I see."

He shrugged. "Just calling it as I see it." His cell phone dinged, and he slipped it from his jogger pants pocket to peer down at it. Looking up, he swatted me on the arm with the back of his hand. "Ayo, listen. I gotta take this, but it was good seeing you, bruh."

"You too, man."

He pointed at me before jogging off and answering his phone. "Don't let Kinston work you too hard," Roman called out. "He can be a beast. Take care."

Knowing he was telling the truth, I grinned while offering him a two-finger salute. Turning, I glided over to Kinston and sat my bag down.

"You're late."

"No, bruh, I'm early. Hella early for me."

Kinston cracked a smile and popped me with the towel. "You got that one."

Stretching my arms, I focused on my brother. "Man, you told Roman about Mr. Fire and Rescue."

Kinston finished his water and tossed the plastic bottle in the nearby recycle bin. "Nah, I didn't tell him about nothing. He saw it play out on social media like I did." He shrugged. "What's the big deal? All of Florida and the rest of the world know about the rescue story of firefighter Kannon and dentist Nissi."

Switching to stretch my legs, I answered, "No big deal. I just—"

"Don't want to be reminded of her at every chance. I get it, especially after what you told me went down at that music showcase club."

"Yeah, thanks, man," I said, plopping down on one of the bench press benches.

I had conveniently left out the Instagram tryst and failed apology dinner. I would never live that embarrassment down.

"So what did you call me out here for? Because I know it wasn't just to work out."

Kinston plopped down across from me with a sinister smirk on his face. "Nissi."

Assuming he was taking a dig at me, I swatted my towel at him.

"Bruh." Dropping the towel around my neck, I lie back on the bench. "What did you really want to talk to me about?"

Kinston stood and walked behind me. With two cleaning cloths, he wiped down the weight bar and then tossed the cloths in the trash bin. I placed my hands on the bar, appropriately spaced apart. Kinston assisted me with lifting the two-hundred-fifty pounds of weight and began to spot me.

"Well, I called you in early today because one of my clients is scheduled for this afternoon, and I didn't want to chance you bumping into her in case she brought her guest again."

Great! Another blast from my past has tracked me down.

A long sigh escaped my lips. "Which of my crazy exes hired you as their trainer to get next to me?"

"None, bro," he said, guiding the weight bar back up. "My client is Aquila Oliver, older sister to Nissi Richards."

My eyes ballooned at his words as I placed the weight bar back in the holder and bent my head back so I could see him eye to eye.

"Bro, how did you link up with her sister?"

"That's the thing. She's been my client for a year. I didn't even know she was related to Nissi until she asked if her sisters could join her session, and they showed up a few nights ago. I recognized Nissi from TikTok."

Sitting upright, my brother had my total attention. He stepped back in front of me as I wiped my forehead and gazed up at him.

"Did you tell them who you were?"

"Yeah, I did. I was so shocked at who she was that I had to speak on it."

"What did Nissi say?"

Kinston retied his shoulder-length dreads on top of his head and shrugged. "Literally nothing. I thought the woman was going to pass out at the revelation. I told her I wouldn't bring you up again, and I carried on with my private class with the ladies."

The wheels in my head started turning. Nissi's sister, Aquila, was a regular and came to the late afternoon sessions on Mondays. I committed that to memory. I felt eyes beaming on me like hot lasers and saw Kinston regarding me with a warning.

"Nope. Don't you dare come up here on Mondays, disrupting my class."

Fueled, I leaped from my seated position. "Bro, you gotta let me come through. It's the only way I can think of to have some time to talk to Nissi."

Kinston rubbed the back of his neck. His facial expression was tight, and I could see the turmoil stirring in his spirit.

"This is my place of business, Kann. I can't do that. Trust is a huge part of my clientele. If I start losing that, I start losing clients. That's bad for business. You know Roman and I are trying to open up more gyms. I can't do that if I'm losing clients. Besides,

I'm not sure if Nissi is coming back with her sister, especially after finding out I'm your brother."

My open palms spread out as I hunched my shoulders. "So why did you tell me that information?"

"To keep you away in the off chance she does show up. Both of them would swear I planned an ambush, and I'm not trying to have that lie growing wings and flying out to other clientele. You're my brother, but this is my livelihood, Kann."

Gripping his arm, I resorted to begging my brother. "Bro, you know I'd never do that. I'll walk away from her before I allow that to happen. But now that I know, I can't just put the coo-coo back in the clock, bruh. All I'm asking for is an opportunity for one shot."

Kinston paced back and forth in deep contemplation. His mind was racing because I asked him to do what he had tried to avoid. I felt terrible, but I needed an "in" with Nissi. There's no way in hell I could pass up any chance I got. The mere fact that her sister was my brother's client spelled out to me that there was something in the cards for Nissi and me. Now that I'd tasted an opportunity to seal the deal, I was ravenous to lockdown any break I came across.

Finally, Kinston stopped and turned to me.

"Listen, I'm probably gonna regret this, but I have an idea that's even better."

"What's that?" I was all ears for whatever suggestion he had.

"Remember our other female trainer, Cami?" When I nodded, Kinston continued. "She popped up in my class that night to invite Aquila and me to her wedding this Saturday. When Aquila introduced Cami to her sisters, they hit it off, and she invited them, too. Each invitation comes with a plus-one invite. I was trying to save my extra invitation, but if you're serious about wanting an opportunity with Nissi, you can be my plus one."

Bowing my head and gripping my brother's shoulders, I exhorted, "Yes. Thank you, bro. Thank you."

"You better thank me. I hoped Nissi's other sister, Angela, would agree to be my plus one."

Wait. Did he say he asked Nissi's sister out? Hold up. Now I need the whole story.

"Wait. Bruh. Wait a minute. You pushed up on Nissi's sister?"

A sly grin spread across Kinston's face. The gleam in his eyes told the whole story. Angela had him just as gone as Nissi had me. What ran in those women's DNA, crack?

"Hell yeah, I stepped to her. That ass called out to me like it was whistling my favorite song, bro."

Howling, I slapped hands with my brother. "Man, I get it. I already know what she's working with if she's anything like Nissi."

"She does favor Nissi more than Aquila in facial features, but Angela is thicker than a Snicker, bruh. Just the right amount of meat on her bones to make me wanna grab and hold on tight. Real talk, she's witty and hilarious, and she rides hard for her family. Those are only a few quirks I picked up on during the class. As attractive as she is, I'd love to explore more with her. Something about her spoke to me like a motherfucka."

Kinston's far-off gaze told me that he had been genuinely pondering over Angela, not just in a sexual way. I understood his plight. I was in the thick of it with Nissi. The fact that he had wanted to go with Angela but sacrificed his opportunity so I could finally rectify my situation and hopefully begin my limitless possibilities with Nissi made me even more grateful for him and indebted. Only brotherly love would do that.

Slapping hands with him and pulling him into a hug, I whispered, "I appreciate you doing this for me, bro. Real talk. I'll do everything I can to ensure Angela and you link up. That's my word."

He pointed his finger at my chest. "You make sure you do what you have to do to land Nissi. I can tell none of them play about their lives or their sisters. If you want that woman, you need to make it plain and finally tell her the truth about you and River."

My head bobbed. Although I had confessed to Nissi that River and I weren't together, I never explained why. Kinston would probably go ballistic if he knew I had the chance and didn't. But I made up my mind that I wouldn't waste this one. He had put his desires aside to ensure that I had mine. Treading light was over.

Kinston leaned closer to me and added, "Fair warning. Nissi asked if she could bring a plus one. So, I'm pretty sure that lame-ass man of hers will be there. But real talk, forget dude."

My scowl punctuated my brother's words. "Then he better step harder than me because I'm coming for what's mine with a vengeance. Believe that."

Playfully, Kinston rubbed the top of my head. "That's my baby brother."

We started our workout again, and I had renewed confidence in my second chance with Nissi. All I needed was a little time and space, and I knew I could make her mine. I knew it. Internally, I laughed at my brother, pushing up on her big sister. Man, it was something about them Richards girls.

Today would be the day I won Nissi back. I felt bad for intruding on Cami's wedding for my selfish gain, but what better atmosphere to secure a relationship than at a wedding? None. Love and romance were in the air.

Nissi could spew whatever she wanted to say out of her mouth, but those tears at the club were real. Calling my name while she reached an orgasm with that rose toy was real, and the intergalactic love we made on the beach was damn sure real. Not only was it real, but it was also right. Whether she wanted to accept it, we were each other's missing piece. Today, I knew it. I knew I was born to love Nissi Richards. I couldn't explain it, but I knew. My only mission for today was to ensure she knew it, too.

Easing out of my truck wearing my tailor-made suit, I strolled to the front of the venue with my wedding gift for Cami and her soon-to-be husband in my hands. My brother was already standing out front waiting on me.

"Boi, you clean!" Kinston said with the top of his fist balled to his mouth. "You came dressed to impress."

"I came dressed to conquer," I corrected before we waltzed up the steps. "So did you, bro." I patted the side of his arm, taking in his attire.

That was no cap. Sparing no expense, I purchased a tailor-made heather blue wool Bespoke suit. I sported a white open-collared shirt underneath with deep brown Ferragamo loafers. A simple white pocket square was my suit accessory while I donned my big face Talley & Twine watch. My curly hair was trimmed low, and my mustache and beard were perfectly shaped. Of course, I wore the same cologne I had on that day at the beach because I came to divide and conquer. *Fuck Ben.*

My brother was dapper in his all-black tailored suit, black open-collared shirt underneath, and black Prada loafers. His locs were neatly twisted into two ponytails on either side of his head and braided together at the bottom. Although I was muscular, his body builder's physique filled out the suit, giving him the appearance of an NFL linebacker. Women always fell out whenever they saw my brother dressed to the nines. I would be interested to see how Angela processed his appearance when she saw him. One thing was for sure: We Jordan boys were bringing our A-game to those Richards sisters.

Once the attendant checked us in, we signed the guest book and left Cami's gifts at the gift table before being escorted inside. Our table was to the left, near the back, with five other people we didn't know. The only person sitting at the table that we did know was Roman. My eyes scanned the crowd and found Nissi seated about three tables up from us. I knew it was her, even though I could only see the back of her head. I also noticed the back of the head of a man sitting beside her. Ben. *So she brought the lame.* I felt sorry for the man, because as soon as the reception started, he was about to be womanless.

We sat through all the pomp and circumstance of the wedding and even sat patiently through the beginning reception traditions, shenanigans, and our plated dinner. Although I was ready to make my move on Nissi, I enjoyed the fanfare. The entire time the wedding took place, it only solidified my feelings for Nissi. From Cami's walk down the aisle to reciting the vows, to the kiss, and even during their first dance, my mind kept picturing Nissi and me. When we finished eating, I felt like I was on the edge of insanity, waiting to get to her.

When I saw women only sitting at Nissi's table, I tapped my brother on the arm.

"Let's make our move."

My brother was a rider. As soon as I tapped him with the command, he didn't skip a beat. When I stood, he was on my heels. We strode up to the table like bosses on a mission, and all three ladies' eyes immediately lifted to see us standing there.

"Kannon?" Nissi said in shock as her eyes roamed me up and down.

"In the flesh," I replied, turning my attention to my brother. "As I've heard, you've met my brother, Kinston."

While I delivered my introduction of my brother, his eyes were locked on who I now could correctly assess was Angela, and hers did the same. I could practically see the drool threatening to ooze off her lips.

"Good evening, ladies," Kinston said, never taking his eyes off Angela.

"Hey, Kinston," they all bellowed, although Angela's was a bit sappier.

Nissi finally recovered from her amazement long enough to introduce me to her sisters.

"Forgive my manners. Kannon, this is my sister, Aquila, and my sister, Angela. You guys, this is Kannon Jordan."

Gracefully, I accepted each of their hands and kissed the tops. They both gave Nissi smitten expressions.

"May we sit down?" I asked.

"Actually—"

"Yes, of course," Aquila said, interrupting Nissi's blatant denial.

Kinston and I didn't hesitate. We pulled out the two chairs in front of us and sat down. While Kinston roped Angela into a conversation, I took that as my cue to focus solely on Nissi.

"I'm glad you're here."

"Why is that?" she asked, sipping on her wine.

"I need to talk to you."

"We have nothing to discuss."

Wagging my finger, I shook my head. "On the contrary, we have a lot to discuss."

Nissi rolled her eyes. I could see the irritation and nervous energy bounce all over her. It was cute. On top of that, her attitude made her look even sexier than she already was. Speaking of which, her dress fit in all the right places. Her naturally curly hair framed her beautiful face, and her pouty lips begged me to kiss them.

"You said everything you needed to say on the beach that night."

I pointed to the plate of cake in front of her. "Are you going to eat that?"

Confused, she shook her head and pushed the plate in my direction. Lifting the fork, I broke a piece of the cake and smoothly slid it into my mouth, letting my tongue slowly lick the fork and darting back and forth between the grooves. Once I swallowed the bite, I licked my lips. Nissi and Aquila stared at me in wonderment.

"Oh my," Aquila said and cleared her throat.

I winked at Nissi and pulled my bottom lip between my teeth. "I'm just practicing for when you don't need that rose toy."

Nissi coughed so harshly that Aquila had to pat her back and give her water. Oh, she was going to talk to me today whether she did so voluntarily or involuntarily. When her coughing fit subsided, she glared at me.

"You're wrong for this," she whispered.

I placed my hand over hers and leaned forward. "But I'm right for you. That's all that matters, Nissi. All I want to do is talk and explain everything. So much has happened over the past few months, and I can't get you off my mind."

"So you don't give two damns that her sister is sitting here, huh?" Aquila quipped and rubbed her earlobe with a sinister gaze.

Yep, she was ready to annihilate me over her baby sister, and Angela was right behind her.

"Excuse me, Kinston. No knock to you because you've been the perfect gentleman," Angela said to him before turning eyes of steel on me, "but haven't you done enough? My baby sister doesn't need to hear more of your liquor-covered lies."

"Whoa, sweetheart," Kinston said, pulling Angela's hand into his. "My brother may have mishandled the situation, but he's no liar." Angela's eyes fell sheepishly, and that's when Kinston gave his attention to Nissi. "My brother is here to rectify his mistake."

Nissi's eyes turned cold as ice when she pointed at Kinston. "See, that's the thing, Kinston. Sleeping with somebody when you know you have a girlfriend isn't a mistake. It's intentional." Then her hardened gaze fell back on me. "The mistake was me believing for one minute that he could be someone I could let inside my yoni or heart. Excuse me."

Nissi stood, throwing her linen napkin on the table.

"Nissi, please. I'm so sorry for that. Wait, please," I pleaded to her back as she headed in the direction of the restrooms.

"Damnit," I bit out in a low growl.

Kinston stood and patted my shoulder. "I'm sorry, bro. I was trying to help."

Nodding, I rubbed my temple with one hand while placing my other hand at the waist of my pants. "I know. It's all right."

Aquila sat back in her chair with her arms folded. "On the strength of Kinston, I'm going to ask you a question, Kannon, and I want you to be completely honest."

Everyone's attention turned to Aquila, and I was all ears.

"Ask away."

"Why are you still after my sister? It was one night, and it cannot be the sex because I'm pretty sure you're well-versed with a limitless supply in that arena. What the hell is it about my sister that, months later, still has you sniffing up her behind?"

Looking back and forth between Aquila and Angela, whom both had a death stare on me, I squared my shoulders and decided to be honest.

"The gospel truth is I'm still sniffing behind her for the same reason she just ran off—because there is more to us than a romp on the beach. Our souls connected that night, and I have not been able to shake her because somewhere during those five hours, she took a piece of my heart. I don't know everything there is to know about her, but deep down in my gut, I know she's supposed to be with me, and I'm supposed to be with her. To me, that's all that matters."

"What about your little girlfriend?" Angela spat.

"That's what I've been trying to tell Nissi. I'm not with her anymore. Haven't been since a month after our date," I explained before exhaling and offering them the whole truth. "My ex knows I want to be with Nissi."

They both gasped, hands flying to their mouths.

"Wait. So why didn't you approach her sooner?" Aquila asked.

"When I tried, she'd already started dating some guy named—"

"I'm so sorry, ladies. I got tied up chopping shop with one of my dental school buddies."

Those slurred words came from behind Kinston and me as Aquila and Angela's eyes grew as wide as saucers. I could tell the man whose mouth they came from had been drinking, but it also sounded eerily familiar. Kinston and I turned around simultaneously to see who was addressing the ladies.

"Benji?" The name flew out of my mouth.

His jaw tightened and twitched as he stared at me.

"Kannon." Then he looked over at Kinston and nodded roughly. "Kinston."

"*The hell?*" I whispered as my thoughts scrambled to come together.

Why would he address Aquila and Angela as if he were here with them, as if he knew them? Then my mind went back to when Nissi was at the fire station. Her phone. I had only caught a glimpse of the name. Her man's name was not Ben. It was *Benji*! Benji Eloi!

My face screwed, and my lips tightened into a growl. "You mutha—"

I didn't get a chance to finish the statement because my fist was flying up in the air to meet Benji's face, but my brother—

knowing me—gripped my arm from connecting and forced it down.

"What the hell?" one of Nissi's sisters said as Benji and I stared menacingly at each other.

"You're foul for this one," Kinston said and wiped his hand over his beard. "Wow."

Benji's eyebrow raised, giving Kinston a cautionary stare before placing his hands in his pants pocket. "There are no fouls in love, my man," he bit out. "Only winners and losers."

With his last word, his rat-like beady eyes landed on me, and I swore I would knock his smug block off this time. Again, Kinston stopped me by stepping in between Benji and me as some of the wedding guests beside us gasped and stepped back, picking up on the tension. Although I was a burning inferno on the inside, I allowed my cooler head to prevail. This was Cami's wedding, and she worked for my brother. Regardless of my woes, I couldn't and wouldn't ruin one of the most important days of her life to coax my ego.

"He's not worth it, especially not here." Kinston's low words pulled me out of the dark abyss of my murderous intentions.

"I'm good." I attempted to sidestep Kinston, and he stepped back in front of me, placing a hand on my shoulder. "I said I was good."

With that, I shrugged him off and made my way to the side exit. I needed air. I needed to breathe. I needed...*Nissi*. She was standing outside right before me when I exited. Her back was to me, and she didn't bother to turn around. Without thinking, I rushed over to her, grabbed her by the elbow, and pulled her to my truck as she hurled protests my way.

"Let go of me!" she said harshly and snatched away from me when we stopped. "Are you insane?"

Swiftly backing her into my truck, I placed both hands on either side of her head and peered into her eyes, positive that my expression was just as maddened as hers.

"Yeah, I'm insane about you."

With a puff, Nissi flailed her hands pointedly as she stressed, "You have a girl—"

"River and I broke up because I want to be with you," I yelled, causing her mouth to clamp shut.

Her countenance fell as realization found its way into her eyes. I couldn't read her. Probably because of the gamut of emotions flowing through her being. I relaxed before I continued, which caused her to relax, too.

"We've been broken up since a month after our date. She left me because she realized I wanted you. Hell, *I* realized I wanted you. Still do."

Nissi scoffed, disgust filling her aura. "So explain you guys being huddled up with each other at the Indie Lovers Club. Obviously, you were there with her."

"Oh my God, woman." I raised my hand, rubbing my fingertips across the furrowed crinkles on my forehead. "I was there with Jovan. He took me out to watch his boy, Kru, perform. I had no clue River was there. We ended amicably, so we still speak. What you saw was two ex-lovers simply enjoying the atmosphere. Nothing more. Nothing less."

Nissi rolled her eyes. "Yeah, right."

My head fell back as I gathered my thoughts. "Nissi, I'm telling you the truth. Think about it. If I were still with River, why would I run after you, especially in front of her?"

She fell back against my truck as if those words had smacked her in the face. I watched as her eyes darted, attempting to look everywhere except at me. She was trying to debunk what I had said—trying to find a way to make my truth untrue. However, she was failing miserably because either way she wanted to slice it, what I had said made sense. I could sense when acceptance finally washed over her.

Nissi's eyes glossed over, and she bit her lip. "Seriously?"

I nodded, bringing my hand to her face and caressing it. "Nissi, it's been four months. Why would I still be pursuing a woman with whom I'd only shared one five-hour date over a woman who held me down for two years if I wasn't serious?"

She attempted to glance away again, but this time, I turned her face back to mine using the crook of my finger, forcing her to drink in what I was saying—not just to her ears but to her heart.

"Nissi, what I did was wrong. It was wrong to River. It was wrong to you. Most importantly, it was wrong for us. But I'm trying to make it right. The right thing to do is be honest about these feelings neither of us understands. The right thing to do was to let River go, which I did. The right thing to do was hunt mercilessly for the woman who stole my soul on one date that lasted five hours. The woman I dream about nearly every night, whose name I call in my sleep. The woman who consumes my daydreams and for whom I had to beg my brother to bring me as his plus one just for a slight chance I could talk to her. It's you, Nissi. It's been you since the moment you walked your sexy ass into Brick."

A tear that she had been holding back streamed down her face. I followed the tear as it trickled down her cheek to the corner of her nose and landed on the tip of her quivering lips. Closing the space between us, I gripped her face between the palms of my hands, brought her to me, and kissed her lips where her salty tear rested. When she didn't push me away, I nibbled on her bottom lip, hoping she would open to me. My reward came when she moaned into my mouth. I deepened the kiss, wrapping my arms around her waist and holding her flush. My throbbing manhood was all the indicator that my loins were calling out to her just as much as my heart. When she wrapped her arms around my neck, that was it.

Still locked in an intense lip lock, I dug my keys out of my pocket and pressed the unlock button on the fob. I didn't even let her lips go when I opened the back door and flipped the front passenger seat up. Lifting her, I placed her in the backseat and climbed behind her. Once inside, I recaptured her lips, and we kissed wildly as if we couldn't get enough of tasting each other. Her kisses tasted like berries and mint as I hovered over her. My thick tongue licked over her plump lips as she lightly moaned against me.

"Kannon," she whimpered, and it was all the encouragement I needed.

Flipping her on her stomach, I tugged her dress upward over her rotund ass, slipped my fingers into the sides of her panties, and slid them down her milk chocolate thighs. As I gripped her at the perfect angle, I licked my lips. I had to taste her. Explore her depths.

"Open up for me, baby."

"Wait, Kannon. Ben—"

Before she could renege for her so-called man, I planted my tongue on her love button. Inhaling her sweet aroma, I swiped her clit slowly and sensually. She tasted like heaven.

"Ahh, Kann...Kannon," she grunted through quivers.

The sound of my name from her sweet lips motivated me, and I sucked her clit between my lips and then swirled my tongue over and over again. Sticking my tongue inside her sopping juices, she let go and rode back on my face as I darted in and out, scooping her essence on my tongue like my favorite ice cream.

"Sweet pussy," I moaned.

Her moans grew deeper and louder as she rode my tongue at a frenzied pace. With the palms of my hands on either butt cheek, I guided her back and forth on my tongue as she squirmed. Using my grip on her, I swirled her ass in a circle while my tongue explored her creamy core. Her juices flowed, wetting my fingers and soaking my mouth, mustache, and beard. Her ragged pants urged me on as her head fell forward, and she pressed her fingertips into the seat cushions. She was nearly ready to come undone. I felt it in her body's reaction, but I wouldn't release her until I was ready.

"Ugh. Kannon. I'm…I'm cumming," she wailed.

I didn't let up. I wanted to taste all her release. She hissed and grunted roughly, trying not to wail out in the throes of passion, but I wanted it all, needed it all. She cried out and shivered, but I gripped her thighs in place and continued to lick and suck while she creamed all over my face. There was no escape. She would have to ride this wave until it crested. Her body stiffened as she tried to crawl away from me, but my grasp on her made that impossible.

"Kannonnnnnn. I can't…I can't…take…please…pleaassee."

She begged through bated breaths until I felt her shudder again, and the front of her body collapsed against my car seat. Raising, I swiped my hand down my face, used the other hand to unbutton my trousers, and pushed them and my boxer briefs down to my knees. When I wrapped my arm around her waist to turn her over, she whimpered and tried to shrug away from me. Her body still shivered from the raging waves of orgasms that crashed through her body. Holding her tighter, I positioned her to straddle me. I wrapped my arms around her waist, and she held my face between her hands as she placed her forehead against mine, still riding out her mini explosions. When her eyes met mine, they were hungry for more. With the hand I had used to wipe her juices, I placed my index and middle fingers against her lips.

"Taste yourself. Taste how good you taste to me."

Gripping my wrist with her hand, she licked her pretty, pouty lips, parted them, and slid both fingers into her mouth. Slowly, she glided my fingers in and out from the tip to the base as if they were another part of my body. My brows furrowed. It turned me on, and my chest heaved up and down at the motion. When she stuck her tongue out and licked my hand, I could no longer restrain myself.

I lifted her and eased her down on my shaft, pushing my way into her softness. Nestled inside of her, I felt cocooned by her love. The connection made us both shudder with delight. Our eyes closed as we relished in our oneness. No one had ever felt like this to me. Her body was my sanctuary, and I could've stayed there in reverence of her temple forever. Surprise overcame me as Nissi began moving her hips up and down my length as my thoughts drifted. The deep, slow roll of her movements caused me to clasp her by her cheeks and push inside to the hilt.

"Nissssiii." My voice came out lowly and gruffly.

She was more than my sanctuary. She was my home.

Seeing the emotion coursing through my being, she didn't let up. My head fell back against the headrest in euphoric bliss. I had wanted to beast out on her, claim her, but she was claiming me. The sound of her juices sloshing as she rodeoed on me made my chest heave and my mind fog over. Nissi was screwing the literal fuck out of me.

"Bae…baby. Ease…ease up," I groaned through bated breaths as I tried to settle my spirit, but she was snatching my soul.

"Kannon," she bellowed so seductively that I almost blew my top. "You feel too good. *This* feels too good," she declared breathlessly.

Gripping her waist, I let her ride me any way she wanted and enjoyed feeling the swell of my thickness inside her warm center. How she managed to feel more incredible with every stroke, I do not know. When her muscles clamped down on me, I shot up, holding her close, causing my stroke to go deeper inside her. I knew I would blow like molten lava inside her, and I needed her to come with me.

"Shiiiittt, Nisssi," I howled to the moon.

Her eyes fluttered as she peered into my intense gaze.

"Can I come inside my sweet, sweet pussy?"

Those deep guttural words must've been more than she could handle because she groaned deeply, and her head fell against my shoulder, unable to control her bearings.

Her next words were gritted and sensual—the melody to my soul.

"I'm coming, Kannon."

Nissi wrapped her arms around my neck and rode herself into oblivion. She came so hard that she belted out her pleasure, my very own erotic ballad composed and performed by her. As soon as I felt her rain shower splash on my tip, I held her tightly with my head nestled between her scrumptious breasts, and I blasted off inside the only woman I had ever experienced without a layer of protection. And I didn't give two damns. She owned my pleasure and me.

As our heads slowly lifted, our silent gazes met. Our breaths were jagged, and we heaved in the air as our bodies began to settle. That's when the reality and gravity of our situation began to come into focus. We were still connected at our cores, but I could feel the gravitational pull of Nissi struggling to snatch herself away from me. While I was in bliss, Nissi morphed into panic, lifting from me and hurriedly sliding her panties over her legs and hips.

"What have I done?" She palmed her forehead with her eyes closed. "I can't believe I did this!"

"Whoa. Wait." After sliding my briefs and slacks back on my waist, I turned to face her.

"No. I can't wait. I need to get back inside. I need to get back to my man!" She scuffled around for her heels.

The wind was knocked out of my sails at her declaration, causing me to fall back against the seat. Lifting my fingertips to my forehead, I rubbed my temple, trying to make sense of what Nissi was telling me. When I saw her hand reach for the door handle, I gripped her, halting her from opening the door.

"Wait a minute, Nissi. Please," I begged, my eyes dancing around just as panicked as she was. "After what we just did, what I just confessed, you're still going back to him?"

Her focus was on my hand covering her arm before she looked back at me with an unreadable expression.

"Kannon," she said breathily, "I just…we're just…maybe… perhaps another time or lifetime…we could've."

She inhaled sharply, unable to develop a coherent thought for what she attempted to say. However, I understood her babbling translation. She didn't want me. She still wanted him. Benji. That prick *Benji*. Despite everything, she would still walk away from me. She would walk away from us.

Leaning forward, I gently grasped her hands in mine.

"Nissi." Her name came out strangled with emotions I didn't know I had been withholding. "You know it should be me by your side as your man. I'm begging you, let's explore what we've known since the day we met."

"But how do you know we're supposed to be together or even that we'll work out?"

"Because I do!" I hollered, my frustration unmistakable. "I know you feel that. I know you see that. I know you want that. As bad as I do. My wrongness stopped us once before. Don't let your mistake do that now."

Her head reared back, and she scoffed. "My *mistake?*"

The offense was damning. She snatched her hands away.

"No, allowing myself to believe you were a different type of man was my mistake. Sleeping with you on the first date was my mistake. Slipping up with you now was my mistake. You were plain conniving. There's a difference." She reached for the door handle, and I didn't stop her this time. "So, yes, I'm going back inside full of guilt and regret to a man who knows how to handle my heart without an intentional *mistake.*"

She opened the door and stepped out, and I stepped out behind her. After taking several steps, she turned around while I was fastening my slacks.

"And another thing, my man may not be packaged as Kannon Jordan, but at least I know he's mine, and he doesn't lie to me."

That's when the burning inferno in the pit of my stomach bubbled over and ripped right through me. My fluid steps closed our gap, and I pointed at her.

"For the record, I own the bad decision I made regarding you, but I'll tell you what…I bet your man ain't owned up to his."

Her eyes flashed with confusion, but I answered her questions before she could even process the question to ask.

"Benji Eloi is my damn dentist and one of my brother's friends and gym clients. I'd bet a million to one that he pursued you after my dental visit, where I discussed with him my TikTok date and how I had messed up. I never knew why he wanted to spend so much time questioning me about it and asking where we stood after the date. But I found out today. Ask him if his actions were an intentional mistake or a coincidence."

She stood there stunned, with her mouth agape, and I waited for her to say something. Anything. She had lost the steam and vibrato of her attitude, but then she turned a blank stare to me, and I couldn't read her expression. When I thought she would say something, her mouth snapped shut. Then she blinked once, turned on her heels, and hightailed it inside the venue.

Refusing to stand there like a bump on a log, I slowly turned away from the venue, got back into my truck, and left.

Chapter Twenty-Six

NISSI

WHAT HAD I *just done?* My thoughts swirled around my head like a whirlwind. One moment I was getting some much-needed air, and the next, Kannon was balls deep inside my yoni. That Judas little twat of mine. I couldn't believe I had let that happen *again*. After all the hurt and pain he had put me through because he had a woman, he'd blown through this wedding and made me no better than him. Soiled. I was now the cheat.

I burst through the hotel doors when I realized I could not go back into the ballroom with the stench of Kannon on my nether region. Switching directions, I ran as fast as possible in my dress, grateful that the line on the other end of the hall was non-existent.

I dashed inside the restroom and quickly checked the three stalls. Once confident I was alone, I locked the main door and rushed to the sink. Turning on the hot water, I waved my hand over the automatic paper towel dispenser several times, gathering as many as possible. The aroma of berries filled the air as I squirted a hefty amount of liquid hand soap onto the towels and then placed them on the countertop to slip my thongs off. A mixture of my juices and Kannon's semen had ruined my undergarment, so I tossed them into the trash receptacle and cleaned between my thighs. Shudders rippled through me as I cleansed around my throbbing bud and folds, evidence of the weakened state I was still experiencing from my forbidden backseat rendezvous. Shaking my head free of those thoughts, I chucked the paper towels, used fresh ones to rinse myself, and then dried off. After washing and drying my hands, I braced myself against the sink with my hands and bent my head to gather myself.

So many thoughts were running through my mind— Kannon's admission of his reason for his breakup with River, his declaration of his feelings for me, and his accusatory stance on Benji. _Benji._ Oh, God. My emotions were torn. Instead of beating myself up as I should have, I was conflicted between confronting Benji about Kannon's confession and apologizing for my infidelity.

There was no way Benji could've done something like that. Benji and I had a history, having been friends for years. Besides, Benji had always been truthful with me about everything. I couldn't force myself to believe Kannon. Benji wouldn't do something like that. Then it dawned on me that I was still hiding out, and my sisters and Benji were probably about to send a search party for me. Besides, nothing would get resolved by hiding out in the hotel's restroom.

Squaring my shoulders, I spruced my curly locks and headed back inside the ballroom to rejoin my sisters and my man. When I returned, I saw Benji and Kinston in what appeared to be a heated debate, but their voices were lowered. As soon as my sisters spotted me, Angela's eyes ballooned as she pointed to Kinston and Benji, and Aquila sprang from her seat to meet me.

"What is going on with Kinston and Benji?" I asked before she could get a word out.

Aquila placed her hands on her hips, and her head fell to the side.

"What the hell does it look like they're doing, singing negro spirituals? Angela is trying to keep the tension between them at bay so we don't get thrown out by security or the bride and groom."

She huffed, swiping her hand across her forehead before she deadpanned on me.

"Where's Kannon?" Her eyes shone with curiosity while her tone was accusatory.

With a shrug and an eye roll, I quipped, "I don't know, and I don't care."

Looking past Aquila, I caught Angela giving me the eye signal of distress.

"Enough about him. We need to get back over there before things get out of hand."

Turning to see what had my focus, Aquila blew a heated breath and followed me.

"This is ridiculous," she muttered as we hightailed it over to Kinston and Benji.

Angela had her hands gripped on Kinston's arms as Kinston pointed a finger in Benji's face.

"I was trying to be civilized to you, but I see you ain't nothing more than a bitch-made punk."

Some patrons heard Kinston and turned to figure out what was happening amid small grumbles of oohs. Reaching them, I stepped in between the two men.

"Hey, hey. Please stop this. I don't know the issue, but this is neither the time nor the place."

"Tell all brawn and no brain that again," Benji slurred, pointing his finger at Kinston.

Kinston tensed, and I swore every muscle hidden behind his suit flexed, indicating his brute strength. It made me extremely nervous for Benji because Kinston was godlike compared to

Benji. If he put his hands on Benji, it would be a murder case, and I was positive that was not how Cami wanted to remember her wedding.

"Run that back again?" Kinston bit out, tilting his ear slightly toward Benji.

My sisters and I turned, pleading with our eyes to Kinston.

"He didn't say anything," I said.

Angela moved beside me. "Please stop this, Kinston. It's not worth it."

Aquila stood on the other side of me. "You're better than this," she said, addressing Kinston.

It was as if our presence and the small set of onlookers flickered Kinston's sensibility. Flipping the tip of his nose, he stood back with his hands raised in surrender.

"Yeah, I'ma fallback. I need to get out of here before I light this wedding up."

Benji smirked at him, but the snarl was still on Kinston's face. His lips tightened into a grimace as he tried to exercise restraint. Suddenly, his eyes fell on me before glancing around the ballroom.

"Where's my brother?"

"I think he left. That's all I know," I answered with my hands raised.

Kinston pulled out his cell phone; he had missed a call. He shook his head and looked over at Angela.

"Listen, I gotta go. I'm sorry about how this went down. I hope we can have a chance to meet on better terms."

Angela nodded. "It's okay. Just go."

Her words were empathic as she placed a comforting hand on his arm. Kinston nodded before he turned and made a mad dash toward the front entrance.

Benji pointed toward him with a glass tumbler in his hand. "Exactly. Fuck him and his brother."

"Benji, that's enough!" I bellowed after noticing Kinston had stopped before continuing his stride out of the venue.

Benji waved his hand in the direction of Kinston. "Punks like him aren't worthy of women like you," he slurred.

My sisters and I turned to look at him with sheer astonishment at his deposition. He walked a few paces and sat his tumbler down before buttoning his jacket and gliding clumsily away from the table back to me.

"Come on, bèl mwen. Let's dance."

Without waiting for an answer, he wrapped his arm around my waist, jerking me close to him. A gasp escaped my lips at the forced connection as Benji snapped his fingers with his other hand and began slowly gyrating against me.

"Benji, that's enough. I think you've had way too much to drink."

The nervous energy swirling in my core caused me to glance around frantically, hoping no one noticed our awkward interaction.

"Damn those two for trying to wreck our good time," he seethed, his words coming out in a low growl. "I just want to share a dance with *my* woman."

Aquila stepped up to us. "I think you need to let my sister take you home and cool off. And that," she pointed her acrylic nail in his face, "is not an ask. That's a demand."

He stared at her, and his slurred laughter accompanied his gaze, indicating his disbelief.

"Oh, come on, Aquila—"

"I do believe my sister said it wasn't an ask because best believe we can give you the answer," Angela intercepted, crossing her arms over her chest. "Get your half-drunk ass outta here before we sober you up real quick."

Benji looked back and forth between the three of us, swallowed, and then straightened up. "All right."

He fished his keys out of his pocket and handed them to me. Snatching them, I glowered at him. "Let me get my purse."

When I grabbed it and returned the few steps where he stood with my sisters, I announced, "I'm ready. Let's go."

When Benji went to walk toward me, my sisters stepped into his path.

"If you get out of hand with my sister, we'll lay hands on you," Aquila quipped with fierce big sister sternness.

Angela pushed him slightly with her fingertips to ensure he understood Aquila's threat. "And that's on Mary had a baby named Jesus."

He lifted his hands. "Okayyy."

My sisters walked with him over to me and hugged me.

"You call us when you make it, and if you need us for any reason, we're a phone call away. You got it?" Aquila reassured me.

I felt like we were little kids again, with my sister-mama Aquila to the rescue.

A warm smile that didn't reach my eyes graced my face. Patting her hand, I assured her that I would be fine. Wrapping my arm around Benji's, we strolled toward the front entrance. He was gibbering about whatever his lushed lips could talk about while I prayed we made it out the door and to his house without further incident.

The ride to Benji's house was quiet, not that I didn't have anything to say to him, but he had fallen asleep before I could get to the traffic light at the hotel entrance. He needed it with his drunken state.

As I drove, my mind began to settle from the calamity of events at the wedding. That only caused my brain to go into overdrive surrounding the little nuisances that started to surface. I hadn't wanted to believe Kannon, but I couldn't deny it was evident that Kinston and Benji had known each other above casual pleasantries. I had been so focused on trying to stop Kinston from pummeling Benji that it didn't dawn on me that they actually knew each other until now. Then there was the fact that Benji was in a drunken stupor. Benji was a man of refinement; he never let his boxers show. It was not like him to allow himself to get two sheets to the wind in public around mostly strangers. In college, the only times he ever got wasted were at his birthday party thrown by his frat brothers and when he was stressed about taking his Jurisprudence exam. He'd been a straight-and-narrow man all the time I'd known him, only doing just enough to have fun without overdoing it. Getting sloshed out of his mind at a wedding where he didn't even know the bride or groom assuredly did not qualify. Mulling over those facts, I had no choice but to consider what Kannon had told me, especially since the number one fact exploded in my mind. Kannon knew Benji's full name and his profession. He had said it in his angered rant to me. *Benji Eloi is my damn dentist.*

"We're here," I announced, lightly tapping Benji's arm.

"Mmm," he grunted as he jumped, then stilled himself before slowly leaning forward and rubbing the sleep out of his eyes with the heels of his hands. "Ugh. What?"

With a sideways glare, I reiterated, "We're here. At your house. Time to get out and go inside."

After removing the keys from the ignition, I grabbed my purse and exited his car. I was up the steps of his house when I saw the passenger side door open. Benji planted one foot on the concrete and slowly emerged from his car. The effects of his drunken good time were on full display. His face looked worn and exhausted, and his dress shirt was halfway out of his pants and wrinkled. He closed the car door, placed folded arms on the roof of the car, and laid his head against them. Impatiently, I shifted my weight onto my right foot as I watched him try to gather himself.

"Benji, let's go inside." I knew my tone came off as heated as I felt.

Lifting his head, he scrubbed his hands down his face amid a deep groan, then stuck his hands in his pockets. When he couldn't find what he was looking for, he patted his pockets and checked his suit jacket pocket. I raised his key fob and pressed the lock button with an attitude. The blare of the lock alarm caused Benji to jump back and throw an irritating glare in my direction.

"I have your car keys because I drove. Let's go in the house."

He grabbed his head. "Okay. Okay. Can you stop yelling?"

"I'm not yelling... yet." I started to press the lock on the fob again to be nasty.

Benji finally straightened up and made his way to the house. He slowly grabbed ahold of the wooden railing and carefully placed each lemon pepper stepper on the steps. It felt like I was watching him walk the green mile; he took so long. When he finally reached the porch, I unlocked the door and stepped inside as he made his way inside the threshold behind me and shut the door.

By the time he entered the living room, I was standing there with my arms folded, already in confrontation mode. Benji took one look at me, shook his head, and released a deep breath before slipping off his suit jacket. He knew the battle was coming whether he was prepared for war or not. Hell, I wasn't even prepared, but we were going to have this conversation, ready or not.

"Benji, I do not want to argue with you—"

"Then don't," he said, cutting me off abruptly. His tone stung a bit.

"Then tell me the truth."

"Tell you the truth," he scoffed, placing his hands in his pants pocket and squaring his shoulders with indignation.

Confused, my head fell back at the hint of audacity in his words. It was the arrogance of it all for me. As if I weren't entitled to the truth. As angry as I had gotten while contemplating the facts on the ride to his place, the last thing he wanted to do was bark up the wrong tree with me. My impromptu sex session be damned.

"I see you have your ass on your shoulders, so I'll get straight to the point." I lit up, tossing a hand on my jutted hip. "So you know Kinston *and Kannon?*"

"I do, and what does it matter?"

"*What does it matter?*" I asked incredulously. "Benji! You know exactly why it matters!"

He put his hand up to stop my rant. "Actually, no, I don't, Nissi. I really don't. Unless you lied to me, you and Kannon were over when we started dating."

"We never had anything to begin with—"

"If that's the case, why are you giving me the third degree when we should be talking about the fact that the bastard tried my manhood tonight by pushing up on you while we were out on a date together?"

Though Benji's point was valid, it did nothing to stop my burning questions.

"It matters because that means you lied to me."

Benji pumped both of his hands to stop me. "Whoa. Whoa. *Lied to you* is a bit dramatic. Don't you think? Did I not reveal information to you? Yes. That hardly qualifies as lying, though."

"Letting me believe you knew nothing about the situation with Kannon or who he was does qualify when you were giving me the third degree about him and his belongings! It's as if you were trying to set me up or something."

Benji scoffed and brought his fingers to the side of his head, massaging his temples.

"Set you up? So you're on some 'stretch the truth' lies tonight. The situation with Kannon happened before us. Clothing and all. So, even if I hadn't known him, the same conversation would've been had between us."

"You were using the situation as leverage over me!"

"No, I leveraged the situation!" he yelled pointedly, using his hand for emphasis. "There's a difference."

His admission was a swift kick to the gut. He had used the situation to play on my emotions. I couldn't believe Benji was capable of such treachery. Until now.

"Wow." I tossed my hands up in the air. "You're perfectly fine with playing on my emotions to get what you want. That's low, Benji. Even for you. And Kinston? He was your friend. You knew he and Kannon were brothers. How could you?"

"*For you!*"

His words boomed like a cannon across the room, leaving us standing in the aftermath of the smoke and mirrors game he had been playing. He rubbed his forehead.

"Gawddamnit, Nissi. Am I friends with Kinston? Yes. Have been for about four years. Is Kannon my client? Yes. He has been since I entered private practice. Did I know they were brothers? Did I already know about your whole TikTok affair? Did I use that to my advantage? Yes. Yes. And hell yes! While keeping that knowledge to myself and pretending I knew nothing about it may be splitting hairs on some level, I didn't do anything wrong because you were never his woman. Being Kinston's friend, should he be upset that I went after a woman I knew his brother wanted? Yes, he has that right, but it still doesn't make me wrong. I knew you. I had you. I *loved* you...well before Kannon knew you even existed. Whether I'm viewed as wrong, right, or indifferent in the way I handled my pursual of you doesn't negate the fact that Kannon screwed his own chances, and you were free and clear for me to pursue just like any other man. Did I do what I had to do to secure you? Yes. All is fair in love and war, and no victor in history has ever made any apologies for that. Neither will I."

A lump formed in my throat because, as deceiving as this entire catastrophe was, he had a valid point. Several actually. Yet and still, I felt used and betrayed by the fact that he simply couldn't or rather chose not to be honest with me. That's the part that hurt.

Walking up to him with teary eyes, I placed my hands on his chest. He clasped his hands over mine, holding them in place.

"If you believe that beyond it being an excuse to weasel out of any culpability, you would've been honest with me. As you stated, there was no reason for you not to be. I wasn't his, and Kannon had screwed himself out of his chance. I'm hurt because you weren't forthcoming with me while demanding I do the same. I'm disappointed in you."

My eyes watered, and I stepped back from him while clearing the droplets from my cheeks. When I looked up, Benji's expression was stoic. He was right. He held no apologies for Kinston, Kannon, or me. That changed my entire outlook on him.

As I turned to leave, Benji called out to me.

"So you're disappointed in me for my lack of honesty, but honesty begets honesty, Nissi. What about you? Hmm? You can stand there on your high and mighty horse, claiming that this little tirade is solely about my lack of being forthcoming, but we both know that's not entirely true. Kinston and Kannon being upset with me, I get. Not you. Your advocation is for Kannon and is hidden behind your disdain of my unwillingness to tell you my connection to them. Why don't you be honest with me about your anger regarding this situation? And you can start by being honest with yourself."

His assertion stopped me in my tracks because he was correct. Yes, I was disappointed in him for his lack of honesty with me, but that reason was twofold. One, I was disappointed because he hadn't been, but I was also upset because I think if I had known, I might not have given him a chance romantically. Hell, I knew that. I knew it because no matter how hard I tried, I couldn't get Kannon Jordan out of my brain or heart. And there it was—my ugly, inexplicable, but extremely honest truth.

Turning back to face him, my gaze fell to the floor as I twiddled with the tassel on my clutch. Honesty begets honesty. I couldn't judge him if I couldn't tell myself or him the truth.

Hitting the sides of my legs, I lifted my head and shrugged. "You're right. It is a partial advocation for Kannon. Truth is, I developed feelings for him that I can't explain and that I have tried my damndest to get rid of, but it is hard to tell you or anybody that because I can't explain something I don't understand for myself."

"Is that why you're struggling with loving me?"

There was the ultimate reason for this inquisition. The waterfall I had been trying to contain broke free with that one simple question, and I dropped my teary face into the palm of my hand, unable to look at Benji. All I could do was nod as I continued shedding the river of tears that wouldn't stop streaming down my face.

After a moment, I felt strong arms encase me. Benji pressed me close to his chest as I released my unshed emotions. His hand brushed up and downward strokes over the small of my back for a long while before I felt the crook of his finger under my chin, lifting my head until we were eye to eye.

"Nissi, I—"

"I slept with Kannon in his truck at the wedding. I'm so sorry," I confessed, the words tumbling from my trembling lips.

Benji's hand dropped from my chin, and his eyes snapped shut. I felt his body stiffen for a moment before he stepped back from me.

"I'm sorry, Benji. We were arguing, and then he was up on me and kissing me, and it just…we just…it happened."

I pleaded for unspoken forgiveness as he stood before me, pacing the floor and wiping his hands down his face. When he finally stopped pacing, he stared at me for what felt like eons. Pinching the bridge of his nose, I saw a few tears drop from his eyes before he released a shaky breath.

"I love you so gotdamn much," he whispered. "Too much." He looked up, then slowly approached me and lifted my hand into his. "I guess that's my karma in all of this. I'm willing to look past your indiscretion, but you must decide where you want to be. I can't make that decision for you."

"Benji—"

He raised his hand, silencing me. "Please don't make a decision right now, but I ask that you allow me to put in my plea for your heart."

I obliged, and he gently slid my wet face between the palms of his hands as he stared into my orbs. Our watery eyes matched each other's pain.

"What you experienced with me may not be shrouded with the allure of TikTok excitement and enveloped in the thrill of some internet-hyped connection, but I'm here— standing right here for you, with you, beside…you. I can't be Kannon. I can only be Benji. I'm not adventurous or a risk-taker, but I'll tell you what

I am. I'm loyal, and I am *yours*. And I love you, bél mwen. When I love, I love for a lifetime, and I hope that can be enough."

Benji's sincerity touched my soul in a way it never had before. How sincerely dope was this man to not only forgive my indiscretion but show his complete vulnerability to me in a moment where my carelessness and thoughtlessness had shattered his manhood? He was a king personified. Therefore, I internally agreed to take truthful consideration of our relationship. I had to soul search for what I wanted, whether with Benji or Kannon, but mostly for me. How blessed was I to have someone who loved me so completely? For that reason alone, regardless of our outcome, I would always have love for Benji because of the heart of this man.

I placed my hand on his cheek and smiled at him. "Thank you."

He returned my smile, and I turned to leave. I needed to go home, shower, and process this day and my feelings. Before I reached the door, Benji called out to me, and I turned to face him again. He stood at the end of the foyer with his hands in his pockets.

"Honesty begets honesty. So, I feel I should tell you this. It wasn't my prying into Kannon's time with you that led me to pursue you." When my eyebrow lifted quizzically, he continued, "I bumped into your sister, Angela, at the gas station the week we reconnected. She invited me to come out to the restaurant that night. She said you'd gone through a rough breakup, so she hoped I could rekindle our flame. Between Kannon's botched attempt and the invite, I felt that was my sign. So, I went for it. I hope you're not mad at your sister or me. I just felt you should know."

Chapter Twenty-Seven

KANNON

"I FIGURED I'D FIND you out here."

Never removing my hands from my pockets, I turned to see Kinston taking slowed steps along the plush greenery toward me. Rather than wait on him to reach me, I re-centered my focus back to in front of me, my head tilted somberly. Kinston placed a firm hand on my shoulder with a comforting squeeze, and I gripped it as a sign of appreciation. He paused before removing his hand and then moved a few steps forward. Once he stopped, he kissed his fingertips before placing them on the top of the smooth marble headstone.

"I love you, Mama," he said softly as he stood in reverence.

After a beat, he stepped back, standing directly beside me. When he didn't speak, my eyes swung over in his direction. He had taken the same stance as me, hands in pockets as he gazed around and inhaled the fresh air.

"I see why you enjoy it out here. It's peaceful. Reminds me of Mama."

It was true. When I was a kid, I was terrified of anything associated with death, especially cemeteries. No way anyone could convince me that visiting a loved one in a graveyard was peaceful, serene, or therapeutic. Until Marie Georgette Jordan was laid to rest. Having been raised in the faith, I understood my mother's soul didn't live in this six-foot-deep hole underneath the dirt, gravel, grass, flowers, and marble stone. No, I was fully aware that my mother's precious soul was dancing in Paradise. However, this was where her remains had been placed as a place of reverence for us. Coming here connected my earthly plane with her spiritual realm; whenever I was here, I felt her overwhelming presence. That was when my view of the cemetery changed because it forever changed my life.

Droplets formed on my lids as I stared at the inscription on the headstone as I had countless times before. I raised my hand, using my thumb and index finger to swipe my eyes before they fell. God, I missed her so much. My mother had been my world—the only lady in my life until I found my Mrs. Forever. My heart panged for the one woman who could provide the clarity I needed. I had been so sure about Nissi, only to have it blow up in my face. If my mother had been here, she would've known and expertly advised me on what to do and say. She probably would've divulged to me that I'd been wasting my time pining away for a woman who didn't want me. Then I could've spared myself the embarrassment of public humiliation and rejection that had shredded my soul. Here I was, out here, hoping to feel something that could allow me to pick up the pieces of my aching heart and bruised ego and move on with my life sans Nissi.

"What happened between you and Nissi, bro?"

Kinston's straightforward question floated into the quiet of the evening air. Gruffly, I exhaled a goaded breath. Sliding the tip of my thumb across the lines in my forehead, I tried to suppress the parking lot fiasco from invading my thoughts, but as soon as Nissi's name fell off Kinston's lips, my mind spiraled with thoughts of our backseat escapades. Flashes of Nissi and me in the throes of passion flooded my memory bank. I could still taste her flavor on my lips. Fresh. Succulent. My mouth watered at the recollection of having her tooted up with my face planted between those pretty globular cheeks sandwiched in my hands. Her scent still wafted through my nostrils, causing my man below to lurch against the zipper of my pants. The remembrance of her wetness gliding up and down my shaft, her hips rolling, pussy sloshing as I touched her walls caused my growing erection. Her breathy moans. The way my name sounded through her bated breaths. It all just...*fuck*! Nissi Richards' vice grip on my entire life was annoyingly maddening. I couldn't even have a decent conversation with my brother about her without losing my damn mind.

"I confessed everything to her. I explained about River and how I felt and even that punk of a boyfriend of hers, and she still rejected me." Turning to the side to look at my brother, I added, "And that was after having the most mind-blowing quickie I'd ever had in my life in the backseat of my truck."

Recognition hit Kinston, and he slowly turned his head to return my stare.

"Wait. Bruh, so you tapped her in the hotel parking lot?"

I didn't reply, and Kinston ran his hand down his face and blew out. "What did she say?"

"She said I made her a cheat just like me and said she made a mistake, before throwing up how perfect and innocent her *man* was."

"That snake *mutha*—"

"Tell me about it. I swear he's catching a fade if I ever see him."

Kinston turned and slapped hands with me. "Oh, he is definitely about to be *faded* then because I fo' sho' got a few tags waiting on him. In the comfort of the wedding and the guise of being drunk, he tried to play me like I'm a sucka after he'd already disrespected my baby bro?" He flicked the tip of his nose, attempting to bite back his anger. "Nah, that motherfucka catching it on principalities alone. I took that 'L' for Cami and

to show Angela that I was mature, but oooh, he got me tight."
Kinston grunted angrily with balled-up fists, his shoulders tense.

I hated seeing my brother angered. Kinston was chill and extremely laid back, so he didn't get riled up easily. When someone managed to anger him, there was an entirely different side of Kinston that surfaced. I always said he had two different personalities—Miami and Dade County. Kinston—at the gym, flexing his muscles, joking, flirting with the ladies, running his business, cooling with his friends and me—that was Mr. Miami. Kinston—head-bussin' ring-a-ding-ding—that was Dade County. Dade County gave zero fucks.

"Don't worry about it, bro. I served the 'L' right back to him with that long stroke, cervix poke in the back of my steamboat to his woman," I quipped, pumping my waist.

Kinston and I looked at each other and barreled in laughter as he playfully boxed me on the shoulders.

"Boi, you wild!" Kinston laughed before we settled down. After a beat, Kinston said, "Thanks, bro. I know you only said that to calm me down. Nissi means way more to you than some revenge ploy."

My gaze fell again, and I was back to square one, muddled over my jacked-up feelings for Nissi. "Yeah."

Kinston shrugged his shoulders. "So that's it? You're just gonna give up on her?"

My jaw flexed with tension as I interlocked my fingers. "There's nothing more I can do. I've done it all repeatedly. There are only so many times a person can tell you they don't want you before you have to believe it. My belief kicked in right after she screwed the hell outta me and chose her fraudulent boyfriend. I want that woman so bad my chest aches, but I can't do this anymore, Kin. I gave her an opportunity to choose me like I chose her, and she chose to walk away." I hunched my shoulders. "So that's what I'm doing."

Kinston nodded with pursed lips. "If that's the case, why are you out here?"

"Praying to God and Mama that it was the right thing to do."

"Hmm," Kinston hummed before giving me three soft pats on the back.

It was the first time I had asked my mother for confirmation, and it hadn't settled my spirit. When I arrived pissed, hurt, and confused, I just knew coming to visit my mother would confirm my decision and make me feel confident walking away. While visiting my mother had calmed my anger, it had done little to release Nissi's hold on me. I had never felt this way about a woman, so perhaps deciding to move forward was enough, and the peace of the decision would come later. Hopefully, letting go of my desires for her would soon follow. I wanted to see Nissi happy, although I felt that happiness was with me. If she didn't feel the same, I couldn't force her, and I was done trying. As much as I didn't want to see her with Benji Eloi, I would be happy for her if that made her happy. Begrudgingly.

The only thing I knew for certain was that love was overrated, and I vowed never to play in that playground again. It wasn't built for me, and apparently, I wasn't built for it. I resounded that the only woman for me had been Marie Georgette Jordan. Bachelor life, it was.

My thoughts were brought to the current moment when I overheard the same prayer I always repeated every time I visited my mother's grave.

"Heavenly Father, thank you for the time we had. Heal me of the hurt from the time we lost. Give me hope for the time when we will reunite. Clarity, peace, and love abound. Amen."

"Amen," I said after my brother.

With that, we both turned and walked away in silence.

Chapter Twenty-Eight

NISSI

"OOP! WELL, HELLO there. It's good to hear that you're at least alive."

My head reared against the arm of my sofa as I muted the television. I don't even know why I answered the phone. I already knew she would be on her BS the second the line connected. To keep my attitude at bay, I pushed a forced puff of air through my pursed lips.

"Don't. You can miss me with the theatrics today, Aquila."

She gasped, obviously taken aback by my words. It was a response she would usually receive from Angela, not me. I was always the laidback, clever comeback type, not the snappy clapback type. That didn't mean I didn't have it in me. There was no doubt I had the skill, especially being the baby sister of two of the biggest clapback queens in history. However, someone had to be mild-mannered between the three of us to bridge the gap, so that was my role. It was how I fit into this power-packed trio to claim my spot of individuality in the Richards' sister clan. Still, I held a little spark and enough sass to smack fire from my lips when I wasn't beat for the BS. The way I'd felt this past week, I was a fire-breathing dragon. Tread light.

"Who pissed in your cornflakes this morning?" Aquila scoffed. "Outside of a quick text that only said, *I'm home, and everything is cool*, we haven't heard a peep from you after that circus show at Cami's wedding, and I'm the bad person for checking in?"

Technically, she was right. These pent-up emotions I was experiencing weren't her fault. But it was her usual condensing tone that set me off. Although I knew that was her natural way, I wasn't in the mood. After what I had gone through, I was allowed to have a mood.

"My cornflakes have been soggy since last Saturday. So, a little less lip service would be greatly appreciated."

A beat passed before Aquila spoke again. "Listen, sis. Last weekend was a complete catastrophe. I'll give you that, but nothing major popped off. Between Kinston, Benji, and Kannon, it could've been way worse. Hell, it should've been worse."

"So what are you saying, Aquila?"

"I'm saying you can't be this upset over that. Something else had to have happened. What is going on, Nissi?"

The concern in her voice melted the ice running through my veins, but not enough to have the conversation she was fishing for.

"To be honest, I don't want to talk about it. It's nothing against you, but I just need time to process things in my head, ya know?"

I could sense her urge to pry, but she chose not to push the subject.

"Okay. Okay. I understand and respect that. I want you to know I'm here for you."

My resolve melted at her relented inquiries.

"Thank you." It floated out weak and almost childlike.

"Oh, Nissi," she breathed out worriedly.

Sucking back tears, I shook my head as I swiped them away. Thank God we weren't on Facetime.

"I'm good, Aquila."

A pregnant pause permeated between the airwaves before Aquila cleared her throat.

"Are you going to the family dinner at Mommy and Daddy's today?"

Heaving a sigh with my eyes closed, I answered, "Yeah, I'll be there."

"Oh, okay then," she said, the perkiness in her voice signifying she was pleased to know I wasn't cutting off all interaction with them. "Okay, sis. Well, I'll see you then."

"All right, sissie. See you later."

"Oh, and Nissi—" she called before I disconnected the line.

"Yeah?"

"Call Angela. She's been calling you and says she hasn't heard from you either. We're both simply concerned. Hit her line."

I grinned as we hung up. Aquila's newness to all things social media was prevalent in her speech.

"Hit her line," I repeated and chuckled to myself.

I placed my phone down beside me as my head lolled backward. I didn't bother to unmute the television as I lay there. My eyes grew heavy, already exhausted, just from the phone call from my sister. I decided I would get a couple of hours of shut-eye before preparing for dinner at my parents' house. Lord knows I needed it.

"We were just about to put out an APB on you."

That was the first thing my mother said as soon as I turned the corner to the kitchen, where my sisters and dad stood laughing and talking around the kitchen island. I hadn't meant to be late, but apparently, I was more exhausted than I realized. I had overslept and decided to take my precious time getting dressed. Dinner started at four p.m. promptly, and here I was, waltzing in at a quarter after five like I didn't have a care in the world. No lie. I hoped they would have been midway through the meal so I could eat and leave as soon as possible.

Everyone's attention turned to me after hearing my mother's comment regarding my tardy presence. Although irritated, I would never pop fly with my mother. My life might have been in disarray, but I still valued it. Abigail Richards was old school. She respected that I was an adult and afforded me the peace of going through my battles, but what I could not do was take those battles out on her lest I was ready to end the battle of life. And Nisante Richards would be right there to beat me down the extra six feet Abigail would have buried me under. While her comment grated one of the few last nerves I was desperately holding on to, I dared not show or speak that to her. Instead, I plastered the biggest fake smile I could muster from the depths of my soul and embraced her with an apology.

"I'm sorry for being late, Mama. I was napping and overslept."

Pulling back from our embrace, I shifted my body to hug my father.

"Hmmm. Overslept? At four in the afternoon? Let me find out Benji had you so preoccupied last night that it made you tired this evening. I like him, but not that much."

Grinning, I playfully slapped my father's shoulder.

"Daddy!" I shrieked, surprise dancing in my eyes.

"Don't stand up here and act like you girls aren't mischievous. I know for certain I didn't give birth to Jezebels, but I didn't give birth to any Ruths either," he teased, much to our chagrin, although it did tickle us.

Angela wagged her finger as she choked out a rebuttal. "Speak on those two." She pointed between Aquila and me. "I am thy humble and loyal servant, Oh Lord."

"As humble and loyal as Delilah," I grumbled as I squeezed Aquila to me about the waist.

Angela and Aquila gasped at my words, both giving me looks of disbelief.

My mother swatted my free hand and pointed at me scathingly. "I heard that. That's not nice, Nissi. Even if you girls do play around too much, some things are too low."

Shrugging, I snatched a chip from Aquila's bag and popped it into my mouth. "Some people are low below, too, Mama."

My head was tilted downward, trying to force the nasty aftertaste of the disgraceful snack posed as a chip, when I felt the hush of silence waft through the kitchen. When I looked up, questioning eyes were all on me.

"What?" I asked nonchalantly.

Angela eased off the barstool and folded her arms, glaring at me. "You're our baby sister, so we know you've honed the art of clapbacks over the years, but it's not you. Is something going on that you want to discuss, sis?"

Her words were laced with concern, but I wasn't interested in speaking with her. I didn't have the strength for fake pleasantries and cooked-up lies. I just wanted to eat dinner with the rest of my family in peace. I hated that I even agreed to come knowing Angela would be there. Why couldn't she get tasked with a last-minute emergency at work or something?

Shaking my head, I offered a feeble shrug. "Nope, nothing." Turning to face my mother, I asked, "When are we going to eat? I'm famished."

My dad nudged me, bringing my attention back to him. "I'm calling Benji."

A strained bit of laughter trickled throughout the room as my mother led the caravan to the dining room, where dinner had been placed on the table. Sunday dinners were always a feast made for a king. My mother threw down in the kitchen, and I only prayed to one day be blessed with her level of culinary expertise. She had that milkshake that brought the boys to the yard and made them move into the house. My daddy has been trapped for over thirty years, and I'm sure part of the reason was her Sunday evening meals.

The table was filled with glazed ham, fried chicken, yellow rice, macaroni and cheese, candied yams, black-eyed peas, collard greens, fresh rolls, and peach cobbler. She had even compromised and made baked chicken for the resident health nut, Aquila. While her plate was only filled with the baked chicken, yellow rice, and her splurge of black-eyed peas, the rest of us loaded up on every menu item on the table before sitting and holding hands while Daddy blessed the food.

"The last thing you need to be doing is praying over that artery-clogging calamity. I don't know how you all continue to do this, knowing it's unhealthy," Aquila fussed.

"Well, dear, that's why we pray over it. So the Lord will allow it to add nourishment, not emergency room visits. That prayer covered your food, too," Mom cackled.

"I'm not saying it shouldn't be prayed over, Mama. I'm just saying. You all should pray to free your tastebuds of those unhealthy desires."

"Don't you start this good Sunday, Aquila," Daddy said, stabbing a pile of greens on his fork. "This is the same food that got you through the first eighteen years of your life. Now, if you want to change up and eat cardboard and plants, that's on you."

I almost spit my sweet tea out, hollering at our daddy. He almost laid our souls low with that foolishness. Angela coughed, and my mother put her head down, almost into her plate, trying to contain the laughter rippling through her.

"Ha! Ha! Laugh it up. I get a clean bill of health every doctor's visit," she touted before sipping her water. "No high blood pressure medicine for me."

"Good because you might need it to fight off listeria from having your salads recalled every other month," Mom chimed in as Aquila's mouth fell agape. Mom pointed her fork at her. "See, I got you with that one. Nothing we eat can fully be trusted, so we pray and eat. Now hush your mouth and eat that baked chicken you begged me to put on this menu."

Angela pointed at Mama. "And that's the part!" With a head toss, she threw more shade at Aquila. "Worry about yourself."

I could not resist. My fingers snapped before I could reel in my emotions, and I pointed at Angela. "No, *that's* the one! Right there. Worry about *yourself.*"

While I resumed stuffing my face, I felt pairs of eyes piercing into me. That's when I realized my words bit out as harshly as my mind had said them, although I hadn't meant them to. Everything Angela did and said got up under my skin these days.

Angela's fork clanked to the plate, and she shifted her body to gaze in my direction.

"Now that's the second time you've come for me. There won't be a third. What's your problem, Nissi?"

"I told you I don't have one." My words oozed out measured.

"Oh, yes, you do," she countered.

My head snapped to the side. "Well, not one I feel like addressing with you now. How about that?"

"Fine, then keep your lips closed from addressing me," she snarled, whipping around to finish her dinner.

"Girls—"

"Like you kept your lips closed about my business!"

The chord Angela had struck caused the confession to spew, thwarting whatever calls for peace my mother was about to demand.

"Here we go," Aquila sighed, placing her fork down and falling back against her seat.

I lifted my dinner napkin from my lap and threw it on the dining table. "You're damn right. Here we go."

"Now, Nissi, you need to watch your mouth in my house and your tone with your sister."

The boom in my dad's voice was usually threatening enough to back us into our corners. But not me. Not today. Not about this.

"I'll watch my tone with my so-called sister when she minds her mouth. She always has something to say and somebody's business to be all up in, except her loveless life!"

"Oop," Aquila gasped, covering her mouth as our parents' mouths fell agape.

Angela slid her chair back with such force that it tilted over and slammed to the floor as she stood facing me. "Run that back one more time."

I would not be deterred. She wanted it with me, and now, she had it.

Crossing my arms, I touted, "Oh, you heard me the first time, *sis*. The only person running something is you with your big mouth."

Our mother stood, slapping her linen napkin down on the table. The anger in her eyes matched the anger in my heart.

"Now that's enough! I will not have this foolishness at my dinner table. You all are too old for this."

Angela placed a finger up. "Wait a minute, Mama. Let her say what she's been itching to say to me." Her arms spread to land on each side of her hips with an air of cockiness on her face.

"You told Benji about what happened with Kannon and me and invited him to the restaurant! How could you? Here I thought it was impeccable timing or some universal fate, and it was just Angela. Angela interfering in everybody else's life!"

She pointed at herself. "You're really blaming me for setting you on the path to hook up with Benji? So what? You were pining away over a man who did you dirty after one date, so I wanted to help you—my sister—get over the scum, and you're seriously upset with me? As if Benji hasn't been the best thing that circumvented that train wreck you were on with Kannon?"

"First of all, it wasn't your place to decide that for me! Second of all, how do you know he has been?" I backed away from the table, fishing my key fob out of my pocket. "Most of all, you should've just told me. Damn!" I pointed around the room, landing my glare back on her and then tapping my chest. "I understand I'm the baby, and everyone wants to look out for me. For that, I'm grateful, but I am also grown. *A grown-ass woman!* If I wanted to go through the mess with Kannon, or even if I didn't, it was my mess and my life to navigate how I saw fit. And maybe, just maybe, if you spent more time devoted to figuring out your love life, you wouldn't have time to muck up mine!"

Angela's eyes were rimmed with tears, and she was visibly shaken. My anger wouldn't allow me to give a damn, but as her sister, I gave all the damns. Yet, I refused to show her that. I would not be weak at this moment. I couldn't be. Although my love for her made me want to recoil and run to her, I needed her— hell, every member of my family—to understand that being *the* baby didn't make me *a* baby. Help, I was open to it all day long. Interference, I was not.

"Wow." She attempted to bite back her emotions. "That's how you really feel?" She flung her hands up as a lone droplet streaked down her face. "My bad. I was only trying to help, but you never have to worry about me again, period."

Cocking my head back, I snapped, "No, you don't get to be the victim here. Next time, ask!" I shoved my loose curls away from my face in frustration as I bounced my key fob in the palm of my other hand. "So many decisions have been made since that un-chance rekindling with Benji that may or may not have been impacted, if only—"

My voice trailed off as I kept my internal thoughts to myself.

Angela swiped her eyes before twisting her head and glancing at me sideways. "Sis, do you… are you… is this about you and Benji or you and Kannon?"

My emotions threatened to overcome me as I swallowed the thick lump in my throat.

"Because of you, I don't know." I turned to our parents. "I'm sorry, Mama and Daddy."

With that, I took off from the house before I broke down in the same messy heap I had been in all week over my confused feelings for Kannon and my heartache with Benji.

Chapter Twenty-Nine

NISSI

SINCE THE EMOTIONAL ebullition at my parent's house, I'd been off the grid. Everyone tried to contact me, from my mom and dad to Aquila and Angela. Even Benji had reached out, but I hadn't spoken to anyone. I texted my mom and dad to let them know I was alive and well, but I needed time to process things. Usually, one of them would go into a tangent about how my sister and I needed to make up and squash our differences, but this time, they told me that they loved me and would talk to me when I was ready. I wasn't sure if the altercation at dinner had made them realize how they chose to interact with their grown children or if they were biding their time to plow into me, but either way, I was beyond thankful for their reprieve, even if it was only temporary.

My isolation from everyone for the week was much needed. The time was well spent reflecting and coming to my realization. Since I had gotten my words off my chest, I'd forgiven Angela. I hadn't told her that yet because I felt horrible for throwing her love life in her face. The breakup between Angela and her ex-fiancé was brutal to her mental, emotional, and physical well-being, and it was low of me to rehash that even if I felt what she did was wrong. Her actions, while ill-conceived, were only intended for good purposes. My words were meant to do precisely what I know they had done—hurt her. The old saying was true. Hurt people, hurt people. That's exactly what I had done to Angela. As soon as I resolved my crappy life situation, I would apologize empathically for that.

All in all, I loved my sisters. We fought like Ghost and Tommy but loved each other like Tia and Tamera. Perhaps that's why my parents didn't pry. At the end of the day, they knew our love for each other would outweigh any rift that ever came between us.

My subsequent realization was that Benji and I weren't going to work because we weren't meant to be. That was the sole reason I was standing at his front door waiting for him to answer. Because the very least I could do was serve him this news in person.

"Bél mwen," he whispered, his words a mixture of relief and thankfulness. He wasted no time pulling me into a tight embrace and kissing the top of my head. "I was so glad you called me today. I've been worried and missed you so damn much."

My only response was to hug him back. I hated this so much. No matter what, I would always love and care for Benji. I couldn't make myself be in love with him. Maybe in the next lifetime, or perhaps we were in a previous one, but in this lifetime, I wasn't. Dragging him along this dead-end destination of a loveless relationship to spare his feelings would not continue to happen. Nor would I continue to ignore my feelings. He deserved so much better than that. He deserved someone who could love him with the same intensity and fervor as he doled out to me. It was me who was underserving.

Benji allowed me into his home, grasping my hand and leading me into his living room. As I followed him, I took in his tall and lean statue. The black slacks he wore with his crisp light blue button-down shirt and the sleeves rolled to his elbows showed he had not long gotten home and had yet to unwind.

As I sat beside him on the sofa, he interlocked his fingers while leaning forward with his arms on his knees. His face bore the tiredness of his day and, if I was a betting woman, the stress of my decision.

"You're here. I've been worried all week."

Relief mixed with uncertainty were laden in his words.

"Yeah, I needed some time to think. You know, be at one with my thoughts." I twiddled my thumbs, a nervous habit.

Nodding, he said, "I understand." His gaze fell to the floor, and there was a long pregnant pause before he lifted his head and faced me again. "So what did you decide?"

His question seemed so hopeful that I almost chickened out and lied to say I hadn't decided and was only there to see him, then take the coward's way out and text him my answer. I wanted to run for the hills because I felt his longing permeating the thick air. At that precise moment, I understood the gravity of his feelings for me, which made my answer to his question that much more difficult.

Turning fully to face him, my knees landed against his as I wrung my fingers together. Nervousness coursed through my system, and I bit my lip to quell it from trembling as my emotions bubbled in the pit of my stomach.

"Benji—"

My tone was so troubled and defeated that Benji raised his hand to stop me before I could move past his name. He had to be on the same energy I was on because he swallowed deeply, and his head fell forward.

"Don't." That one word came out with the strength of a thousand pains. "Nissi, please. Don't do this to us."

Finally, he lifted his head, and my heart shattered when his eyes fell on me.

"Not again." His tone was gruff and laced with unshed tears.

Closing my eyes, I inhaled a huge intake of air before slowly releasing it. "I'm so sorry."

"Time. You just need more time," he reasoned before bouncing to his feet. He paced as he rested his chin on the cuff of his hand. "That's it. Just more time."

I hated this. Regardless of how Benji came into my life this second time, I knew his feelings for me were real—just as real as when we were in dental college together. Though I gave it the old college try, my heart wasn't in this relationship. The same way it wasn't back in college. As much as I hated to hurt this man who was guilty of nothing but loving me, it was time for both of us to face the facts. The fact was that no matter how good of a man Benji was and was to me, he wasn't the man for me.

I slid my hands along my thighs to clear the mist of sweat that had built up on them before I slowly stood and walked up to him. Gently, I pulled his warm hands into my clammy ones.

"Benji."

He refused to look at me, opting to focus on the wall to his right. Using my fingertips to guide his face to mine, the dam he had barely been holding back broke as his floodgates sent a slow and steady stream down his face that he tried to sniff away.

"You deserve someone who wants all of you the same way you want all of me. It's not fair to give you a portion when I have your whole."

"Then give me your whole!" he boomed, the wind from his breath pushing out harshly.

He paused, pinching the bridge of his nose.

"I don't mean to yell, but you know how I feel. I love you, Nissi. Only you. I'm here. Please meet me halfway, baby. If you took an honest chance on me, I could be the man you need."

Gripping his face between the palms of my hands, I shook my head. "And therein lies the problem. We can go through life pretending, but we both know I'm not the woman you *need*. And...you're not the man that I *want*."

Utter defeat swept across his entire being as he dropped his forehead into the palm of his hand. I stepped backward away from him to give him a moment to let what I said fully sink in. Wiping the tip of his nose, he cleared his throat before lifting his bloodshot eyes to me.

"You can't make it any clearer than that. I get it now. You want him...Kannon."

"It sounds crazy, I know. It was one date and one night, but I couldn't shake that man. I don't know if he and I will last forever. What I do know is that I owe myself an honest chance at something I want deep down, and you deserve that same chance at happiness. It's not that Kannon is winning and you are losing in this situation. I can wholeheartedly admit that whether or not this thing with Kannon existed, we weren't meant to be, Benji. And I'm so sorry because I know that hurts you just as much as it hurts me to say it."

After several minutes of contemplation, Benji stepped back and patted his chest.

"Maybe one day in the future, I'll believe that. Right now, my heart doesn't feel that way, but I can't and won't force you to stay where you don't want to be. We both deserve far more than that." Placing his hands on my shoulders, he sighed, looking deeply into my eyes. "I love you too much to be the source of your misery."

"And I love you too much to make you feel miserable."

"And herein lies the impasse." He sighed, cupping my face between the palms of his hands as he caressed my cheeks with his thumbs. "You'd be the woman of my dreams even in my misery."

A smirk traced the lines of my face. "Uh-uh, don't sell yourself short."

He shrugged. "What can I say? Misery does love company."

We burst into laughter at his dark humor. As the moment died off, our gazes turned solemn, and an unspoken understanding passed between us. We had made peace with the decision. Benji was a good man; he just wasn't my man. I prayed he found a woman who could fully take care of his precious heart.

"I guess I better go," I said, easing away from him.

Our hands trailed each other's arms until we clasped hands together. His eyes zoomed in on me, and the look he gave me sent chills up my spine and pierced my soul.

"If he fumbles your heart—"

"You'll be in a long line of kick-assers, but I swear I'll give you your fair share at a go-round with him."

Nodding, he bent his head and planted his lips against me, delivering the softest forehead kiss I had ever experienced. "Be good to yourself, Bél mwen."

"You as well."

I paced the floor in my condo, biting the tip of my thumb after unblocking Kannon's number in my phone. Nervous was an understatement. I had denied this man three times. How would I look crawling back to him on some "Oh, by the way, I changed my mind" tip? He would probably think I was looney and thank his lucky stars that he had dodged a crazy chick bullet. No lie. I would.

How selfish of me to fear rejection when he put himself out there only to be rejected.

I was fresh off my breakup with Benji, but I had decided this couldn't wait. Kannon and I had already deprived ourselves of precious months. There was no sense waiting any longer. I'm sure my sisters would have said to take a day to recoup, but they didn't understand how much I needed to have this conversation with Kannon, which was urgent like a mutha. If only I could find the courage to send the text.

Screw it. Instead of a message, my finger pressed the Facetime button. I figured if he could see my face, he would not only hear but see that I meant what I said as I bore my heart to him.

Just before the line disconnected, his face appeared. From the background noise and the only visibility I had, it seemed he was at the firehouse.

"I'm sorry. I didn't know you were at work."

"Give me a second."

I could hear his footfalls as the background noise grew further in the distance. He had to be moving to a quieter area. Suddenly, his face reappeared, and a mixture of shock and confusion beamed from his eyes.

"I'm back," he said, exhaling a long breath. "Nissi Richards. I'm surprised. What pleasure do I owe for this unblocked phone call?"

The hint of sarcasm was ever-present in his tone. Typically, I would have a smart-mouthed comeback, but his indifference was understood. I had iced him a thousand times over and was now on his line out of the blue. I would feel a way about it, too. Therefore, I owed him a straight-up explanation. As my mouth opened to pour out the contents of my heart to him, my throat felt as if it were about to close, and my body temperature rose. Either I was nervous or about to have a panic attack.

"Nissi?" he asked, impatience dancing in his voice.

Both. It was definitely both: nervousness and a panic attack.

"Kannon, I…I wanted to…umm…the funny thing is…I—"

Scratching his beard, he stared at the phone with a blank expression. "Listen, I'm not sure what this is about, but I'm at work and need to go. So—"

"I know. I know," I said with rushed frustration. "Kannon, I just—"

"Nissi, just say whatever it is you have to say."

"It's been you for me, too, Kannon. Ever since I spotted your sexy ass at Brick. I'm telling you that I let my mistake stop us from exploring what we could be. I'm saying that I see this. I feel this. I want this. I want *this* to be an us. I'm saying that I'm not walking away this time. I'm here, and if you forgive me, I'm ready to be yours."

Damn near verbatim, the words he had spoken to me at the wedding spilled from my lips. Yes, I remembered every plea that had flowed from his lips and permeated my heart even then when I was in denial that he was the man I truly wanted. While I was lost in the fairytale of our moment, I realized Kannon hadn't said a word. Not one single solitary word. Hell, he hadn't even uttered a peep. He just stood there staring blankly at the screen. He was so quiet and still that I thought the Facetime call had frozen.

"Kannon?"

Biting his bottom lip, he inhaled sharply. "I'm still here."

"Did you hear me?" I asked, worried that perhaps he'd missed what I had said.

"I heard every word." He swiped a hand over his face, swiping away a myriad of emotions. His clenched jaw and stoned face stared back at me.

The pit of my stomach gurgled with apprehension and expectancy. Easing onto my sofa, I leaned back and ran my free hand up and down my pants.

Swallowing deeply, I asked, "So you don't have anything to say about what I just shared?"

His face bunched with his eyebrows squinted as his lips curled into a grimace.

"Anything to say?" he repeated as if in disbelief. "I can't believe this. You know what, I can." He huffed and folded one arm across his chest. "Yeah, I do have something to say. Since you're all about repeating words, let me repeat some for you. I made a mistake in pursuing you. I was wrong for revealing my feelings to you. I was wrong for thinking that a woman I'd met once was the woman I should hitch my relationship wagon on. Maybe we could've had something in a different lifetime. But in this lifetime, you were right the first time."

A hollow point to the temple would've felt better than his words. The feeling in my belly was replaced with the heartbeat from my heart falling from my chest cavity into the pit of my stomach. Emotions gripped me as tremors overtook my body, and tears I hadn't realized formulated began to trickle.

Sniffling, I nodded. "Okay." I breathed. "Okay, I deserved that. But, Kannon, I wasn't right then. I'm right now. And I know you're at work, and maybe this isn't the best time. And I know you're upset with me, and you have every right to be. I would love the chance—"

"The same chance I asked for? Pleaded for? Begged for? *That* chance?"

His heated words dealt blow after devasting blow.

Closing my eyes, all I could whisper was, "Kannon, please."

This time, it was my tears that poured like a broken faucet.

I reopened my eyes to see the hurt and anger dancing in his. He was conflicted. His once stoic stance softened as his shoulders relaxed. He moistened his mouth with the sexiest lick to those smooth, plump lips. Why did everything about him have to be exponentially sexy right now? As I desperately wiped water droplets that refused to stop flowing with my shirt sleeve, I watched through blurry eyes, hoping he had only been spouting vitriol out of hurt and not the intent. Hurt I could dismiss because it was temporary, but intention was precisely that—intended. It meant he *meant* every word he'd spoken. It meant permanent.

"Nissi—"

"Kannon." My voice cracked under my trembling lips. "I made a mistake."

This time, his eyes closed as he pressed his lips together. He began to shake his head, and when he reopened his eyes, I knew without him having to formulate a word.

"I'm sorry, Nissi. I can't. At a certain point, we must realize this dance we've been dragging each other into will not work. At some point, someone must exit the dance floor. That exit came for me back at the wedding. I hope you find the man you need in your life, and I'm sorry that couldn't be me."

With that, the Facetime call ended, and I was left sitting on my sofa, holding the phone in my hand and feeling an emptiness that left me gutted. I might not have known Kannon well or for long, but I knew permanent. And this was permanent.

Leaning back against the sofa cushions, my hands fell to my sides as I allowed my cell phone to fall beside me on the seat cushion. Streams of tears streaked down the sides of my face, and instead of wiping them away and forcing myself to pick up the pieces, I let them fall. For once, I allowed myself to process my feelings, the rejection, the pain—all of it. I had to because Kannon made it perfectly clear that he had moved on, and now, I had no choice but to do the same. As the gaping hole in my heart swelled with unending agony, I couldn't help but think this had to be how River and Benji felt. There were no winners here. All of us suffered significant losses from our actions. Actions that we would forever have to live with.

The incessant knocking at my door wouldn't stop. I had no clue who it was, but I knew today was not the day. It had barely been twenty-four hours since I broke Benji's heart and had my own caved in by Kannon's rejection. I had no patience left for messy Aquila, my meddling parents, or my nosy friends. Angela and I hadn't spoken, so I figured she'd get her information secondhand until we tried to reconcile our differences.

Slinging the comforter off my body, I swung my legs over the side of my bed and shoved my feet into my house slippers. I ran my fingers through my dry curls and peered at the bedside alarm clock, which read 4:13 pm. I had wept and slept the entire night and day away. That thought made me take a glance in the mirror. The reflection that stared back at me caused me to jump before I realized it was me looking like death deep fried and baked over twice. *Dear Lord.* My eyes were puffy and red from what I could see of them. My cheeks and lips were swollen. My face was slightly ashen from dryness, and my hair seemed like the finger rake only added volume to the matted dehydrated curls atop my head.

Before I could consider my appearance, I became aware of the continued thumps on my door. Annoyance heated my core as I stomped through my condo toward my front door. Peering through the peephole, I saw the last person I ever expected to see standing there.

Snatching the door open, my chest heaved as we held a stare-off. But when my bottom lip began to twitch and my eyes brimmed, her eyes softened, and she rushed inside, clutching me in her arms. I collapsed inside the cocoon of Angela's arms as she held me tightly to her bosom. The levy of waterfalls I had reproduced sprang forth and leaked all over us. She walked me slowly to the living room and helped me sit on the loveseat.

"Oh, sis. It's going to be okay."

She rubbed small circles against my back as my tears continued to fall while she whispered encouraging words to me.

"He doesn't want me anymore, Ang," I finally said between whimpers.

"Who, honey?"

"Kannon."

I felt the wind leave her, knowing the feeling. The air had been knocked out of my sails for nearly a day, and I still couldn't catch my breath. Standing, she moved across the room where a box of Kleenex sat and brought the entire box over to me. Pulling a few of the tissues, I began wiping my eyes to cork the faucet in my eyelids.

Patting my knee, Angela cast the sincerest gaze on me and asked, "What happened, sis?"

As angry as I had been with her, the pleading in her voice and the fact that I needed the love and support caused me to open up. I disclosed everything that happened between Benji and me and then with my conversation with Kannon. By the time I finished, I had no more of anything left inside of me. I had drained my spirit and my dam dry.

Angela's eyes leaked as she glanced over at me. "I'm so sorry, sis."

"It's not your fault—"

"But it is. I never should've invited Benji behind your back. Your love life was for you to figure out, and my intervention led to a trainwreck of events. Now you are left without the man you truly wanted in your life. I should've minded the business that pays me." Reaching over, she pulled me into another embrace. "You were right, Nissi. I'm sorry, and I love you."

Squeezing each other tightly, we lingered there for a few moments, basking in our rekindled closeness. When I felt strong enough, I pulled out of her embrace and touched her arm lovingly.

"Ang, I understand exactly why you did what you did. You were doing what a great big sister does, trying to help your baby sister. At first, I blamed you. So, I lashed out at you, which was wrong, but all of that was a cop-out. I had every opportunity to go after who I truly wanted, but I chose to stay in a relationship that I knew wasn't serving me. We all had a hand in our individual actions, but my missed chance with Kannon has more to do with him and me than River, Benji, or you."

It was her turn to pat my arm. "We were both wrong. We have to be more careful to account for each other's feelings and allow each other to handle our situations. It's water under the bridge, seriously." Then she wagged her finger at me. "Umm, but don't let Benji off the hook that easy. He knew that man had a thing for you, and he was dead wrong to go after his client's love interest, knowing that would cause damage."

I couldn't help but laugh, and boy, did I need it.

"All is fair in love and war, I guess." I giggled with a shrug.

"And that's why he's by himself right now."

"Angela!" I shrieked, barreling over in laughter.

She shrugged. "What?"

"I cannot with you!"

She pushed me on the shoulder. "Maybe not, but what you *can* do is go shower and get yourself together because this, baby sis…" She waved her hands up and down at me. "…ain't it."

Oh no, she didn't just gameshow host wave me. Hell, I couldn't argue. She was spot-on. I knew I looked and most likely smelled unbecoming, so I rolled my eyes and stood to go and tend to my upkeep.

"Once you're dressed, I'll take you out for a little sisterly bonding time."

"You don't have to drag me out. I'm hurt over Kannon, and I must learn to deal with that."

"So you can't learn to deal with it over Cheesecake Factory and Nordstroms?" Angela quipped.

"Uhhh, on second thought—"

"Mmmhmm." She giggled. "Go get yourself together, and let big sis treat you."

Gasping, I pointed to myself.

"On that note, who *are I* to turn down a good time?" I playfully questioned before scurrying to my bedroom.

I stopped in mid-stride, tossing a smile back toward Angela. "I love you, sissie."

Leaning back on my sofa, she blew a kiss my way. "I love you more."

Walking down the hall, I knew that I may be hurting now, but with the help of my sisters, I would eventually be all right, and that was enough for me.

Chapter Thirty

KANNON

*E*VER SINCE NISSI'S phone call, I'd been in the dumps. The easiest thing for me to do would have been to give in to her pleas. They weighed on my heart heavily to the point I could barely function. Everything in my life had been a task over the past two days. Eating, sleeping, showering, and even getting out of bed was a feat. I wanted that woman more than anything but couldn't allow myself to fall into the Nissi saga again.

It wasn't that I didn't believe her. I could see it in her eyes, hear it in her voice, feel her soul connecting to mine. Honestly, I was afraid. That was my manned-up truth. Afraid that if I gave in to her, she would capture my whole heart and snatch hers away as she had before. Rejection I could take. Not abandonment. Not from her. Besides, nothing I'd said had made a difference—not about River, Benji, and even my feelings. If she could deny me three times knowing all those things, how could I trust that this change of heart wasn't temporary? I couldn't, and that was problematic for me. My feelings for her were not fleeting. They were permanent and urgent, like a muthafucka.

"What are y'all looking at?" I asked my bros in the fire station after I came out of the bathroom into the common area.

A few of the men were gathered around Jovan as he played something on his cell phone. All of them seemed highly intrigued with whatever nonsense he was showing. Knowing my boy, it was probably some scantily clad social media vixen doing a sensual dance or sexual simulation. And knowing the other men in the firehouse, or in general, they were enjoying the virtual festivities just as much as Javon.

They all looked at me with the same blank expression, causing me to rear my head back and squint my face.

"What?" I said, a slight chuckle escaping.

They looked at Jovan as he stared back at them. Captain shrugged and finally said the words it seemed no one else had the courage to speak.

"Tell him, Daniels."

Jovan released a deep breath and looked over at me, raking his hand down his face. My eyes fell on him, noticing the unsettled spirit about him. Captain recaptured my attention when he asked everyone to clear out to give me and Jovan the room. Now I was worried. I walked over to Jovan and took a seat across from him.

Leaning forward with my hands clasped together on the table, I gave him an inquisitive stare. "So you wanna fill me in on what everyone else knows except me?"

Jovan shook his head. "Not really," he replied, leaning back in his seat and tapping his cell phone on the table.

Irritation heated my core as I knocked my knuckles against the table. "Man, just say whatever it is. The mountain of disappointing news I've received over the past month can't be any worse than that."

"That's the thing. I know what you've been going through, and the last thing I want is to drag you back into the mess you've been trying to relieve yourself. As your boi, I'm not trying to put you through that again."

My gut feeling told me it had something to do with Nissi. With the small station house, our core team knew things didn't work out between Nissi and me. While I only told a couple of the men who had inquired, the news eventually reached everyone because even men gossiped. No matter how we blamed women for that pesky habit, men were just as horrible with the rumor mill.

I may have been setting myself up for another headache behind Nissi, but I was curious why my boi and fellow comrades were flustered. And because deep down, I always wanted to hear about any news concerning Nissi, I would endure the gut-wrenching revelation that Jovan had to share.

"I appreciate you looking out, but I promise it's all right. Go ahead and hit me with the news."

Jovan took me in, contemplating whether to reveal the information he was withholding. After a few seconds, he shook his head and slid his phone over to me.

"Replay the video."

Nodding, I picked up Jovan's phone off the table and saw that the video was by someone by the TikTok name of @AngSoRich. When I pressed play, I realized the video was created by Nissi's sister, Angela. I sat back and listened attentively.

"My sister is going to kill me because I interfered in her love life once before without knowing where her heart lies, and my actions mucked up some things. Even though I'm still interfering in her business, I feel it's my responsibility to correct this wrong. My sister is the dancing dentist who was trapped in the elevator and rescued by the fireman. I'm here pleading to him not to blame my sister for her actions. That other man intervening was on me. She felt like it was a sign, but she knows and understands the truth now. She realized one important thing even before knowing the truth. She knew and understood that it was you then, and it is you now. She doesn't know I'm doing this, which is why I'm not tagging her, but I hope with all my might that this tag reaches you before she sees it. And since I know you girls in cyberspace like to tussle, please know this is my sister. So while I may be stepping outside my place again, I'm one thousand percent sure she'll appreciate it this time. If it works."

The video ended, and I read the caption that stated *@ KingKannon94, this is for you. Please HMU! Signed, a Concerned Sister #MrFireAndRescue*

Pulling out my cell phone, I tapped the app, saw the slew of notifications on my TikTok, and went to her page. Sure enough, she had posted the video about five hours ago and tagged me. I hadn't seen it because I had turned off my notifications. Since Nissi blocked me and I had random strangers contacting me about the state of our relationship, I opted to view my profile whenever I went into the app, which was very seldom since most of my brand ambassador stints had been fulfilled.

"Man, listen, I know Nissi is a sore subject for you. If you ain't feeling her, ignore her sister and keep moving with your life. You don't owe her nothing," Jovan said matter-of-factly.

Slowly, I stood up from my seat and slapped hands with him. "Good looking out, my boi."

He nodded as I handed him back his phone. "What are you going to do about that?"

I tucked my phone away in my pocket before pushing the chair back under the table.

"Nothing, bruh."

With that, I walked away to start my duties in the station house.

Chapter Thirty-One

NISSI

LAZILY, I STROLLED up to the elevator. My weekend had been an emotional rollercoaster and had left me drained. Angela's impromptu shopping spree worked temporarily, but once the fanfare was over and I was left to my recognizance, all I could think about was my lost chance with Kannon. I knew one day I would look back on this moment and receive it as a learned lesson, but today, I had no energy to peer on the bright side of this hell. Hence why I was running late into the office.

Since I didn't have any appointments until after lunch, I figured I would spend my morning taking my time to boost my mood and come in. I hadn't planned to be an hour late, but such was life. As the elevator opened, I was surprised to be the only occupant. Anxiety coursed through my veins when the doors closed because it was my first time riding in the contraption since my incident. Oddly, I prayed the elevator would get trapped again and that Fire and Rescue would be needed to free me, and hopefully, Kannon would be my rescuer again. Pathetic, I know. I guess my incident was enough to have them do the necessary repairs because not only did it not break down, but it seemed to transport me to the ninth floor at lightning speed.

With a heavy sigh, I gripped my satchel and exited the elevator. Straightening my posture and tossing my hair back,

I shrugged away the worries of the weekend and prepared to begin my life anew. It was time to get back to my life as Dr. Nissi Richards and move forward sans Benji and Kannon. I kept the faith that the one who was meant to be would appear one day. All I could do in the interim was live my life.

"Good morning, Sheena," I greeted on the way to my office.

She was hot on my heels with a folder in one hand and a cup of coffee in the other.

"Good morning, Dr. Nissi," she said as I placed my satchel on my desk and pulled on my white coat.

Taking the coffee from her hands, I pulled out my leather chair.

"I am going to chart until my first patient."

"Okay, I'll come and get you when it's that time."

"Thanks, Sheena."

When she closed my door, I got started with my day. After a couple of hours of work, my desk phone rang. Peering at the line, I saw it was Ciara. A smile graced my face as I answered.

"Dr. Nissi Richards' office. You break it. I crown it."

Ciara burst into laughter. "OM to the effin' G! I called to check on you after your eventful past week and weekend, but I see you are just fine with your crazy self."

I matched her giggles before calming down. "It's better to laugh than to cry."

"Aww, Nissi," Ciara cooed, turning serious.

"No, ma'am, none of that." I wagged my finger as if she could see me. "I've decided I'm done with the pity parties. Today is a new day. I won't pretend I'm not hurt about Kannon's decision, but I will learn to be okay with his wishes. In the end, all I want is for him to be happy, and if that is without me, that's what it is. I wish him nothing less than the best."

"Yasss, hunty! I'm proud of you. And you know I've got your back."

"I know you do, girl."

"And no worries. The right man will come along, and you'll know when he does. I'm happy to see you're not letting this situation defeat you."

"No lie, girl. The struggle is still very real, but I have so many things to live for. So, I can't allow it to keep me down. Still, I'm not completely over it because Kannon…whew, chile."

"Ha!" Ciara hollered. "You don't have to tell me. I remember Mr. Fire and Rescue."

"Anyway, I need to get ready for my first patient."

"No lunch break today?" she asked.

"Even if I was, I'm not scheduling lunch outside the building with you. That elevator was kind to me this morning. I am not trying to test those waters," I joked.

"Right? You need to stay right there in your office."

"How about you bring me back something?"

Ciara scoffed. "In your words, you got *bring back* money?" she joked.

"Bye, bish!" I rolled my eyes.

"Bye!" she said with a chuckle before we hung up.

I sat there for a few more minutes charting before clocking the time on my watch. I stood to prepare for my patient. Just then, Sheena walked through my door.

"I was just about to come and get you," she said, leaning on the open door. "Your patient is waiting in exam room nine."

"Thanks, Sheena," I answered, grabbing the paperwork. "A new patient consult. Simple enough."

Reaching the door as I trekked down the hall, I quickly reviewed the paperwork for the patient's information. Opening the door, I put on my best smile and said, "Hello, Mr. Desman Isready. Did I pronounce—"

My eyes glanced up, and I dropped the paperwork as I stood frozen. Standing beside the exam chair and holding the most beautiful bouquet of red roses was Kannon, looking as sexy as ever in a short-sleeved Polo top, slim-fit chino pants, and white Air Force Ones. His chin beard and goatee were shaped nicely with his low-cut wavy Caesar. His crisp and light scent wafted through the air as he donned those brilliantly bright white teeth directly at me.

"That's right, baby. *This man is ready.*"

"Kan...Kannon." His name came out shakily.

"Yes, baby. It's me. I want you to know I heard every word you spoke, and with the help and a little talking to by a certain sister of yours, I want you to know it's you for me. It was the moment I saw your sexy ass walk into Brick, and it still is today. I hope that you—"

His words were cut off because all I could do was run into his arms and plant a kiss on him that I had wanted to plant since the day I stopped lying to myself about how much I wanted him. Wrapping my arms around his neck, he placed the bouquet on the exam chair and embraced me as we tongue-lashed each other with fervor. The only thing that stopped us was the catcalls and whistles behind me. When we broke the kiss, I turned to find Sheena, my entire office staff, and Ciara, Aquila, and Angela standing there, gawking happily at us.

"I hope you're not mad at me," Angela said with an unsure expression.

"I should've known." I wagged my finger at her. "I can't believe all of you were in on this." I gazed around in sheer amazement.

"Not everyone," Sheena said. "Mainly, Angela brought me, Ciara, and Aquila into her perfect plan, and you know I had to notify the office."

Everyone laughed, including me, as I waved my sisters over. "This is one time I'm happy for your meddling ways."

We hugged each other, and Angela winked at Kannon.

"Make it count," Angela warned him.

"Or you can count your days," Aquila added with all the big sister energy in the world.

Kannon chortled throatily. My God, everything he did exuded sex appeal.

"You have my word." He pulled my face toward his so that we were staring eye to eye. "This time, I have no intention of letting her slip away."

"Me either, Mr. Jordan," I agreed as we pecked each other's lips again.

"Okay, that's our cue. I can't take too much of this PDA," Aquila joked as they began to file out.

I turned to everyone. "Thank you, guys, for real."

They all gave me their wishes, and Ciara stopped before walking off.

"As I said, you'll know when the right one comes along." She winked at us and disappeared out the doorway.

Turning back to Kannon, I grabbed his chin softly with my hand. "How about I take you to lunch?"

"Oh, you're treating me?" he asked, sexily licking his lips.

Nodding, I said, "Oh yes, Mr. Jordan. I sure am."

Taking his hand, I led him down the hall. Once we reached the door, I ushered him inside, followed, closed the door, and twisted the lock. He turned around and looked at me suspiciously.

"I thought you were treating me out to lunch?"

While slipping off my white coat, my head bounced in agreement.

"I am. I will feed you a side dish of Nissi's nipples tossed over a bed of Nissi's sweet treasure drizzled with Nissi's succulent juices and, if we have time, a dessert portion of Nissi's head."

Kannon was on brick with my nasty talk. The lip bite and moan showed how excited he was with emphasis.

"Well, come on and serve it up then because I'm hungry, and I've been craving this meal for a long time."

"Say less, Mr. Jordan," I said while sauntering over to serve him this full-course meal.

Our lunchtime lovemaking was otherworldly as we freely explored the depths of our connection. After sexing each other to exhaustion, we lingered there for a long while, finally accepting what we had tried to run from for so long—our love.

Finally gazing at me, he joked, "You know, baby, you didn't give me a chance to ask if you'd be my lady."

We burst into laughter as I gazed down into his eyes.

"Baby, consider that question asked and answered."

Our shared chortles slowly faded and gave way to the seriousness of the moment. Basking in each other, I slowly stroked my fingertips down the waves of his hair as he drew small circles against the small of my back. As I gazed into Kannon's beautiful light brown orbs, they were stormy with unshared emotions.

He swallowed deeply before licking his lips. "I love you, Nissi," he whispered softly, yet confidently.

Leaning my forehead against his temple, I uttered the same sentiment. "I love you, Kannon."

And both of us meant it. We'd fallen in love one night at a restaurant over drinks and appetizers, and it felt good to express those feelings on our shared journey of discovery.

"What do you say we get out of here and start building this relationship together? Sheena's orders were to reschedule your other appointments."

"Then let's get the first day down of a lifetime to go."

He gazed up at me and pecked my lips. "A lifetime. I love the sound of that, Dr. Richards. I love the sound of that. And I know the perfect place to start."

"Where's that?" I asked as we stood straightening ourselves.

He pulled me close and placed a soft kiss on my lips before gazing deeply into my eyes. "I want to introduce you to my mother."

Epilogue

ONE YEAR LATER

"Come on, Papa Kain, you gotta get in on this!" Nissi let out a boisterous laugh as he begrudgingly moved toward the group of them.

"I'm only doing this Tikky Tokky for you, Nissi," Kain said, shaking his head. "Especially on this remix song. Why can't we do the original version?"

"Because we can't, Pops. Now, come on. You heard my fiancée." Kannon pulled his dad in step so they could start their electric slide version of Beyoncé's "Before I Let Go" for TikTok.

"I love the sound of that," Nissi said as she turned to kiss Kannon.

"A'ight, enough of that. Let's do this dance!" Nissi's dad, Nisante, shouted.

Nissi and Kannon had been engaged for a week and were set to get married in six months, sealing the lifetime union of The Dancing Dentist and Mr. Fire and Rescue. Both families had come out to celebrate Nissi and Kannon's engagement and decided to go with an old-school barbecue at the Richards' house. The buzz was all over Miami, but in their true private fashion, they decided they would only share their wedding moment with family and a few close friends. That still didn't stop them from sharing the fun of their union with the place it all started—TikTok. Hence the dance video. They all electric slid to the song, laughing and messing up but recording it to share with their virtual friends all the same. Once it was finished, everyone continued to enjoy each other—dancing and talking.

"May I have this dance?" Kinston asked, walking up behind Angela.

She turned to him from a conversation with her cousins. Although she tried to hide her blush, it was evident his request smote her.

"I didn't think you were going to make it."

He shrugged. "I wouldn't miss this day for anything in the world."

"To celebrate your brother's engagement to my sister, I know."

He filled their space and tilted her chin up. "To have the opportunity to see you."

"We'll see you later, Ang," one of her cousins said as they giggled and walked away.

Offering his hand to her, he whispered, "May I?"

She placed her hand in his and batted her eyes. "You may."

As they eased up to the dance area where the other dancers were, Kannon catcalled his brother.

"A'ight now, bro! I see you!"

"Stay over there where your fiancée is."

Kannon peered down lovingly at Nissi. "I've always got my eyes on the prize. Believe that. Ain't that right, Mrs. Jordan?"

"Mr. Jordan," she responded with a kiss. "Absolutely."

THE END

ACKNOWLEDGMENTS

Thank You and Love to:

My husband – My partner in this thing called life.

My children – My blessings in this thing called life.

My friends – My riders in this thing called life.

My Skye's Sweethearts (supporters) – My motivation in this thing called life.

My publisher (Black Odyssey Media) – My pen vessel in this thing called life.

Myself – My believer in this thing called life.

My God – My everything in this thing called life.

Special thanks to N'Tyse, Briana Cole, and Danesha Little for your raving endorsements. Danesha – my pea in a pod, your sisterhood means the world.

Life – We only get one go-around at this masterpiece. But if we live it and love it right, then once is enough. Live your life, sweethearts. But most importantly, love it.

~Aries Skye

#SkyeStories #ThisSkyeIsLimitless

AUTHOR'S NOTE

This book is dedicated to the real-life headline of Dr. Hailey Logan and Firefighter David. Your brief viral story inspired this fan-fiction love story.

My name is Aries Skye, and I want to thank you all for joining me on my debut journey. I hope you enjoyed this tale of Nissi and Kannon and continue with me as I pen the beauty in black romance. Please continue to follow me via my mailing list at authorariesskye.carrd.co (I promise not to spam you) and follow me on social media at Author Aries Skye on Facebook, @ariesskye_ on Instagram and follow me on TikTok @authorariesskye.

AUTHOR'S BIO

This fiery Aries lady—Aries Skye, believes in the power of black love. She sets her focus on highlighting the realities of beautiful black individuals finding their way in life through love. That's exactly what her #SkyeStories bring—penning the beauty in Black romance. A natural-born writer, Aries Skye has been crafting stories since she was a preteen and went on to major in English – Creative Writing at ASU. When she's not wielding her magical black girl pen, she's cocooned in the peace and comfort of her family with her adoring husband of two decades and their four energetic and artistic womb fruits. *Love on the Ninth Floor* is her debut novel.

Aries Skye is an alter pseudo for Author Untamed.

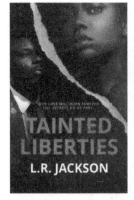

TAINTED LIBERTIES
OUR LOVE WILL BURN FOREVER TILL SECRETS DO US PART...
L.R. JACKSON

EVERY BLACK GIRL DANCES
a novel by
candice y. johnson

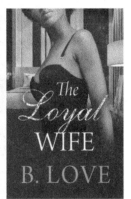

The Loyal WIFE
B. LOVE

SOLDIERS OF LOVE
BEAUTIFUL SCARS
N'TYSE & UNTAMED

A THRILLER
INNO CENT INTENT
K.C. MILLS

THE KNOWING
CAROLYN MITCHELL BOYKIN

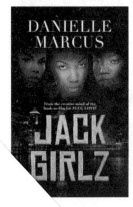

DANIELLE MARCUS
From the creative mind of the book-to-film hit PLUG LOVE!
JACK GIRLZ

ERICK S. GRAY
"A suspenseful tale with a twist that you won't see coming."
— K'WAN, national bestselling crime novelist of Animal
GUN

AMERICAN GUNNER 2
CIVIL LIBERTIES
EDDY CLARK   D. ANDREA WHITFIELD